LAURIE GERMAINE

Tinsel in a Twist

Scattered Whimsy

To Kreh
You've put up with my highs and lows,
my doubts and insecurities,
with a grace and patience only a strong man of God could wield.
I am a blessed woman.
I love you.

Contents

Who's Who

KRINGLE FAMILY:

Meister K—Niklas's grandfather, Santa Claus

Madam Anne—Niklas's grandmother, Mrs. Claus

Meister Nico—Niklas's father, next-in-line for Santa

Madam Marie—Niklas's mother

Kristof—Niklas's younger brother

Onkel/Herr Stoffel—Meister K's brother, Niklas's great-uncle

Fritz, Elke, Lukas—Onkel Stoffel's grandchildren, Niklas's second cousins

DONATI FAMILY:

Marco—Gina's father

Elise—Gina's mother

Logan—Gina's brother

Aunt Cat—Gina's aunt, Marco's younger sister

Nonna—Gina's grandmother, Marco's mother

Papa Campi—Gina's great-grandfather, Nonna's father.

One

Tinsel—Nov 21 A New Beginning

Riding sidesaddle behind Niklas Kringle, one arm hooked around his torso, I nudge the blindfold covering my eyes. How is Eggnog's gait so even? Were it not for the fact both reindeer and Kringle fear flying (an inconvenient phobia for one destined to become Santa Claus), I'd bet a stocking's worth of gumdrops the reindeer carries us across air, not ground.

Niklas shifts and grabs my mittened hand. "No peeking."

"You sure we're not airborne?"

He chokes on a laugh.

The frigid-yet-bearable temperature of Flitterndorf's November arctic air drops like Santa down a chimney, signaling we've passed beyond Christmas HQ's borders. The wind slices through my leggings, and I tighten my hold about Niklas. "Where are you taking me?"

"You'll see," he says, a smile in his tone.

I chew the inside of my cheek. "Will we be gone long? I'd hoped to squeeze in one last training session with the reindeer before leaving

1

for Germany."

Niklas's body tenses as usual at the mention of our trip, but his tone is gentle when he asks, "Didn't Jangles suggest that extra rest—not an extra lesson—would improve the Third String's listless behavior?"

Yeees. And since Jangles is my boss, I'd do well to obey him. Except, I'll be in Germany with Niklas and his parents for the next three weeks. By the time I come back, the Third String will have gotten rusty on their progress with the Peppermint Twist. In getting rusty, they might not have the Twist nailed down for the Mastery Tournament in mid-January. And if they—we—aren't ready for the tournament, Meister K might promote another elf instead of me when Jangles advances to the Major Flight Team. And if I don't become the Minor Flight Team leader, how will I stop the whispers behind my back?

Whispers that have grown louder these past few weeks.

I rest my forehead against Niklas's back. *Calm down, Tinsel. You'll figure it out.* "You know," I say aloud to silence the advancing doubts, "the Third String would make twice the progress in half the time if you flew with us."

"You're teaching them the Peppermint Twist before they've mastered the easier moves," Niklas replies. "Nothing about that will go fast."

"They know the Twist individually." It's when I string seven hotheaded reindeer together that things get … complicated.

"Even the Second String hasn't perfected the Twist."

"That's because your father's team isn't as gifted as yours."

Niklas chuckles. "I won't tell him you said that."

"It's more than the move itself, though." I prod his coat-clad shoulder with my chin. "Only the two closest reindeer can hear my commands when we're flying, and they take too long informing the others before the commands get executed. So, when something unexpected happens, it ends in a mess." Like last week, when I broke three leather traces in one flight. "If you came with me, you could use your Santa powers of telepathy to show them what to do. *Kein Problem.*"

"No problem? Big problem—I don't fly."

"Yet."

Niklas stiffens again. "I hope that's confidence in my abilities and not a reminder of our frostbitten flights to Germany."

I suppress a grin. "Yes. That's it. Absolutely."

"Cheeky elf. Thank Christmas I'll be too sedated to remember flying."

Though I can't see, I know Niklas well enough to guess that his jaw muscles pop. "You don't have to attend the Initiation Ceremony."

"It's tradition. And Great-Onkel Stoffel is a stickler for tradition."

An ancient edict we memorized as students at Flitterndorf School of Talents pops into my mind: *Every firstborn Kringle, on the eve of St. Nicholas Day in his twentieth year, must present himself before the representatives at Weihnachts Manor and pledge allegiance to Christmas.*

"Think of where you and I would be," I say, "or rather, where we wouldn't be, had you stuck with tradition and followed the edict prohibiting romance between Kringles and elves."

"Now *that* was a tradition worthy of purging." Niklas shifts as I sense Eggnog slow to a stop. "We're here." His body disappears, taking the heat with him. I shiver and adjust the newsboy cap over my elfin ears, yelping when Eggnog tilts forward, then backward. The ground materializes beneath my feet, and Niklas helps me dismount.

I smooth a hand over my *dirndl* skirts, ensuring they lay properly. "How fast did you travel this time, Eggy?"

"'Twasn't fast at all," the flying-averse reindeer answers. "Lots o' twists 'n turns slowin' me, so maybe a hundred forty miles an hour?"

"Give him a straight, clear shot like the Third String has above the trees," Niklas says, "and he'll leave them in the snowdust."

I smile. "Well, we know which one of them is your favorite."

Niklas laughs and kisses my nose. "You ready?"

"Yes, please." I reach for the blindfold, but he intercepts my hands with his own.

"No, are you ready to follow me?" He gently tugs me forward.

I slide my booted feet along a flat surface in my coal-black world. "What if you lead me into a tree or something?"

He laughs again. "Would I do that to you?"

I take a few more cautious steps. "Once upon a time." When he used to mask his feelings behind mockery and pranks.

"Have I not redeemed myself in the past two years?"

The corner of my mouth lifts. "Almost."

"Watch your footing—you're about to climb three steps."

His grip tightens, and I ascend one step at a time. Bells chime above, and warm air brushes my cheeks. Niklas leads me onward. A rich coffee aroma twirls about, and I inhale on a greedy breath. "Waaiiit. Are we …?"

Niklas removes my blindfold. "Now you can look."

I blink several times in the soft lighting. Around the room, comfy armchairs have been arranged into small groupings, and loaded bookshelves create alcoves for tables that seat up to four people. A coffee machine percolates behind an ordering counter.

"You brought me to the Huggamugg Café." I clasp my hands, then frown. "Where is everyone?" Ever since Gina Donati, my best friend, took over management eighteen months ago, this place bustles morning and afternoon despite Waldheim's meager population. Saturdays are no different, yet the café stands empty.

In the dining area, white fairy lights dangle above two striped armchairs angled toward each other. Over one drapes a masculine, calf-length coat trimmed in ivory faux fur, its green velvet embellished with intricate embroidery. Over the other chair drapes a glorified dirndl boasting three layers of ankle-length skirts, the top skirt matching the coat in fabric and trim.

Moving closer, I tug off my mittens and run a hand along the skirt. "It's beautiful." Bright red embroidered rosemaling motifs sweep up both sides of the top skirt, starting broad at the bottom hem and tapering to points at the waist. The measurements that Madam Marie, Niklas's mother, had taken a few months ago flood my memory, and my stomach flips. "Are these for the Initiation Ceremony?"

"Mmm-hmm. One for you, and one for me."

I toss Niklas a glance. "Which one's mine?"

He winks, removing his beanie and shaking out his pale blond locks.

"I've never owned anything so elegant." I trace a swirl of embroidery on his coat. "And you've never worn green before." The color of my elf clan.

"Turn it over."

Taking it by the shoulders, I carefully lift the coat. Bright red rosemaling sweeps up the back. "It has the same design as the dress."

"Yep."

My heart thumps as I replace the coat on the chair. "Is that significant?"

"It is."

An empty coffee shop. Romantic lighting. Special outfits. Niklas is up to something. Am I ready for it to be *the* something?

Strike that. I am. But what about the other Christmas elves?

"Tinsel." Niklas's low timbre compels me to turn around. He lowers to one knee, and my breath hitches as he takes my left hand. "I know that growing up, my actions didn't always reflect my emotions, but ever since you swiped my cheek with that loaded paintbrush, I've pretty much been a goner."

A laugh bubbles up at the memory of my seven-year-old self. "You said my painting of a reindeer resembled a warped Christmas tree."

"It was constructive criticism."

"You killed my inner artist."

"And paved the way for your future job working with my reindeer." The emerald flecks in his eyes sparkle beneath the hair flopped over his forehead. He raises his hand. A ring glints between thumb and forefinger, its multiple diamonds forming a snowflake pattern. "Tinsel Kuchler, I love you. You bring out the best in me. Will you do me the honor of becoming my wife?"

Yes! I open my mouth, but unbidden anxiety swirls in my belly, and out pops, "What will the elves think?"

A line appears between Niklas's brows. "That's your answer?"

"No. I mean—" I clasp his hand between both of mine. "I'm sorry. This morning I overheard some of them talking about me, dissing my clan, and—"

"So they've been a little off lately. We don't need their approval to get married."

"Niklas, if they don't approve of me now, as a Minor Flight Team member, how will they approve of me as the team leader when I get promoted?" I stare at our hands, the ring glowing with possibilities. "And if they can't do that, they'll never approve of me as a different kind of leader."

"What if you're not promoted?"

My jaw slackens.

Niklas pushes to his feet and cups my elbows. "My point is, we can't wait for the perfect timing. 'Perfect' will never come. If the elves can't see how amazing you are by now, that's their problem." He rests his forehead against mine. "Don't let something like a few elves—"

"A couple thousand elves."

"—keep you from becoming Mrs. Tinsel Kringle."

The name triggers a grin. "Okay, yeah, I kinda like the sound of that."

"Just 'kinda'?" His hands slide along my waist, his clove scent wrapping me in a hug. "Am I still having to redeem myself here?"

I clutch the lapels of his coat. "You've come far in the last few minutes."

Eyes darkening, Niklas claims my mouth in a slow, sultry kiss. Heat travels from my pointed ears to my toes. Two years and I still melt like a slushy snow maiden.

"I love you," he whispers against my lips.

"I love you, too."

"Then marry me." Niklas lifts the ring between us. "Reject the doubts and choose me instead." His dimples emerge in a mischievous smile. "I bet I'll keep you warmer at night than they will."

A laugh escapes. "You know I can't resist your Kringle charm." And never let it be said this elf chose fear over love. "Yes, Niklas, I'll marry you."

Two

Tinsel—Nov 21 Strung Up

"Then Gina came out with squeals and congratulations and gushed over the ring as any friend would." I grin at the seven reindeer staring at me in the FTA, or Flight Training Arena, as I wrap up our engagement story. Niklas secures the last few traces on the reindeer's harnesses that tether them to the practice sleigh. "She showed us to a secluded, candlelit table, served food Niklas had catered in, and afterward, Eggnog took us home."

Niklas winks over the animals' backs. Okay, so I may have left out the mushier moments.

"It's abou' time he popped the question," Chip grumbles from his position among the two rows of reindeer. "He's dithered over it fer months now."

Peppermint exhales a happy sigh. "'Tis romantic."

"Who ken the eejit had it in him?" Licorice adds with her odd mix of affection and sarcasm.

"I'm right here." A lopsided grin plays about Niklas's mouth. "I may not understand your words, but I can read your images loud and clear.

Snowballs, you'd think I'd have earned my team's respect by now." He ambles around the Third String, catching my eye. "But then, we both know which one of us is *their* favorite."

I rock onto my heels and look skyward.

"You all set for flying?" he asks, his phone chiming.

"Ach, she's fine. We're fine." Cocoa lets out a huge yawn. "Let's git goin' so's we can git back already."

Niklas smooths a finger along his bottom lip as he checks his screen. I turn to Cocoa. "You don't want to fly?"

"Aye." The reindeer's eyelids droop. "And nay."

"Remember what Jangles said about them." Niklas pockets his phone again and pulls me into a loose embrace.

Chip cocks his head. "What'd he say abou' us?"

But Niklas addresses me. "I've got to get home. Grandpop's requested a last-minute family meeting."

"Oh?" I link my arms about his neck, my engagement ring flashing as it catches the light. "What does Santa need this time?"

"It seems my brother showed up today."

My eyebrows rise. "I thought Kristof had two more months abroad. He was planning to attend your Initiation Ceremony."

"Apparently, that changed. I'm sure he'll tell me why."

"And here I'd hoped to tempt you to come fly with us."

Niklas laughs. "Short of a lobotomy, that won't happen for a long time."

"Didja hear that, team?" Chocolate lets out a yawn to rival Cocoa's. "He didna use 'never' this time."

Niklas rolls his eyes. "Great image, Chocolate." He frames my face. "See you tomorrow?"

"Eleven-thirty. I'll be ready."

The lines tighten around his mouth. No doubt he's imagining the flights to Germany awaiting us and his parents. Three flights spanning three days, long layovers included. My fingers curl over his wrist. "You don't have to do this. Your great uncle might get his *lederhosen* in a twist at the thought of breaking with tradition, but—"

"I'm not doing this for tradition, Tinsel. I'm doing this for you." Niklas sweeps a strand of hair from my cheek. "You deserve to experience sights beyond Flitterndorf, and I want to be with you when you see them."

My mouth opens in a small 'o,' and he captures my lips in a promising kiss. His hands travel down my back, urging me closer.

Something pokes my upper arm, and Niklas jerks as though he were poked, too. "All right, lovebirds," Butterscotch rumbles, "leave room fer th' Christmas spirit betwixt ye."

"Roasted chestnuts, Butterball." Niklas rubs his arm. "I barely kissed her."

I push aside Butterscotch's antlers. "What image did you get from them this time?"

"A monstrous one," Niklas says. "Oversize antlers, red eyes, and billows of steam."

I cock an eyebrow at the lead reindeer. "I didn't know the spirit of Christmas looked like that."

"He disna, but I will." A warning saturates Butterscotch's tone.

Chuckling, Niklas backs toward the front entrance. "This is why our fathers don't worry about chaperones."

After he leaves, I jog to the FTA's back entrance. "Okay, you all made your point—pun intended." I heave open the doors. "So, let's get flying. You up for another go at the Peppermint Twist?"

"You're nutty as fruitcake if you think anyone's flying today."

I jump at the words, peanut brittle sharp, as Leif, a fellow Minor Flight Team member, marches into the Lower Stables from the side door.

Cocoa groans. "Fer the love o' chew toys, what is it now?"

Leif's curly-toed red boots stir up dust, and an odd scent drifts past, gone before I can place it. The elf puffs out his chest, buttons straining on his shirt, and glares at me from his forty-inch height. He looks like a Jangles-wannabe. "What are you doing with these reindeer?"

He sounds like a Jangles-wannabe. Why so cranky? "I was going to let them stretch their legs. They've been idle in their stalls all day."

"That's because they've been sluggish."

From the front of the line, Butterscotch jerks his head about. "Did he say we're lazy?"

Licorice paws the ground. "Ach, he's one ta talk."

Cinnamon shakes her antlered head. "We'll show 'em who's—" She freezes with a wince. "I shouldna done that."

Frowning, I approach Cinnamon. "You okay?"

"See?" Leif wags his finger at the reindeer. "Sluggish. Off their game. Something's wrong. Jangles wants them left alone until tomorrow."

"I'll be gone tomorrow," I murmur, scratching Cinnamon's neck. Her coat lacks its usual sheen.

Leif pushes back his jacket and tucks his thumbs behind his suspenders. "I'll be here."

My stomach clenches. While I'm overseas, the other Minor Flight Team members will either ruin the progress I've made over the past four months with the Third String or take credit for it. Both scenarios could jeopardize my shot at that promotion.

I swivel my engagement ring, the ungracious thoughts tasting bitter on my tongue. Now who's the cranky one?

My fiddling draws Leif's gaze to the ring, and his eyes widen. "Oh, no," he whispers. Spinning on his heel, he scurries back to the Lower Stables.

I sigh. Even though I warned Niklas this would be a common reaction, the elf's dismay stings.

"Dinna listen ta him, gel." Chip straightens to his full height. "We're the Third String, after all. Let's prove him wrong."

Cinnamon nods. "Me head prob'ly hurts cuz I havna done anythin' all day."

A chorus of "ayes" and hoof stomps follow.

"You're right." I throw back my shoulders. "We'll show them, won't we?" I march to the sleigh and position myself behind the dash. I'll prove Niklas's faith in me isn't misplaced and prove to Meister K that I'm the best replacement for Jangles. Then the elves will see I'll make a decent Mrs. Kringle. Giving the reins a slap, I shout, "To the skies, team!"

The Third String pounds through the back entrance and vaults into the air.

* * *

Twenty minutes later, I use the emergency kit's skinning knife to free the reindeer from tangled traces and the practice sleigh, which took out two trees before cracking and getting caught in a third.

Ninety minutes after that, once I've returned the Third String safely to their stalls and survived a verbal lashing from Jangles, I stare at the office door of my boss's boss. A.k.a., Meister K.

Santa Claus.

My future grandfather-in-law.

Somehow, I don't think that last fact will spare me from another Penalty.

Three

Tinsel—Nov 21 Just a Legend

From behind his massive oak desk, Meister K regards me over his spectacles, his blue eyes sunken in his haggard expression. His fingers comb through his long, white beard in a repetitive motion. On the wall to his left hang portraits of his father and grandfather, their jolly faces out of place amidst the room's tension.

The silence lengthens.

I squirm on the armchair.

To Meister K's right hangs another portrait, a recent addition to the office, and the man's leering grin mocks my discomfort. One hand clutches a horned, devilish mask near his face; the other wields a long, black switch. A shiver drills down my spine. Karl Krampus. The patriarch of a family responsible for the growing opposition to Christmas, and for the entrenched rumors staining the beloved holiday.

Why is our enemy on display in Meister K's office?

Meister K clears his throat, and I startle, my gaze snapping back to his. He steeples his hands atop his desk. "Jangles informed me of what happened with the Third String," he says, his deep voice tired. "Now I would like to hear your version of the story."

I clench the folds of my dirndl skirt. "The Third String was gung-ho to leave the stables, sir. They'd been cooped up too long, you see. But I misjudged their mental stamina. Once they began acting loopy in the sky, I should've stopped any attempt at the Peppermint Twist despite their insistence—"

"The Twist!"

Swallowing, I run a fingertip along a stripe in the chair's fabric. "Yes, sir. They're getting the hang of it. If Chip hadn't started on the wrong lead, or maybe if Cocoa and Cinnamon hadn't rotated the wrong way—" I bite my lip. "I tried to warn them, correct them, but they couldn't hear me, and before I knew it, we were out of control, and … we crashed."

Rubbing a meaty hand over his mouth, Meister K heaves a long sigh. "I'd hoped to congratulate you and welcome you into the family before doling out another Penalty."

Heat creeps up my neck. It's been several months since my last Penalty. Doesn't that count for something?

Meister K lifts a steaming mug from his desk and takes a sip. He thunks it down again with a grimace. "For the love of marshmallows, what did those half-pints put in my eggnog?" He shoves the mug aside. "How is it they mess up a standard recipe after all these years? Of all the incompetent—" He halts as my eyebrows hike at his un-Santa-like behavior. His shoulders sag, and Meister K removes his glasses to rub his eyes, the spectacles dangling between his fingers. "Tinsel, Jangles seeks your suspension from the team, and I'm afraid I must agree with him."

"What?" I grip the chair cushion. This Penalty is worse than my phony banishment two years ago. "Meister K, I—"

He holds up his hand and my mouth snaps shut, pressure welling behind my eyes. "You showed a lack of foresight this evening. I know you would never wittingly put those 'deer in harm's way, and they, in turn, would do anything for you. The fact is, however, you did put them in harm's way. The one elf who should have known better than the rest of us that they're sick—"

"They downplayed it."

The eyes in Krampus's portrait turn accusing, and I shift on the chair again.

"You ignored the signs," Meister K says. "I would be remiss to ignore this breach of trust."

My throat aches at his stern words and deep frown, but he's right. I let the reindeer stoke my pride, which stoked a need to prove myself, which overran my good sense and sound judgment—and almost ended in disaster. "I'm sorry, sir."

"So am I." He replaces his spectacles. "For now, I shall allow the suspension. You'll have opportunities in Germany to show your competence with my brother's reindeer herd, and Jangles's anger may lessen during your absence. We can revisit this issue when you return."

I work to keep the hot tears from building on my eyelids. "What if you were to take away my trip instead of my job?" It's the one thing I excel at.

His mouth tightens. "We need you in Germany, Tinsel." Meister K stands and pivots to stare out the window. In the distant east, moonlight glimmers off the snow-capped Mount Trost. "What do you remember about the legend of the Silver Reindeer?"

At the random switch in topics, I blink away my blurred vision. Sifting through memories from my school days, I recite the nursery rhyme. "'If silver is born to the reindeer herd, Krampus will rise, new powers unfurled. Together Santa and 'deer must toil. Two years have they, the Krampus to foil.'"

15

"Mmm. Two years for the Silver Reindeer to mature and bond with the current Santa." Meister K clasps his hands behind his back. "Two years to prepare for an uprising. That animal would be key to Krampus's defeat, *nicht wahr?*"

"It's a fairy story. The few times in past generations that the Krampus family tried to usurp the mantle of Santa Claus, the elves defeated them with no help from some mythical Silver Reindeer."

His fingers twitch. "And yet, legends don't spring up without some origin in truth."

I stare at him. "Are you saying a Silver Reindeer existed in the past?"

"I'm saying what happened in the past has suddenly become more relevant." Meister K turns from the window and clears his throat. "Because Kristof discovered a Silver Reindeer last week."

Reality shifts, and I rock back in the armchair.

"She's being cared for by a rancher and his family a few towns over from Weihnachts Manor," Meister K continues. "Allegedly, someone had separated the reindeer as a newborn from her herd on purpose and left her in the Black Forest to die." He dips his head to look at me over his spectacles. "Had the Hoffmanns not found her and taken her in, we would've never known she existed."

"Never known." My fingers trail the pattern in my apron's embroidery. "So then, if the legend is true, we'd never have been able to defeat Krampus this time." Within his portrait, Krampus's eyes glint and his leer deepens. *Together Santa and 'deer must toil; two years have they, the Krampus to foil.* "How old is she? How much time do we have?"

Meister K tugs on his beard. "The Hoffmanns believe she was, uh, born two years ago this past June."

I jump to my feet. "She's two-and-a-half years old? That means we're running on borrowed time. How will you communicate with her now? How will we plan a victory? Christmas is five weeks away.

What if the Krampus family attacks before then? How—"

Again, Meister K holds up a hand. The faintest twinkle emerges in his eye. "I told you we need you in Germany."

I sink back onto the chair. "I don't under—" Oh. "You wish *me* to communicate with the Silver Reindeer? What about my ... suspension?" The word burns my tongue.

"The two are unrelated. Just don't put the SR in harm's way." He settles back at his desk. "One thing you must bear in mind, however. As far as we can tell, no one at Weihnachts Manor knows you can converse with reindeer, and we'd like to keep it that way."

My brow knits together. "I'm supposed to hide my talent?"

"Someone didn't want us to know about the SR. That someone could be a Krampus, but we haven't kept tabs on the descendants, and you know their mantle doesn't pass from firstborn to firstborn like the Kringles.'"

No, it gravitates to whichever family member is the most determined to claim and foster it. Thus, during one generation, Krampus could show up in North America. During another generation, in Europe. A third generation, in Asia.

"Surely your kin at Weihnachts Manor would pitch in and help us. Why the secrecy?"

"Over the last few years, the quality and quantity of work coming from my brother's outpost have deteriorated, while the discord between the elves in the Blue and White Clans has increased." Meister K reaches for his mug before jerking his hand back again. "That indicates a possible Krampus influence. I don't think it's a coincidence that the Silver Reindeer was born in that area and an attempt was made to snuff out her life. Until we know exactly who was behind such actions, word can't get around that we know about the SR, or that you have the ability to communicate with her. Understood?"

I nod.

"Now, head home and get some rest. You have several long travel days ahead of you."

Mind whirling, I rise and then hesitate at the door. "Do Meister Nico and the others know about this?"

"About the Silver Reindeer? Yes."

My fingers tighten on the doorknob. "And my suspension?"

"Not yet."

"If you don't mind, may I be the one to tell them?"

Meister K gives a curt bob of his head. With a whispered, *"Danke,"* I leave his office.

Cold envelops me as I exit the Workshop, my emotions wavering between elation and sorrow. The Kringles need my talent—yay. Except, a legend has proven true, we've lost all time to prepare against an enemy attack, I'm suspended from my beloved job and must inform Niklas of my folly.

Great gobs of dirty snow.

Descending Huff 'n Puff Hill, I hug my arms to my knotted stomach. How am I supposed to tell my fiancé I damaged the practice sleigh and endangered his reindeer? Will he side with his grandfather and Jangles in their decision to suspend me? Will he later question reinstating me on the team?

My boots drag along the path. What if this causes Niklas to second guess his proposal? After all, what forthcoming Santa would, in his right mind, unite with an elf who jeopardizes his reindeer? And though I was never irresponsible with the Third String before, now that it has happened, who's to say it won't happen again?

I mull over the plausible, unsavory outcomes down the hill and through town until I reach the Town Square. The recent addition of a gigantic snow globe whirrs at its center, a gift sent months ago from Meister K's brother, Stoffel. Snowflakes spiral out from a hole in the top on a constant stream of air. Inside the glass dome, flakes swirl around a scaled-down version of Weihnachts Manor, the original Christmas headquarters. In a few days, I'll behold the real deal.

Somewhere near that real deal is the Silver Reindeer, whose knowledge can make or break the future of Christmas.

Stray snowflakes land in my eyelashes as a stray thought lands in my mind. If my talent can help stave off an enemy uprising, surely that will restore my good standing in the eyes of Meister K and Jangles. And wipe away any future doubt that might plague Niklas in having proposed to such a bumbling elf.

This is perfect. I'll save Christmas from any nefarious Krampus plot *and* save my engagement.

A few days can't come fast enough.

Four

Tinsel—Nov 24 New World

My fingertips dance against the windowpane as the train races toward Munich's Hauptbahnhof. Bare trees and brown grass cover the gentle hills and fields of the German countryside, and while some might despair at the forlorn autumn view, I smile.

A new world awaits out there, and it's beautiful.

It's also huge. The chaos from the Frankfurt airport lingers on me like flour from my parent's *Konditorei*, The Flaky Crust, lingers on their clothes. So many people, speaking a dozen different languages, going in a hundred different directions to live a thousand different lives. And that was just one sliver of one city.

I fiddle with the tatted choker my parents gave me before I left Flitterndorf, three flights and two loooong layovers ago. Since then, I've reached for it often, seeking some semblance of comfort. A mini reindeer pendant hangs from it, lying in the cradle of my collarbone. Do Mutti and Vati know the "mission" I'm on, or is the reindeer merely a representation of the motley crew I've come to love in the Third String?

A crew that, if they know about my suspension, didn't hear it from me.

"Sugarplum for your thoughts," Niklas murmurs in my ear, his hand slipping around mine. A voice announces our destination through an intercom. "Your smile drooped. Thinking about the Third String?"

The jet lag-induced headache at the base of my skull ratchets up a notch, and my gaze flicks to Niklas's parents sitting on the bench seat opposite. "Why would you ask that? Have you heard something?"

Niklas snorts. "I know you. Sometimes, you're a little too preoccupied with my reindeer."

"Oh." I let out a relieved half-laugh.

"Kristof will check on them and let us know how they're doing. We've got a different reindeer to worry about, now that we're done with those frosted airplanes." Niklas shudders.

I search his face. Less green than it had been at the airport. "Grateful to be on the ground?"

"Grateful the worst is behind us." His expression grows sheepish. "I'm sorry I put you through that ordeal. I acted like a wuss—"

"Don't apologize." I finger my engagement ring. Its double-twisted band had left a temporary impression on my skin when Niklas seized my hand during the last flight. "It's not often I get to be the strong one. I'm happy to carry the burden once in a while." I prod his shoulder with mine. "We all have our weaknesses."

From my dirndl pocket, my cell phone (a combined present last year from Gina, Niklas, Kristof, and my parents) chimes with an incoming text. I pull it out to read the message.

Good morning! Gina writes. **Or I should say, good afternoon, since that's your present reality. ;) Got your text from earlier. Thnx for the travel updates. Pls tell me you're not still in Frankfurt—this has got to be the longest trip across the world ever!!**

Her enthusiasm oozes through her words, and I chuckle. We may be physically separated for three weeks, travel time included, but thank Christmas we can still "talk." **On the train, heading to Munich,** I reply. **There are villages out here bigger than twice the population of Flitterndorf and Waldheim combined! I feel tiny.**

A human-sized elf … tiny? Gina adds a laughing emoji.

I respond with the one looking heavenward.

Have you told you-know-who about you-know-what? she asks, referring to my lengthy text from the other day when I vented about my suspension.

Shifting on the seat, I glance at Niklas and type: **No.**

Coward, she shoots back.

I choke on a laugh. **Am not! Trying to gauge the best time to tell him.** And gather enough courage for the task.

Sooner rather than later, she responds. **Duh!**

"Best time to tell me what?" Niklas asks, resting his chin on my shoulder.

"What?" I slap the phone against my chest and edge away. "N-nothing. What makes you think it's about you?"

He laughs. "You claim my eye twitches when I lie, yet you don't exactly have a poker face yourself. But all right"—he holds up his hands—"keep your secrets for now. Seems I'll find out *sooner or later.*"

I stick out my tongue, and Niklas laughs all the more.

Once the train pulls into the station, we gather our belongings and follow his parents to the exit. As we disembark onto the platform, I succumb to a yawn, and the din of the Hauptbahnhof thrums in my ears. Squealing train wheels and whining machinery add to the warbled drone of a few hundred people coming and going in the gigantic steel building. A woman recites an announcement in German through the overhead PA system. Even the busiest day at the

Workshop pales in comparison to the noise and activity here.

My headache wraps toward my temples, and I scrounge in my backpack for the pain reliever Mutti insisted I take, "just in case."

God bless mothers everywhere.

"I've visited Weihnachts Manor once before," Madam Marie says beside me, her manner calm and unruffled. "It's hidden in a remote valley north of the Austrian border." She scans the bustling crowd before turning her merry gaze to me. "Serenity and seclusion—and a long nap—sound like heavenly peace at the moment."

We exchange a grin, and I offer her my pain reliever.

"Do we have everything?" Meister Nico asks, counting our luggage. At our nods, he smiles through his short gray beard and grips the handle to his suitcase. "Follow me. We're to meet my uncle at that American coffeehouse—Star-something-or-other."

Madam Marie falls into step beside her husband, with Niklas trailing behind them and me taking up the rear, lugging my gray-and-white checkered suitcase. People brush past me, some going the same way only faster, others going in the opposite direction. A few have their heads down, focused on their phones, and almost everyone wears some form of black coat and hauls a sleek, compact black roller.

I sidestep a man who pays more attention to his cyber world than the tangible one beneath his feet. "Does the coffeehouse offer drinking chocolate? I'm desperate for one of Mutti's Kandi Cups."

Chuckling, Niklas switches his suitcase to his other hand and reaches back to pull me alongside him. "No one can do chocolate like your mother."

I squeeze his fingers. "Trying to score brownie points with your future mom-in-law?"

"Nah, she's too savvy to fall for my Kringle charm." He winks and angles me away from an approaching gaggle of teenage girls who laugh over a shared phone.

23

We wend around a large family in the midst of a reunion, and I cling tighter to Niklas. "How do you Kringles do it?"

"Do what?"

"Not collapse under the pressure to reach everyone with the Hope of Christmas?" And how will I contribute once we're married? "Tucked away in our little corner of Flitterndorf, I never grasped how big the world is, how many people it holds."

"We don't do it alone, Tins." Niklas releases me to readjust his backpack straps. "Every Christmas believer helps shine a light in their own little corner. If we could see those lights through satellite imagery, it would make for a spectacular picture." He gives me a reassuring smile. "There are more believers than people suspect these days."

"Ho, *ho!*" The booming laugh cuts through the swirl of German conversations. "*Grüß Gott, meine Familie.*" A thinner version of Meister K steps into view beneath the coffeehouse's white block letters.

Meister Nico issues a belly laugh in return. "Onkel Stoffel! *Guten Tag.*"

"Nico." Spreading out his arms, Santa's look-alike rattles off more phrases in German, clapping Meister Nico on the shoulders. Then he swivels to Niklas. "And this must be Nicky. How big you've grown."

"Guten Tag, Great-Onkel Stoffel."

The bespectacled, bearded gentleman waves aside Niklas's words. "You're in Bairisch country now. We say *Grüß Gott*, not *Guten Tag.* And none of this 'great' stuff. Makes me feel old. Onkel Stoffel is perfect." He speaks with a hint of an accent after decades of living in Germany. Lowering his brow, he gestures to me. "Who is this? I thought you were bringing your little elf friend."

Niklas coughs. "This *is* my little friend—uh, my girlfriend"—he rolls his eyes—"my fiancée, Tinsel. Tinsel, meet my Onkel Stoffel."

Smiling, I hold out my hand. "Guten—er, Grüß Gott, Meister Kringle."

"'Meister'?" He peers at me over his glasses. "Flattering, but that title isn't mine. We keep things simple, *ja*? You may call me *Herr Stoffel*. So. You are the elf." He assesses me with faded blue eyes. "Tall, indeed. What do you do? Are you a Toy Maker?"

"I work with the reindeer." Used to.

"Oh? How so? You muck their stalls?"

I bristle at the implication. "I'm on the Minor Flight Team." Was. "In fact, my talent—"

"She has a calming effect on my 'deer." Niklas slides his arm around my waist, and I wince at my near slip-up. "I couldn't do without her."

Herr Stoffel's gaze sharpens. "Yes, well, it's good to be needed. I look forward to getting better acquainted."

As he greets Madam Marie, I murmur to Niklas, "Sorry. I forgot my talent's a secret."

He kisses my temple. "No harm done."

Yet.

"*Weihnachtsmann?*" A wee hand tugs on the hem of Niklas's coat.

His expression brightening, Niklas crouches to address the little boy, whose mother rattles off a spiel of German words. I catch the beginning: *Entshuldigung Sie*. She's apologizing, probably for the boy "mistaking" Niklas for Santa Claus. I give her a reassuring grin as Niklas engages the boy in conversation. She has no idea how often this happens when Niklas leaves Flitterndorf's borders.

And Niklas has no idea how easy he has it, to jump from language to language with nary a thought, thanks to the magical perk of being the future Santa Claus. As for me? Aside from the words we use in our daily speech back home, I've fought for the bit of German I know.

Which, after listening to the conversational snippets around me, isn't a whole lot.

"Come along, *Kinder*," Herr Stoffel calls, motioning to us as he walks past the coffeehouse. "*Mein Auto* is this way."

After some parting words to the boy and his mother, Niklas straightens and watches them walk away. "That's what it's all about, right there. Spreading the Love. Sharing the Hope." He runs a palm along his chin, brow furrowed. "We have to find that Silver Reindeer before Krampus's running start clinches his win."

Five

Tinsel—Nov 25 Weihnachts Manor

Light presses against my closed eyelids as I emerge from sleep. Stretching my arms and legs across the satin sheets, I seek the edges of my twin mattress ... in vain.

My lips twitch in a smile. I'm not in my twin bed.

A faint "Ho, ho, ho," echoes from far away.

Nor am I in my family's apartment above the Flaky Crust.

Although jet lag leaves my head feeling like the Toy Makers stuffed it with cotton batting, and news of the Silver Reindeer marks this trip with a measure of gravity, I bound out of bed with an excited squeal that would make Gina proud. Racing to one side of the partially opened curtains, I pull a silken cord.

The velvet drapery parts farther, and sunlight streams through the lattice windows, chasing away the room's morning chill. I press my forehead against the pane. Located in a wing on the third floor of Weihnachts Manor, my room offers a grand view of the exterior façade angling away from me.

Manor, indeed. A misleading moniker for the Kringles' original residence. Chiseled stone walls expertly meld with the same Tudor architecture as the Workshop, but where four corner towers anchor the boxy Workshop, this place is a rambling castle with multiple wings and rooflines, turrets and spindles, nooks and crannies. A literal feast—no, dessert—for the eyes. With Christmas icing on top.

I intend to explore as soon as possible.

My stomach growls.

Or maybe I'll explore right after breakfast.

Rubbing my pajama sleeves, I turn from the window, and my smile grows. Bathed in sunlight, the bedroom's maroon walls exude warmth, the murals spring to life, and gilded portraits sparkle. Beside the four-poster bed stands a stone fireplace, where the nighttime fire still crackles—oddly enough. Long-needled garland festoons the mantelpiece. A chaise lounge and wardrobe share the adjacent wall, while a private bathroom juts into the room along the window wall. This suite is large enough to fit the entire Third String without feeling squished.

I grab my phone off the nightstand and pull up my text thread with Niklas as I pad over to the wardrobe. **You awake?**

Inside the wardrobe, my clothes either hang from the rod or rest in the column of shelves to the right. A new scent escapes the furniture's confines, and I take a deep breath. No, not new. Where have I smelled it before?

Another muted, "Ho, ho, ho," floats under the bedroom door, followed by a high-pitched peal of laughter. Herr Stoffel, no doubt, and one of Niklas's second cousins. I search my memory for their names. Fritz, Elke, and Lukas. Siblings who came here six years ago to live with their grandfather after their parents died. Maybe Niklas already enjoys a hot breakfast with them, since it is half past ten.

I finger through my clothes options. Provided I can find my way to the dining room, do I join them wearing my customary dirndl or attempt to blend in with skinny jeans?

The back of my neck prickles, and I spin around.

"Who's there?" The words fly from my mouth though I stand alone in the bedroom. The portraits and life-sized murals peer out from the walls. Could they …? I scoff. "No one's watching you, Tinsel." I stare down each figure, one at a time. "They're nothing but empty faces."

Still, I have a sudden hankering for flesh-and-blood company. After snatching a dirndl off a hanger and a long sleeve blouse from the top shelf, I hurry into the bathroom to freshen up and change.

* * *

Ten minutes later, I exit the suite, clasping my new choker into place, my phone in my pocket in case Niklas finally texts me, my gray newsboy cap atop my head. Although the manor's cloaking spell still exists within its borders—the one Nicholas Kringle created in the sixteenth century to protect the resident elves' identities—who knows if the magic will cloak elfin guests as well. Fingering the outlines of my pointy ears, I reassure myself they're hidden.

A long hallway extends in both directions, ending at corners that curve out of sight. Which way to the stairs?

I hold up my index finger. When in doubt, default to *Kindheit*. Childhood.

Eenie meenie minie mop
Time for work up at the 'Shop
Building toys, we never stop
Eenie meenie minie mop

Left it is.

I venture along the carpeted corridor, idly tapping the wall sconces as I pass. Two years ago, I broke one in a Workshop tower, which ended up being the mechanism needed to lower a wall and get a retired sleigh to Santa. One of several secrets I discovered that Christmas season.

How many secrets does Weihnachts Manor hide?

Glancing over my shoulder, I tug on a sconce. It doesn't budge. Ah, well.

At the corridor's end, I hesitate. Silent night, this new wing goes on forever. I could get lost until Christmas Day and not have exhausted all my options. I shoot another text to Niklas: **How do I get to the dining room?!**

Up ahead, the fifth door on the right stands ajar, opening into the hallway and blocking my view of the room's interior. Approaching it, I knock first, then peek around it when no one answers. A narrow stone corridor extends into blackness. I wrinkle my nose at its earthy smell and close the door.

A soft gasp issues farther down the hallway.

"*Was machen Sie hier?* What are you doing?" Emerging from an alcove with a stack of towels in her arms, a teenage elf with big brown eyes hurries toward me, brown hair tucked beneath a pointed blue cap, cobalt blue dirndl skirts swishing with each step. Her gaze darts beyond me, behind her, up at me. "*Sie sollten nicht hier sein.*"

I shouldn't be here? "*Es tut mir leid,*" I apologize. "*Ich suche ...* um ... *Wissen Sie wo ...* uh ..." I worry my bottom lip. Seriously? After spending the last two years studying German for such an opportunity, I forget everything I learned? I give her my friendliest smile. She's smaller in stature than many of my peers in Flitterndorf, but she can't be more than a year or two younger than me. "*Sprechen Sie Englisch?* I-I'm looking for the dining room. Or is it the breakfast room? Um ... *Frühstuck?*"

"No food on this floor," she responds with an accent. She readjusts her towels and makes shooing motions with one hand. "*Bitte,* you go.

Schnell. Before *Frau* Wissen sees—"

"*Was ist heir passiert?*" a sharp voice calls out.

The elf winces, her hold tightening on the bottom towel. An older female elf has emerged from the alcove, her features stern, her dirndl ivory in color and long in the skirt. She marches toward us, glaring first up at me, then straight at the other elf, and issues a stream of foreign words too fast for me to catch. The teenage elf lowers her chin, gives a quiet response with a curtsy, and hurries back the way she had come.

Pivoting her glare back to me, the older elf—Frau Wissen, I assume—points in the opposite direction, spewing another round of German words. I catch one because I know it well: *verboten.*

As in the now-defunct-thanks-to-Niklas edict, "Romance between elves and Kringles is verboten."

What am I forbidden from now? "*E-Entschuldigung.* I'm looking for—"

She stomps a foot, her eyes bulging. "*Verlassen Sie sofort!*"

Yikes—I'm leaving, I'm leaving! I scamper back along the hallway, risking a last glance at the corner. The elf's face remains rigid, her nostrils flared. Good garland, she's more militant than Frau Tanz, my former dance instructor at Flitterndorf School of Talents.

After several backtracks and U-turns, I emerge onto a wide gallery that runs along the inside wall of an enormous entrance hall. The hall stands three stories high with marble floors and columns, and filigreed molding in the ceiling. Light pours through an upper bank of windows on the opposite wall, below which a pair of glass doors lead outside to a terrace, its furniture protected under canvas for the winter. A bare Norway spruce stands in the hall's center, stretching toward the ceiling, mammoth in size yet modest in appearance compared to its opulent surroundings. Several presents find shelter beneath the branches, but where are the Christmas ornaments?

Three elves appear below and cross the entrance hall to toss—toss!—more presents under the tree. *"The quality and quantity of work coming from Weihnachts Manor over the last few years have deteriorated,"* Meister K told me.

Meister Nico says the Kringles would've remained in Weihnachts Manor had the outside world's population growth not encroached on the manor and threatened the elves' ability to expand and multiply. When Christofel Kringle set off to find a new location after the German War of 1866, the majority of elves accompanied him, and they eventually established Flitterndorf and its protective barrier in northern Canada.

What about the elves who stayed behind? Did they stay willingly, or were they forced?

A fresh wave of laughter carries from below, and I follow it down the wide, curving staircase to a pair of oak doors standing ajar. I poke my head inside the room. Niklas, his second cousins, and Herr Stoffel sit around an oval table strewn with half-finished breakfast plates, glasses of orange juice and water, and mugs of hot liquid. Dare I hope it's drinking chocolate?

"Guten Morgen," I say, venturing into the cozy breakfast room with its pale green walls and more gilded paintings. Niklas breaks off his conversation with a pretty brunette and hops from his chair.

"There you are." Eyes gleaming, he engulfs me in a hug. "I was beginning to think you'd gone to tour the manor on your own."

"More like a *de*tour, and completely unintentional. Didn't you get my texts?"

"What texts? My phone's been quiet all morning."

"You talk of Handys? Cell phones?" The brunette sidles up beside Niklas and lays polished fingernails on his upper arm as she addresses me. "Messages and calls can be so-so inside Weihnachts Manor." A delicate accent colors her words, and she smells faintly of roses.

"Some rooms get two bars. Other rooms get no bars." She points out the window. "The terrace gets four."

Niklas grins. "In other words, better to communicate face-to-face."

I glance at the table, where eight-year-old Lukas and his older brother, Fritz—who could pass for Niklas in age and looks, save for his auburn hair—talk with their sister, Elke. I turn back to the brunette, whose hand still lingers on my man's arm. "I don't think we met yesterday. You are ...?"

"Entschuldigung. Where are my manners?" Her lips spread in a smile, white teeth against rose lipstick. "I'm Gretel Brunner."

My stomach contracts, and the air vacates the room.

This polished woman is Niklas's ex-fiancée.

Six

Tinsel—Nov 25 First Impressions

Forcing my own smile, I shake Gretel's hand. "Pleased to meet you. I'm—"

"Tinsel Kuchler, of course." She flicks her sleek hair behind her shoulder. "I finally meet the girl who captured our Nicky's affections."

Nicky? Squeezing the reindeer pendant on my choker, I take in Gretel's heart-shaped face and curvy frame. Not at all how *our Nicky* painted her. I raise my eyebrows at him.

Though he smiles, his eyes are pinched, like he consumed a bad batch of figgy pudding. He motions toward a sideboard lined with covered dishes. "You hungry, Tins?"

"Bitte, help yourself," Gretel says. "We have a typical Canadian breakfast for your comfort, but you must promise to try *Weisswurst*, our traditional Bavarian sausage."

"We? Our?"

A soft laugh escapes her, soothing yet subdued, like it never fully developed. It draws Fritz's appreciative eye. "The Kringles, I mean. I visit so often, the manor feels like home." Waving aside her words, she sashays back to her place at the table. Caramel-toned hair bounces around her shoulders, her heather gray sweater and black pants hugging her in all the right places.

I adjust my newsboy cap, wishing I'd asked Gina to tone down my copper hue when she cut my hair last week, and whisper to Niklas, "You once said she'd fit the Santa outfit better than you."

He guides me to the food as I tug at my wrinkled dirndl skirt. "She's obviously been on a diet," he whispers back, offering me a plate.

"Obviously." I heap the plate with fried potatoes.

"And she must have done something different with her hair."

"Mmm-hmm." I should've chosen my skinny jeans. Even Niklas has forgone his lederhosen today.

"And had her teeth fixed."

"And then what? Plastic surgery?"

"Tinsel—"

"You could've warned me." I scoop a hard-boiled egg onto my plate. "She's your ex-fiancée, for garland's sake."

"We were never engaged," he murmurs.

"An opinion not shared by the masses."

Niklas cups my elbow. "You believe the elves over me?"

"I believe you never considered yourself engaged, but what did it say on paper?"

"There was no paper because there was no arrangement because there was no agreement."

I cock an eyebrow. "Seriously, *Nicky*, how often will she be here?" Because whenever we're in a room together, people will compare the two of us, and I already know which one will come up lacking. Ugh. I plop a link of Weisswurst beside my egg and grab a bread roll.

Niklas presses his lips to my cheek. "I picked you, Tins. Never forget that." He catches my gaze, his green eyes flooded with affection.

My posture softens. He did pick me. And he didn't have to. Where is this insecurity coming from?

Herr Stoffel clears his throat from his position at the head of the table. Niklas pulls away with a wink and leads me to a pair of chairs across from Lukas and Fritz.

"*Sind Sie eine echte Elfe?*" the little boy asks, freckles dotting a wide-eyed face beneath a mop of golden-brown hair.

Fritz elbows him in the arm. "*Auf Englisch.*"

"It's okay, I understood him." Piercing a potato wedge with my fork, I smile at Lukas. "Yes, I'm a real elf."

"You're big."

"She's *tall*." Fritz smacks the back of Lukas's head.

Lukas shoves him off and stares at me. "Why?"

"Why am I tall?" I pop the food in my mouth and swallow before answering. "I'm one-eighth human on my father's side."

"Oooh. A *Mischling*."

"Lukas!" Elke hisses. "Do not be rude."

Herr Stoffel peers beneath bushy eyebrows at his grandson. "Not quite a half-breed, Lukas. We must pay better attention to your math skills, nicht wahr?" Steepling his fingers, he turns to me. "How do you like your room?"

I tug my gaze from the young boy, deciding not to take offense. "It's beautiful, sir. Beyond what I imagined for a guest room. *Vielen dank.*" I cut into my sausage and bring a piece to my mouth.

Herr Stoffel watches me. "Is it customary in Flitterndorf to wear hats when you eat?"

"N-nein." Cheeks stinging, I lower the fork. "I've heard Weihnachts Manor receives many visitors, and …"

Herr Stoffel reaches for his ceramic mug. "And?"

"My ears, sir."

"What about your ears?"

I glance down the table at Gretel, but she already knows about me.

"They're pointed."

His nostrils flare. "I heard the elves in Flitterndorf are educated, so how is it you are ignorant about the magic instilled on these grounds?" "I'm not ignorant, sir." My hands fist in my lap, and Niklas covers them with one of his. "I know about the cloaking spell, and that visitors to the manor see the elves as humans and their village as nothing more than a vast, green lawn." Heat pours over me. "Yet I'm a guest here—"

"What does that matter?" Herr Stoffel sits back with a *harrumph.* "An elf, by any other birthplace—or height—is still just an elf."

Just? I return his cool stare.

Niklas squeezes my hands. "Good news for me, then."

Herr Stoffel cocks his head. "Oh?"

"Mmm. I'm rather fond of her ears." Niklas slips off my newsboy cap, the air cooling my ears as my layered curls spring free. His face hardens at his uncle. "They're arguably her best feature and shouldn't be forced into hiding the entire time we're here."

Movements halt around the table as the unspoken challenge sparks between Herr Stoffel and his great-nephew. Gretel emits a delicate cough into the lengthening silence.

"My, it smells wonderful in here," says a tired voice as one door swings wide. Meister Nico ushers Madam Marie into the dining room, dark circles shading his eyes. His gaze rakes over the subdued crowd, and he slips his thumbs behind his lederhosen suspenders. "Eh, good morning, everyone. I trust it's not too late to say that."

Niklas gives him a strained smile. "Officially? No." He rises to kiss his mother on the cheek.

Herr Stoffel motions toward the food. "There is still plenty of *Essen* to enjoy." As they fill their plates, he asks, "Have you discussed your plans for today?"

"I'd love an official tour of the manor." Madam Marie laughs. "We got lost finding the breakfast room."

At least I'm not the only one. "Could we also visit the reindeer stables? I promised the Third String I'd take pictures of the herd."

Niklas exchanges a weighty look with his father. Did I speak out of turn? Maybe they want to first visit the Hoffmann ranch and see the Silver Reindeer.

"The stables are my favorite place here," Fritz says, redirecting my attention. I'm struck again by his resemblance to Niklas.

"Mine, too." I chuckle. "I-I mean, it's my favorite place in Flitterndorf. Even Niklas doesn't mind going there anymore."

Fritz's forehead puckers. "Anymore?"

Niklas stiffens beside me, and I cringe inwardly. Fruitcake. Me and my stupid mouth.

Gretel cradles her coffee cup. "Isn't Santa's place with his reindeer?"

"Santa's place is wherever Santa is needed." Meister Nico takes a seat to the right of his uncle and reaches for the pepper. An awkward silence descends.

"Want to know my favorite place?" Lukas pipes up in his light accent.

His excitement eases the tension like a favorite Christmas carol eases stress, and Niklas grins. "The library."

"Nein." Lukas scrunches his nose.

Running a finger along his bottom lip, Niklas pretends to think. "The media room?"

Lukas giggles. "Nein!"

"No? Hmm." Niklas shrugs. "I give up. What's your favorite place?"

"The dungeons. It is perfect for"—he squints at the ceiling—"*ein Versteckspiel?*"

"Hide and Seek. Ah. I'm afraid I'd have the advantage in that game." When Lukas's forehead puckers, Niklas leans toward him, resting his arms on the table. "Do you know that as a future Santa, I possess the ability to locate children anywhere in the world?"

Lukas's eyes grow round. "No fair."

Niklas smiles. "I suppose I could ignore that Santa-sense, if you want to play sometime."

I fiddle with my choker. "Why does Weihnachts Manor have dungeons?"

"They are from the original structure," Gretel says. "But when Nicholas Kringle moved into the abandoned manor to create Christmas headquarters, he used them for storage."

Lukas says something in German, his voice taking on a spooky tone, his mischievous gaze darting around the table.

"You exaggerate about the dungeons, my boy." Herr Stoffel pushes aside his plate. "We shall take a tour of the manor when everyone finishes eating." His gaze slides to me. "Then you can see our storage for yourself."

As conversations deviate, Gretel walks around the table and slides into the vacant chair beside me. She points to my choker. "That is lovely."

"Thank you. My parents gave it to me."

"I make something similar." She pulls back her sleeve cuff to reveal a hemp bracelet around her wrist, beads alternating among the intricate knots.

Niklas stretches across me to take her wrist in hand. "Wow. That's beautiful. You made this?"

Gretel nods, a smile curving her lips. My chest tightens. Outshone once again.

Niklas sniffs, and that's when I smell it, too. Subtle and pleasing. "Is that coming from the bracelet?" I ask.

"Mm-hmm. Ylang ylang, rose, and other essential oils. Rubbed into the hemp."

"What if we added that stuff to your necklace, Tins?" Niklas bumps my shoulder with his. "That'd be cool, huh?"

Why? So I can smell like Gretel?

"We could do that." Gretel withdraws her wrist and looks at me. "If you want. I could also teach you how to make one of these bracelets while you're here."

Niklas laughs. "Knots on a reindeer harness Tinsel can handle. Tiny knots like this? You should've seen the sewing projects she tried to do for school—" He cuts off, blinks, and meets my frown with his own. "I'm sorry. I shouldn't poke fun."

He hasn't done so at my expense for a long time. At least he apologized. Angling toward Gretel, I force a light-hearted tone into my words. "Niklas is right. I'm all thumbs when it comes to knitting or sewing. That said, I don't shy away from trying something new. Will you teach me?"

Her answering smile reveals a crooked bicuspid. Not perfect, after all.

Okay, so she's my fiancé's pseudo-ex-fiancée, but she doesn't act like an embittered ex. Perhaps she hated the idea of an arranged marriage as much as Niklas did, in which case, there's no reason to feel threatened or not to like her. I was predisposed to dislike *Gina* when I first met her simply because she enjoyed a close friendship with Niklas. Now she's my best friend. What if I find a similar ally in Gretel, despite her history with Niklas?

Besides, this time I've got the guy. Why waste energy being jealous?

Seven

Tinsel—Nov 25 Quite the Personalities

If ever I need a reminder for where jealousy can lead a person, it hangs in the ballroom, our current stop on the impromptu tour.

Sunlight pours through an upper row of windows in the cavernous room, bouncing off pale walls and gilded accents, and shimmering through crystal chandeliers. Elegant patterns in the hardwood floor meander beneath a Christmas-themed mural stretching across the ceiling. Bas-relief of poinsettias and holly berries decorate the walls alongside frescoes of past Kringles—rosy-cheeked men who wore the mantle of Santa Claus, Sinterklaas, Père Noel, Babbo Natale, and more, throughout the ages.

Yet for all the splendor in the room, corruption seeps behind a few Santas in the form of Krampus, denoting times in history when Santa and his elves came under attack.

All because Krampus coveted Santa's role and desired power.

Power in benevolent hands promotes life. Power in jealous hands destroys it.

I glance again at Gretel chatting with Madam Marie. Gretel has probably exchanged more words with Niklas's mother in the hour-long tour than I have in my nineteen years of life. Were I that good at making small talk—

My gaze cuts back to the nearest Krampus fresco with his cold eyes and sneer, and I lift my chin as some in the group filter from the room. "If you're what ultimate jealousy looks like, I want no part in it." I turn abruptly, bumping into a solid form, but a silver glint in the fresco catches my eye.

"*Vorsicht*," Niklas says, gripping my arms. "Careful."

"Sorry." I flash a smile, my focus on the fresco, and strain to make out the silvery-white form leaping in the sky above Krampus's head. "Hey, is that the Silver Reindeer?" I grip Niklas's arm. "Meister K said the legend must be based on some truth. What do you think it means, that an SR is depicted with these two particular men?"

"What do *you* think it means?"

What's with Niklas's sudden accent? Auburn hair registers in my peripheral vision, and I recoil from Fritz, putting distance between us. "Now that's freaky. I thought you were Niklas."

"Entschuldigung?" Fritz frowns.

"You sound like him. Well, the timbre of your voice. Not in pronunciation." I search for tousled blond hair among the others. Niklas crouches beside Lukas as they talk. "You look like him, too."

Fritz appraises his second cousin. "I do not see it." He gestures at the fresco. "So, you think Silver Reindeer is significant?"

"Um…" I stare at the muscled animal, thick antlers arching above its back. Panic buzzes in my head. Had I said something important? Did I let something slip? "It certainly is magnificent. I'm told it sparkles even in the dark."

"*Es funkelt sogar im Dunkeln*," Fritz says, repeating my words in German. He quirks an eyebrow. "Silver Reindeer is not real."

I shrug to offset anything I may have said. "It's fun to imagine what it might be like to meet one." Soon, I'll get my chance.

"You cannot meet what does not exist."

Who's he trying to convince, me or himself? *Did you know one was born over two years ago?* I want to argue. But I stay silent, since it was by accident that Kristof found out about the SR while interning at the Russian Outpost, and we don't know if Fritz can be trusted.

Someone squeezes my arm, and I jump. Niklas—the real one—chuckles. "Already spooked and we haven't seen the dungeons."

I offer a tight-lipped smile as we exit the ballroom onto the gallery overlooking the naked evergreen tree. Although I worried leaving the tree branches unadorned was a slight against Christmas, it turns out Weihnachts Manor celebrates the German way, saving the tree decorating for Christmas Eve. A lone elf adds two more presents under the branches. Earlier in the tour, we peeked into several of the elves' workrooms peppered throughout the manor—candy-making in the kitchen; teddy bear and toy stations on the fourth floor; woodworking in what was originally the conservatory—but I haven't glimpsed my favorite area.

Sunlight winks through the glass terrace doors, beckoning me to the grounds that lie beyond. "Instead of the dungeons, could we visit the stables now?"

"Would you like to visit the stables now?" Fritz asks at the same time.

We share a grin, even as the humor fades from Niklas's eyes. "Stables. Of course. Because we love those reindeer." He claps Fritz on the shoulder. "Lead the way, cousin."

* * *

Bundled in our coats and gloves, we cross the wide, flagstone terrace, last night's rain puddling here and there on the stones. A dormant fountain in the center portrays a mighty reindeer rearing on its hind legs, head tucked, antlers angled toward the heavens.

My phone chimes with an incoming text. Then chimes again. Beside me, Niklas's phone does likewise. Once. Twice. Three times. I laugh. "Seems we found a signal. Fritz, you must come out here often to chat with your friends, huh?"

Fritz lifts a shoulder as Niklas pulls out his phone, and we descend the terrace stairs.

In the distance, sprawling across the extensive grounds, lies the elves' village. Their homes reflect the manor's colors, smoke curling from some chimneys, round-topped windows like friendly eyes. Fritz follows a path along the village's outer curve before veering off toward a thick copse of evergreens. Our proximity to the elves' homes reveals the peeling paint, warped wooden shutters, missing shingles, and cracked front walks of what I thought were well-kept cottages. I nudge Niklas to glance up from his phone. This is a stark contrast to the tidy abodes in Flitterndorf. The few elves milling about narrow their eyes as we pass.

I clear my throat and address Fritz in the uneasy silence. "Tell me about the manor's magic boundary. I heard it begins at the gatehouse on the northwest side. Where does it go from there?"

With his hand, Fritz indicates the forest that wraps behind the elf dwellings. "Almost two kilometers into the forest, and one kilometer east of the gatehouse."

"Those *are* tight confines. No wonder the Kringles felt the need to move."

"Leaving behind the unlikelies."

Niklas looks at him. "Excuse me?"

Fritz nods back at the elf village. "Not everybody went to Flitterndorf."

"But why call them the 'unlikelies'?"

"Christofel Kringle left them behind. He believed they had nothing to offer and were expendable."

The muscles in Niklas's jaw bunch. "He did not believe that. Everyone has something to offer."

"Perhaps they wanted to stay," I suggest, slipping a hand around Niklas's arm.

Fritz looks at me askance as we pass among the evergreens, beyond which spreads a long, one-storied stone building. "Ask them sometime. See what they tell you. Here." He points to the building, two mini cupolas atop its slate roof. Four wide, red doors mark four entrances. "Our stables." He ushers us through one entrance into a dimly lit interior.

I rub my arms. Dust motes hang in the air, and a solitary black carriage sits in a corner. "No elves today?"

"Our operation is not like yours. Few of our reindeer fly, and we don't have flight teams, so stables are in name only. They hold tools and food supplements. No animals."

Niklas picks up a random shovel, inspecting it. "Surely some elves work with the reindeer."

"That is *my* job." Fritz ducks through a back doorway.

I follow him. "You?" Behind the stables, a wooden fence separates us from a pasture where a dozen reindeer graze.

"Just not the way you think." Fritz smooths a finger along his lip, like Niklas does sometimes. "Mostly I teach them tricks and get them used to pulling a sleigh and meeting children at the *Weihnachtsmarkt*."

I grin. "You take them to the Christmas market?"

"The ones I trust. Though even then, they sometimes surprise me."

Niklas hasn't joined us. Propping my elbows atop the split-rail fence, I glance at the stables. He paces the exterior wall, phone pressed to his ear, face taut with concern. Hmm. I refocus on Fritz. "Reindeer do have quite the personalities."

Fritz cocks his head. "Capabilities, sure. Personalities?"

One reindeer trots over to the fence and puts her snout in my face. I laugh. "Hi, there. Who are you?"

"This is Bonbon. She's proving to be a great jumper."

"Well, hi, Bonbon. Or should I say, Grüß dich." I scratch behind one ear, and she pushes into my hand.

"Dinna react ta my voice," the reindeer whispers in a rush, "but if ye understand me, scratch m'other ear, then tap me nose twice."

My heart leaps at the familiar brogue even as a tremor careens down my back. Why would she communicate with me, when no one here knows about my talent? Do I respond or not?

I can't help it—I scratch her other ear and tap her nose.

Bonbon pumps her head. "Good. They said ye could, though I dinna believe it."

They, who? A shame my skills don't include mind-reading.

"I must talk with ye alone. There's a tall, spindly pine at the edge o' the woods beyond the elf village. Can ye meet me there after midnight, once everyone is asleep? Rub me neck if the answer's aye."

I comply as a brawnier reindeer approaches, a white patch of fur surrounding his left eye below the jagged remains of a brow tine.

"What're ye doin' with that elf?" Dipping his head, he jabs Bonbon's side with his good brow tine.

"Muskat!" Fritz pushes at the larger reindeer's shoulder. "Stop that."

"I told ye no' ta talk with her." Muskat jabs Bonbon again and she jumps away. "Git goin'. Back ta th' others."

Fritz slips between the rails and swats the animal's rump. "What's gotten into you?"

Muskat's eyes narrow at me. "Whate'er she said, ferget it. They're lost ta ye, so dinna bother lookin'. Go back where ye came from." He blows out a breath, blasting me with hot air, and trots away.

Coughing, I wave a hand by my face, my heart clunking behind my rib cage.

"I stand corrected—they have strong personalities." Fritz's brow furrows as Muskat moves through the herd. "What was that about?"

Muskat doesn't want me talking to Bonbon? Who's lost, and how concerned should I be? That settles it. Even if I have to set ten alarms to wake me, I'm showing up at that spindly pine tonight. Fritz studies me, and I knead the tension from my forehead. Must pretend I didn't hear anything from either of them. "Maybe he doesn't like me?"

Fritz props his boot on the bottom rail of the fence. "Muskat does not even know you."

"Neither does your grandfather, and he doesn't like me." I pinch my lips closed. Didn't intend to share that little observation.

Fritz sighs. "Opa Stoffel likes tradition. You challenge tradition."

"How so?"

"You're an elf, yet you're tall."

"Not by choice."

"You're engaged to a Kringle, yet it's verboten."

My hands tighten on the top rail. "We scrapped that edict two years ago. Didn't you get the memo?"

He spares me a sidelong glance. "You should not have come to Germany, Tinsel." His accent thickens with agitation.

I huff. "All the more reason to stay, then."

"You do not understand—"

"I understand that Niklas wants me here for the Initiation Ceremony, and Meister K wants me to—" I look down and pick at the railing. *Make contact with the Silver Reindeer.* Good garland, how many times will I almost let something slip today? "Meister K wants me to have a good time," I finish lamely.

"People don't always get what they want." Fritz's gaze slides past me toward Niklas. "Not even your Weihnachtsmänner."

Santa Clauses. Plural form. Is there a double meaning behind his words?

Niklas saunters over, stashing his phone in a coat pocket. He smiles, but it's his fake one. "Sorry about that. Grandpop called, and I decided to take it while I had reception. What'd I miss?"

Eight

Gina—Nov 25 Not a Brother

~⸲ᗒᗕᘔ~

Waldheim

I flick my finger and send a pen spinning on the desk's surface. The spreadsheet on my laptop screen blurs before my tired eyes, and I let my head drop back to stare at the office ceiling. As the owner of the Huggamugg Café, Claire will be happy with the increase in the shop's numbers, thanks to some recent creative changes I implemented—but mostly thanks to Dad's advice for turning a profit.

It was Dad and my brother, Logan, who suggested I take over local management when Claire wanted to open a second café in Calgary. Since Logan created a good life for himself far away in Terrebonne (conveniently forgetting he'd planned to come back and set up an auto repair shop here in Waldheim), it's natural he'd want me to experience the same sense of success. I agreed because it seemed the next logical step.

Now I'm wondering, the next step to what?

My gaze drifts to the doll standing atop the corner file cabinet. I named her Caterina after my aunt because they have the same elegance and chic fashion sense. Its face is the canvas for my latest attempt at a repaint, yet in the harsh office lighting, the doll's lips look too thick, and the hue clashes with the lavender-pink I used to paint the cheeks. Maybe after my workout with Aunt Cat at the gym this afternoon, I can try again.

Finger-combing my hair over one shoulder, I separate out some blue strands from the black as my laptop alerts me of a new email. I wind the blue lock around my finger and toggle between programs to check my inbox. Café spreadsheets can wait.

My heart trips at the latest message. It's from Doll Haven. Ever since their contest ended a month ago, I've anticipated, dreaded, hoped, feared, longed for their announcement. I click into the email, worrying my bottom lip.

Dear Ms. Donati,

Thank you for your entry into the Doll Haven's Repaint Contest. We were at once undone by the hundreds of applicants we received and astounded by their many talents and creations. While each artist made a lasting impression upon us, we could only choose the top three winners to join us for Doll Haven's Doll Making Workshop.

We regret to inform you—

I sit back, a combination of disappointment and relief swirling in my heart. I'd entered the contest on a whim, a way to test the proverbial waters. Had they announced me as a winner, I don't know that I could've left Waldheim to attend the workshop. Validation of a latent talent would have been nice, though.

Instead, they rejected my work. And no matter what anyone says, rejection of one's work still feels personal.

Caterina taunts me from atop the file cabinet. In a matter of steps, I cross the room and rotate her to face the wall. "Silly idea, anyway, Gina," I whisper, fluffing the doll's dark hair. "Stick with what you're good at."

Which, apparently, is managing a café.

A knock sounds on my door. "Gina?" Mikal, my right-hand gal, hovers in the office doorway, a smile on her round face. She wags her eyebrows. "Sorry to disturb you, but there's a guy here to see you."

Chuckling, I join her in the hallway. "What's with the giddy-schoolgirl vibe?"

She fans her cheek. "He's super cute—like the tourists you're always dating—and it got me wondering." Smile widening, she pushes open the door that links the café's "Employees Only" rooms to the front dining area. "What if one of them returned to woo you? Wouldn't that be romantic?"

"'Woo'? Have you been reading Jane Austen again?" Mikal's suggestion is ludicrous, of course. After Isaak broke my naive teenage heart a few years ago, I adopted a three-date policy—hence why I only date tourists. By the third date, they're leaving town, and I remain unscathed by love. (Plus, I'm holding out for a real-life Legolas from The Lord of the Rings movies. Few men these days can attain that level of awesome.)

What if, however, I left one of *their* hearts wounded? Or even worse, hopeful?

Oh, dear.

Behind Mikal, I adjust my burgundy tunic sweater, brush lint from my leggings, and brace for whoever awaits me.

A young man in a knitted black cap leans an elbow on the ordering counter. Broad shoulders fill out his black ski coat, and a gray knit scarf loops about his neck. Gracious, Mikal was right. Not a Legolas, yet definite hunk material. Our gazes catch, and my stomach scrambles when his mouth lifts in a grin.

Wait, I know that grin. "Kristof? Omigoodness!" Abandoning my reserve, I rush forward and rise on tiptoe to fling my arms about his neck. His arms wrap around my waist, and a combination of sandalwood and vanilla compels me to press my nose into his scarf and take a deep inhale. "What are you doing here?"

"Came to town to gather supplies at the hardware store." Kristof gives me a tight squeeze, then relaxes his hold. "I couldn't very well skip seeing my favorite person in Waldheim."

"You're not even supposed to be in the country." I shift in the loose circle of his arms and tilt my head back. "What'd they feed you in Russia? Last time I saw you, I was, like, eye-level with your chin. Now, you're a full head taller."

"I credit the stuffed *pelmeni* and truckloads of potatoes."

"When did you get back? Does Tinsel know? She didn't mention anything in a text."

Kristof's hazel eyes crinkle. "You two talk about me? Should I be concerned or flattered?"

His teasing reminds me we stand in a semi-embrace, and I withdraw before we attract unnecessary attention from Mikal and the regulars in the dining room. Gesturing for him to follow, I head for the back door. "We can chat in private, and you can tell me why you're here rather than exploring another abandoned castle or carving up a frozen pond in the German village on your hockey skates."

"Plans changed," comes his frank response. By the time we enter my office, however, his countenance has dimmed.

I close the door and sit atop my desk, my booted feet swaying as I wait for him to expound. Silence grows instead. Removing his cap, Kristof plows his hand through spiky dark blond locks. His eyebrows rise, and he points to the corner. "What are you hiding over there?"

"Hmm?" I visually trace the path of his finger to my doll. "Oh. Nothing. Tangible proof of where my gifts lie. And where they don't."

He walks over and picks up Caterina. "Not bad. The Doll Makers at the Workshop would have suggestions for improvement, of course, but compared to the pic you sent me of your first attempt ..." He grins.

I wince, the memory a burning sore, rather than comforting nostalgia, after receiving the contest's rejection. "I never should have sent it. Seems silly to have been so proud."

"Hey"—Kristof replaces Caterina in the position he found her—"I'll take pictures of dolls any day over the ones of your doofus tourist boyfriends."

I flash him a Cheshire grin as he perches beside me on the desk. "How else could I get you back for those drool-worthy shots you kept sending from Russia? And Italy. And France! Did you even intern?"

His eyes brighten again. Good.

My gaze wanders over his face, his form, the hard planes and angles he didn't have when I saw him last New Year's. Gone is the cute teenager I hugged goodbye when he left for his internship. In his place sits this brawny young man radiating confidence he must have picked up overseas. He cocks an eyebrow at my scrutiny. I shrug, pulling at the cuffs of my knit sleeves. "You look different. Older."

A grin plays about his mouth. "Once again I have to wonder if I should be concerned or flattered."

I fight off a surge of heat. Even though I'm older than Kristof by two years and eight months, we've enjoyed an easy friendship for almost a decade. No need for that to change just because he suddenly looks like a guy I'd date rather than the kid who tagged along with me and Niklas.

"Well, you look great, as usual," he says when I remain silent. He tugs a lock of my hair. "I see you've added another blue stripe."

"I can always count on you to notice the little details."

"When the subject matter interests me." He crosses his arms. "And your aunt? How's her visit going?"

I toss my head back with a smile. "It's great. She's great. She adds a spark to our mundane lives, you know? When she's awake, that is."

"Awake?"

"Aunt Cat is barely in her forties, but that woman can nap with the best of grandmas." I reach for a nearby pen and play with its clicker. "Seriously, Kris, why are you home early? Didn't you enjoy Germany?"

"I loved it." He unzips his coat and loosens his scarf. "Hoping to return after the holidays, in fact."

His words settle around my heart in a funny way. "Return for good?"

"Possibly."

"Oh." For some reason, I thought his internship had an end date, and he'd be a regular at the Huggamugg Café again. "So, you came home to spend the holidays with your family, when you're supposed to be overseas for Nik's ceremony."

"Plans—"

"Changed. Yeah, yeah." My mind's whirring now. "You said you're in town to gather supplies, except your family never travels this late in the year for that stuff. By now, you're up to your eyeballs with"—glancing at my closed office door, I lower my voice—"Christmas preparations." I tap his leg with the pen. "What's really going on?"

Kristof scratches the stubble along his jaw, his gaze mirroring my path to the door and back again. "This is between us, okay?"

I scoot closer.

A wisp of a smile crosses his lips. "We need materials to repair damage done to the FTA."

"Damage? What, did a reindeer bust a hole through the wall or something?" I joke.

"More like a *pack* of reindeer busted through the back entrance."

I hold up my hands. "Whoa, you're serious?"

"Unfortunately, yes." Kristof kneads the back of his neck. "Two nights ago, the Third String went missing, along with the practice sleigh. We found damage on the FTA interior walls and back doors, but no runner markings in the snow. Which means they immediately took to the skies, and we have no way to track them."

I blink several times. "No one heard anything inside?"

"The Big Eight and Second String might have—if they hadn't been drugged to sleep."

My mouth unhinges. "How are you so calm? This is crazy. Tinsel must be going out of her mind. Why hasn't she said anything?" She's texted about spotty cell reception, a bizarro reindeer encounter, and oh-so-casually dropped the bomb that she met Niklas's ex-fiancée (!), but as to her precious Third String disappearing? Crickets.

I swivel for my phone beside the laptop, and Kristof catches my wrist. "Remember, this is between you and me."

"You mean—" My eyes widen. "Tinsel doesn't know?"

He shakes his head. "Nik asked to be the one to tell her at the right time."

"Those reindeer are practically family to her."

"Tinsel has looked forward to this trip for months, yet we've already taken away some of her excitement with news of—" He drops his gaze and coughs once.

"She told me about the Silver Reindeer, if that's what has you nervous."

Kristof gives a lop-sided grin. "Of course she did. Then you understand that news like this will kill any chances for her to enjoy herself. She'd likely hop the next flight home, and for what? We already have teams of elves out searching, and we need her in Germany. If we're lucky, we'll find the Third String before Nik has to say anything."

I click the pen twice more and set it aside. "Let me help." The words escape before I give them thought. "For Tinsel's sake. If she can't be here, let me help in her stead. I can search the woods—"

"The reindeer *flew* out of the stables the other night. They could be anywhere in the world by now."

"Or they could still be in the area, and your elves can only cover so much ground." I hop off the desk and walk around to pack away my laptop. "I'll stay here through lunch, in case Mikal and Titus need me, and afterward I can, like, borrow Dad's snowmobile and cover the northwest trail—"

"Nein, Gina." Kristof takes my elbow. "As much as I appreciate your offer, I don't want my family's problems interfering with your schedule."

"The café closes at three, anyway. My staff doesn't need me for that." He opens his mouth, but I add, "Your family problems have the potential to affect young lives all over the world. Please. Let me help."

Kristof narrows his eyes. "You're going into the woods no matter what I say, aren't you?"

"Yep."

He works to hide his amusement. "Fine. Go, if you must. Just don't hold out hope of finding anything. Stick to the familiar trails. Your sense of direction is atrocious, and I don't want you getting lost."

"I'll be okay."

"Don't stay out too late, either. The sun doesn't linger long above the horizon these days and—"

"And I know how cold it gets, *Dad*. Is that all, *Dad*?"

Kristof's gaze pierces mine. "You better not think of me as a dad."

I used to think of him as another brother. Today, however ….

A lazy smile drifts across his lips, snapping me out of my stupor, and I veer him toward the door. "Get going. Buy your supplies. I'll call you if I find anything this afternoon."

"Thanks." Kristof tugs his beanie over his head as I accompany him into the hallway. "It was good to see you, G. Maybe you can carve out time for me amongst all your dates while I'm back." With a wink, he exits through the doorway into the dining area.

I stare at his retreating back, the prospect of seeing Kristof again appealing to me in a way seeing Logan never will. Definitely *not* brother material.

That doesn't make him dating material.

If only we got enough tourists this time of year to clutter up my social calendar.

Nine

Gina—Nov 25 Into the Woods

∼⊙⟲∞⟳⊙∼

The treads of Dad's snowmobile churn up the fresh snow as I zip through the woods, taking the trail I've seen Tinsel use whenever she leaves Waldheim. If I follow it long enough, will I reach Flitterndorf, or does Tinsel's path veer off somewhere?

I tried finding the village once, after I learned Tinsel is a Christmas elf and jolly ol' Saint Nicholas does, indeed, exist. He's none other than Meister K, in fact, whom I've known since forever because he does business with Dad's hardware store every year.

Miiind blooown.

That summer, I had delusions of being the first to discover Flitterndorf, despite Tinsel's claims I wouldn't get beyond some barrier that prevents humans from breaching its borders. Curiosity drove me to try, anyway, with a couple of unsuspecting friends, until they wanted to turn around—*needed* to get back home, they said—and I didn't force the issue.

I won't give up so easily in searching for the Third String, even though I've been criss-crossing these woods for over an hour with nary a sign of them. Staying out much longer, however, will make me late for meeting Aunt Cat at the gym.

Pff. Like I can focus on my glutes when my best friend's animals are missing. Tinsel needs my help, whether she knows it or not. My regularly scheduled program will have to wait.

And how rewarding will it be to call Kristof with the news that I found the Third String? To hear the appreciation in his deep timbre, imagine the warmth in his eyes—

I give myself a shake. Kristof's a heartthrob, sure, but he's a friend. And too young to consider him as anything more. And he's no Legolas. And—new twist—he plans to return to Germany.

And, and, and.

Where was I going with these thoughts?

Where am I going on this snowmobile?

Unfamiliar groupings of trees blur together as I zoom along unfamiliar slopes and around unfamiliar bends in the trail. I may have taken an accidental detour at some random spruce in the last, oh, twenty minutes or so. Am I still headed in the right direction? Yeah, yeah, I should've grabbed my compass before starting out. Hindsight so not helpful.

"Just a little farther, then I'll go back," I promise myself. Now, if I were a reindeer, where would I hide?

I peer through the passing trees, the low-hanging sun swathing everything in a magenta hue, when the snowmobile sputters beneath me. What? I press the throttle to give it more gas. The engine revs, then conks out.

"You've got to be kidding me." The fuel gauge says I have over half a tank. What's the deal? Checking that the kill switch and key are in the correct positions, I pull the cord. Silence greets me instead of a warm purr. "Awesome." I punch the handlebar. "Of course you'd give out miles from civilization."

A twig snaps in the distance. My scalp tightens, and I lift the visor on my helmet. Frigid air bites my nose. Gnarled trees surround me, their branches stretching into the path ahead. Deepening shadows produce unnatural shapes in 3D. I envision big four-footed creatures and even bigger antlers roaming in the background. Or big creatures with even bigger teeth. A spasm ripples up my spine. While we don't often find man-threatening predators in this area (and wouldn't bears know enough to hibernate?), an occasional exception will ramble through. I vote for not being the prey of said exception.

Something rustles to my left. I yank the pull cord again, but the snowmobile is dead. Stupid machine.

The rustling grows louder, like an animal crunches through the snow and debris. A large animal. Heart thwacking, I slowly reach for the saddlebag pocket holding the bear spray and peek out of the corner of my eye. *Please don't be a cranky, sleep-deprived grizzly.*

Or a sadistic slasher looking for its next victim. (This is what I get for watching *Scream* as a kid.)

A dark brown form moves among the trees. Skinny legs. Antlers. I let out an audible sigh and relax. Just a reindeer. I straighten again. A reindeer!

"Hey! Uh, excuse me." I remove my helmet. "Are you one of Tinsel's friends?" Good heavens, I'm talking to an animal.

One that ignores me and continues on its way.

A wild animal should have run from my voice; a tame animal would have at least glanced in my direction. This one does nothing, as if I don't exist. Head low, it drags its hooves through the snow. After several paces, it stumbles, then rights itself. My lips purse, and I hop off the snowmobile, setting the helmet on the seat. The animal stumbles twice more, angling away from me. It sways, trips ... Can reindeer get drunk?

I pull a wool cap from my jacket pocket, yank it over my head, and start after the animal. The air thickens with one step. My movements become sluggish, as though I'm stuck in an invisible wall of jello. I strain to propel myself forward, and the jello resists me.

Turn back. Go home. Forget what you saw.

Forget— What *did* I see? The trees six feet in front of me waver. A sticky web cloys my brain. "What am I … doing here? Where is 'here'?"

Go home.

"Home." My posture slackens. "Where's home?"

Turn around.

Yes. Home … behind me. I should—

In the quivering distance, a reindeer slips into a line of tightly packed evergreens.

Reindeer. Follow the reindeer.

The web tightens its hold. *Why?*

Don't know. Just must.

Must go home.

No. I lean forward and wrestle against the invisible jello.

Hooooome.

"Reindeeeer." At last, with an almost audible *slurp*, I stagger free. At the same time, the web snaps inside my head.

Tinsel! I'm tracking the reindeer for Tinsel. To see if it's one of the missing Third String. How could I forget that? And who turned up the heat? The temperature must have risen thirty degrees. Loosening my scarf, I take off after the animal and pursue it through the evergreens.

A wide clearing unfolds on the other side. Several reindeer stand there, heads slumped, eyes glazed. I lurch to a stop. Other reindeer lie on their sides. Dead?

"Good gravy, what's going on?" I approach a prone reindeer, hands outstretched to ward off any erratic behavior. "Hi, there, big guy. Or girl," I coo, crouching near the animal. "I promise I won't hurt you."

It stares with vacant eyes, its side rising and falling in shallow breaths. Still alive. For now.

I tug off my gloves and grab my phone from my ski pants' pockets, even though reception out here is spotty—whoa, one bar? Sweet. I tap Kristof's number, and his phone rings four times followed by a staticky, "Hey, what's up?"

My extremities buzz at his warm tone. *Focus.* "Remember when I texted that I was heading into the woods?"

"You got lost, didn't you?" His voice reverberates with mirth.

"No." I consider my curious surroundings. "Well, maybe, but that's not why I'm calling." The animal beside me lets out a moan. "I've stumbled across some reindeer. No clue if they're the missing ones—"

"Wait, you ..." His voice cuts in and out. "... can't understand ..."

"Kristof?"

"Where ... woods ... are you?"

Guessing at his missing words, I answer, "Some sort of clearing. I don't know exactly." I slip the scarf from my neck and toss it aside. "'Cause you're right—I'm lost."

He says something unintelligible.

"Hello? Kris?"

Dead air. Snow crunches behind me, and the hair rises at the nape of my neck. I adjust my cap with a covert glimpse around. Nothing but reindeer.

"... na? Can you hear me?"

"Yes! What should I do? We have a poor connection, and my battery won't last long in the cold." A nearby reindeer sways, eyes glassy. "These guys are acting so strange. Like listless zombies, except without the decay. One's barely breathing and—"

Something hard and small presses between my shoulder blades. "No sudden movements, girlie," growls a voice at my back. Dread pours over me like iced coffee. "Hands where I can see 'em. Now."

Ten

Gina—Nov 25 Flitterndorf

I raise my arms as someone snickers.

"'Hands where I can see 'em'?" says a squeaky voice. "What are you, Benny, the mafia?"

"Shut up, Herb." Benny (innocent name for a low-life) plucks the phone from me. "I'll take this, danke."

"Hey!" I begin to turn.

"Ah ah ah." The object in my back presses harder. "No peeking."

My head snaps forward. A tinny "Gina?" emits from my phone. Can Kristof hear what's going on?

"Who is this, your boyfriend?" Benny sneers behind me. "Buh-bye, boyfriend. Tibbs, catch. You know what to do."

Clothes rustle, footsteps scrunch, and a resounding *thwap* cuts the air. I wince, bracing for some kind of impact. Instead, a few branches crack elsewhere in the woods.

"What do you want with me?" I ask, pulse hammering in my ears. There are at least three thugs and possibly one gun behind me. How many thugs can I take out before they take *me* out?

"Cooperate and you won't get hurt," Benny says in his growly voice. "Back away from the animal." I try to rise, but he pokes me again. "On your knees. Keep your hands in the air."

I obey, the crusty snow buckling beneath me.

When I'm about a man's length from the reindeer, Benny yells, "Now, boys!"

Someone tackles me from behind, plowing me face-first into the snow. My chin stings. A weight drops onto my legs, another onto my shoulders, and a wayward boot bats me in the head as my arms are yanked behind me. Strong, narrow binds cinch my wrists together, followed by my ankles, then my knees. As fast as they materialized, the weights depart.

"All right, you can get up now. If you can."

Chortles and sniggers follow Benny's words. I rotate my head to spit out a gob of icy granules and clench my teeth against the tears crawling at the back of my throat. Kristof was right—I shouldn't have messed with my schedule.

"Herb, bring the SnoMo."

SnoMo? My breathing stills. Someone besides Tinsel and the Kringles uses that term?

I roll onto my side, propping up on an elbow. A handful of children stand several feet away, armed with ... toys? "You're kidding me." I rock myself to a sitting position and glare at their water guns and slingshots. "I was trussed up by toy-toting tots in less than five seconds?"

"Watch your mouth, lady." The kid with Benny's voice jabs his "weapon" toward me. "We're not 'tots.'"

Neither are they thugs. Relief loosens my tongue. "You can't seriously think I'd be intimidated by a water gun."

"It's a water *blaster*."

"You can call it a water cannon, for all I care. It won't stop me from doing this." Springing to my feet, I hop across the snow-covered field in the direction of my snowmobile, the kids hollering behind me.

* * *

Well, that attempt to escape was short-lived.

The ground races past inches from my nose as I jostle to the motion of Benny's miniature snowmobile. Its seat cushion digs into my stomach with each bounce, since I'm—grrr—flung across it like a captive across a horse in an old American Western. These kids even put a gag around my mouth. My chin stings anew, and my head pounds with the blood rush.

Cold air tunnels through my sodden ski jacket and pants, and a shiver rattles my body. My scarf got left behind, as did my hat when it flew off after a well-placed blast from the kids' guns. Water droplets trickle along my soaked scalp and down the frozen locks dangling over my shoulder.

Nobody told me those blasters were connected to backpacks bulging with water.

My eyes narrow at the kid following Benny on another snowmobile. Defeated by mere children. How humiliating.

The bumpy trail flattens beneath the vehicle's treads, and my chest constricts. They mentioned something about taking me to see the boss. Is he—or she—the one grownup among this motley crew? What will happen to me then? I didn't even do anything.

Shouts parry between my abductors and others. I lift my head. We travel past buildings and houses in the Tudor style reminiscent of an old European village with extra Christmas flare. Red-and-white striped corner trusses stand like candy cane sticks. White painted snowflakes embellish green balconies. Red shutters sport gingerbread men cutouts.

And all in miniature. Like a village built for Hobbits.

Except that children, not Hobbits, run amok everywhere. Coming out, going in, greeting one another, arguing. A few even ride reindeer. Many stop to gape at me.

Um, hang on.

Shaking stiff strands of hair from my eyes, I contort as much as my position will allow and peer at Benny driving the snowmobile. No chubby cheeks or soft skin like a kid. Instead, he has the hard planes and crow's feet of an adult. Yet his proportions aren't like those found in people with dwarfism; rather they're in keeping with an average-sized adult male, but on a smaller scale.

And he has pointy ears.

"You're Christmas elves!" I yell to be heard over the drone of the vehicle, and the gag warbles my words into, "Ya kee-ahsh ehsh!" Benny curls his lips in response. From my sideways position, I study the other elves' details as we pass. The intricate designs on their lederhosen and dirndls. The myriad hues of red and green. Their matching, curly-toed shoes.

Gasp. Christmas. Elves. SnoMos. I'm in Flitterndorf!

Aw, man. I hang my head. Bound and waterlogged is not how I imagined taking my first tour of Flitterndorf.

Wait. If Benny's a Christmas elf, that means his boss is Santa Claus. And Santa is Meister K, whose order of eggnog-with-a-shot-of-huckleberry I fill every time he comes to town and visits the Huggamugg Café. A bark of laughter escapes me. "Oh, are you going to be in trouble," I warn Benny around my gag.

Of course, he doesn't understand me.

The buildings dwindle, the bumps return, and soon the snowmobile's angle increases as we ascend a steep incline. My body rocks on the seat, and I squeeze the cushion with my thighs and upper torso so I don't roll off this vehicle and under the one behind us. Too many minutes later, we level out, and Benny finally brings us to a stop. Thank goodness. An ache pounds in my shoulders, my body shivers relentlessly, aaaand I'm about to lose my lunch.

"Tibbs, get Meister K," Benny says, his feet appearing in the snow beneath my face. Aww, he wears pointy shoes, too. (How did I miss these telltale details before?) "As for you"—he rights me into a sitting position with the help of another elf—"stay put. Any funny business and I'll—"

"Do what?" I garble around my gag, another shudder racking my body. "Pelt me with coal from your slingshots?" Benny rolls his eyes.

Beyond him, an imposing Tudor castle rises several stories high. Its timber framework makes geometric patterns on the outside walls, interrupted by evenly spaced lattice windows. Towers flank the structure at each corner, their pitched, red metal roofs piercing the sky. Two cranberry red doors mark the entrance, and a rustic wooden sign hangs above it with three block numbers, 0-3-1.

Santa's Workshop. It has to be.

"Th-that's am-ma-mazing," I stammer. The shivering intensifies the ache in my shoulders with my arms pinned behind me. My trembling legs agitate the zip ties around my knees and ankles, but since my jacket and ski pants have stiffened into ice packs padding my body, I can't stop.

Just as I'm contemplating swapping half my doll collection for a cup of cocoa, the Workshop's front doors bang open, and Meister K marches outside in a maroon coat trimmed in white fur. When visiting the hardware store, he dresses in overalls and a cowboy hat. Here, there's no mistaking the jolly fat man (although at present he sports a more severe demeanor). His powerful stride gobbles up the distance between us. "I'm here, Benny. What's this about an impost—"

"Gina!" Kristof appears from behind his grandfather, and my heart does a silly leap as he hurries forward. Surely my reaction has everything to do with imminent freedom and nothing to do with the fact he's rocking a fitted, black cardigan over forest green lederhosen cinched at the knee, his gray knee-high socks defining stellar calf muscles.

Oh, so now I pay attention to details.

Meister K flails an arm in my direction, his mouth forming a black circle inside a bushy white beard. "Why is Miss Donati trussed up like a Christmas goose?"

"We caught her red-handed, sir," Benny says, smiling broadly.

Kristof drops to his knees in front of me, his spiky, dark blond locks ruffled to perfection. "Sorry about this," he murmurs, leaning close to untie the gag's knot behind my head. I inhale sandalwood. He pulls the gag away and frowns, gently touching my scraped chin. Our gazes collide. Though his hazel eyes lack the visceral punch of Nik's green ones, they carry a heat that swarms my belly.

Definite huggable material, this one.

The corner of his mouth lifts. Drat, did my thoughts play across my face? What's my deal, anyway? He's Kristof. Resident of the friend zone. "W-why're you smiling? What's s-so funny?"

He flips open a pocketknife and cuts the zip ties at my wrists, knees, and ankles. "You remind me of a stuffed animal that's gone through the wash."

Seriously? Let the man stay in the friend zone. Limbs free, I massage my wrists and press cold fingertips to my sore mouth.

"Here." Kristof removes my wet jacket, unbuttons and shrugs out of his cardigan, and drapes it around my shoulders. I sink into his lingering body heat, tugging the edges together beneath my chin.

"Why is she soaked?" Meister K demands, hands on hips.

"She was trying to escape, sir," Benny answers.

"But why apprehend her in the first place?"

"She's dangerous."

"Dangerous?" Pushing to his feet, Kristof crosses his arms, his red gingham shirt molding to his biceps. Hot dang, when'd he get the muscles? "Gina is Tinsel's best friend."

Benny rubs a knuckle across his forehead. "She was harming the reindeer."

"I was not!" I stand, but my feet smart with pins and needles, so I sit again. "W-was not. I wanted to see w-what was wrong with them. If I c-could do anything to help. I was on the phone with K-Kristof when you came upon m-me." At the mention of my phone, I look from one elf to the next. "Where did you p-put my phone, anyway?"

Benny and Tibbs shift on their feet and exchange glances.

"Oh, no." Another shiver wrenches my body. "What'd you d-do with it?"

Tibbs jiggles his slingshot with a nervous chuckle.

I groan. "The tree b-branches snapping ... that was my phone?"

"First you attack her, then you take her phone?" Meister K yanks on his beard. "What were you doing outside the barrier?"

"We weren't outside the barrier, sir," Tibbs says. "*She* was *inside* the barrier. In Cookie Meadow."

Kristof's head whips in my direction, his eyebrows bunching together. Meister K claps him on the shoulder. "Not here. Take her to the apartment where it's warm and private. I will check on the reindeer. As for you five"—he peers over his spectacles at Benny and the other elves—"you have a phone to find."

69

Eleven

Gina—Nov 25 Hobnobbing with Santa

"Here, child." Madam Anne, Kristof's grandmother, offers me a green mug decorated with red, gold, and blue rosemaling. Her wrinkled cheeks pull into a smile. "This will revive you from the inside out."

Huddled before the stone fireplace on a tufted ottoman, I reach for the mug, Kristof's cardigan still draped over my shoulders. "Thank you." The tea's peppermint notes relax my muscles, and I take a sip, the liquid sliding down my throat to warm my belly. "This is wonderful."

Across the apartment, Kristof paces in the Tuscany-inspired kitchen, one hand at his waist, phone pressed to his ear as he speaks with Meister K. I meet Madam Anne's gaze as she settles on the sofa opposite me. "Will the reindeer be okay?"

"I hope so." She arranges her long skirts about her legs. "I can't promise anything, mind you, until we know what we're dealing with. But"—she winks—"I do know Santa has a way with animals."

"I'll meet you there in a little while," Kristof says into the phone. He taps the screen with a thumb, slips it into his pocket, and grabs his mug from the island counter.

He weaves around the worn farmhouse table and sofa to stand beside me, and I raise my eyebrows. "Well?"

"Well." Kristof stares into the flames. Nearby, my jacket and ski pants hang on the coat rack repositioned from the foyer to the hearth. "Grandpop found the 'deer you mentioned."

"And?"

"They're not the Third String. Nevertheless, as they're part of our larger reindeer herd, they require our care." He glances back at his grandmother. "I suggested we turn the Prep Stables into a temporary animal hospital for the sick 'deer, so Grandpop is going to talk to the elves about making that a reality."

My fingers tighten about the mug. "I'm sorry."

"It's not your fault." He nudges my upper arm with the back of his hand. "You warm and dry now?"

"Almost." I take another sip of tea, lifting my gaze to the thick timber supports that arch across the ceiling. Their dark coffee tones contrast with buttercream walls and the embroidered ivory linens hanging in the windows. Off to my left, a spiral staircase ascends to a cozy loft overlooking the living room, its railing made from rough-hewn logs. Rosemaling accents and Christmas flair beautify the furniture.

The old-world charm in the Kringles' apartment gives new meaning to the words, "Home Sweet Home," and if the reindeer's illness didn't cast a pall over my current circumstances, I'd think I was dreaming.

Kristof squats in front of me. "You okay?"

I poke him in the shoulder.

He snorts. "What was that for?"

"Is this for real?"

Kristof pokes *me* in the shoulder. Hard.

"Ow."

"It's for real."

"Hmph." Placing the mug at my feet, I snuggle deeper into his cardigan, his sandalwood scent blending with the apartment's apple-cinnamon flavor. "Just for that, I'm not giving this back yet."

A slow smile meanders across his lips. "Keep it as long as you need it."

That's the problem—I don't need it. I want it.

A blue lock of hair drapes over my shoulder, and Kristof pinches its ends. Two beads of water plop to the floor. "I apologize again for the elves' behavior," he says. "Grandpop will talk to them."

"Please don't punish them on my account. They were protecting the reindeer and their turf from uninvited company."

Kristof swaps a look with Madam Anne as he moves to the sofa. "Gina, how *did* you get past the barrier?"

"I don't know what barrier you keep talking about." Angling sideways on the ottoman, I stretch toward the flames frolicking behind the protective glass. "All I saw were trees and a meadow."

"The barrier's invisible, and it deters anyone who's not a Kringle or an elf from crossing into Flitterndorf." Kristof sets his mug on a side table and leans forward, elbows on his knees. "You're neither Kringle nor elf, yet Benny found you in Cookie Meadow. How?"

"I followed a reindeer."

"You followed a reindeer and"—he mimes walking with his fingers—"waltzed right in."

"Yes. No. Kind of. There was a section of woods that ..." I rub my hands along my fleece leggings. "Okay, this is going to sound crazy, but like, something got into my head and tried to convince me to go away."

"That's the barrier." Kristof's eyes brighten. "If humans try to cross it, they'll either get an urge to turn around and go home, or they'll alter their course and travel parallel to our borders."

"Huh. Well, I would've given up, had I not spotted the reindeer a second time."

A line forms between his eyebrows. "You shouldn't have been able to physically pass the barrier, no matter what reason you had."

I pick up my tea and take a sip. "If it's any consolation, it did feel like I was encased in jello for a moment."

Kristof drills a hand through his spikes, mussing their perfection. He frowns at Madam Anne. "Gram, could the barrier be failing?"

"Oh, I don't think so," Madam Anne says, pulling a knitted work-in-progress out of a cloth bag beside her.

"No? First, the Third String disappears, and now Gina shows up. How do you explain that?"

"I can't." Madam Anne's needles click as she works a pattern from memory. "That doesn't mean an explanation doesn't exist."

"Are the two connected, you think?" he asks.

Madam Anne's pale gaze connects with mine over her knitting. "Gina, how did you travel so deep into the woods today? You couldn't have walked."

"No, I borrowed my dad's snowmobile." I trace the mug's handle with my thumb. "Which reminds me, it's still in the woods. It conked out right before I saw the reindeer. No warning, either. One minute it's working. The next, it's not."

"Conked out, you say?" Madam Anne pats Kristof's knee. "There you go. The barrier remains intact."

"Then how'd Gina get through?"

I squint at Madam Anne. "Wait, so Dad's snowmobile died because of the barrier? How am I supposed to get home?"

"Pull it away from the barrier, dear. It should start up again."

"Oh. Well, that's easy enough." Standing, I feel my jacket and ski pants. Dry. The ends of my hair are damp, and I'll need to borrow a hat, but aside from that, I should probably head home. A knot hardens behind my diaphragm, and I mirror Kristof's earlier stance, staring into the flames. I'm not ready to leave.

The fire pops. A line from *The Night Before Christmas* runs through my head, and I spin about at the comical image it generates. "Does Meister K ever 'lay a finger aside of his nose' and fly up this chimney?"

Kristof coughs on his tea and sets it aside again. "Fly? He used to when Nik and I were little and easily impressed."

"Can Nik do it?"

"Yeah. He's fast, too."

The fire warms the back of my legs. "So, Nik will fly up a chimney, yet he won't fly in a sleigh?"

"It's a matter of altitude."

"What about you?"

Kristof scratches his scruff. "I don't have the full arsenal of magic at my disposal like the firstborn does."

My gaze falls to where his gingham shirt pulls across his chest. "You have more muscles than Nik does." I gasp and slap a hand over my mouth. Madam Anne giggles behind closed lips, and a pleased twinkle sparks in Kristof's eyes. Face heating, I shed his cardigan and throw it at him.

He catches it one-handed, laughing. "I take it you're feeling better."

"Uncomfortably warm at the moment." Averting my face, I grab my mug and bring it into the kitchen. "I should get going, actually." Whether or not I want to. My vision blurs as I set the mug in the sink. Good gravy, why so emotional?

"Kristof," Madam Anne says, the sofa cushion shifting, "why don't you show Gina the PD Wing before she goes?"

I glance across the island counter to the living room. "Isn't Meister K expecting you?"

"This won't take long." Kristof grins. "You'll love it."

* * *

After I don my ski pants and say goodbye to Madam Anne, Kristof ushers me from the apartment back into the narrow corridor I shuffled through, half-frozen, forty minutes earlier. Maroon wainscoting and creamy white upper walls bask beneath the soft glow of carriage lanterns hanging at measured intervals in the hallway. When we come to a "T," Kristof motions us to the right, and I fall into step beside him, our boots scuffing against the dark, wooden floorboards, warped and worn by time's passing.

Respect for tradition and a rich understanding of heritage steep not only within these walls but within the whole of Flitterndorf. A legacy carried over and cherished from their roots in the Old World. How long ago was that, exactly?

"When did your family settle here from Germany?" I ask, drawing a finger along the wainscoting.

"It wasn't a direct shot from one place to the other. They left Germany in 1866 and didn't settle here until 1869."

"Still, that's almost a hundred years before Waldheim was incorporated."

"Which is when your family came over, right?"

"Dad's grandparents actually came earlier, when Waldheim was still just a settlement." I pluck at my jacket folded over my forearm. "They relocated from Italy with four kids in tow to start a new life. My Great-Grandma Campi, however, called it quits after eight years in the 'grueling climate of the Arctic Circle.'" I use the air quotes with a grin. "She went back to her *bella Italia* and took the children with her. My grandma, *Nonna*, was seventeen at the time. Papa Campi, on the other hand, stayed behind to ... I don't know, freeze?"

"To operate the hardware store he had the foresight to open—which proved a blessing for my family. And our business was a blessing for him."

"Mmm, true." Had he not stuck around, Dad wouldn't have visited

Papa Campi as a young man, met Mum, and decided to take over management of the hardware store. And I wouldn't now be walking the halls of Santa's Workshop beside a handsome Kringle.

I hip-check Kristof as we travel down another hallway. "So, what's this PD Wing?"

"You'll see." He swivels to walk backward in front of me, a teasing grin on his lips. "If my grandfather can make you gooey-eyed, I suspect this will make you drool."

"Gooey-eyed?"

"I saw your expression outside the Workshop."

My cheeks prickle. That may have been my expression for Kristof, not for his grandfather. "Um, try awestruck. He *is* Santa Claus."

Kristof descends a flight of stairs. "You've known that about him for the last two years."

"I never saw him as Santa in his Christmas village, though," I say behind Kristof, trailing my hand on the stair railing. "There's a difference between believing in something without having seen it and then, like, experiencing it with my five senses. I mean, I can still taste Madam Anne's peppermint tea, I smell cinnamon, and this banister feels smooth and solid beneath my palm."

Kristof turns down a broad hallway with green-and-white striped walls, and I double my pace to catch up. "I admired your family's lovely apartment and listened to—" Grabbing his arm, I stop him and point at the ceiling, where faint Christmas music plays from inset speakers. "And listened to cheesy songs piped throughout the Workshop." I smile and squeeze his arm. "Kristof, I'm sorry the reindeer's illness is what brought me here, but I'll never forget this day as long as I live."

His gaze roams over my face, the pleasure in his eyes warming me faster than any fire, drink, or cardigan.

I wet my lips. "What?"

Kristof clears his throat and moves away. "I've never seen you so animated, that's all." He approaches the lone door on the right. "Try not to go bonkers in here, okay?" Rotating the handle, he gives it a push. "Welcome to the Production Wing, where we make Christmas wishes come true."

Twelve

Gina—Nov 25 Production Wing

As a child, I read about Santa, his elves, and the toys they make. I pored over pictures from artists' imaginations, watched movies reflecting a director's vision, even entertained my own ideas. The real version astounds me in a heady rush.

Hundreds of elves talk, laugh, and sing as they create in a ginormous area quivering with energy. *Ping*-ing, *whirr*-ing, *clack*-ing, *whack*-ing, and any other imagined work-related verb rises on the peppermint-tinged air to meld in joyous cacophony. An immense double-sided, river rock fireplace rises from floor to second-story ceiling in the center, its mantel loaded with garland swags, white lights, and oversize ornaments. Two timber frame lofts cozy up each end of the cavernous room, and a miniature train bustles along a suspended track, its cars loaded with fluffy stuffed animals, smiling, curly-haired dolls, and other colorful toys.

"Projects that require welding, power saws, and the like are created in another area of the Workshop," Kristof says, guiding me among the worktables. Cherry-stained floorboards creak underfoot.

"Everything else, however, we make here in the Production Wing."

Mixed paraphernalia strewn across the tabletops indicates the focus at each station. Nuts, bolts, and metal hardware cover a table where elves assemble fire engines. Yards of fabric, scissors, pins, and measuring tape spill across another table for cloth building blocks. At a third table, elves fashion jewelry with hand tools, colored metallic wire, and multiple jars of beads.

Eagerness unfurls inside my core. Inspiration swirls in my mind. I drift toward an empty seat at a nearby painting station, my fingers twitching to create.

A familiar smell floats by, and I pause, breathing deep. Coffee?

There, tucked in another corner, stands a coffee kiosk looking like an amplified child's playhouse. Two elf baristas bustle behind the counter, filling orders. More elves wait in line, dressed in red or green dirndls and lederhosen. Several gawk at me.

In fact, most activity has come to a halt around us, the noise level dying. I edge back to Kristof's side, murmuring, "Why are they staring?"

He chuckles. "Most have never seen a non-Kringle human in the flesh. And they've *never* had one visit the PD Wing." Offering the elves a winsome grin, he calls out, "Everyone, this is Gina, a friend of mine and Tinsel's." His voice booms throughout the space. "I'm giving her a tour this afternoon, so I trust you'll treat her to a hearty, Christmas welcome." As they shout greetings and return to their work, Kristof beckons me with a hand. "Come, I want to show you something I think you're gonna love."

He leads me to a loft via a curved staircase, the circular treads hailing from one mammoth tree trunk, cut and splayed in an upward spiral. Thick log rails run the length of the loft, and diamond-shaped windows open to a starry sky. At the tables, elves concentrate on—

My breath catches. Dolls.

From every stage of development other than baking the molds, elves fashion ball-jointed and polymer clay dolls. Some elves sand and assemble body parts. Others sew doll clothes. Still others sculpt faces from clay. One table displays mini paint jars and brushes for painting, and another, the telltale skeins of yarn and elf-sized straight irons for making wigs.

Twirling a lock of my own hair, I approach the wigs when shouts erupt from a far table.

"Shove over, Red. Give me some room."

"Me, shove over? You Pukeys hog the table a little more every day."

Two elves elbow one another, their faces contorted and snarling, their commotion jarring the loft's tranquil mood.

"Who're you calling pukey?"

"You. Seen the color of your clothes lately?"

Frowning, Kristof heads over. "What's going on, guys?"

"You need your eyes checked." One elf jumps up, plucking at his lederhosen. "This is forest green, not puke."

"Is that what your mother told you?"

"Leave my mother out of this—"

"Hey, time out." Kristof steps between them, yet they don't heed him until he clasps each of them on a shoulder. Their voices drop to an inaudible level.

"So, you're Tinsel's friend," comes a voice near my waist.

I startle as a female elf looks up from the table beside me, a four-inch paintbrush in one hand, a porcelain head in the other. I return her smile. "Yes, I am."

Lowering her gaze, she pulls a fine line of black paint above the doll's eye socket to thicken the eyebrow. "I always admired Tinsel. Clumsy, for sure, but she has spirit and grit." The elf wears a dirndl similar to Tinsel's, except this one's scarlet with a black apron embroidered in holly berry motifs.

"Did you say you've *always* admired her?" I ask. In the distance, Kristof crouches at eye level with the two elves as he speaks. "She was under the impression no one did."

The elf shifts on her chair and steals a glance with her coworkers. "I didn't voice my opinion. Sometimes the right view isn't the popular view." She holds out a hand. "I'm Bellamy."

Bending, I engulf her Lilliputian palm in mine. So this is why Tinsel feels colossal. "Nice to meet you." My gaze moves to the doll head. "What are you working on?"

She tilts the ceramic face, showing me its slanted eye sockets and pointy ears. "We received a letter requesting a male goth elf. Frau Kleider in Doll Costumes is working on the outfit, and I'm scheduled to start on the wig in another day or two, but it has me stumped."

"Is that why you're so pokey today?" a male elf grumbles beside her. Her eyes narrow at him.

An idea for a wig pops into my mind, but the rejection letter follows on its heels, silencing me. Kristof returns, anyway, slipping his phone into his pants pocket. "Got a call from Grandpop. I'm afraid we need to go." Though he smiles, tight lines rim his eyes.

"Okay, sure." I wave to Bellamy. "It was a pleasure to meet you." Her cheeks plump as she grins. "I hope we see you again."

Not likely. I hesitate before descending the stairs. Bellamy resumes her work, her creative energy rising to join the others' pulsating the air. Something wrenches behind my rib cage. Even had I been a winner in the Doll Haven contest, a human workshop could never compare to the magic and wonder here.

At the bottom of the stairs, I hasten after Kristof, who strides across the Wing in a different direction than we entered. He slips out a side door into an unfamiliar hallway. If he weren't my guide in this place, I would be totally lost.

And if he doesn't slow down, I *will* be totally lost. "Wait for me." I jog along the hall to catch up. "Is everything okay with your grandfather? Why were those elves fighting?"

Kristof scratches his jaw. "I don't know why. I don't think the elves knew, either."

"Oh. Well, kudos to managing it tactfully."

"I have to." Hooking his thumbs into the pockets of his lederhosen, Kristof turns down another random hallway. "At present, I'm in line to become Santa Claus after Nik."

"How would that work, since you don't possess the firstborn magic?"

A shadow clings to him, hunching his shoulders. "If Nik can't fulfill his role as Santa, or if he dies and leaves behind no children, his magic would transfer to me."

"Kristof." I step in front of him and put a hand on his chest. His somber eyes deflate the residual gaiety from the Production Wing. "What's the matter? What did Meister K tell you?"

He messes with his hair again, further mashing his spikes. "I'm to give you a ride to the Prep Stables, which is near the southern border where your snowmobile stalled. The elves have started rearranging the stables into a makeshift hospital, and Grandpop's assessing the sickest reindeer." He meets my gaze, his muscles tensing beneath my palm. "One reindeer has already died."

Thirteen

Tinsel—Nov 26 Reindeer Rendezvous

Weihnachts Manor

Banking on most everyone being asleep by twelve-thirty, I leave my bedroom a few minutes after that, clad in jeans, a wool sweater, and winter accessories. Under normal circumstances, a midnight rendezvous with Bonbon would've required shots of caffeine, but my internal body clock thinks it's only late afternoon.

Aided by my phone's flashlight, I creep downstairs to the terrace doors, where a metal key protrudes from a keyhole. I quietly rotate it and depress the handle. Locked.

Pursing my lips, I turn the key to its original position, and the door swings open. It was already unlocked? Is that normal, or did someone exit ahead of me?

Or is this to allow someone in?

A chill slips beneath my scarf.

Once outside on the moonlit terrace, I hug the manor's shadowed wall and slink along the stone exterior until the spindly pine comes into view. It towers over the others like an arrow piercing the starry sky. Since the shortest distance between two points is a straight line, I break from the shadows and, praying I go unnoticed, race across the brown lawn past the elves' village.

Reaching the pine, I pause to catch my breath, then whisper, "Bonbon?" My phone says it's 12:46. Did she give up waiting for me?

Several minutes pass. Branches sway in a gentle breeze, shifting the shadows, creating illusions. Twigs snap to my right, and my scalp tightens. Once again, the sensation I'm being watched flutters over me. Friend or foe?

Two glints of light appear in the shrouded woods, and my heart knocks into my throat as they move closer. I plant my feet, ready to run, when a splash of moonlight reveals Bonbon's slender form.

Exhaling, I sag against the tree trunk. "You scared me. I mean, I was expecting you, but"—I motion around us—"who knows what else is out here." Smiling away my unfounded fears, I adjust my beanie. "So, what's going on? Why a clandestine meeting?"

Bonbon picks up her head, her ears flicking forward. "They said … help … sent me ta …" After a pause, her eyes widen, like she expects a response.

"Uh, I didn't catch some of that. Help? Is someone in trouble?"

She takes two steps toward me. "I thought … me. This canna … ta find yer … third …" Her voice cuts in and out like a bad connection, and I shake my head.

"I-I'm sorry, Bonbon. I don't—"

"They need …" She stomps a hoof. "… fer a few days … and that bully … sumthing's … right and ye—"

"Bonbon!"

I jerk as Muskat rears out of the darkness, inserting himself between me and Bonbon. He growls something in German, and his words, like Bonbon's, are broken by stretches of silence.

Suddenly, he strikes her with his antlers, and she stumbles to the side.

"Hey, quit that." I rush forward to intervene. "Leave her alone."

Snapping his head in my direction, Muskat narrows his eyes, his white patch pronounced in the moonlight. He paws the ground, shoulder muscles rippling. Gulp.

I throw out my mittened hands in placation. "She didn't do anything wrong. Please, don't—"

He lunges. I shriek and bolt, dodging through the trees. His hooves thunder behind me, ever closer, and I race faster, my lungs searing. I trip over an exposed root and skid along the needle-strewn ground. Knees stinging, I scramble to my feet. A branch swipes them out from under me.

Not a branch. Antlers. They dig into my side and flip me onto my back. Muskat looms over me, his head rearing back—

"Stop!"

Muskat convulses at the command as someone materializes nearby. "Get. Away. From her."

Tears spring to my eyes. Niklas.

Muskat plants a hoof on my sternum. Panic flares within. One thrust could break several ribs—or worse. I paw at the hoof, my mittens clumsy and ineffective.

"In the name of Christmas," says Niklas in an authoritative tone I've never heard, "I order you to back off."

Muskat growls, yet he dips his head and retreats two steps.

Niklas rushes to my side. "Are you okay?"

As he helps me to my quaking feet, I nod, not trusting myself to speak, and brush the debris from my jeans. A new hole gapes at my knee.

Niklas glares at Muskat. "Return to your herd. Onkel Stoffel will hear about this in the morning." As Muskat angles away, Niklas adds, "And leave Bonbon alone." He straightens to his full height, the commanding quality in his voice again. "If I see so much as a scratch on her, you will answer for it."

With an angry snort, Muskat melts into the woods. Niklas gathers me in his arms, and I tremble against him, burying my face into his shoulder. "Sweet little drummer boy, what was that about?" he asks.

I shake my head and clutch him tighter.

"Thank Christmas I don't need to understand reindeer for reindeer to understand me. And obey." He kisses my temple through my beanie.

"Thank Christmas you were around. What're you doing out here?"

"I couldn't sleep, so I went to the terrace to text with Kristof." Niklas stiffens and pulls back. "Then I saw Fritz come out and head for the stables. A few minutes later, you emerged skulking around, and I thought—" His gaze falls away. "Sorry. I forgot you said you were meeting Bonbon."

Was he about to say he thought Fritz and I ...? No, that can't be right. Hugging my arms, I scan the blackness between the trees. "Where'd Bonbon go, anyway? Bonbon?" Silence answers me.

"Were you able to talk to her before Muskat interfered?"

"Kind of. Her words came out disjointed, but she kept mentioning a 'they,' and I caught the words 'help' and 'bully.'" I yank on the brim of my beanie. "I understood her well enough yesterday. Why not now?"

"You're tired?"

I let out half a laugh. "I'm so keyed up, it'll be lunchtime before I fall asleep."

With a lop-sided grin, Niklas wraps an arm about my shoulders and steers me toward the manor. "Let's at least try to sleep. I need you sharp for tomorrow morning when we visit the Silver Reindeer."

My heart skips. By tomorrow afternoon, I'll have the skinny on how to defeat Krampus and be a step closer to regaining my position with the Third String. "Who's taking us?"

"Pa arranged to borrow Onkel Stoffel's car." Niklas winks. "GPS will be our navigator."

* * *

Come mid-morning, I stare at the empty stall as Niklas and Meister Nico converse with Herr Hoffmann. The foreign words spin around me as despair roils within, seeking a place to lodge.

Gone.

The Silver Reindeer is gone.

I loosen my scarf and reach for my choker. According to the Hoffmanns, she ran away two days after Kristof's visit, well over a week ago. By now, she could be anywhere in the world.

What made her leave?

The Hoffmanns don't know.

Is there any chance of finding her?

The wrinkled brows on the men's faces tell me the odds aren't good.

I reject their answers and the despair. Because if we can't find the SR, Krampus has essentially won, and I refuse to let that be our reality.

Fourteen

Tinsel—Nov 26 Crumbling

Despite my attempts to evade it, despair pursues me throughout the day. For something else has disappeared along with the Silver Reindeer.

I kick a clump of dead leaves in the path as I trudge up the wooded slope behind Weihnachts Manor. Lukas scampers among the trees, while Elke, Niklas, and Gretel chat beside me, the pseudo-ex-fiancée acting as our guide to the local abandoned castles. Ordinarily, I would've engaged in their discussion of former Santas, yet the gray clouds churning above the barren branches match my mood, and I withdraw from conversations.

After returning from the Hoffmanns' ranch earlier, I hurried to the stables where I found Fritz working with the reindeer in the corral. Bonbon trotted over and nudged my hand. By her head movements and hoof stomps, I knew she was trying to communicate—something important enough that she continues to risk Muskat's wrath—but I heard only grunts and snorts.

I couldn't understand her. At all.

Has my talent seriously gone defunct two years after I discovered it? Right when I need it—when the Kringles need it—the most? Light drizzle seeps into my coat, and I rub my arms against the chill. My talent can't be gone for good. Imagine never again talking to the Third String!

Of course, if I can't communicate with the Silver Reindeer (should we find her), we can't stop Krampus from destroying Christmas. If we can't stop Krampus, will there even be a Third String to go home to?

"Say, where's your smile gone?" Niklas chucks my chin. "I haven't seen one since breakfast." He weaves his fingers between mine, and warm tingles race up my arm. "Don't worry," he whispers for my ears alone. "We'll figure something out. For all we know, the SR could be in these woods this very minute."

The drizzle becomes a delicate rain, and with a smirk, I flip my hood over my newsboy cap to protect my neck. "You would employ the one incentive for me to stay out in this weather."

Niklas thumps a fist against his chest, feigning affront. "Hiking to an abandoned castle with your lovable, amazing, charming fiancé isn't incentive enough?"

"Do not worry, *meine Freunde*." Gretel ups her pace to pull ahead of us. "Tomorrow will be sunny."

Elke snaps a twig from an overhead branch. "And tomorrow evening, the Weihnachtsmarkt opens."

At the promise of sun and Christmas, I smile. "Fritz told me about it. I can't wait."

Niklas's brow wrinkles. "Fritz?"

"He said Herr Stoffel plays the part of Father Christmas each night at the market. And next week is Brückenstadt's *Krampuslauf*—the Krampus Run—which takes place a few days before the actual Krampus Night."

Elke gives an exaggerated shudder. *"Krampusnacht.* I hate—"

"I love Krampusnacht!" Lukas hollers, jumping across our path and barreling between the trees on the other side.

I lean into Niklas. "Fritz says people dress up in Krampus costumes and parade through the streets and frighten children. Sounds freaky to me."

Niklas continues to frown. "Fritz told you all this? When?"

"I saw him when I checked on Bonbon after visiting the Hoffmanns."

His hold slackens and then tightens around mine. "So, how is Bonbon?"

I pull in my bottom lip as a gray structure becomes visible beyond the trees up ahead. "She's fine."

"Were you able to"—his voice drops to a murmur—"talk to her?"

"No."

"Maybe you can try this evening."

Right, because Niklas thinks we simply didn't have the opportunity. Ugh. I need to confess. "Niklas—"

"Come on, *ihr Langweiler.*" Gretel waves from beneath a stone archway. "How do you say it in English? Ah—slowpokes. I thought you wanted to see an abandoned castle."

A crumbling front wall rises from the hillside about five meters in height, bare tree branches waving overhead from inside the structure. My eyebrows lift. "That's abandoned, all right." A wooden door stands in an alcove at the far end. Above it, bricks plug a lone window.

Lukas tugs on my hand. "Come see."

He pulls me through the archway, and we leave the woods behind for a smaller wooded version inside. All that remains of the original structure are the thick exterior walls, pockmarked with an occasional window. The roof has long since disintegrated, and earth, dead grass, and trees have reclaimed the floor, which now slopes like the hill outside.

As Lukas tumbles about the area and Gretel launches into a story of the duke who once lived here, I turn in a slow circle. Strange to think that several hundred years ago people found this a place of security and shelter, and called it home.

My gaze travels along the wall through which we entered. Seamless, save for the main archway and plugged window. Wasn't there a doorway beneath that window? I duck outside as the wind stirs. Yes, there's the alcove's shadow breaking up the exterior wall. And yet ... I return through the archway to study the interior. No door. Not even a bricked-up doorjamb to indicate an entrance.

I slip outside again. The wind fiddles with my hood, and I pinch my coat collar closed, crunching through leaves as I approach the alcove. A hefty iron ring serves as a doorknob. Above it, someone carved an intricate emblem of intertwining reedy branches that end in rounded leaves and berry clusters. Raindrops splatter against the iron ring, and I grasp it, giving it a twist. The door doesn't budge.

Fruitcake. I wipe the damp rust flakes from my palms. The screws anchoring the iron ring's plate to the door gleam in the timeworn surface, and I squint closer at the six-lobed heads.

As a Christmas elf, I had to learn all manner of fasteners and hardware in school. If memory serves me right, this screw head didn't exist until after the mid-1900s. Modern screws in supposedly ancient hardware. Interesting.

Backing away, I study the wooden door itself, knotted and weathered. Or maybe it's made to *look* weathered. Who would bother replacing a door that doesn't lead anywhere?

The hair at the nape of my neck rises with the sensation of being watched. Not again.

I whip around. Among the evergreens, blending with the shadows and clumps of pine needles, a dark form breaks up the line of branches, like a head ... with horns.

Like Krampus in that ballroom fresco.

"Tinsel?"

I yelp as Niklas approaches from the archway. He chuckles. "Jumpy much?"

"I—" My throat closes. I point toward the branches, but the head—or whatever I saw—is gone.

The breeze picks up, blowing off my hood, and raindrops sting my cheeks. Decaying leaves swoosh and twirl across the ground. One attaches to my leg. I bend to free it when a flash of white winks from deep in the woods.

Niklas tenses beside me. "What was that?"

I shake my head.

"Something ran past. Like a stag or—" We exchange looks, and he squeezes my elbow. "Be right back." He takes off through the trees, twigs and leaves snapping and rustling underfoot as he goes.

Gretel approaches, arms crossed, Elke trailing behind her. "Men," Gretel says. "Does he think he can catch whatever wild animal he saw?"

I shrug. "He *is* Santa. Or, he will be. That comes with certain blessings, one of which includes having a way with animals." Particularly those in the deer species, though his communication skills are—were?—one-sided without me.

"It is too bad not all Kringles enjoy those same"—Gretel glances at Elke—"blessings."

"Pardon?"

"We talked to Kristof when he visited. He, like Stoffel, is a second son with hopes and dreams, but without the full magic of a firstborn."

Elke works her fingers into a pair of gloves. "Kristof thinks the … what is that word?" She rattles off something in German.

"Hype," Gretel says.

"The hype is unfair around a firstborn," Elke says in her thick accent, "yet what can he do?"

"Is that what he told you?" I ask.

Gretel unties and adjusts her scarf. "His eyes told us. His tone, too."

When Kristof left for his internship in January, he'd been comfortable with his role as Santa's second son. Had something occurred overseas to alter his stance?

"He said if something happened to Santa's direct lineage," Gretel continues, "the powers transfer to the next closest kin. *Ist das richtig oder?*"

I jerk my head, frowning at Gretel through the rain. Elke scuffs the sodden ground with her boot, and Lukas throws rocks at a nearby tree trunk, his ear cocked. "Yes, that's right," I say. "Otherwise, the absence of Santa Claus would leave a void in the world."

Gretel lets out that subdued laugh. "Not everyone thinks highly of der Weihnachtsmann. Some might welcome a void."

Shivering, I tug my hood back over my head and search the woods for Niklas—and Gretel's words for an underlying message. "A void doesn't remain empty. Something would fill it, and we risk replacing a positive with a negative."

"Perhaps it was positive. Once. But some people think a 'holy' day driven by greed, money, and ... *Materialismus* ... is a day better left like this castle." She nods behind us. "Abandoned."

My gaze narrows at Elke, a Kringle herself. "Do you believe that?"

The young teenager lifts a shoulder.

"The Kringles were commissioned to reflect the Light of this world," I say, "to share the Hope and Joy of Christmas, and to plant seeds of Faith." *Niklas, where are you? Please tell me you found the Silver Reindeer.* "We mustn't abandon Christmas, even if cultures distort Santa's message into one of materialism. The foundation is still solid."

Pulling out a slender tube from her pocket, Gretel tilts her head. "Then what do you suggest?" she asks, squirting lotion onto her palm.

"Me?"

"You know the saying, 'Behind every powerful Santa Claus is a powerful Mrs. Claus.'"

The lotion's scent carries on the breeze, similar to the essential oils she added to my choker yesterday. "You mean, 'Behind every *great* Santa Claus is a *great* Mrs. Claus.'"

She caps the tube, tucks it away again, and rubs the lotion into her skin. "Same thing. If you become Mrs. Claus, how will you help fix this distorted view of Christmas?"

If? I squirm more from her actual question, however, than her veiled suggestion. "Niklas and I haven't even set a wedding date. Since his parents will take the mantle before we do, envisioning my role as Mrs. Claus—er, Mrs. Kringle—seems premature."

"When I believed we'd marry, I had my entire first five years planned out."

Five years. Is that expected? Is marrying into the Kringle family like marrying into royalty? Requirements and protocols to meet and carry out? A marketing plan with extravagant flow charts, dazzling graphs, and innovative solutions to guarantee Santa's success?

Am I up to the task? I can't answer that when there are so many unknowns.

Except, the young woman beside me was prepared.

Footfalls sound in the woods seconds before Niklas reappears, alone, jogging among the trees. Lukas makes a sound of disgust. "You didn't catch it?"

Niklas bends over to brace himself on his knees, shaking his head. "It's long gone," he pants, "whatever it was."

"Did you see anything else of interest?" I ask. Like a horned beast?

"No." Blowing out a breath, he glances at me and straightens with a laugh. "You look soaked."

I roll my eyes. "In case you haven't noticed, genius, it's raining."

"My toes have gone numb," Elke says. "May we go home?"

I brighten at the idea. "And warm up with a mug of drinking chocolate."

"Chocolate!" Lukas whoops and leaps about.

"All in favor?" I raise my hand. Elke and Lukas mimic me with hesitant grins.

Niklas glances up the trail. "What about the other castle? You're going to let a little rain drive you inside?"

Is this one of the unspoken expectations? Will I get docked "points" if I don't conform? "I'm heading back with Elke and Lukas. You do what you want."

"Tinsel." Slipping a finger into my coat pocket, Niklas tugs me toward him. Our gazes hold and dance for a moment. An emotion glints in his emerald eyes but vanishes before I can name it. "All right, I'll meet up with you later. On one condition."

"What's that?"

"Promise me some mint kisses when I return." His dimpled grin softens my irritation. "And I don't mean the candy variety."

Fifteen

Tinsel—Nov 26 Suitable Match

In the kitchen, elves bustle up and down step stools from stoves to sinks to fridges. Lingering near the door out of their way, I scope the area for dishes and mugs. A long marble-topped island counter cuts the room in half, bakeware and frying pans nestled in its open shelving. Gray light pours through upper windows, reflecting off creamy walls. A cheery-looking room, yet melancholy pervades the air.

"*Was machen Sie hier?*"

I glance down at a craggy-faced elf, his blue lederhosen dotted with flour, much like my father's clothes back home. A fellow baker. I smile. "May I have a snack and some cocoa, please?"

"*Der Frühstücksraum.*"

"Breakfast room?"

"Yes, yes. You'll find snacks and hot water for cocoa or tea in the breakfast room," he snaps in perfect English.

"Oh." I blink at his bitter expression. "Do you mind if ... That is, I prefer warm milk in my cocoa, not water. Could I—"

He grunts and his features harden, deepening the lines already etched in his skin. "Stay here." Grumbling under his breath, Herr "Craggy-Pants" stomps toward the adjoining butler's pantry. Perhaps that's what has soured the elves around here: having to drink cocoa made with water.

A moment later, something flat smacks me from behind. "Ow—hey!"

"Do you mind?" says a muffled voice.

I move aside as a square wood panel in the wall swings outward, revealing a tunnel. An elf in a white top and ivory lederhosen emerges, cradling a red leather pouch the size of a tennis ball.

"You know not to block this entrance," he complains (also in perfect English). "I got another supply—"

"Dieter!" Herr Craggy-Pants strides from the pantry, a green mug in his elfin grip, milk sloshing along its rim.

Dieter looks up, then at me. Color drains from his face to match his shirt. Shielding the pouch, he kicks the panel closed and hurries away with a muttered apology.

Where have I seen his overbite and weak chin before? My gaze flits to the panel. And where does that tunnel lead?

"What are you gaping at?" Craggy-Pants demands. I snap my mouth closed. "Who are you, anyway?"

"Tinsel Kuchler, sir. An elf, like you."

His upper lip curls in a sneer. "You're not like us. Here." He shoves the mug at me, droplets of heated milk splashing onto my skin. "Now go away."

Frosted windowpanes, his attitude matches that of Jangles before I left Flitterndorf. Clutching the mug, I backtrack through the hallways. Why is everyone so moody? Even I've been irritated.

Lukas bolts from the breakfast room as I enter, and Fritz glances up from where he pours himself a cup of coffee at the sideboard. "You returned already, too?" he asks.

"It was raining and chilly."

"Chilly? You live in the Arctic Circle."

"That's a different kind of cold." I peruse the drink options on the sideboard until I find the powdered chocolate. It'll have to suffice for now. "Germany has a damp chill. Seeps into your bones faster."

"Lukas says Gretel and Niklas are still hiking."

"Niklas wanted to see more ruins." I scoop powder into my milk. "Me, I'd rather visit a castle that's been maintained, like when we tour Neuschwanstein next week."

Fritz adds cream to his coffee. "I'm surprised you left them alone together." He offers me the small carafe.

I take it with a confused smile. "Why surprised?"

"Because of their history. Their engagement."

"That was never official."

"To some, it was. Opa Stoffel believes Gretel would have made an excellent Mrs. Claus. She's smart, good with people, creative, royalty—"

"She's royalty?"

"Distant. But what of you?" His eyebrows rise, and I fidget under his scrutiny. "Mmm." Fritz gestures toward the door with his mug. "I go to the morning room, to play cards with Elke and Lukas. You may join us."

I turn to the spread of cheese, crackers, and fruit atop the sideboard, and grab a plate. "I'll think about it. Danke."

Though Fritz leaves the room, his unspoken words remain, pinging louder than Jangles's commands in the FTA.

What if Herr Stoffel isn't alone in thinking Gretel would make an excellent Mrs. Claus? What if Gretel believes it, too? Had Niklas disappointed her, after all, when he declared he wouldn't marry her? She hasn't acted like a woman scorned, yet she confessed to making plans, and clearly someone groomed her for the role. Now that she's interacting with Niklas again in person, might this visit stir up old emotions?

Snack and drink in hand, though I'm no longer hungry, I cross the spacious entrance hall toward the morning room at the opposite end. Approaching the naked Christmas tree, I give it a pitying glance. Tradition or not, someone should put a few ornaments on its boughs. Or would that offend the Bavarian Kringles?

"—not even a Toy Maker at that. She works with animals."

The faintly accented words echo off the walls of an alcove as I pass. Their malice and contempt stop me. Herr Stoffel?

"Working with the future Big Eight is an admirable position," a recognizable voice replies. Meister Nico. I squint through the darkened alcove into the open doorway of an office. Lamplight bathes the far wall.

"Niklas is like a prince who owns many fine horses," Herr Stoffel says. "She, a mere stablehand who cleans their stalls. The two don't belong together."

They're talking about me. My grip tightens on the plate.

Meister Nico scoffs. "Since when does your side of the family look down your noses at the elves?"

"Since when does yours mingle with the help?"

"They're our backbone."

A shadow moves across the patch of light, and I shrink from view. "This is not how we operate," Herr Stoffel says. "It goes against the ancient edicts."

"It's because they're ancient that some of them have been overruled."

"Some are timeless, no matter which way the stocking swings."

"Agreed, and we adhere to the foundations of Christmas. Within those borders, however, we have much freedom. We've made an exception where Tinsel is concerned, and we stand by our decision."

"Our family did not build a legacy making exceptions."

"This isn't about *our* legacy, Onkel."

"The world is changing, Nico," a third voice says, his accent thick and his tone commanding. "Kringles are no longer in people's good graces. You must abide by the rules. No exceptions. Unless you want to be responsible for the breakdown of Christmas."

"Of course not—"

"Good." Herr Stoffel again. "Then end the engagement, Nico. I do not condone it."

"It's not yours to condone."

"Kringles are part of the royal bloodline—"

"A diluted bloodline—"

"But not *polluted*. Which is exactly what you invite by letting Niklas marry that elf." Herr Stoffel pauses. "End their engagement, Nico. Or I will."

"Grüß Gott. *Kann ich Sie helfen?*"

I start at the voice behind me, sloshing cocoa onto the floor. A woman with dark chocolate eyes watches me, her fitted lab coat open over a navy blue jumpsuit, one arm holding … a reindeer figurine?

"Um, nein, danke, I don't need help." Heat rushes into my cheeks. "I-I'm on my way to join Fritz and the others."

Her lips lift in a closed-mouth smile that reminds me of Gina. "A Canadian. I know many Canadians," she says in fluid English, her manicured fingers combing a wisp of deep brown hair into her soft updo. "As for Fritz, he's in the morning room with his siblings." She points behind me.

Play dumb. "Vielen dank." I nod at the reindeer. "Beautiful figurine."

"Isn't it? It took me a while to perfect it."

I lean closer. Its details look incredibly lifelike, from its fur coat to the exceptional antlers, from its glass eyes to the intricate lines around the nose and mouth. "You made this?"

"You could say that."

"Ina?" Herr Stoffel's frame fills up his office doorway. Another gentleman with a thick mustache peers over his shoulder. *"Alles in Ordnung?"*

A flicker of disdain crosses the woman's elegant features. "Everything is fine, Stoffel. Are you ready for our meeting?"

Herr Stoffel shifts his attention to me, his mouth mashed into a straight line. "Do you need something, Tinsel?"

I press the edge of my plate into my breastbone. Does he know I was eavesdropping?

"Tinsel?" Ina says my name as though she's heard it before. Snowballs and icicles, they're all talking about me.

"Yes, ma'am, that's me. Nice to meet you." Dipping my head, I pivot and hurry toward the morning room, guessing Herr Stoffel watches me like a forest predator. *Do not trip. Do not trip.* Now more than ever, I must downplay my incompetence, my defects. Not just with Niklas, but with his whole family. Otherwise, Herr Stoffel will convince everyone I'm not a suitable match.

A vivid picture of the perfect bride sears my brain: Gretel, wearing my Initiation dress, savoring the warmth of Niklas's smile.

Where's the nearest bathroom so I can throw up?

Sixteen

Tinsel—Nov 27 Secret Tunnel

"Tinsel, you're not thinking rationally," Gina says, using her parents' house phone since she lost her cell the other day (the details of which remain foggy).

I glare at the moon from my position on the terrace, the cold flagstones seeping into my jeans. "You didn't see the joy on Niklas's face when he and Gretel returned from their hike," I argue into my cell. "Joy that had nothing to do with me." I huff and lean against the manor wall. "I should've never left them alone together."

Gina laughs on the other end. "That guy is besotted with you, not Gretel. Like, never Gretel, if you recall."

"I still haven't told him I put his reindeer in danger. Or got suspended."

"He'll forgive you, Tins. That bling on your finger represents a depth of emotion and commitment not easily shaken. Have faith. Stand confident."

Her words keep my growing doubt in check. "Thanks, G."

"Anytime." Something clatters in the background followed by her quick intake of breath.

"What are you doing?"

"Working on a doll wig. My straight iron dropped. Had to rescue it before it burned a hole in my—" She halts. "Hang on a second."

"What's up?"

"It happened again."

I push to my feet. "What did?"

She doesn't answer. Movement sounds, then silence. I pull the phone away to check the time and groan. Four-thirty. I'm gonna be a zombie at breakfast.

With a lengthy sigh, Gina gets back on the phone. "Remember I told you about that *whump* I heard a couple of nights ago outside my bedroom door?"

"Yeah."

"I just heard it again."

The stone wall digs into my back. My eyes strain against the nighttime darkness. "You checked it out this time?"

"Yes. Nothing out of the ordinary—unless you count the skewed pictures on the hallway wall and the swaying spoons on Mum's souvenir rack."

I shudder, and the darkness presses closer. "You're giving me the Krampus-crawlies."

"The what?"

"It's Christmas-speak for the shivers. Y'know—the heebie-jeebies, the creeps."

"Okay, but what's a Krampus?"

"Oh, no." I shake my head, inching closer to the terrace doors. "I'm alone, outside, in the dark. Google it for yourself."

"'Google it.' Listen to you, throwing around contemporary speech like a pro." Gina gives an exaggerated sniff. "I'm so proud."

I chuckle, some of my fear dissipating, and it morphs into a yawn.

"So, everything's okay there?"

"Peachy."

"Then I'm heading back to bed. Have fun with your wig, and whenever you find your phone or get a new one, I want a pic of the finished product."

"It might suck."

"What was it you told me earlier? Have faith and—"

"Yeah, yeah. Get to bed, elf. Talk to you later."

Smiling, I return to my chilly bedroom, change back into my pajamas, and slide into bed. The comforter settles around me, and a whiff of vanilla and a scent now familiar yet still unknown whooshes into the air. My smile fades, Gina's encouragement taking on a mocking tone. I roll onto my side and stare at the wall mural opposite the windows.

Have faith? Stand confident? How does an elf stand confident when the confidence is leaking out of her?

Scriiitch.

My ears prick at the sound coming from behind the mural, tinged red from the glow of fireplace embers. Is that a mouse in the wall? Or something worse? Images of deviled horns and a forked tongue swim before my eyes. I shouldn't have mentioned Krampus to Gina.

A dull *pop* follows, like wood expanding, and a section of the mural swings inward on silent hinges. Whispered rustling and muted white sleeves reveal a childlike form entering my room.

Ice washes over me, freezing me in place. Who's skulking through secret doorways in the wee hours of the morning? My fingers curl into my pillow. While too soft to act as a weapon, it might distract long enough for me to nab something sturdy.

Carrying a bulky object, the figure moves toward the fireplace, inadvertently drawing closer to the bed. Wait—I recognize that *swish*. Dirndl skirts. An elf! Which explains the small stature, but not her early presence.

She crouches by the fireplace that quit emitting heat a few hours ago. In quiet movements, she transfers her load to the struggling embers, piece by piece. I want to knock my forehead with the heel of my palm. She's here to help, not harm.

A flame flares to life on the long match she holds, its light playing on her features as she ignites the kindling. It's the teenage elf from the other morning. The one with the stack of towels. Her head swivels toward the bed, and I snap my eyes shut. When I peek again a moment later, she's pulling at the ties of a leather pouch similar to the one that elf had in the kitchen yesterday.

A pouch he didn't want me to see.

She dips her fingers into the pouch and tosses a powder substance into the fire, which pops and hisses.

I rise on one elbow. "What was that?"

The elf jerks with a squeal, loses her balance, and lands on her rear. My eyes narrow, but a pleasing fragrance drifts by. I inhale and sit up straighter. "That smell. Is that …?" I grope for my choker on the nightstand and bring it to my nose. The scent has faded, yet I can make out the base notes. Comparable to what I smell now. I look at the elf petrified on the floor. "What did you put into the fire?"

"F-fragrance, ma'am. Vanilla, lavender, ylang ylang, and others. You do not like?"

"No, it's nice." I pluck at my comforter, its scent probably absorbed from the fire. "My name's Tinsel. And I'm nineteen, so please, forget the 'ma'am.'"

"Yes, ma—" The elf gives a small grin. "Yes, miss."

"Tinsel. You are?"

"Poppy."

"Do you come into my room every morning, Poppy?"

"Ja, to tend the fire. When you leave for breakfast, I return to change towels and bed sheets."

I point to the wall mural. "You enter through hidden tunnels?"

Poppy nods. "We elves use them to travel and work between rooms."

Like the tunnel Dieter used. "Do they link together? If I took this passageway, would it bring me around to that corridor I saw the other morning?"

"What corridor?"

"The one I found when we first met. It was behind the fifth door."

Her face pales, noticeable even in the inadequate firelight. "There is no corridor." Fisting her cobalt blue apron, she glances around the room. "D-do you have dirty clothes to be washed?"

Why the change in subject? "Sure, I've got a growing pile in my suitcase, but I can do my own laundry."

"I hear you are an elf, ja?"

I pull back my hair to show her my pointy ears.

"So you know about talents and our jobs. Laundry, ironing, folding—those are my talents."

"They are?"

Her nostrils flare. "You think this kind of work needs no talent?"

"I never gave it much thought."

"You do not clean clothes in Flitterndorf?"

I grin. "We don't have community laundromats, if that's what you mean." I cock my head, a hazy memory coming to me. "The Workshop does have a laundry room. We took a tour one year when I was in school. Elves folded painter smocks and barista aprons faster than I could spell the words. Others created origami-like sculptures out of napkins and tablecloths. It was fascinating." And I'd forgotten about it over the years in my quest to find my own talent. How self-absorbed can I get?

"Nothing pleases like freshly pressed and folded laundry," Poppy says, a smitten glimmer in her eyes.

My eyes held a similar shine after discovering I could communicate with the reindeer. Far be it from me to eclipse such joy from a fellow elf. "In that case"—I slip to the floor and pull the suitcase from under the bed—"I have some laundry for you."

"*Wunderbar.*"

I wad the clothes into a heap. "Poppy, if the elves at Weihnachts Manor are working according to their talents, why is everyone grumpy?" I recall what Fritz told me the other day. "Is it because your families were left behind all those years ago?"

"Left behind?" She scrunches her nose. "Ah, you talk with a Kringle. Nein, our families chose to stay behind. We knew our work here would still be important. The Kringles that return here are the unhappy ones."

I lift an eyebrow. "I've met a lot of grumpy elves."

"That is new. Their joy, their ... *Befriedigung?*"

"Um, contentment?"

"Ja, it fades about a year ago. It gets worse these last weeks."

"Yet you aren't affected. How come?"

Poppy merely shrugs.

Seventeen

Tinsel—Nov 27 Just a Closet

After Poppy leaves, I sleep for a few fitful hours, dreaming of tunnels and hidey-holes and Krampus leaping from shadowed recesses. With heavy-lidded eyes, I toss aside the bed covers mid-morning and stand before the wardrobe. Staring at my reflection in its mirrored door to fasten my parents' choker, I debate wearing my all-time comfiest dirndl, but Fritz's accolades about Gretel drown out Gina's encouragement. I choose skinny jeans and a ribbed turtleneck.

Pulling a sweater over my head, I leave the bedroom intent on breakfast and a visit to the reindeer.

"Paß auf!"

My head pops through the neck hole, and an elf snarls up at me. "Entschuldigung," I mutter as he tromps down the hall to the left.

Hang the mistletoe—that's Dieter from the kitchen. His familiar face tugs at my brain, though no last name surfaces with it. At the corner, he shoots a glance over his shoulder, eyes flaring when he catches me watching. His pace quickens, a red pouch clinking at his waist as he disappears down the corridor Frau Wissen forbade me from entering. Why is the corridor forbidden, anyway? Because of that tunnel Poppy didn't want to talk about?

Curiosity roused, I tiptoe along the hall and peek around the corner. Dieter passes the third door … passes the fourth door … slows as he nears Door Number Five—

"What're we watching?"

I squeak and jump around. Niklas gives a lop-sided grin, handsome yet un-Kringle-like in blue jeans and a cabled sweater. I smack his arm and whisper, "Don't do that to me. Why are you here?"

"You hadn't come to breakfast, so I wanted to check on you. Plus, Pa thought we should borrow the car again to search for the Silver Reindeer, and I didn't want you to miss out." His eyes twinkle. "We spying on someone?"

I hazard another glance around the corner. Door Number Five swings shut, leaving an empty hallway. Clasping Niklas's arm, I pull him with me. "Technically, we're not supposed to be in this wing—"

"Says who?"

"An elf chewed me out two days ago."

"Lucky for you, I'm a Kringle." He winks. "No place is off-limits to me."

"Pff. Door Number Five might be."

"Door what-now?"

I slink up to the door in question, a tingle racing through me, and explain how I discovered a long, spooky passageway behind it, before Poppy saw me and Frau Wissen yelled at us.

"Spooky?"

"And drafty." My hand grasps the knob of its own accord, despite the fact Dieter could still be in sight on the other side. The cold metal seeps into my skin. "Then an elf emerged through a hidden tunnel in the kitchen—"

"Hidden tunnel?"

"I didn't tell you that, either?" Glancing in both directions, I launch into a hurried retelling of the elves entering rooms via secret passageways. "And a moment ago, one went through here. At least, I think he did, even though Poppy claims this passage doesn't—" My gaze snags on a symbol centered above the door. A crisscrossing of vines and berries. "Hey, I saw this same emblem yesterday at the abandoned castle."

Niklas wags his eyebrows. "Intrigue and secrets. I like it." He rubs his palms together, mischief coloring his expression. "Let's go snooping."

Biting back a smile, I open Door Number Five. The hallway light exposes a shallow recess in the wall. A few cardboard boxes rest on the overhead shelf, one vintage coat hangs on the rack, and several more boxes clutter the floor.

My eyebrows knit. "What is this?"

"Best guess? A closet." Niklas pulls on his mouth to mask a grin. "You know, kind of like a wardrobe, except not free-standing."

I jab him with an elbow. "This had been a passageway two days ago."

"You sure you have the right door?"

"Dieter just used it."

"Yet, he's not in here. It's probably this one." Niklas moves to open the door on the left, which reveals the black and white tiles of a bathroom. "Or not." He closes it and walks past me to the door on the right. "So, it's this one." He tugs on the doorknob. Locked. His shoulders sag. "Muddy snowballs, I wanted to go snooping." He jerks his thumb at the locked door. "This is your hallway. Dieter must've locked it behind him."

Ignoring Niklas, I step around the boxes to the closet's back wall and push.

"You think it's a façade?"

"Well, the elf didn't simply vanish." I feel the corners and gasp at the chill. "Niklas, there's a draft." A muffled noise sounds from the end of the hall, and my eyes widen. "Someone's coming." I scramble from the closet, but my foot catches on a box, and I pitch forward.

Quick on the reflexes, Niklas grips my flailing arms, his mouth lifting at the corners. "Clumsy elf. It's not a crime to roam the halls." His gaze drifts past me, and his smile fades. "The boxes didn't move when you tripped."

"Because they're heavy." Righting myself, I beckon him with a wave. "C'mon, let's go."

He taps a box with his foot, then kicks it. It doesn't budge. Crouching, he shoves the stack. Nothing moves or shifts.

"Ey!" Frau Wissen charges toward us, yelling in German.

I yank Niklas to his feet, and we race back along the corridor, around the corner, down that hallway, and into my bedroom. The door clicks shut, and I collapse against it, trying to catch my breath. "What'd I tell you? Flippity fruitcake, do you think she'll tell Herr Stoffel?" I want to regain my position, not solidify my suspension.

"Solid wood," Niklas murmurs, kneading the back of his neck.

"What?"

"Those boxes in the closet. They're a solid chunk of wood, carved and painted—and affixed to the floor."

"For what purpose? It takes up so much room."

"Inconvenient." His gaze finds mine. "If that was a real closet."

"So, it *is* a façade." My fingertips pulsate with the memory of the cool draft. "What's at the other end of that passageway they don't want others to discover?"

Eighteen

Tinsel—Nov 27 Here We Come a Whistling

No sooner do we descend the stairs to the entrance hall than Niklas is called away by his mother, and I wander into the breakfast room to wait for him. Ten minutes later, I send him a text to meet me at the stables instead, trusting he'll receive the message when he gets reception somewhere.

After grabbing my winter accessories, I slip out the back and make for the reindeer pasture. If hopes could become reality, yesterday's snag in communications was purely a glitch caused by stress or jet lag, and my talent's still intact. I want to hear what Bonbon has to say, and ask if these reindeer know about the SR. They might even know where we can find her.

Perhaps that's what Bonbon wants to tell me.

As I walk through the stables and near the fence separating me from the herd, three whistle blasts pierce the air. Fritz stands in the field, a group of reindeer lined up at his right. Several more mill at the field's far edge, where a reindeer lands. Fritz blows the whistle another three times, and the stately reindeer at the front of the line takes off running. It builds up speed until it launches in the air, sails for a second, then lands again.

"Neat trick," I call out.

Fritz whirls about, eyes wide.

"Sorry." I put my mittened hands to my mouth. "Didn't mean to startle you."

He issues a long, trilling peal on his whistle, and the reindeer disperse, some pawing in the dried grass, others trotting farther into the field. Fritz jogs to the fence. "Grüß Gott."

"Sorry if I'm intruding on your lessons." I point toward the reindeer and stand on tiptoes. "Just wanted to come see them. Is Bonbon around?"

"Ja, she is out near the trees."

"And Muskat?"

Fritz grins. "He leaves her alone."

"Good." I study his features, so like Niklas's, yet I'm beginning to see little differences. Fritz's eyebrows are thicker, his chin broader, and he lacks Niklas's dimples. I indicate the whistle he holds. "You use this to issue commands? Whistles would come in handy back home when our Flight Teams are airborne." When *I'm* airborne with the Third String. "Speaking of flight, let me know if one of your 'deer develops the ability to fly."

Fritz rotates the whistle between his fingers. "It's not likely. I'm told the last time that happened, Meister K was a teenager."

"Crumbling candy canes."

"Why?"

I pull off a mitten and pick at the fence railing. "Niklas's team has been down one member since we learned Eggnog's afraid of heights two years ago."

"A flying reindeer scared of heights?" chirps a youthful voice to my right.

I spin around. The elegant black carriage from inside the stables now sits outside, tucked against the stables' back wall, and Lukas bounces at its dash. He slaps a set of reins, as though pretending to direct a team of horses. Or reindeer, I suppose.

"If he can fly," Lukas says, "how do you know he's afraid?"

I pick harder at the railing, glancing between the brothers. "Niklas figured it out. You know how Kringles can tap into their reindeer's emotions."

"Not all Kringles." Fritz props an arm atop the fence. "And you are not a good liar."

My mouth opens and closes several times. I can't deny it, but neither do I have to verbally affirm it.

"*Wann können wir die Dungeons sehen?*" Lukas trills, slapping the reins again.

I let out an uncomfortable chuckle at the boy's question. Never. Never is a good time to see the dungeons.

"Auf Englisch, Lukas," Fritz chides him.

"I understood him." I frown at the line I've dug into the railing. "Trying to think of when we can go. This afternoon is out. What about tomorrow?"

"We have dance practice."

A chip of wood breaks free beneath my nail. "Dance practice?"

"For Nik's Initiation Ceremony." Fritz eyes my obsession with the railing. "Opa Stoffel mentioned it that first morning after you arrived."

Mentioned it to Niklas, perhaps, and possibly to Meister Nico, but not when I was around to hear.

"Can we go before dance practice?" Lukas grins, his teeth glinting like a predator.

I shake off the comparison. He's eight years old, for garland's sake.

"Sure, why not?"

He cheers, then hops from the carriage and races away through the stables.

Fritz's mouth curves in a Niklas-esque grin, and an eerie tremor runs through me. "You're a generous elf, Tinsel, to indulge him. It's almost a shame that—"

"What's got into Lukas?" Niklas emerges from the stables, hiking a thumb over his shoulder. "He nearly knocked me over back there."

"He's excited." Snowman, what had Fritz been about to say?

Niklas slides an arm around my waist. "So, there's been a change to our afternoon plans. Onkel Stoffel is giving us a tour of Brückenstadt instead."

No searching for the Silver Reindeer? Considering I haven't heard a peep from these reindeer, I should be relieved, yet now we're spending an afternoon with Herr Stoffel. I slump against Niklas. "Does it have to be your great-uncle?"

Niklas chuckles. "He won't bite."

"He'll glare." I wave a hand at Fritz. "Why can't you show us around?"

Fritz inclines his head. "I'd be honored to show you more sights another time." He gives the railing a slap. "For now, I return to the reindeer."

I watch him go, and Niklas rumbles at my side, "You'd rather have Fritz as a tour guide?"

"He's nicer." I motion toward the trees. "He's even making sure Muskat leaves Bonbon alone."

Niklas withdraws to lean against the rail. "I gather you two have a lot in common."

"In the sense we both work with reindeer." I adjust my hat. *Worked.* I *worked* with the reindeer. *Niklas, I put the Third String in jeopardy and got suspended. I'm sorry.* Why is that so hard to say?

Maybe because in adding, *Oh, and I lost my talent,* there won't be anything left of me to love.

Fritz whistles a command, and a dozen reindeer trot over to surround him. Grunts issue from two reindeer in another group, their antlers clacking across the frosty air as they spar with each other.

"What's up with those two?" Niklas asks. "Is that in jest or anger?"

Fritz shouts at them, but they continue their struggle. One is missing a brow tine. "The one on the left is Muskat, so it could be in anger, for all I know."

"How can you not know? They must be squawking at each other. What are they saying?"

I shift on my feet as Fritz blows the whistle again and gestures toward me and Niklas. Or just Niklas, the future Santa. "They're, uh, speaking a barrage of German I can't understand." My face prickles from the lie.

Niklas chuckles, propping an elbow on the railing. "Odd to think of them speaking German. If Chip were here, he'd be out sparring with those two." He points to a nearby group of females. "How 'bout those three there? What are they talking about?"

"N-nothing." That I can hear, anyway. Niklas zeroes in on me, his green eyes razor sharp. I force a smile. "They're a quiet bunch."

"Hmm. You put Licorice, Peppermint, and Cinnamon together, and I'm inundated with mental images from their nonstop chatter." His mirth fades, and he studies his gloves. Uh-oh. What about the Third String triggered his bleak expression? Has he heard about my suspension, after all? "Tinsel ..." He turns to me. I swallow. Fritz's whistle carries across the field, like the measure of a song, and Niklas scowls. "Why is he using a whistle?"

"To issue commands. Isn't it great?" I blow into my mittens, happy to change subjects. "We should implement something like that."

"We don't need whistles. Santas can read minds."

Several reindeer strut in a line before Fritz, raising their forelegs high like dressage horses. "Except, I'm not Santa, and you refuse to get in the sleigh." An image of my failed attempt at a Peppermint Twist with the Third String streaks through my mind, and I wince. "The team can't hear my voice at three thousand feet, but they'd hear a whistle." Had I used one, our near-disaster might have been averted. Perching my arms atop the railing, I lean my chin on my linked hands. "Do you see how they respond to Fritz? Like he's got his own brand of magic."

"That appeals to you?"

A new image replaces the old one, blurring with the reality before me. Succinct, measured movements. Tight, precise spirals. Peppermint Perfection. A shoo-in for Jangles's replacement. I smile. "Definitely." I tilt my head, the ideal Twist looping in my mind—until Meister K's face pops out of nowhere.

Jangles seeks your suspension from the team, and I'm afraid I must agree with him.

Figgy pudding. What if my lost talent persuades Meister K to make my suspension permanent? All the whistles in the world won't help me then, and I'd bring disgrace to the Kringle name if Niklas married me. Which means he wouldn't—couldn't—marry me.

You'll have opportunities in Germany to show your competence with my brother's reindeer herd, Meister K said.

If Fritz could teach me some commands with the whistle, and if I mastered them prior to baring my faults, maybe I can still convince Meister K I'm the best replacement for Jangles, regardless of talent. And convince Niklas I'm still worth marrying.

I peek at him from the corner of my eye—then straighten and turn in a circle. "Niklas?"

He's gone.

Nineteen

Gina—Nov 27 Odd Man Out

Waldheim

The doll sits on my desk, her bald head tilted as if to say, "Get on with it already."

I secure several more lengths of yarn around the thin dowel, give them a firm tug, and grab my flat iron. "Have patience," I mumble to my childhood toy. "Brilliance doesn't happen overnight." Case in point, the wig I tried making last night while talking to Tinsel ended up in the trashcan.

Yet I won't quit. The tour Kristof gave me of Santa's Workshop ignited something long dead inside my bones, and right now, I'm heeding that creative call. Time will tell if I've opened the door to an ally or a monster.

A monster like the one Tinsel mentioned—Krampus—which I later researched. The horror movies I used to watch may have desensitized me to a lot of creepy stuff, but that dude is hideous, no mistake.

The Mickey Mouse house phone clangs beside me on the desk, and I jump, dropping my iron. After the elves lost my cell, I confiscated

Mickey from the living room. Though cuter than a smartphone, he's way too loud.

Lifting the receiver from Mickey's arm, I put it to my ear and lean over for my iron. "Hello?"

"Hi, Gina? This is Kristof."

My stomach cartwheels, and I fumble with the iron again. "Hi."

"I'm at the café, looking for you. Mikal said you went home early. You feeling okay?"

"Fine. I wanted to … work on something."

"Not getting ready for a date, are you?"

I laugh, setting the iron atop the desk. "No, no date. Why?"

"Mind if I swing by? I have something for you."

"Sure." My stomach trips again. "Yeah, come on over."

"Great. See you in a few."

I hang up and stare into Mickey's plastic eyes. Good gravy, Kristof's coming. I lift my work shirt to my nose. With a grimace, I shut off my iron and hustle to change, comb my hair, and check my makeup.

Not that I care how I look. It's Kristof, after all.

… Okay, so creativity might not be the only spark ignited the other day in Flitterndorf. But I can't encourage it. Even if Kristof were to make it past my three-date policy, someday he'd break my heart like Isaak, and our friendship would be ruined. No thanks.

Whump!

A spray of ice skitters along my skin at the now-familiar sound. I set down my hairbrush, slink across the carpet, and place an ear to the door. Silence. Grasping the doorknob, I give it a yank.

Aunt Cat teeters at the top of the stairs, a hand flying to her chest. "Goodness, Gina. You scared me. I didn't know anyone was up here."

"Sorry."

Her manicured fingers smooth over her dark brown hair. "Aren't you supposed to be at work?"

"Came home an hour ago." A *ting ting* comes from Mum's spoon rack across the hall as some spoons sway. "You didn't happen to hear that a moment ago, did you?"

Aunt Cat hides a yawn. "Hear what, Sweetie?"

"There was a noise, like something falling."

"Oh. No. I just woke from a nap."

Judging by her expertly made-up eyes, the black, crisp jumpsuit, and soft gray cardigan, I'd guess she came from an executive business meeting, not a guest room. That's classy Aunt Cat for you.

She places a hand on the banister. "I'm going to make some coffee. You interested?"

Hovering in my bedroom doorway, I tug on a blue lock of my hair. The spoon rack hangs crooked against the green and ivory Victorian replica wallpaper. "No, thanks. Kristof's arriving any minute."

"Kristof?" Aunt Cat's eyebrows rise. "Is he another tourist fling?"

"Oh, please." I tilt the rack to the left. Too far. "He's firmly entrenched —cemented—rooted—in the friend zone." Emphasis for my sake or Aunt Cat's?

"Ah, he's the guy whose employees pulled a prank on you and lost your phone."

"Yes." I tilt the rack the other way, my wrist bumping a photograph of my grandmother. "Those little twerps."

"'Little twerps'?" Aunt Cat laughs, a light, tinkling sound I've tried to emulate over the years, and starts down the stairs. "Honey, what more can you expect? They're men."

Right—men. Gotta remember that little white lie I told my folks and Aunt Cat surrounding my phone's disappearance. Had I blamed it on "imaginary" elves, I'd have lost their respect.

I straighten Nonna's picture, the censure in her dark gaze as stark now as it had been during my childhood. She hadn't lived an easy life, uprooted from Italy at age nine to settle here, then uprooted again

120

when her parents separated several years later. It wasn't until Dad was born that she allowed her own father, Papa Campi, back into her life. I gravitate to his sepia-toned picture beside hers. A sweet old man with a thick Italian accent who lived with us until he died when I was six. I have fonder memories of him than I do Nonna.

With a lingering grin, I return to the spoon rack, determined to right it, and my focus drifts as usual to the emblem centered above the rack. Reedy branches intertwine multiple times in an area about the size of a teacup saucer, their ends disappearing behind rounded leaves and petite berries. An odd design that doesn't fit or repeat with the wallpaper's pattern of scrolls, flowers, and curvy vases. I've always wondered why.

Downstairs, the front door opens on creaky hinges. "Man, is it ever cold out there today," Dad says, stomping his boots on the tiled area by the door. "Gina!"

I take the stairs two at a time. "Hey. Finally home for lunch?"

"Yes, and guess who I ran into coming up the drive." Dad beckons someone behind him as a swirl of arctic wind hits me.

Kristof enters the house, flashing me a grin, and Dad closes the door. "Thank you, sir. I won't take long."

"No problem. Good to see you again." Dad hangs his coat in the closet. "You two want anything while I'm in the kitchen? Water? Pop?"

"We're good, Dad, thanks."

As he leaves, Kristof removes his beanie and rifles a hand over his gelled locks. My heart skitters at the rumpled result, and I clear my throat. "How's your day been?" *How's your day?* Can I get any more awkward?

"I didn't come to unload my troubles." Kristof reaches into his back pocket. "I came to give you this." And he holds out my phone.

"They found it!" I clasp it to my chest, then press the home button.

The screen lights up. "You charged it, too. Thank you." I scroll through the ribbon of notifications. "Heavens, have I got catching up to do."

Kristof angles close to peer at my screen, smelling of sandalwood and vanilla again. "FYI, Nik hasn't told Tinsel you found your way into Flitterndorf."

"I still can't tell her?" I drop my head back. "You guys are killing me."

"He thinks it would raise too many questions and undue concern."

"What about the Third String?"

"That's off-limits, too."

"What's Nik waiting for? This could backfire on him." Then again, Tinsel has her own confessions to make. This could backfire on them both.

Kristof scrubs a palm over his five o'clock shadow, fuller than the other day. "I don't agree with how he's going about this, but you can't fault the guy for wanting to protect Tinsel."

"She's not some exotic flower that'll whither under adversity."

The kitchen door opens and Aunt Cat comes through the living room, cupping a steaming mug between her hands. "Gina, honey, there's more coffee in the pot, if you want a cup." She does a double-take, her eyes flaring at Kristof, before her features school into a welcoming smile. "Hi, there."

"Aunt Cat, this is Kristof. Kristof, this is my aunt, Caterina."

"Kristof." Aunt Cat says his name like she's sampling wine. "*Not* another tourist."

He cocks an eyebrow at me. "Talking to your aunt about me, too, huh? If I were one of your air-headed tourist dudes, I might get the wrong message."

I swat his arm. "They're not airheads."

His eyebrow arches higher.

"Not all of them."

He and Aunt Cat share a grin, then he gets a funny look on his face. "Have we met before?"

She plays with the beaded necklace at her throat. "You may have glimpsed me around town without knowing it."

"Except Kristof recently returned from overseas," I say.

"Ah." Aunt Cat cradles her mug. "Well, people have often said Gina and I look alike. That could be what has you confused." She points to the stairs. "I must be off. Research awaits. Nice to meet you, Kristof."

His pensive gaze follows her across the room and up the staircase. "What's her line of work?"

"She's a chemist. Currently experimenting with aromatherapy, I think. What do you want to bet she's, like, asleep in five minutes?" I tease. "She calls it 'beauty rest.'"

Kristof's attention swings back to me, his eyes crinkling. "I could take that comment down so many tangents, yet I'll refrain so I don't get myself in trouble. Speaking of trouble"—he tugs his beanie into place—"I should head home before I'm in a different kind of trouble with Grandpop."

"Did you come all this way just for me?" I glance out the front windows and frown. "That's not your snowmobile."

"I borrowed Gary's SnoMo to get here."

"Gary-the-café-custodian Gary?"

"Yep." Kristof pulls on his thrummed mittens with a sly smile. "My ride is hiding in the woods near his house."

"Hiding."

At the front door, he pauses. "Do you have a few minutes? You can come see."

"I have the whole afternoon." I grab my coat and winter accessories from the closet.

"Evening, too?"

My movements slow as I push my arms into the coat sleeves. "Why?"

His cheeks tinge pink, but he looks me square in the eye. "Will you have dinner with me?"

"As in, a date?" My heart kicks behind my ribs.

"Would that be such a bad thing?"

"No." I bite my bottom lip. "And yes."

Kristof chuckles. "Then we won't call it a date, and we'll eat with my grandparents."

My world stops tilting, and I relax. "In that case, I'd love to have dinner with you. Let me tell my folks. I'll meet you outside."

Twenty

Gina—Nov 27 Prized Reindeer

Mum's at work, but Dad's finishing up in the kitchen, and his demeanor turns haunted when I inform him I'll be with Kristof for the rest of the day.

"I don't think that's wise," he says, rinsing off a plate.

My fingers flex around my gloves. "Why not?"

"I'm concerned about you spending too much time with Kristof."

"Since when? Besides, we'll be hanging out with his grandparents. You know, Kris Kringle? You've done business with him for years."

Dad stares at the wall above the sink. "I'm not worried about the people."

"What is it, then?"

He waves me off, avoiding eye contact as he sets the plate in the dish drainer. "Just be careful."

I've already survived getting trussed up by water-wielding elves. What worse things could happen? Shrugging, I leave him to his moodiness and join Kristof outside, where he straddles the snowmobile.

"Ready?" He pats the remaining sliver of seat cushion behind him.

"Hop on."

I hesitate. "No helmets?"

"We're switching transportation in five minutes." He tugs me forward. "I promise to keep you safe in the meantime."

Minutes later, Kristof pulls into a driveway about a quarter-mile into the woods. A spotlight shines above the front door, but otherwise, the house looks quiet. Kristof cuts the engine, dismounts, and lifts a small duffle bag from behind me.

"So, now what?" I don't see another snowmobile or vehicle or even a pair of skis anywhere.

Kristof flashes his white teeth. "Now we walk." Flinging the bag over his shoulder, he sets off across the driveway and deeper into the woods.

Arranging my scarf to cover my nose and mouth in the subfreezing temps, I dash after him. "Waitwaitwaitwaitwait. You can't mean walk all the way to Flitterndorf, right? 'Cause that would be insane." Dried underbrush mixed with snow crunch beneath our feet.

He chuckles. "Relax, G." He brandishes his arm toward a cluster of paper birch trees, beside which stands a ginormous form. "We're flying."

I suck in a breath. Massive antlers branch out from atop a head raised in confidence, neck muscles rippling down into shoulder muscles, power radiating along its hide. "Whoa." Roughly the size of a Canadian moose, this reindeer is far more magnificent than the one I saw two days ago. I pluck Kristof's coat sleeve. "Can I pet it?"

"*It* is a *she*, and yes, you may." He guides me closer, the reindeer's head towering above us. She wears a bitless bridle fitted over her muzzle and behind her ears, and leather reins loop across her shoulders. "Blaze, meet Gina. Gina, this is Blaze, one of Grandpop's Big Eight and a direct descendant of Prancer."

"No way." A smile tugs at my lips, and I remove a glove to run my

126

hand down her neck. "This is surreal. I'm seriously about to fly on one of Santa's prized reindeer?"

"They're faster than a SnoMo, and I couldn't afford to be gone long." Kristof sets the duffle bag near the reindeer's rump, where a wide strip of leather protects the animal's hide, narrowing to wrap around its underside.

"Now the snowmobile cover-up makes sense."

"Yeah." Kristof's mouth quirks. "Can you imagine your family's reaction if I showed up at your doorstep riding a reindeer?"

I shake my head. "Mum and Dad still can't look at Tinsel the same way after they witnessed her talking with that reindeer a couple of years ago."

Kristof concentrates on securing the bag to the strapping via a series of knots, and my gaze wanders over the hard planes in his face and golden flecks in his stubble. He might be only eighteen, but there's nothing boyish about him anymore.

His movements pause. "Do I have dirt smudged on my face?"

"What? No." My cheeks ignite, and I grapple for a response other than, *Admiring your general hotness.* "You, uh, sure Blaze can manage the weight of us plus the bag?"

Blaze tosses her head, and Kristof laughs. "You insulted her."

"Oh, goodness, I'm sorry." Stepping forward, I pat her shoulder and send Kristof a mouthed, *Whoops.*

He grins, and this time it's his gaze that lingers. "You know, I'm curious about something."

"Hmm?"

"When I asked you to dinner earlier, you were reluctant at the thought of it being just us. We've been friends for years, though." He makes a sweeping motion, and my brow hikes when Blaze bends her front legs to kneel in the crusted snow. "So, why would a date with me be a bad thing?"

127

"Most of my dates are 'bad things.'"

Kristof straddles the animal's back and chuckles. "That's 'cause most of the tourists you date are idiots."

And none of them could wordlessly command a beast several times their size and weight, or mount said beast with the ease of Legolas in the LOTR movie trilogy.

Excuse me while I mop up my drool.

Scooting closer to the duffle bag, Kristof creates a space in front of him. "Your turn."

Right. I'm supposed to get up there, too. "Don't expect me to be as nimble as you." Gripping his mittened hand for balance, I stretch my leg across Blaze's body, and Kristof helps position me behind her shoulders.

Reaching past me for the reins, he slips his other arm around my waist and anchors me against him. My stomach flip-flops. There are two layers of coats between us, you say? Tell that to the wires in my brain that have short-circuited.

"Ready to fly?" he asks.

I give a vigorous nod, my vocal cords currently inoperable.

"And for what it's worth, G," Kristof murmurs in my ear, a quiver dancing along my spine, "I'm not like your tourist guys."

Yeeaahhh. I'm beginning to think he's not like most guys.

Twenty-One

Gina—Nov 27 In Common

I fit my scarf tighter over my nose, squinting against the icy wind stinging my exposed skin. "This is incredible," I holler, angling my head so Kristof can catch my words as Blaze zips through the air. "Even though I can't feel my face."

His chest vibrates with a laugh. "I knew you'd like it."

"But you should really wear helmets." Below us, the forest passes in an inky blur. "I mean, why bother wearing them on snowmobiles or downhill skiing, if you're not going to, like, wear one on the back of a reindeer flying several hundred feet in the air?"

"Reindeer won't let you fall."

"Ohhh." I give Blaze another well-deserved pat. Stars glitter in the dark sky overhead and all around. Living in a remote location, I enjoy the cosmos display each night, yet up here, the stars feel close enough I could snatch one for my own. "How much longer?" I ask.

"To get home? A few minutes."

Home. Kristof's home, maybe. Never mine.

An image flashes in my mind of a painted picture cut from my childhood coloring book: Santa flying over rooftops in his sleigh, elves waving from workshop windows, and a sign in the corner that reads, "North Pole."

I clench it in my tiny fingers and, with a glance at my grandma, Nonna, asleep on the couch, I approach Papa Campi in the recliner. A cloud of white hair surrounds his head and face, like the Santa in my picture. He has a pudgy belly. Like my picture.

The old man smiles and beckons me close, using those funny words I don't understand. My gaze darts to Nonna again. Still sleeping. Papa Campi points to the picture, and I show it to him. He chuckles. "Babbo Natale, sì?"

What? I shake my head. "Santa Claus."

"Ah. Santeh Claus." *He purses his lips, jabbing his chest with a thumb.* "Never saw Santeh wit purple ... cappotto ... eh, coat." *He shrugs.* "But I no see him often."

I inhale. "You've seen Santa?" *I climb onto his lap and peer into his filmy brown eyes.* "What's he like?"

He laughs, a jolly ho, ho, ho sound. "A good man."

I poke my picture. "I'm gonna live there someday."

"Veramente? Will you make giocattoli? Mmm ... toys?"

"Mmm-hmm." *I bounce on his leg.* "I'm gonna make dollies and ride a reindeer."

"Ride a reindeer?" *Nonna's sharp tone spikes the air, and I huddle into Papa Campi as she rises from the couch.* "What is going on here?" *She wags her finger in the old man's face.* "You tell foul stories again, no? What's this?" *Nonna snatches my picture from him and makes a tsking noise.* "Gina. This no good. You say you make dolls?" *She shakes the paper in front of me.* "You no have talent."

Papa Campi clears his throat. "Coraline—"

"Don't you 'Coraline' me." *Her mouth thins.* "You are traditore to our kin, Papà. Gina"—*she rips the picture in half and my insides hurt*—"you *no listen to him. All lies,* capisci?" *She crumples the pieces. "I have better plans for you,* bambina—"

"No!"

"Gina?" Kristof's arm tightens about my ribs. "You okay?"

My scarf has slipped, exposing my nose and cheeks. Nodding, I fix the scarf and force myself to relax as Blaze veers toward a glow beyond the craggy mountain range. Just a memory. One of the last before Papa Campi died the following year. While I have more memories of Nonna before she died when I was ten, she wears the same vexed expression in all of them.

I never could make Nonna proud.

The air temperature changes like it did the other day when I passed through the barrier. Warmer than the negative digits of Waldheim, though still below freezing. Up ahead, lights glisten from the Christmas village nestled in the valley. "It's like something out of a fairy tale," I breathe.

"An apt description, considering many people believe we are a fairy tale."

"How do you stay hidden when those lights are a dead giveaway to planes flying overhead?"

"If we weren't astride a reindeer right now, the ancient magic protecting Flitterndorf would shield the lights from view."

"Magic seems too simple an explanation."

Blaze's angle sharpens well before the town's outskirts, and I rear back against Kristof as the rambling roofline of a lone structure rushes to meet us. The reindeer touches down alongside the grand building, and I wait for my stomach to catch up with me.

"Not everything has to be complicated in order to believe it," Kristof says, dismounting. A sheet of cold air hits my back, and I shiver. "Neither must one understand all the complexities before exercising faith in something." He pats Blaze and grins. "You demonstrated that

131

when you rode a flying reindeer. Pretty simple, huh?"

I peek at the ground. "Is there a simple remedy for getting off without making a fool of myself?"

Chuckling, Kristof seizes my waist and helps me slide from Blaze's back. My knees protest as I stand, and I cling to his coat sleeve. Several elves scamper between the peak-roofed building that looks similar in style to the Workshop, and the field beside it, in which many reindeer stand or lie down. "Where are we?"

Kristof cups my elbow as I steady myself. "This is the Prep Stables. Grandpop asked me to stop by on my way home."

"What do you normally do here, when it's not used as an infirmary?"

"The reindeer that don't make it onto a Kringle team train here for other jobs around Flitterndorf. Not every elf utilizes SnoMos."

In the distance, Meister K walks among the standing reindeer, offering them something to eat, patting their heads, or scratching their necks. His mouth moves in what I suspect are words of encouragement. "How are they doing?" I ask.

A shadow dims the light in Kristof's eyes. "Another 'deer died yesterday. Several more are in critical condition. Grandpop fears it's a matter of time before whatever sickness they have overtakes the Second String or Big Eight."

"I'm so sorry."

"And who knows what state the Third String is in." He unties his duffle bag, the lines tightening around his mouth. "It's only been a few days, but the longer it takes us to find them, the less certain I am of success."

"You came to my house to deliver a phone when you're needed here?" I punch him lightly in the arm. "I could've waited."

"Yeah, except"—a boyish grin flits across his lips—"you'll end up being the one bright spot in my day, and that couldn't wait."

"Meister Kristof!" From the stable entrance, an elf emerges armed with a clipboard, her red jacket open over a red dirndl.

Kristof waves in greeting. "Frau Chemiker, any news?"

She hurries toward us, her eyebrows pulling together above her glasses as she stares at me. "Y-yes, sir." She continues to stare.

"Oh, sorry." Kristof clears his throat. "This is Gina Donati, a friend of mine and Tinsel's. She's, um …" He adjusts his hat. "I invited her to dinner. Please, Frau Chemiker, an update? How are the reindeer?"

The elf yanks her gaze from me and pushes her square frames up the bridge of her nose. "Some reindeer are stable, some grow sicker, and one …" Her attention jumps to Meister K. "Another died in the last half hour, and none of us know how to tell him."

Kristof winces. "I'll tell him." Sighing, he hoists the duffle bag over one shoulder. "Any word on the autopsy results to know what illness we're dealing with?"

"That's one of the problems, sir." She hugs the clipboard to her chest. "The autopsy shows this is not an illness. It's poison."

I exchange a look with Kristof. His Adam's apple bobs. "What kind of poison?"

"We don't know. That's another problem." Her lips purse as two elves barrel out the stable doors, voices raised, their words heated and cruel. "And that is the third problem. The quarreling has worsened among the elves." One elf stomps away to the SnoMos, and the other marches off on a pair of snowshoes. Frau Chemiker groans. "It appears Herr Verwalter is down two more helpers."

My heart wrenches in sympathy. "I can fill in for a bit. What does he need?"

Kristof gives me a grateful smile. "You'll find Herr Verwalter inside. White hair, short beard. His office is on your left when you enter."

As Frau Chemiker and Kristof make for his grandfather in the field, I roll back my shoulders and enter the stables. How bad can elf work be, anyway?

Twenty minutes later, I take a selfie, my smile pained as I stand ankle-deep in muck and soiled straw. I have a new appreciation for the year-long Penalty Tinsel endured.

* * *

I walk the aisle between reindeer stalls, hunched over to push the elf-sized wheelbarrow overflowing with dirty straw (apparently, the human-sized wheelbarrow is stationed at the Lower Stables). I've lost count of how many times I've made this trek in the past hour. Seriously, I could haul more straw in my arms than this toy can. At least I have my phone again—and access to my music. Easier to suffer the rancid work with Skillet songs motivating me.

Herr Verwalter passed me off to an assistant, who passed me off to one of hers, a Herr Bote. He, in turn, being the lowest in the pecking order, loves telling me what to do. I've cleaned out three stalls so far—mucked, scoured, and relined with fresh bedding. On my way back from dumping my present load in a growing pile behind the stables, Herr Bote informs me the next stall requires a full hose-down. I don't ask why. The reason is etched on the other elves' haggard faces.

When will Niklas or Kristof tell Tinsel about the reindeer? The Third String may be her favorites, but her sympathies don't stop there.

"Frau Donut!"

Herr Bote's holler jolts me from where I stand outside the empty stall, and I pull an earbud from my ear. His eyebrows mash together. "That stall won't clean itself. I said you need a hose."

Gotta love being bossed around by an elf with an overbite who can't get my name right.

I take a calming breath. No one forced me to volunteer. "Where can I find one?"

Herr Bote mutters at the ceiling about the ones already in use in the different areas (the Prep Stables are deceptively large). He snaps his fingers. "Should be two more in the supply closet."

Supply closet. He pointed it out to me in passing a while ago. If I recall, it's relatively close. How lost could I get? Still, to be on the safe side .... "Could you show me where that is again?"

He rolls his eyes, and I follow him from the stalls into the stables' grand foyer and down a wide hallway to the second door on the left. This he opens with an exaggerated flourish. "Don't dawdle."

If my answering smile borders on sarcastic, it's because I'm biting back a snarky comment.

I step into the room, and a light blinks on overhead. My eyes widen. This closet is bigger than my living room. Open shelving units loaded with cleaning supplies, paper goods, linens, and other miscellaneous items create long aisles, while human-sized cabinets flank the walls. Some cabinets are accessible, some have items piled in front of them.

Halfway down the third aisle, I find a black hose coiled on the top shelf, out of reach. A further search rewards me with a short ladder propped against a cabinet door.

Whoa, fancy door pull for a storage cabinet. I flick it, then trace the molded curves of its metal plate. Vines and berries. Vines and—

I crouch at eye-level with the plate, and my mouth parts on a gasp. This is the same emblem above Mum's spoon rack.

Why do my house and Santa's supply closet have this peculiar emblem in common?

"Gina, you in here?"

I hop from my crouch as Kristof comes into view. "Hey. Hi. You startled me."

One side of his mouth lifts. "Sorry. Herr Bote said I'd find you here."

"Yeah, uh"—I cast about for the step stool—"I needed a hose." Face warming from getting so easily distracted, I open the stool in the aisle and stretch to grab the black coil. "Did you need me for something?" Hose acquired, I descend too quickly and misjudge the distance between the elf-sized steps. I trip, but Kristof catches me from behind.

His hands linger at my waist, and the warmth in my face increases. "Came to take you to our non-date dinner."

Non-date. I grin, keeping my potentially red cheeks averted. "Is Herr Bote okay with that?"

"He got extra help for almost two hours. He'll be fine." Kristof plucks the hose from me as I return the ladder. "Imagine my shock, however, when I heard they'd put Gina Donati to work mucking reindeer stalls."

I lead us from the supply closet. "Yes, can you believe I scooped poop for you?"

He laughs.

"And took orders from someone half my size." I send him an arch look, pulling the door closed. "I don't do that for just anyone."

His eyes twinkle. "Yet you won't accept a date with me."

I feign indignation. "I have a policy."

"Then I'm complaining to management."

My stomach growls, echoing off the walls, and I clap a hand over my belly. "Come back during office hours. The manager's on a supper break."

Kristof laughs again. "Fair enough. Let's give this hose to Herr Bote, and we'll get you fed." Looping an arm about my neck, he guides me down the hallway.

Twenty-Two

Gina—Nov 27 Not a Date

Entering his family's apartment, Kristof directs me to hang my belongings on the nearby coat tree. I toe off my ankle boots and slide them under the cushioned bench.

"Kristof? Is that you?" a voice calls from around the corner.

"Yes, Gram. Gina, too." He puts a hand at my lower back, an electric spray radiating through my torso from his touch, and propels me down the narrow foyer and into the kitchen.

A rich aroma wafts from the oven, and Madam Anne leaves a saucepan bubbling on the stovetop to greet me with a hug. "This is a welcome surprise." She frames my face in her papery hands. "What brings you here again so soon?"

"Kristof invited me to dinner. I hope that's okay."

"It's wonderful. Kristof"—she receives a kiss on her cheek from him—"how did it go this afternoon with the reindeer? Your grandfather already told me not to expect him for dinner."

Kristof blows out a breath. "Grandpop's on the verge of a nervous breakdown, Gram. Until we can figure out what's going on, he's turned the Workshop—and its problems—over to me so he can focus on the reindeer. But filling in for Santa Claus?" He clenches the countertop as Madam Anne returns to stir the contents in the saucepan. "Those are big boots to fill, tailored more for Pa or Niklas than me."

"Unless Santa's boots aren't what we need at this time," she says.

"Over a dozen elves have quit their jobs at the Workshop in the last thirty-six hours. Five of them Doll Makers." Kristof scrubs at his already mussed hair. "I'm supposed to know how to handle that? Niklas and I should switch places. I'm better utilized in Germany."

"Don't underestimate your skill set." She pats his cheek before opening a box of biscuit mix sitting on the counter. "You're glad Kristof's here, aren't you, dear?"

Kristof beats me to an answer, his eyes glinting with mischief. "Yeah, she's so glad, she declined a dinner date with me."

I splutter for an explanation so as to not offend his grandmother, and Madam Anne chuckles. "A little rejection is good for these Kringle men." She measures dry mix into a red bowl. "I remember how Niklas would get tied up in a Christmas knot when his charm wouldn't work on Tinsel. Kept him humble. Well, humble-ish."

Chin in hand, I smile. "He used to go on and on, venting about her. I knew Tinsel's name long before I met her."

"While you crushed on Niklas in secret," Kristof singsongs, pulling a drinking glass from the cupboard.

My face flares in heat all over again.

"Kristof." Madam Anne swats his arm. "Quit teasing your friend."

"She's cute when she blushes." He tosses me a wink as he opens the fridge.

Madam Anne wags a wooden spoon in my direction before dipping it into the mixing bowl. "Don't let him goad you. Ask him about *his* first crush."

I perk up. "Oh? What's this?"

Kristof blanches, setting the container of milk on the counter. "Gram."

"Who was she?"

"You mean who is she," Madam Anne says.

"*Gram.*"

Her grin broadens. "The thing you must bear in mind about Kringle men, Gina, is that once they fall for something, it's unlikely something else will tempt them away."

Red tinges Kristof's neck and ears. "That's enough, Gram."

"Aw, but you're cute when you blush," I coo, nudging him in the arm.

He stands close enough I notice the gold flecks in his hazel eyes, and a slow smile meanders across his lips. He has nice lips. I take a ragged breath, my lungs filling with his sandalwood scent, and force myself to retreat a step. Flirting with him is dangerous.

I give Madam Anne a too-bright smile. "May I help you with dinner?"

"That would be lovely, dear. If you want to wash up first, you can use the bathroom down that side hallway. Second door on your right."

"Don't get lost," Kristof murmurs into his glass as I pass.

I hip-check him on my way, the action making him dribble milk down his chin. His laugh follows me along the hall, and I duck into the bathroom, breathless. My reflection in the mirror reveals bright eyes, pink cheeks, and a giddy smile.

What's my deal? In all the times we've hung out with Tinsel and Niklas or other mutual friends, his smiles never tripped me up the way they have today. He's only ever been "Niklas's younger brother." Why should today be any different?

Washing at the sink, I whisper to my reflection, "But it *was* different once, wasn't it?"

Last Christmas season, before Kristof left for Russia, there'd been that afternoon of skiing and later, a weekend movie marathon of LOTR and The Hobbit trilogies, when his smiles turned my insides to mush, and a few brushes of his fingertips sent shock waves up my arm.

Then—*then*—that hug goodbye when he kissed my cheek and the corner of his lips missed the corner of mine by a millimeter, and I wanted so badly to shift so our lips would meet.

At the time, I convinced myself I was imagining things since he's almost three years my junior. Yet the older we get, the narrower the age gap looks.

Why am I fighting this attraction, again?

He plans to return to Germany, my practical side argues, *which would leave you once again broken if you don't keep your heart in check. Best to stick to your policy. No exceptions.*

I stare at my reflection. And since Kristof's not even a tourist, he doesn't get a date. Like, ever. Too risky.

"Enjoy his friendship, nothing more." Giving myself a firm nod, I snap off the light and open the bathroom door.

An array of photographs covers the entire opposite wall. Matching eight-by-ten frames in the top row showcase the different Santa Clauses over the years—similar suits, unique faces. Beneath them are photos of Santa shaking hands with prominent world leaders throughout the last few centuries; Santa photographed with children; Santa with his own family. Young Santas. Old Santas.

"What is this? The hall of fame?"

Kristof joins me, grinning. "More like the hall of memory."

"So these are your kin." I circle my hand near a cluster of smaller Santa pictures and peek at Kristof. "You may not have all the powers of a firstborn, but you look like a Kringle." Straightening, I move to a new section.

From the confines of a wooden frame, slitted eyes glare at me, and I yelp. "What. Is. That?"

The portrait shows a man from the waist up, holding a mask as though he's just peeled it from his face. Giant, gnarled horns and an elongated tongue curl from the mask's forehead and mouth like the online pics I googled last night. Something I'd expect to find in a haunted house rather than Santa's hallway.

"That," Kristof says, "is Karl Krampus, the first Krampus that started our family feud after Nikolaus Kringle—not to be confused with *the* St. Nicholas—received the mantle of Santa Claus."

A tremor surges through me. Not caused by the demonic mask, but by the man himself, leering at the viewer, arrogance in his eyes, his lips curled in a vengeful smirk.

The male version of my grandmother.

A ridiculous notion, of course. Despite lacking in the empathy department, Nonna wasn't Halloween material.

"You said a family feud? So he's a real person?"

"Some aspects are real, some aspects are myth. Like Santa Claus." Kristof indicates the man's mask. "Tradition holds that Krampus is a hairy, devilish figure who frightens children into behaving, instead of rewarding them for good behavior, as Santa does. He roams the streets on Krampusnacht, the night before the Festival of St. Nicholas, whipping children, sometimes stealing one or two away to eat them."

I stare at the nose and chin identical to Nonna's, then hasten to the kitchen, where Madam Anne has piled dinnerware on the countertop.

Behind me, Kristof continues. "The tradition is on the rise again in parts of Europe and making headway in some parts of North America. People in Krampus costumes will run up and down city streets, much to the warped delight of spectators. Sometimes they'll incite those on the sidelines and pretend to whisk away a child."

I take the stack of plates. "So, what's the *myth*?"

141

Kristof trails me around the table, arranging flatware beside each plate. "The myth is in thinking Krampus wants people to behave. Just as Santa is a man on a mission to spread the true Spirit of Christmas—the Hope, Love, Peace, and Freedom found therein—Krampus is on a mission to spread chaos, lies, panic, and fear."

My movements slow. "Why?"

"Karl was jealous of the Kringles and their perceived power, Santa's worldwide recognition, his status in the hearts of children." Kristof folds the cloth napkins and slips one beneath each fork. "Karl wanted Santa's position for himself, and that jealousy has fueled the Krampus family ever since."

"So, they spread chaos, lies, and fear to endear people to them? That doesn't make sense."

He shrugs. "The Krampuses don't care about endearment, as long as the end result is the same. It's easier to sway people's support and influence their conduct through fear and lies than trying to earn their loyalty."

I don't know much about Dad's ancestry, but I can't ignore the fact that, given the right wig, Karl Krampus looks exactly like my grandmother. Are they related? Would that be through her mother's line, or her father's? Her father ... Papa Campi ... who remained in Waldheim, alone, immersed in a foreign way of life, exposed to harsh temperatures, long after his wife and children had left him. Why would he do that?

Unless he knew Santa Claus lived over the next mountain range.

Sweet Papa Campi, a filthy Krampus? What would that make me?

The room sways, and I clutch the tabletop.

"Gina." Kristof rushes to my side as my knees give way.

My fingers splay against his chest. "I-I'm fine."

"You're whiter than Santa's beard. Sit." He pulls out a chair and lowers me into it. Spots cluster in my peripheral vision, and I shake my head to clear them. A glass of water bumps my elbow. I take a grateful sip as Kristof rubs my back. My eyes drift closed.

"You should take her home," Madam Anne says, her voice far away.

"No." I force the word past my thick lips. "Please, I'm okay. Just need ... a minute." I need to talk to my folks. Either Nonna's face on that Krampus is a freaky coincidence and life goes on the way it always has, or I have foul blood running through my veins. From the little I now understand about Krampus and his kin, they're trouble for the Kringles and those who love Christmas.

I could be trouble for them.

For Kristof.

"Yes," I whisper, heat building behind my eyes, "take me home."

Twenty-Three

Gina—Nov 27 Family Tree

We make the trip to my house in weighty silence. I can't bear to end things on such a heavy note, however, so upon reaching the front door, I send Kristof a grin where he hovers on the top porch step. "Even though I scooped poop for you but never got dinner, I still had a good time." Overall.

One corner of Kristof's mouth lifts. "Put that way, I'm glad this was a non-date." He stuffs his hands in his coat pockets. "I'll make it up to you."

"Would that be before or after you return to Germany?" I tease. Joking makes it easier to evade thoughts of a potential skeleton in my family's closet.

"I don't know that I will go back."

"You want to."

"I think Weihnachts Manor holds more potential for me than Flitterndorf, so yeah, I do." He leans a shoulder against the porch post. "Would you begrudge me for pursuing my passions?"

"I envy you for it."

Kristof steps forward. "You had a chance when you applied for and were offered that job in Alberta. It was the perfect fit and opportunity, yet you rejected it. You never told me why."

A thread of regret rouses at his words. I squelch it. "I have to go. Thanks for bringing me home." Rising on tiptoes, I give Kristof an impulsive hug, and his arms close about me, keeping me there. Fitting me against him. Warm and safe in his embrace. I bury my face into his neck, breathing in his sandalwood scent. One breath. Two breaths. Three—I force myself to withdraw, pressing my lips to his cheek as I retreat.

"That felt like goodbye," he says, his voice hushed.

If I'm related to his enemy, it may very well be. Avoiding his eyes, I grope behind me for the doorknob.

"Gina, what aren't you telling me?"

I find the knob. "G'night, Kristof." Ducking inside, I close the door on his confused expression. So much for ending on a lighter note.

Mum, Dad, and Aunt Cat sit in the living room, watching a movie while eating dinner on tray tables. They startle when I snap on the foyer light. I study Aunt Cat and Dad, seeing them with new eyes. They have Nonna's nose. Karl Krampus's nose.

"Gina?" Mum aims the remote at the TV and the screen pauses. "We didn't expect you home this early." Her forehead creases. "Are you okay? Did something happen?"

I touch the tip of my own nose. Am I being paranoid? Is this an innocent coincidence? If I start asking questions, how will I know I'm getting honest answers? I twist a lock of hair.

Aunt Cat picks up her plate and drink. "I'll take this to my room so you three can chat."

Mum pats the couch cushion between her and Dad, and I reluctantly sit. "What is it, sweetheart? Did you and Kristof have a fight or something?"

I hug my arms. *Blurt it out and gauge their reaction.* "Have you guys heard of a mythical figure called Krampus?"

Mum glances at Dad. "Yes. Why?"

"Mind telling me why Nonna looks just like him?"

"Gina!" Mum gasps. "What a thing to say." But Dad's olive skin tone pales.

"Not the masked creature, Mum. The man behind the mask. Karl Krampus. I saw his portrait in the Kringles' apartment."

Dad leans forward to knead his temples. "I knew this would happen if I let you spend time with that Kringle boy."

"So it's true? We're related to him?" Unexpected tears spring in my eyes. I'm a filthy Krampus. Then the implication of Dad's words registers, and I wrap my coat tighter around me. "How did you *know* I'd find out about Krampus by hanging out with the Kringles? Do you know that Meister K ..." I hesitate, unsure how to continue.

"That Meister K is Santa Claus, and he and the elves make and deliver toys to children on a global scale?" Irony lines Dad's voice. "Oh, yes, we know."

My jaw drops. "Since when?"

"We found out the same time you did," Mum says quietly. "When we saw Tinsel talking to that reindeer on our front lawn two Christmases ago."

Dad drags a hand over his face. "We didn't want to believe it at first. Then it opened a floodgate of questions, the answers to which I didn't have for a long time."

"Yet you have the answers now?" I glare at Dad. "How long have you been hiding the fact we're related to a demon-figure who was—and whose descendants still are—enemies to my closest friends?"

"And how would you suggest I drop this kind of bomb on my grown children?" Dad stands and paces the room between the TV and the coffee table. His gaze darts to the stairs, then to me. "Growing up, I didn't know much about my family's history. I thought the stories I heard were tall tales, and no one gave me a reason to believe otherwise. By the time I moved here to live with Papa Campi and he began hinting that those stories were real, I took it for old age and dementia."

Dad grips the back of his neck and lowers his voice. "Until a couple of years ago when Tinsel stayed with us. She 'wore,'"—he uses air quotes—"those too-lifelike elfin ears. And then to see her talk with that reindeer? Suddenly, Papa Campi's ramblings made more sense. I tried to glean information from relatives about our ancestry, careful I didn't sound like a lunatic myself in case no one else had made the connection. If anyone knows anything, they haven't come forward." With another glance up the stairs, Dad gestures Mum and me to follow him into his study. "Then about a year ago, I was going through Papa's old ledgers from the hardware store." He stops at his bookshelf in the corner and slips a narrow, leather-bound book from among the thicker volumes. "I found this."

He extends the book to me. I thumb through pages and pages of words in the beautiful, slanted script from a bygone era. "I can't read this. It's in cursive."

Dad grunts. "It's also in Italian. Your great-grandfather's journal." He lowers himself into his office chair, sifts through a desk drawer, and holds up a memory stick. "Over the summer, I translated about half of it and saved it here."

"Did you learn anything?"

"I learned Papa Campi is not the full-blooded Italian like we believed." Dad taps the memory stick on the desk. "Prior to his mother settling, marrying, and raising a family in Italy, she had immigrated from Germany. Her maiden name ... was Krampus."

I sink onto the stack of old encyclopedias Mum and Dad refuse to toss.

"Papa Campi's mother raised him and his siblings with full knowledge of their Krampus heritage, expecting them to continue in their ancestor's footsteps with the intent to one day supplant the Kringles." Dad peers at the ceiling. "But when Papa was in his late teens, he discovered his best friend was a Kringle descendant, and he became a covert Kringle-sympathizer. Because of this, he didn't pass along his family legacy to his future wife or children. At least, not in its historical context." Dad gives a wan grin. "Papa couldn't resist couching his heritage in the form of tall tales and bedtime stories."

Mum perches on the corner of Dad's desk. "Fast-forward twelve years when he began hearing talk among his kin about the North American location of Santa's village. Papa Campi packed up his young family and moved here, where he hoped to—in his own words—act as the gatekeeper and dissuade or reroute any Krampus who made it this far."

"None ever did." Dad leans forward, resting his arms atop his desk. "Unfortunately, Papa Campi didn't tell his wife the truth behind the move, and you know the rest of the story."

I drum my fingers against the journal. "Great-Grandma Campi left him after eight years and returned to Italy with the kids. With Nonna."

"And since Nonna didn't know the truth, either, she grew bitter and angry, believing her father had deserted the family. So even though she married a Californian and moved to the northern Pacific Coast, she didn't speak to or visit Papa Campi for years." Dad winks at Mum. "Thank goodness she didn't stop me from visiting him before I was to go to university."

Dad had met Mum that summer. Needless to say, he never made it to university. "What became of Papa Campi's siblings and their families?" I ask. Could one of their descendants be causing trouble for the Kringles today?

"We don't know, but Papa suspected one of his brothers had a hand

148

in the turmoil surrounding World War II."

I point to the memory stick. "May I borrow that and the journal for a few days?"

"Remember I haven't finished translating." He hands over the stick and glances at the office door. "Listen, your Aunt Cat doesn't know about our lineage. Nonna rarely talked about Papa's side of the family, and Cat was too young to remember the stories we heard as children. Nor did she visit Papa, like I did, to hear his crazy talk, or meet Tinsel to put any pieces together." He shakes his head. "Some might think I'm just as crazy, believing good and evil magic exists in the world today."

"Not crazy. Informed." The memory stick's edges poke my palm. "And the Kringles have good magic, so why were you concerned about me going with Kristof into Flitterndorf?"

"Because we don't know if your physical presence there would have a negative effect on the Kringles or the elves." Dad sighs and meets my gaze. "I hate to say it, Gina, but you may have to curb your friendship with Kristof."

Twenty-Four

Gina—Nov 28 More Secrets

Hours later, I lean against my bedroom doorjamb, fingering the sleeve cuffs of my hoodie, the ever-faithful nightlight brightening the hallway. From the opposite wall, the reedy emblem screams at me now that I know it also exists in Flitterndorf.

And now that I've seen it illustrated on a page in Papa Campi's journal. Yep. Same stems. Same leaves and berries. Coincidence? I think not. Beneath the picture, he drew a stick figure, a vertical line, and an arrow pointing to several encircled words. Using Google Translate, I might glean the gist of what Papa Campi wrote—if I could first read his cursive script.

A giant yawn escapes me, and I cover it with a glance down the hall, but all is quiet at one o'clock in the morning on a Saturday. My gaze drifts back to the emblem and catches on a thin shadow below it.

I squint, craning my neck forward. A horizontal crack runs a few inches above Mum's spoon rack in an unnaturally straight line. I step close. Beyond the rack to the right, the horizontal line meets another straight line running perpendicular down the wallpaper's seam. I follow it with a hand, its edge chafing my skin, until it vanishes behind the baseboard.

Two feet to the left, I discover a third crack paralleling the second.

"What in the …?" Stepping back, I visually trace all three lines. "Omigoodness."

There's a secret door in my hallway.

Do Mum and Dad know about this? Is it another thing they've kept from me? Where does it lead? Seeking a doorknob or hinges and finding neither, I crouch by the baseboard and poke around. "C'mon, open sesame."

The mirrored medicine cabinet in our bathroom is held closed by a spring magnet, requiring a push at its base before it will open. Perhaps this door works the same way. I push first against the lower right side, then the left. Nothing happens. I do the same with the top corners. Still nothing.

Pushing around and on the rack itself causes spoons to sway and ting against each other. Grrr. I brace my hands on the wall, flanking the rack, and hang my head. There's got to be a way to open this thing. What am I missing? I strike the baseboard with my slippered foot.

Shhh-ick.

The secret door swings inward, and I stumble forward, tripping over the fixed baseboard, my palms smacking onto dusty floorboards. Wincing, I push to my feet. The nightlight's insipid glow outlines my shadow extending along the floor in a narrow, empty room. Empty? Why conceal an empty room?

Behind me, the door moves, and I jerk about. "Mum?"

No one's there. The pool of light decreases as the door closes.

Wait, I don't have—

Whoosh-ick.

—my phone.

Darkness engulfs me. No phone means no flashlight.

I suck air into my lungs but am still starved for breath. From the glimpse I got, this room looks like an unfinished attic with exposed two-by-fours, cobwebs, and half-embedded rusty nails. Too many horror movies involve such a scene. I squeeze my eyes. Never again. I'm never watching a horror movie. Ever. Again.

So leave already! Common sense shouts into the mounting panic.

Eyes popping open, I search along the door in the absolute darkness. My suspicion proves correct: no doorknob. It was hard enough to open this thing when I had light. How am I supposed to figure it out in the pitch black?

And what if the room isn't truly empty? What if my eyes missed something crouched in a darkened corner, ready to spring at me?

My heart beats an erratic pulse, and I press my back against the door, senses alert. As my eyes adjust, a pale gray horizontal line materializes in the distance, and I almost cry in relief. A thread of light, no matter its size, never fails to dispel the ominous quality of darkness. After a moment, I make out some wall studs. A moment after that, the empty corners.

Whew.

Now that Jack the Ripper isn't about to snatch me, I take cautious steps toward the gray light, about five meters away. Is there enough house for such length? Halfway across the room, plaster takes over the two-by-fours, and a shift happens in the air, an electric spray raising the hair along my arms and the nape of my neck.

The light turns out to be a crack where the floor meets the wall at the other end of the room. A second crack travels upward. Another door. This one with a doorknob.

Holding my breath, I grasp the knob. It moves readily, silently. The door inches open to reveal built-in shelves on an adjacent wall filled with books, trinkets, and an assortment of lab equipment. I push the door further. Reindeer figurines populate the next section of shelves, and a cluttered desk sits in the center of the small room.

Someone's office. A paneled door faces me from the opposite wall. As Kristof would say, where in the winter wonderland am I? It can't be my house. There's not enough structure on the other side of the upstairs hallway for an attic room and office.

Neither does my house border another building, so how am I not standing outside, freezing my butt off?

A headache gnaws at the base of my skull, and one foot slides back in retreat. I force it to stop. I'm not leaving until I figure this out. Grabbing the wheeled chair at the desk, I drag it over and prop open the door—cleverly disguised as more shelves—so it can't close on me. Sunbeams angle in through a narrow window beside these shelves.

Sunbeams in the middle of the night?

I move to the window. Sure enough, sunlight reflects off dirty snow piled along a sidewalk, and storefronts across the cobblestone street boast foreign words.

Cobblestone. Foreign words. I get the feeling I'm not in Waldheim anymore.

Closing my eyes, I breathe slowly to calm a heart begging to freak out. "Later," I whisper. "Right now, determine why your house connects to this office."

I scan the desk's surface: a cup holding pens and pencils, letters addressed to one *Ina Donath*, splayed papers written in German, a German dictionary. Papa Campi's mother was German. A cardboard box the size of a shoebox sits beside the dictionary, its flaps open, several burgundy pouches nestled within. I bend closer. Golden swirls emboss the pouches, and golden cords cinch them closed. I trace a swirl with my finger—and a pleasant tingle races up my arm.

My gaze flits to the office door. Before I second-guess myself, I ease a pouch from the box, a *clink* sounding from within. Its soft contours radiate warmth and energy into my palm.

153

I tug on the cord. Little blue glass vials rest inside the pouch, and I remove one, liquid sloshing against its sides. More tingles zing through my veins. I unscrew the cap. A rancid odor escapes the rollerball and hits my nose. Then it's gone, leaving behind a flowery scent.

It smells like freedom.

Tipping the bottle, I apply the roller to the inside of my wrist. A heady rush of … power? strength? confidence? … courses through me. Restricting barricades crumble from my mind to expose an expanse of untapped potential and endless possibilities. My spine straightens. I'm invincible. Not in a superhero way, but in my capabilities. There's nothing I can't accomplish. Whatever I set out to do, I will succeed. The coffee shop. Relationships. Dolls.

Dolls.

An image of *the* perfect wig springs to mind, along with the instinctive know-how to create it. I must get home before the idea escapes me.

I return the bottle to the pouch and tuck the pouch back in the box. The minute I let it go, however, loss washes over me and dims my sight. Magic. That's what I've been sensing. I don't know what kind, I don't know how it's possible, yet I never want to be without it.

Something bangs in the distance, and voices carry to me, heels clacking on a tiled floor. I can't be found in here—wherever here is. Lunging forward, I grab the pouch again and stuff it into a pocket of my pajama bottoms. I arrange the other pouches in the box to fill the void and press the flaps closed.

The printed name in the flap's address field leaps at me: *Brückenstadt*. Isn't that where Kristof went? Where Tinsel and Niklas are at present?

Papers in German. Storefronts with German names. Cobblestone streets. Sunlight rather than moonlight.

Have I somehow traveled to Brückenstadt?

I waver on my feet, but the voices grow louder, jolting me from shock. Fleeing into the hidden room, I give the chair a shove toward the desk and yank the door shut before someone enters the office. Darkness shrouds me, and I blindly stumble across the expanse to the other door and search for a way to open it. I kneel. Since this door opened when kicked, there might be something on this side that will allow me to—

My fingers flick a piece of protruding hardware near the floor, and the door swings inward. Yes! The nightlight's yellow glow greets me, and I scurry over the baseboard into the hallway. My blessed hallway. I smile, and the door shuts behind me—with a too-familiar *whump*.

Icy tentacles tiptoe up my neck. So this is where the sound comes from.

Someone else in this house has been using the secret passageway.

My headache resumes, like a dozen elf-sized hammers beating against my brain. Trembling, I escape into my bedroom. Should I tell Mum and Dad someone's going in and out of our house via a hidden door? What if they're using the door?

What if it's Aunt Cat? Just because Papa Campi drew the emblem in his journal doesn't mean the passageway and office are affiliated with a monster. Aunt Cat could know about it, even if she doesn't know about Krampus.

Pressing against the pain in my head, I stagger toward my bed. Something bumps my thigh with a *clink*.

I pull the burgundy leather pouch from my pocket, my skin tingling again. The swirly pattern swims before my eyes, and my body sways. In the span of five meters, I traveled thousands of miles, jumped eight time zones, crossed an ocean, and arrived in Germany.

Pinpricks of light invade my vision. The room tilts, my knees buckle, and the carpet rises toward me.

Twenty-Five

Tinsel—Nov 28 Dance Practice

Weihnachts Manor

One, two, three. One, two, three.

I grind my teeth, my palm sweaty in Niklas's hand as we circle the ballroom with the other couples. And I thought dancing was bad when the entire Flitterndorf community watched us perform the Festival Dance two years ago. Who'd have guessed I'd prefer two-thousand-plus pairs of eyes on me over one specific pair?

Lifeless yet shrewd, Herr Stoffel's gaze tracks me across the hardwood floor, and I flounder through my steps. Niklas does little to help me look the part of a competent fiancée. He's fluctuated between cool and lukewarm ever since he left the reindeer pasture yesterday. I didn't even get a kiss goodnight.

After an abysmal display of my (in)capabilities, Herr Stoffel mixes up the partners for the next dance, pairing me with Meister Nico, and Niklas with Elke. Unfortunately, Meister Nico doesn't make a better partner, his eyes hollow and his countenance slack as he leads me in a stiff square, functioning on autopilot. A faint scent of jasmine hovers in the air.

We stutter about the floor for another minute before I whisper, "Are you well, Meister Nico? We don't have to dance if—"

He gulps some air, his fingers tightening around mine. "Tinsel," he rasps. "Be vigilant."

Unease slips under my collar. "Sir?"

"I fear I won't hold out much longer, but Niklas is stronger than I am. Adhere to the truth and you will endure." Meister Nico casts a wary glance at the other couples. "Don't give up on him, even when they adjust their tactics."

I swallow, attempting to make sense of his words.

"Promise me," he says, eyes wide beneath his eyebrows. "Promise me you won't abandon Nicky."

"I-I promise."

His expression relaxes, and moisture collects along his lids. "You are good for him. I happily admit Niklas chose better for himself than I or his mother would have done. I wish now that he proposed a while ago, for then you would be married. Untouchable. Sadly, engagements can be broken," he ends on a tortured whisper.

His words thunk in my stomach like a lump of coal. "What are you saying?" Is Herr Stoffel still pressuring him to end the engagement? Are they pressuring Niklas?

"May I cut in?"

Lukas beams up at us, the innocence in his face obscuring the sneaky tendencies I encountered earlier. Despite my clandestine distress signal of a tightened grip, Meister Nico relinquishes me without another word, his face once again vacant. "Please be okay," I murmur after him.

"He is fine." Lukas assumes a stance with his shorter, boyhood frame, and tugs me into the dance. "He *und* cousin Nik play hide-and-seek with me this morning."

157

I stumble at his erratic movements. "You've been busy today." Considering he also gave me a mid-morning tour of the dungeons, which included locking me in a dank, dark cell for fifteen panic-filled minutes. Poppy eventually rescued me, and when I confronted Lukas, he groused that I couldn't take a joke. "How long did it take Niklas to find you?" I ask as Lukas pulls me in a circle.

"He never found me."

Niklas must have played along for the sake of his second cousin. Santas always know where to find children. "He's a good sport," I say aloud.

Lukas jerks me in the opposite direction, and I trip over my feet. "He's a weak, greedy man who destroys Christmas."

"Niklas?"

"Santa Claus." Lukas pulls me into a frenzy of circles, going faster and faster until my stomach bucks.

I yank from his grip, my vision spinning. "Enough."

He smirks, mocks a bow, and walks away. In the dizzy background, Herr Stoffel watches us. I stagger to the wall to wait out the vertigo. Meister Nico and Madam Marie dance past. Then Fritz and Elke. Niklas and Gretel whirl by, Niklas twirling her away and back in with a laugh.

My throat closes. They look good together.

Her caramel hair offsets his pale blond locks. Her black ribbed shirt complements his mulberry wine sweater. Her curvy shape fits with his lean build. Even the difference in their height has visual appeal.

The ballroom goes out of focus. Couples become fuzzy. What had Herr Stoffel said yesterday when we left for the tour around town? "A shame Gretel couldn't clear her schedule. She's a natural leader and would have made the perfect guide." Yes, his not-so-veiled implication came in loud and clear. Since leadership is a useful trait for any Mrs. Claus to have, Gretel would make the perfect choice there, as well.

I tug on my choker's reindeer pendant as darkness clouds my heart. Niklas should be with her, but I'm standing in their way of a "happily ever after." If I bow out now—if *I* break off the engagement with a Kringle—I can do so with my head held high. I'd end it and—

"Tinsel!"

I gasp. Niklas grips my shoulders, eyebrows pinched. Light floods my vision, and the darkness retreats. "Are you okay?" The music has stopped. People mutter to one another while staring. Niklas gives me a gentle shake. "Tins."

"You looked stunning dancing with Gretel," I whisper.

He lifts my chin with a knuckle. "I didn't want to dance with Gretel."

I meet his gaze. His aloofness from earlier has disappeared, replaced with tender strength. Sanctuary. Love. He gathers me close, and I snuggle into him, gratitude soothing my hurt edges. How could I think of relinquishing Niklas to Gretel so easily?

"I need fresh air," I say.

"You and I both." Niklas takes my hand and, ignoring Herr Stoffel's shouts, leads me onto the balcony that runs the length of the ballroom. Cold air brushes my face and rushes down my neck. The drizzle from earlier has turned to snow, and fat flakes kiss my cheeks.

Laughing, I lift my arms to collect the precious surprise. "Oh, I've missed this." I move to the railing. Snow-capped mountains rise in the hazy distance, a boon to Brückenstadt's hospitality industry when winter tourists and weekenders flock to the nearby ski slopes. "It's beautiful here. But it's not home."

"Agreed." Niklas leans his forearms on the railing beside me. "Seriously, you okay? You didn't seem like yourself back there."

Below us, the faint snow covering resembles a lacy white blanket over the dead grass and gravel driveway. "Did you see your dad? He's stressing."

"This is turning out to be a stressful place." Niklas kneads the

159

fingers of one hand. "Tell me you feel it, too. The oppression that saturates Weihnachts Manor."

I nod.

He pivots to stare at the ballroom's exterior. "These Kringles might live in a castle while my family and I live in an apartment, but they've lost their joy, their childlike wonder." Niklas crosses his arms on a shiver. "Rather than inventing, creating, or dreaming, these elves assemble toys from muscle memory. I wouldn't trade places for all the castles in the world."

Though I press my lips together, the words still eek out on a whisper. "What about for a curvy brunette?"

His gaze snaps to my face. "What?"

"You were enthralled with Gretel while dancing."

"Nein, Tins." Niklas tucks a short lock of hair behind my ear. "I'm hyper-aware of *you*. I know when you're sporting a new apron, when you're wearing makeup, and when Gina's touched up your hair for an overseas trip." He tugs on my belt loop. "I notice when you wear jeans two days in a row instead of your dirndl, when your dancing partner mistreats you"—he folds his arms again—"and when you hit it off better than expected with a certain second cousin."

My eyebrows knit together. "Who? Wait, Fritz? Sure, he's okay—"

"Just okay?" Niklas's jaw muscles pulse in the muted daylight. "This morning you slipped away to hang out with him and the reindeer, and yesterday you said he has definite appeal."

"This morning I studied how he implemented the whistle while working the reindeer. And yesterday, I said no such thing."

"You did. If you'd been a cartoon, your eyes would've had hearts in them."

I think back to our conversation, to the situation at the time, and laugh.

Niklas's eyes narrow. The vulnerability etched in his features, the jealousy mirroring what I felt inside moments ago, tempers my outburst. I uncross his arms and move into the space, sliding my hands about his waist. "You're the one who mentioned 'appeal.' I thought you were talking about the whistle."

He scowls. "Who cares about a frostbitten whistle?"

"I do. It would make my job a piece of fruitcake."

Niklas studies my face. "I've been insecure for almost two days because of the way you ogled a whistle?"

I trail kisses along his jaw to hide the chuckle fighting for release. "You have nothing to be jealous about when it comes to Fritz." His fingers dig into my back, urging me closer. I kiss the corner of his mouth. "So, the next time you see me working with him and the reindeer, don't read into anything, okay?"

Niklas cocks an eyebrow. "Next time?"

"I've asked him to teach me some tricks with the whistle."

His dimples come out for the first time today. "For that task, you'll need strong lips."

Grinning, I rise on tiptoes. "Know of any good exercises?"

"The best." Cupping the nape of my neck, he slants his mouth across mine and guides me through several breathtaking lessons. The zeal in his kisses edges out my envy; the warmth in his caress erases my doubts. When we at last ease apart, the fire gleaming in Niklas's green eyes reflects the one he's ignited within me.

"For sanity's sake," he murmurs, setting me away from him, "we should head back inside." He winks. "And keep your head down. You look thoroughly kissed."

I jab him with my elbow, but the ballroom stands empty and quiet when we return. "Where'd everybody go?"

"Afternoon meal, most likely."

"Should we join them?"

"Might as well." Niklas smooths a thumb over his bottom lip, studying the portraits of Kringles-past. "On second thought, let's swing by that closet again."

"Now?"

"I want to investigate those wooden boxes. What better time to do it than when everyone is occupied?"

"What if Frau Wissen catches us again? Your Kringle charm didn't work yesterday."

"That's because *someone* didn't give me the chance to win her over."

He doesn't get the chance today, either. Door Number Five is locked.

Twenty-Six

Gina—Nov 28 Mistlefeude

∽᷑᷒᷑᷒᷑᷒᷑᷒∼

Waldheim

An angering crick in my neck pulls me into consciousness. I groan, my face mashed against a rough surface, and wipe the wetness from my mouth. Flashes of a bizarre dream assail me, and my eyes pop open. I push to a sitting position with a frown.

What am I doing on the floor? Across the room, my laptop rests on the pillow, the comforter taut and tidy beneath it. I shuffle to the bed on my knees and tap the laptop to life. Six-twenty in the morning. Why didn't I sleep in my— I glance at my hand white-knuckling a burgundy pouch, soft tingles prancing along my fingers.

"Aw, man." My breathing escalates. It wasn't a dream. I actually traveled to Germany.

Hopping to my feet, I dash to the bathroom to splash water on my face—and to be near the toilet in case I puke. "On the bright side," I mumble into the towel as I dry off, "I've got some awesome perfume-y stuff to alleviate the insanity of what happened."

Yeah, perfume you stole, my inner voice pipes up.

I gape at my reflection. Omigoodness, I'm a felon. What's worse is I know I should give it back, yet I don't want to.

Whump.

My heart nearly rockets out of my chest. Someone used the hidden passageway. Friend? Foe? What if it's a foe? WhatdoIdo? WhatdoIdo?

I glance around the bathroom and heft the toilet bowl plunger like a club. Throwing my shoulders back, I whip open the door and jump into the hallway.

Aunt Cat freezes in her bedroom doorway, eyes wide as healthy color drains from her face. I drop my arm holding the plunger. "Aunt Cat?" My gaze rakes over her professional day clothes—and snags on the reindeer figurine she carries. I choke and point at the spoon rack. "Did you ... Are you— I heard ..." I gulp, struggling to take in air.

She moves forward and grips my shoulder. "Gina, honey, it's okay. I didn't mean to scare you. I went downstairs to get some water and—"

"Stop." I shrug from her and wave at the figurine. "I know where that came from. You went through the door." I snap my fingers as though that will help conjure up more details from last night—er, early this morning. "That office—the one on the other side of the secret passageway—it belongs to someone named Ina Donath, I think. Do you know her? All that chemistry paraphernalia ... do you work with her?"

Aunt Cat glances at my parents' bedroom door, then beckons me back to my room. I drop the plunger beside the bathroom sink and follow Aunt Cat. By the time she closes the door, her cheeks have regained their color. She smiles, and her eyes sparkle. "Yes, I do work with Ina. She's the patron for my latest project."

"What kind of project? Is she linked to"—dare I say it?—"to Krampus?"

Aunt Cat sets the reindeer atop my vanity. "What is a Krampus?"

Whew, she doesn't know about him. I breathe easier. Aunt Cat puts an arm around my shoulders and walks me to my bed. "Come sit. I'll explain what I can, so long as you understand some of my work is confidential." She looks down, squats, and picks up something at her feet. "What's this?" Rising again, she dangles the burgundy pouch between us.

"Um ..." I pull on the sleeves to my hoodie. "I might've borrowed it?"

Her eyebrow quirks.

I sigh and sink onto my mattress. "I'm sorry. I totally took it. Stole it. Is Ms. Donath gonna be mad? Call the cops? Will I be arrested here or in Germany?"

Aunt Cat laughs, shaking her head, and settles beside me. "Gina, you're not in trouble. I'm just trying to understand."

"So am I."

"Then let's help each other. Tell me what you know."

I pick at my sleeve cuffs. How to explain without mentioning Krampus? "I, uh, happened to notice the lines in the wallpaper last night, and after a little prodding, I figured out how to work the hidden door. It took me to an office. Ms. Donath's, judging by the papers on the desk." I nod at the reindeer on my vanity. "I saw some of those on her shelves and then"—my gaze travels to the pouch, and I wet my lips—"I found a box filled with those pouches, and I applied the perfume and ..." I meet her gaze. "Aunt Cat, what is that stuff? Magic, yes, but what kind? Good magic?" Please, not the bad Krampus-kind-of-magic.

"If you applied it, you already know it's the best magic." Tugging at the drawstring, Aunt Cat proceeds to tell me about the different people she's met on her many journeys, from all walks of life, the most amazing of all being a family with the last name of Kringle. "I met them long ago, kept in touch over the years, and ultimately put the pieces together to realize the family's patriarch, Stoffel, thought he was a relative of Santa Claus himself."

"You believed him?" Does she know *I* know Santa Claus?

"Not at first. Then he introduced me to Ina Donath, who shares a love for chemistry, and we became fast friends. Over time, she confided in me about magic portals and her experiments involving this." Aunt Cat holds a bottle up to the light. "The liquid in here is called mistlefeude—*Feude* means *joy* in German. It also comes as a powder. Apparently, there's a dark shadow threatening Santa, his family, and the elves. Threatening Christmas. Ina wants to circulate mistlefeude among the elves to help ward off this dark threat."

Aunt Cat looks at me. I drop my gaze and chew the edge of my cuff.

She bumps my shoulder with hers. "You don't have to pretend with me, Gina. No, I haven't met Santa Claus, but I know your friend, Kristof, is somehow related. And although I haven't met an elf, I know Flitterndorf is nearby."

That makes things easy. "Okay, so we're both believers. Then answer this. If Ms. Donath's office is in Germany, how can she get to Flitterndorf to help the elves?" My mouth forms an 'o' as I recall the emblem in the Prep Stables. "You said portals, plural. Is there a portal that links Germany to Flitterndorf?"

Aunt Cat shakes her head. "She has a liaison inside Santa's village to aid her. She gets the mistlefeude to him, and he disperses it."

I stare at the bottle. "Does the mistlefeude affect the elves like it did me?"

Aunt Cat gives me a knowing grin. "Fabulous, isn't it?"

"That's the understatement of the decade." I glance at my wig-making materials on my desk across the room. "A pity its effects don't last long."

"Ah, therein lies the beauty of mistlefeude. With each application, the effects last longer and longer, up to several days." She drops the bottle into the pouch and cinches it closed.

My insides feel the pinch of separation, and I have to hold my arm from reaching for the mistlefeude. "Does Ms. Donath … I mean, do you think she might spare … That is, could—" I bite my lip.

Aunt Cat chuckles. "Here." She takes my hand and places the pouch in my palm. Recognizable tingles race about. "I will talk to Ina, and we'll figure out a way you can repay her."

A lightness spreads across my core. "Aunt Cat," I breathe, "thank you so much." As I scrabble to apply more mistlefeude, Aunt Cat smiles, picks up the reindeer figurine, and leaves the room. I have the coolest aunt in the world. A chemist who works with magic.

Rolling the perfume along my neck, I close my eyes with a sigh. Tempting images of doll wigs and face repaints swirl in my head, and I move to my desk. With one grand sweep, I push yesterday's wig wefts to the side and pull out a new skein of yarn from my stash. Soon, I will work my own brand of magic.

Twenty-Seven

Tinsel—Nov 28 Something Amiss

Brückenstadt

In fascination, I meander along the pedestrian-only *Hauptstraße*, or main street, in downtown Brückenstadt as a live band serenades the Saturday night crowd enjoying the Christmas market. Rows of wooden huts sparkle beneath white lights and garland swags, and sellers beckon me from behind counters laden with their wares. Glass ball ornaments, angel figurines, wax candles, children's toys and games, sweets such as strudels and gingerbread hearts, gourmet chocolate, fudge, candy sticks, tea, mulled wine ... the list goes on. It's a shopper's paradise, whether one celebrates the Feast of St. Nicholas next weekend or Christmas a few weeks later.

With my phone, I capture a sleighful of pictures for Gina, knowing she'd love this scene. As for me, the holiday vision vies for space alongside visions of locked doors dancing in my head. Interior locked doors hide secrets, and I'm anxious to unearth the ones behind Door Number Five. So, who has the key?

Several huts away, *Lebkuchenherzen*—gingerbread hearts—dangle along lengths of ribbon hanging vertically in the kiosk's opening. That must be where Niklas texted me to meet him in a few minutes. Reorienting in that direction, I lift my phone to take a picture of the neighboring *Nußknacker*, or nutcracker, kiosk, and a familiar face moves across the mid-ground of my screen. Gina? I look up.

No, it's that woman I met at the manor. Ina. She carries another reindeer figurine, this one with pale fur, its body in a rearing position. Even while toting a child's toy, she manages to glide through the crowd with a grace I will never possess, her confident air reminiscent of Gina.

I sneak a pic and send it to Gina with the caption: **Personality-wise, you outshine this woman in every way. Visually, Ina Donath reminds me of you. Miss you!**

Ina turns to stroll down a different row of huts as Lukas and a friend race across her path. They weave between legs, shouting with laughter. My lips curve in a smile. Lukas may not have endeared himself to me, but I don't begrudge him his fun. After all, when's the last time I heard anyone else in his family laugh?

Tucking my phone into a coat pocket, I lengthen my stride toward the gingerbread hut. A few steps later, I falter. Niklas waits there, all right, standing close to Gretel, their heads bent toward each other, intent on a gingerbread heart in her hand. She lifts her face to his as he says something, and her mouth spreads in a dreamy-eyed smile. The aura outlining them quivers, like heat waves radiating from Vati's enormous brick oven back home.

My insides burn hotter. Is he flirting with her? Or she with him? *See? They do belong together.*

Light-hearted shrieks and laughter rise in the distance, jarring the traitorous thought from my head, and I give myself a shake. Earlier today, Niklas said he's aware of me, not Gretel. I shouldn't jump to conclusions. For all I know, I'm reading the situation wrong.

New shrieks erupt close by, and a large fuzzy shape moves in my peripheral vision. I glance over. A horned beast with red, glinting eyes, a distorted mouth, and long, skinny tongue lunges at me.

Screaming, I stumble backward, tripping into one person, colliding with another, losing my balance. I land in a tub of squishiness and pitch backward. Shouts rise in both English and German.

"Tinsel." Niklas grabs my arms and pulls me upright, my rear wedged in a large wicker basket. "Roasted chestnuts, are you okay?"

My heart races, and I scan the area. "Did you see it? Where'd it go?" People gawk and point, laughing and shaking their heads.

"See what?" He struggles to free me, tipping the basket so my feet touch the ground. Small stuffed animals litter the cobblestones.

"The devil. Except it wasn't red with a pitchfork, but—"

"Brown and furry?"

Standing, I readjust my coat and sweater. "*Genau!* Exactly."

"Like that?" Niklas motions behind me to where a man's head pokes out of a beast's body, his gaze on me as he speaks with Gretel and another woman. "It's a Krampus costume, Tinsel. The guy's been carousing around tonight, building excitement for next week's Krampus Run."

The man approaches, the beast's head under his arm, and I straighten my beanie over my ears. "*Entschuldigen Sie,*" he says, yet his animated face and excited gestures belie his apology as he rattles off unintelligible German.

Gretel grins. "He says he's sorry he gave you a fright, but he also thanks you for a great reaction. You made his day."

I grimace at the Krampus head. "He made my nightmares."

"And we've made more work for this poor seller." One at a time, Niklas picks up a stuffed animal, brushes it off, and tosses it in the wicker basket.

"I'm so sorry." Comprehending afresh the toys scattered on the ground, I grab those nearest me. My foot rolls on something soft. I pick up the mini stuffed blackbird with floppy legs and wipe off the dirt, but a dark smudge persists on its yellow foot. A woman, presumably the seller, speaks with Gretel and Fritz, windmilling her arms, shaking her finger in my direction. My skin heats as I imagine what she's saying. Rifling through my backpack purse, I find my wallet and pull out some paper money.

"*Wieviel kostet es?*" I ask, seeking Fritz for guidance. He thumbs through the banknotes, takes the five Euro note, and gives it to the woman. She accepts the money, then shoos us away.

As we leave the area and lingering spectators, Gretel smirks. "Nicky, when you said she was clumsy, you didn't tell us she can't go out in public."

Stung, I frown at Niklas, his lips working to smother a grin. "Really? Of all the things you could've told her, that's the one you went with?"

"Not the only one."

Fritz snorts as we start across one of several pedestrian bridges in town, the placid waters of the Hohenbach rippling underneath. "That was not clumsy. She got scared by the Krampus. Anybody could see that."

"Danke." I fold my arms on a shudder. "You all would've freaked, too, had it sprung on you like that." Reaching the middle of the bridge, I lean against the stone wall. The others follow suit.

"Where to, now?" Gretel asks, brushing flecks of mortar from the wall into the river. "Back to the Weihnachtsmarkt or home?"

"Home?" My gaze connects with her, and her cheeks darken in the lamplight.

"I spend much time there," she says, "it's like my second home."

Shouts rise above the Weihnachtsmarkt, likely "Krampus" striking again. I rub the smudge on my ill-acquired stuffed blackbird, a scarf knotted around its neck. "Why do you spend so much time there?"

"I'm Stoffel's unofficial secretary and keep his office organized." She prods Fritz. "I have worn a path through the woods from my place to yours, *oder?*"

He smiles, his gaze clinging to her even after she looks away.

The commotion grows louder. Beside me, Niklas stares into the waters below, moonlight bouncing off his granite features.

"I'm sorry if I embarrassed you back there," I whisper.

He startles. "Nein, that's not—"

"Niklas!" Hurrying along the bridge, Herr Stoffel puffs toward us, a mustached man at his side. Meister Nico and several middle-aged men and women trail behind them, their faces craggy, and their eyes sparking with wisdom and strength. My gaze returns to the man with the mustache. Didn't I see him in Herr Stoffel's office when I met Ina the other day?

"*Vati, was ist passiert?*" Gretel asks, latching onto the mustached man's arm.

Vati. The word I use to refer to my father. The German word for *dad*. So this man is Gretel's father. Herr Brunner. His reasons for wanting to split up Niklas and me make sense now.

Herr Stoffel speaks to Niklas in rapid German, his words agitated and terse, bushy brows drawn in concern. The others huddle close, occasionally adding to the discussion. When Herr Stoffel shifts his attention to Fritz, I slip a mittened hand into the crook of Niklas's elbow. "What's going on?"

"Two boys are missing, and one of them is Lukas," Niklas murmurs. "Onkel Stoffel is assembling a search party and asked me to join him."

"I'll come with you."

"No."

I flinch at the finality in his voice. "Why not? I saw Lukas not too long ago. He can't have gone far."

"Onkel Stoffel forbids it. He says …" Niklas's gaze collides with mine before skittering away again. "He says you're making me weak."

My mouth unhinges like one of the nutcrackers. "You're not going to let him talk about me like that, are you?"

"Well, no, but—"

"There's a 'but'?"

"Tins, his grandson is missing—"

"And I want to help."

His eyes go flat. "Onkel Stoffel doesn't want your help." He glances at the stuffed blackbird in my fist. "Considering how often you bungle things, it's best if you stay out of it."

I recoil, his words stinging like a physical slap.

Niklas blinks. His mouth parts. "Tinsel." He grabs my arm as I edge backward, a stricken look in his eyes. "I didn't mean that the way it sounded."

"You said exactly what you meant."

"Niklas"—Herr Stoffel claps Niklas on the shoulder—"*komm schon.*" Behind him, Herr Brunner watches me, his dark gaze severe. With a last look tossed in my direction, Niklas lets them lead him away, leaving my heart bruised like my blackbird's foot.

Twenty-Eight

Tinsel—Nov 28-29 Lost and Found

❧⟡❧

Fidgeting with my engagement ring, I pace the music room while Madam Marie sits in a chair with her embroidery hoop and needle. Elke plays random ditties at the grand piano. If only I could channel my nervous energies into something productive.

Like helping my fiancé rescue a missing child. His pseudo-ex-fiancée got to go. Why not me?

Onkel Stoffel says you're making me weak …. Considering how often you bungle things, it's best if you stay out of it.

I spin on my heel and stalk away from the painful thoughts. It's been two hours. Why has it taken so long to find Lukas? Niklas should have located him in record time.

As a diversion, I check my phone again for an answering text from Gina, now that she's recovered her own phone. A thud sounds in the foyer, followed by a flurry of voices. They're back. Exchanging a glance with Madam Marie, I race to meet them. "Did you find—"

"*Und* when it reared again," Lukas says, barreling into the entrance hall from the foyer with a wide grin, "Krampus fled. *Es war fett.*"

I hesitate beside the Norway spruce. "Krampus was awesome?"

Lukas scoffs. "Nein, Krampus was mean, scary. He put us in a sack."

"He did what?" I look from Niklas to Fritz to Meister Nico to Herr Stoffel as they enter from the foyer, but only Fritz meets my gaze.

"We found Lukas and Peter wandering in the forest," he explains, adding in a stage-whisper, "Spouting nonsense."

Lukas glowers. "Not no-sense. Krampus stole us *und* if shiny reindeer hadn't come—"

"Enough." Fritz grips Lukas's shoulder as warning bells sound in my mind. "It was a man in costume who got overly excited about Krampusnacht." He glares at his grandfather.

Elke puts an arm around Lukas's small frame. "Let's get you washed up and to bed."

"Wait, wait." I crouch before Lukas. "What do you mean by 'shiny'?"

"It was *wunderschön*." He skips toward the staircase. "Es funkelt sogar im Dunkeln."

It sparkles even in the dark.

Lukas saw the Silver Reindeer?

As Fritz trails his siblings upstairs, and Meister Nico and Herr Stoffel file into the music room with Madam Marie, I turn to Niklas. He stares at the floor, hands shoved into his front pockets.

"Did you see the SR, too?" I ask. Reluctance wars with elation, since I can't communicate with the reindeer. "I suppose we should—"

"When were you going to tell me?" Niklas lifts his gaze to my face, a hard glint in his eyes.

My insides knot. "Tell you wh—"

"Tell me Grandpop suspended you from the Minor Flight Team. Because you put my reindeer in jeopardy."

The floor seems to drop away, and I waver on my feet. Someone told him. I had several chances to do it first, yet I squandered them. Foolish, selfish decision. "I'm sorry."

Niklas steps close, towering over me. "That's all you have to say? I'm the future Santa Claus"—he gestures to a random wall—"and that's my reindeer team. Responsibility for their welfare and the elves I put in charge of them falls to *me*. I have a right to know what happens with both animal and elf, especially when one party has been negligent and—" He clamps his mouth shut and redirects his glare at the spruce.

I hang my head. "I'm sorry. It was an accident. I promise it won't happen again."

"You're right," Niklas says in a strained voice. "It won't."

He approves of the suspension, then.

Hot tears sting my eyes, and I dash from the hall. "Brava, Tinsel," I hiss, stumbling up the stairs. "Herr Stoffel needn't convince Niklas you're his weak link, because you'll have done it for him."

As an elf, hidden and protected by the Clandy-Stein Mountains, I've lived in a bubble all my life. The Kringles, however, being human, don't exist solely behind those mountains. I understand that now in a way I never could before this trip. And while I might "shine" in Flitterndorf, as Niklas once said, lulling me into believing I'm his match, in the real world I look more like a candle at the end of its wick.

What do people do with weak links and spent candles?

They throw them away.

* * *

Members of the Third String rear onto their hind legs, shaking their heads, their antlers raking against the confining stone walls. I rush to calm them but move like I'm waist-deep in snow. Someone throws a thick chain over Butterscotch's neck and pulls, restraining the animal's struggle. Someone else plunges a needle into his hindquarters, and he collapses.

Alarm rips through me, an inferno that channels into my hands. Still, I fumble at a rescue as the faceless enemy pins down my reindeer, one by one.

Peppermint stands with head bowed, chains binding her legs to the dank stall. Chocolate and Chip kick at their captors. In the end, they each succumb to whatever substance lurks inside those needles.

I wail in frustration, my skin like hot iron.

A black presence rises above me. I scream—

"Hey, hey, shhh. Tinsel, it's okay."

I work to open my eyes. As I do, the stalls and darkness fade, replaced by a blanket of stars and waning moonlight. Niklas leans over me, my hand engulfed in his.

"You're all right. You're safe. Though why you're sleeping in a field is beyond me." He kisses my knuckles. "Thankfully, I know you well enough to look for you among the reindeer before growing concerned when I didn't find you in your room."

Blinking, I prop up on my elbow. An afghan clings to me. Thick stockings keep my legs warm beneath my dirndl, and Bonbon grazes several meters away. I sigh and lie back down. "I came here to think and must've fallen asleep. What time is it?"

"Two-thirty." Niklas settles beside me on the ground. "Were you having a nightmare just now?"

For the umpteenth time tonight, my eyes flood with tears. "I dreamt about the Third String. They were in trouble. In captivity." The stars blur overhead. "Someone was poisoning them. They called for help, but every time I tried to rescue them, I failed. I was useless." A lone tear treks from the corner of my eye, and my jaw clenches. "I'm not useless."

Niklas's finger brushes the underside of my wrist. "I certainly don't think so."

"You don't, huh?" Pulling from him, I roll away and tuck my hands under my cheek. "Why did you come looking for me, Niklas?"

"I couldn't sleep."

"Jet lag?"

"Guilt. Shame. Embarrassment. Inadequacy." A soft sigh escapes him. "Mind games."

My eyebrows knot, and I angle slightly back toward him.

With two fingers, Niklas sweeps the hair alongside my forehead. Sprays of electricity run amok inside me, and I try to stifle it. "Being near you alleviates the mind games," he says. "In you, I find sanctuary. Clarity. Home. So, here I am."

Sanctuary. That's what went through my mind when he pulled me from my manic thoughts in the ballroom. With another sigh, I shrug aside the Afghan and sit to face Niklas. "What sort of mind games?"

He cringes. "Thoughts keep popping into my head. Suspicions. Things I know aren't true, yet I can't shake them." He takes my hand, turns it over, and traces the lines in my palm. "I didn't come here to talk about that, however. I came to apologize." His voice sounds husky, pained. "Tinsel, I don't deserve your forgiveness, but I'm so sorry for what I said at the Weihnachtsmarkt and in the entrance hall. Every time I think about how I treated you, I'm ashamed. To love you is to embrace your clumsiness, not find fault in it. As to the Third String, we both know they can be persuasive and sneaky."

"I shouldn't have kept the Peppermint Twist fiasco a secret, though."

Niklas presses his lips to my palm, heat flaring along my veins. "I'll forgive you if you forgive me."

"So quick and simple?"

"You know I can't stay mad at you for long." Holding my hand captive, he draws me close with a wink. "And you can't stay mad at me. It's part of my Kringle charm."

My lips twitch. "Cocky Kringle."

His gaze drops to my mouth. "Kiss and make up?"

Grinning, I close the gap between us, then squeal as he snakes an arm about me and hauls me into his lap to deepen the kiss.

Like any good chaperon, Bonbon breaks up our make-out session before it gets too steamy, and we fold up the Afghan and return to the manor. As we say goodnight at my bedroom door, Niklas studies the wood paneling and murmurs, "I have an idea. Originally, I was thinking we should search for the SR tomorrow after church."

I draw in a breath, fingering my choker out of habit. If keeping my faux pas with the Third String a secret has taught me anything, I better confess my missing talent ASAP. "Niklas, about the Silver Reindeer—"

He puts a finger against my lips. "Now, I'm thinking you and I need to get away for the afternoon instead. Alone. A chance to clear our heads, set aside our worries for a few hours." He gives a dimpled smile. "We'll be like those annoying tourists. Loud, always taking pictures, boisterous."

"I'd love to. Honest. But shouldn't we be trying to save Christmas?"

Niklas's gaze again flits to my door. "So we put in some effort tonight. What about that secret door in your room?"

"What about it?"

His eyes twinkle in the dimmed light from the wall sconces. "Let's find out where it goes."

Twenty-Nine

Tinsel—Nov 29 Day Trip

Gina texts me the next morning as I sit in a church pew between Niklas and Fritz.

I promise I'm not blowing you off! Would you believe I spent my entire Sat working on a wig & doll repaint?! Mum had to drag me downstairs earlier to make sure I ate dinner. :D The doll looks ah-MAZE-ing! I can't even. Swoon. And the creative juices keep flowing—I don't want to stop, even though it's almost 2AM. Gah! Must get some sleep. I hvn't read all your texts, but I promise I will tomorrow. Miss you!

Smiling, I tuck the phone away. At least one of us is having fun.

It's not that I don't have my moments of fun, but the stress of Krampus and the Silver Reindeer colors everything. Our adventure last night through hidden passageways brought us to the other bedroom suites in my wing, not to the hallway closet like I'd hoped. And although I tried earlier to engage the manor's reindeer herd in a game of "Twenty Questions" about the SR (there are fewer 'deer today, and I didn't see Bonbon), I left unsuccessful.

Yet that aside, and ignoring the weight of my unconfessed secret, the mood between Niklas and me has improved since we talked. In fact, he's so attentive this morning, it doesn't faze me when Gretel squeezes into the pew beside him as the service begins. And when we return to the manor and Herr Stoffel calls for another dance practice before the midday meal, Niklas draws me close, saying to the group, "Tinsel and I are sitting this one out."

Herr Stoffel narrows his eyes. "You cannot skip practice." Behind him, Dieter emerges from the office, head ducked and pace swift, before turning a corner. Something swings from his fingers.

"You'll have to excuse us this one time, Onkel," Niklas argues. "I'm taking Tinsel to Salzburg."

Salzburg? Ribbons and bows!

Gretel clasps her hands. "The weather is perfect for that." She nods at Fritz, then smiles at me. "We come with you, ja? I show you the great shopping—"

"No." Niklas winces and pinches the bridge of his nose. Faint shadows darken his eyes. Have they been there all morning? "Just me and Tins."

Herr Stoffel sputters. "I-I must protest—"

"Oh, let them go, Stoffel," Madam Marie says in a quiet voice. She, too, rubs her forehead. "They can make up the practice when they return."

Niklas gives her a kiss on the cheek. "Thank you, Mum." He smiles at me. "Grab your passport and anything else you might need for Salzburg. I'll meet you back here in five minutes."

Energized by the promise of an afternoon with Niklas all to myself, I hasten up the two flights of stairs. As I round the corner to my hallway, however, an elf disappears at the far end. Dieter? Bypassing my bedroom door, I tiptoe along the hall after him, a jingle-jangle perking my elfin ears. I peek down the forbidden corridor. Sure enough, Dieter stands at Door Number Five, wiggling a key into its lock. Where have I seen him before? Reindeer spring to mind. And stables.

Bote.

Dieter Bote.

The name conjures a memory of a Prep Stables' worker, green lederhosen smudged with dirt and straw.

My pulse quickens. What's an elf from Flitterndorf doing here?

Stepping into the closet, Dieter pulls the door closed behind him. I wait for a moment, and like last time, he doesn't reemerge. After checking that I'm alone, I scurry down the hall, take a fortifying breath, and open the door.

An empty closet greets me, the vintage coat swaying on its hanger.

* * *

"You look content." Chin propped in his hand, Niklas regards me across the table in the St. Peter Stiftskulinarium. The restaurant is one of the oldest in Europe and built into Mönchsberg, the mountain in the heart of Salzburg. He taps my foot with his. "Admit it. You're glad we came instead of staying behind to inspect a closet that may or may not have led somewhere."

Wrinkling my nose, I pop the last bite of soup-soaked bread bowl into my mouth. Okay, I may have balked at leaving the manor once Dieter unlocked the closet and promptly vanished. Where did he go, and why is an elf from the Green Clan wearing white and working at Weihnachts Manor? Niklas has no answer for the first part, but he reminded me that elves from the manor have, on rare occasions, transferred to Flitterndorf in the past, so he figures the reverse is possible.

"I still hope to solve this closet mystery, but, yes"—I lean into the table's edge—"I'm glad we escaped the manor for a bit." What better way to spend an afternoon than touring Salzburg on the arm of my fiancé, away from the heaviness of Weihnachts Manor or Herr Stoffel's watchful eye? "Your color has returned, and I haven't had to compete with Gretel, so this was a win for both of us."

Niklas draws a finger along my left hand and toys with the engagement ring. "I don't like Gretel in that way. Never have, never will."

Nearby, a Christmas tree glistens with white lights. Here in the restaurant's ancient rock cellar, columns and arches visibly separate groups of tables while fancy, antlered chandeliers dangle overhead. My words are less fancy as I whisper, "That's not what it looked like at the Weihnachtsmarkt."

He stands and pulls me to my feet. "What do you mean?"

"I saw you, Niklas." I swallow as he helps me into my coat. "Flirting with Gretel."

"What? No, I wasn't. When?"

"Before I made a spectacle of myself with the stuffed animals." I button my coat, studying his face. "You two were on the verge of kissing."

Brow furrowed, Niklas leads me from the restaurant. Dusk has settled across Salzburg, and the brightest stars wink in the clear sky. I tighten my scarf against the crisp air. Somewhere, a choir sings seasonal tunes, their voices skimming over rooftops.

Walking beside me, Niklas takes a deep breath. "Tinsel, I ..." When he doesn't continue, I glance over. "I think I'm being set up. I think *we're* being set up."

"That's your excuse for almost kissing Gretel?"

His jaw muscles bunch. "We weren't 'almost kissing.'"

"I know what I saw."

"You think you know what you saw. Apparently, I'm not the only one suffering from mind games."

The choir grows louder as we enter the Domplatz. Salzburg's own Christmas market is in full swing, and several times larger than the one in Brückenstadt. I tuck my chin into my scarf. "All right, Kringle, I'll bite. Who do you think is trying to split us up? Your great-uncle immediately comes to mind."

"Roasted chestnuts, no." Niklas swipes off his cap and shoves a hand through his hair. "I'm talking about Krampus."

"Herr Stoffel makes more sense."

"It's true he doesn't favor you, but split us up?"

"Remember when we went hiking the other day, and I returned to the manor early?" As Niklas skirts us around the kiosks overflowing with food and goodies, I launch into a summary of what I overheard Herr Stoffel tell Meister Nico about ending our relationship.

A stony expression clouds Niklas's face. "Onkel Stoffel doesn't have the authority to make those decisions, or to enforce them."

"Authority or not, he's doing a great job at it."

The muscles pop repeatedly in his jaw. "All of this must tie in with Krampus, yet I don't know how, and it's driving me crazy." Niklas ducks through a narrow archway, and I follow him onto a side street, pre-lit garland stretching between the buildings. "I snatch a thread here, grasp a thread there, and start to see a pattern, only to watch the threads slip through my fingers"—he curls his into claws—"and turn around to trap me. Bind me."

"Why would Krampus waste time on you? On us? Wouldn't he go after Meister K?"

"What else explains us seeing things that aren't real and jumping to wrong conclusions?"

"You're telling me you weren't inches from Gretel's face last night."

"I don't like Gretel."

I stop him in the street, pedestrians passing us on both sides. "I didn't ask if you liked her."

Niklas stares at me, green eyes hard with resentment. Does he not remember their chummy position? Or is he right, and I, too, am plagued with mind games? Slowly, the lines about his eyes soften, and he skims his fingers along my cheek. "The next time you think you see me in some questionable situation, you have permission to kiss me."

"What?"

"You heard me." His thumb grazes my bottom lip, and I sway toward him. "Just plant one on me. One kiss from you clears the muddy waters. My muddled mind." His dimples surface in his classic grin. "Though you needn't restrict yourself to the questionable moments. I'll welcome a kiss from you whenever." Niklas takes my hand. "Except right now. Right now, it's time for your surprise."

With the Hohensalzburg Fortress presiding in the background above the city's historic center, Niklas leads me toward a lone horse-drawn carriage parked beside the sidewalk. A man dressed in dark brown lederhosen and a button-up black jacket with green embroidery stands by the carriage.

"Grüß Gott," Niklas calls out.

The man responds in kind, shaking Niklas's hand. They converse for a moment before Niklas motions me into the hackney. I ascend the mounting step and scoot along the bench seat as he hops in after me.

"I'd have ordered snow for a sleigh ride," Niklas says, draping a blanket over our legs, "if that kind of power were mine to wield."

"I read somewhere these carriages stop operating by late afternoon in the colder months. Given that it's now evening, you wield some power."

Niklas nods at the man taking his place in the driver's seat. "When I told Herr Müller I wanted to impress my fiancée, he made an

185

exception for you."

These aren't the actions of someone with a wandering eye. My offense dissolves. "I don't deserve you."

The carriage jostles to life, pressing me against the seat cushion. The horses' hooves *clip clop* along the pavement, their pace slowing time itself as we leave the city behind and make for the lower paths of Mönchsberg. Once in a while, I glimpse the river Salzach, its water speckled with the reflected city lights. Niklas's phone chimes at one point, but he ignores it. Wrapping an arm about me, he tugs me close and kisses my temple.

"I love you," he says. "Please remember that. We can beat whatever Krampus is planning if we stick together. Have faith in me. In us."

"I'm trying to."

Niklas's hold tightens. "You inspire me, you know. You're like a sprig of holly defying the winter in Figgy Forest. Challenging death's grasp." A shudder ripples through him. "Death. That's what I've been sensing. Like I'm dying. Ripped apart from the inside."

I sit up in alarm. "Because of the mind games? Then let's go home. What's keeping us here? Your Initiation Ceremony? The Silver Reindeer? They're not worth it. We'll find another way to defeat Kramp—"

A flash of white streaks from the trees and arches directly overhead. The horses rear, the carriage jostles, and Herr Müller curses in German.

Niklas grips the door sash. "Is that…?" His forehead puckers. "She's small."

Thirty

Tinsel—Nov 29 Confession

I swivel on the seat and let out a breath. As if conjured by our words, a silvery-white reindeer stands before the draft horses, shimmering antlers splaying over her trim back. Though her head doesn't reach the horses' shoulders, the equines prance side to side, like they want to escape in a frothing gallop, but something restrains them. Gripping the reins, Herr Müller exchanges terse words with Niklas.

The Silver Reindeer angles her head, her gaze boring into mine. Crumbling candy canes, she wants something. How am I going to decipher what that is? Biting my lip, I push aside the blanket.

"Tins." Niklas grabs my arm. "What are you doing?"

"You want me to talk to her, don't you?" I slip free and fumble with the door latch.

"I'm coming with you."

The reindeer snorts and sidesteps the horses, shaking her head as we exit the carriage. The driver shouts a warning. Even though we, too, stand taller than she does, we approach the reindeer with cautious steps. She bobs her head and strikes the pavement with a

187

hoof, her toffee eyes blinking.

"It's okay, I'm a friend." I stretch toward her, palm out. "Maybe you already know that. We've been searching for you—"

The SR makes a guttural noise, noses her neck, and stares at me.

Aw, snowman. I tug the brim of my newsboy cap. "I'm sorry. I don't … I can't—"

She rears and paws the air. The horses neigh. I stumble backward into Niklas, whose arm comes around to anchor me as he pivots us both, putting himself between me and the reindeer.

Suddenly, he's gone with a shout. I turn just as the SR flings him onto her back by her antlers.

"No! Niklas!"

She rockets into the air, and I wave my arms over my head. "Come back! What are you doing?"

The carriage rattles behind me, and I spin about, my mouth dropping as Herr Müller takes off, shouting at his horses. "Wait, where are *you* going?" I race after him, but he travels too fast and vanishes around the bend.

Bumbling to a stop in the empty lane, I glance at the sky. There's no sign of the SR. Where did she take Niklas? Is she bringing him back? I cup my mouth and holler, "Niiiklaaaas!" Holy holly berries, this is a disaster.

Silver flashes above. Two seconds later, the Silver Reindeer lands and shakes Niklas off her back. He crashes to the ground beside the bushes lining the path.

"Niklas." I hurry over to him, glaring at the SR. For a slight creature, she's got attitude. "Whose side are you on?"

She brays, stomps her hoof, and disappears into the sky again. Groaning, Niklas pushes onto all fours and retches into the bushes.

I kneel beside him and rub his back. "I'm so sorry. Are you okay?" Of course he's not okay. A mad reindeer gave him the flight—and fright—of his life!

Niklas collapses onto his side and swipes his mouth. "I don't care what the legend says. That reindeer is not our ally."

"This is my fault. I didn't want to tell you, because I didn't want you to think less of me than you already do. First I put your reindeer in harm's way. Then I got suspended. Now I can't even help your family save Christmas. I don't have the makings of Mrs. Santa Claus and—"

"Tinsel, slow down." Niklas shifts onto his back, throws one arm over his eyes, and searches for me with the other, latching onto my hand. "Let's get one thing straight. I don't love you because of some talent or a measure of success. I love you because you're strong in your convictions and stubborn when it counts. You're compassionate, loyal to those you love, a defender of Christmas—"

"I can't communicate with reindeer anymore," I blurt out, staring at our linked hands. There's no way Niklas can defend me, now that he knows I'm lacking.

His body stills. He peeks at me from under his arm, and I angle away, my vision blurring. "Can't communicate? That's your talent. Waitwaitwait." Niklas grunts to a sitting position. "When did this happen?"

"A few days after we got here."

He drills a hand through his hair. "This is because of Krampus. It's got to be."

I'm not the only one suffering from mind games .... We can beat whatever Krampus is planning. "He's messing with my talent?"

"And mine."

"What do you mean?"

Niklas rests his arms on his knees, dropping his head to his knuckles. "I can no longer locate a child, Tins."

"You found Lukas—"

"We found Lukas and Paul, thanks to the police, not me. And I'm having trouble understanding people in a foreign language other than German. Knowing Krampus is behind this doesn't fix anything. The doubts keeping piling on. Plus ... my biggest problem precedes him."

"Your fear of flying."

He nods. "I'm the firstborn. The future Santa Claus. I'm supposed to spend hours flying around the world, and I can't last thirty seconds on the back of a reindeer." Lifting his head, Niklas looks at me. "You think you're not worthy of me, but it's the other way around. Why else would I have waited so long before asking you to marry me? I wanted to prove myself worthy of *you*." He lets out a half-laugh. "Clearly, I gave up on that. I'm gonna go crazy if I have to wait much longer before making you mine." His eyebrows draw together. "Except that's selfish. Because I'm half a man. Incomplete. You deserve—"

"Don't." I grip his forearms. "No one's half a person, Niklas. You already possess everything you need to become a great Santa. It's in your DNA. It's in the spirit of Christmas." I press a hand against his heart. "It's right here, waiting for you to tap into it." My gaze holds his, and I whisper, "If you saw yourself through my eyes, you would never doubt your worth or potential."

Niklas's lips quirk at one end. "I'd kiss you for that, but I should probably brush my teeth first." He pushes to his feet, then pulls me to mine. "So, my dear Future-Mrs.-Kringle, with our talents nullified and the Silver Reindeer gone rogue, what do we do now?"

"Find a new way to stop Krampus. And I think I know where to start."

Thirty-One

Gina—Nov 29 Inspiration

Waldheim

"Honest opinion, 'kay?" I flip the camera view on my phone to show Kristof the two dolls standing on my desk and study his facial reaction in our video call.

His eyebrows shoot up. "They're marvelous, G. Bring me closer."

I smile at his praise and oblige him, zooming in on the dolls' repainted faces and fresh wigs. "I've been working on them since yesterday morning."

"You're kidding."

"Nope." One doll has pale lavender space buns with a butterfly cheek tattoo. The other has sleek auburn locks with an ethereal repaint.

"Gina, it's four o'clock in the afternoon." Kristof's expression turns skeptical. "You completed wigs and repaints in that short amount of time?"

I sink into my desk chair, careful to keep the camera on the dolls. "Some aspects I'd started earlier. I did have two dolls going at the same time, so I could work on one while the other dried."

"Still, if I understand correctly, most dolls take a few days to complete."

"Right? That's been my usual experience." I fiddle with the mistlefeude Aunt Cat let me keep. The stuff truly did bring on the joy. "But I knew what I wanted and how to make it happen and went ahead and did it."

"With a fantastic outcome." Kristof rubs his scruff, his eyes narrowing slightly.

I know that look. "You're contemplating something."

He chuckles and shakes his head. "Wishing it were possible to hire you at the Workshop. At least until Christmas."

A light clicks on inside, and I flip the camera to face me. "Kristof, that's perfect. Let's do it."

He laughs. I don't. He sobers. "What about your job at the Huggamugg Café?"

"Oh. Right." I deflate, then perk up again. "Maybe I bring my laptop, and during breaks, I work on the spreadsheets and orders and things that don't require my physical presence at the café. My staff can take turns opening and closing, and I'll go in on weekends. We could test it for a week or two, couldn't we?"

I gaze at my doll collection. How fortuitous! I could offer to be another liaison for Ina and administer mistlefeude on the sly among the elves. Imagine the empowerment this would bring them. A spritz here, a spritz there—their negativity would disintegrate. Yes, I'd be helping myself in the process with the tips and tricks I could glean from the Doll Makers at Santa's Workshop. That's not a crime, is it? We're talking about a dream come true—a dream I had buried when Nonna ripped up the page from my coloring book.

"You can't say no," I plead with Kristof through the screen.

He laughs again. "Who are you, and what have you done with the real Gina? She's not prone to leave her comfort zone and wade into unchartered waters."

"That was before I got tackled by rogue elves and trotted off to Santa Claus's headquarters," I tease. Before I learned I have a monster in my family closet and a portal in my house that links to Germany. "Stuff like that messes with one's head."

"Point taken. I need to run this by Grandpop first. Send me some pics and a quick video of those dolls, and we'll see what he thinks."

I roll a scrap of yarn between my fingers. "What do *you* think?"

His background shifts as he lowers into an armchair. "Professionally, I think you'd be an asset to the Doll Makers when they need it the most. Selfishly, I'd love having you work in the same building as me." A grin meanders across his lips. "That's a lot of lunch dates."

"Lunch get-togethers."

"You say Christmas Tree, I say Tannenbaum." He winks, the action having the same stomach-flipping effect it does in person.

My mind returns to that impulsive hug I gave him Friday night. How well I fit in his arms. If his hugs are that delicious, what would that make his kisses?

Not that I have any business thinking about kissing someone cemented in the friend zone.

I clear my throat. "Okay, I'm hanging up. Call me once you've talked with Meister K."

"I will, but, Gina"—Kristof rubs his forehead—"be forewarned. Outside of a Kringle, no human has ever held a position at the Workshop."

"So I shouldn't get my hopes up. I know. I'll be fine." I show him a toothy smile and end the call.

What Kristof doesn't realize is that Meister K will be so blown over by my creations, he'll beg me to work for him. My newly acquired abilities are that good.

I squeal and kiss the bottle of mistlefeude.

Thirty minutes later, Kristof calls back. "How soon can you be ready?"

* * *

In the backyard, Dad's ax slices through the log he's chopping into kindling, his expression solemn ever since I explained (minus the part about the mistlefeude) why I'll be in Flitterndorf for the next week. Though I don't need my parents' permission, I would like their blessing.

"Living with Tinsel's family and working alongside the elves in Santa's Workshop isn't what I had in mind when I told you to read my grandfather's journal," Dad says, breaking the stretch of silence.

Wood smoke carries on the breeze, the frigid air numbing my cheeks, and I tighten my scarf. "We come from a twisted family, Dad. Forgive me for trying to untwist it a little."

He fine-tunes his hold on the ax, his breath fogging in front of him, and swings again. The log splits in two. "What if you make things worse for the Kringles?"

I scoff. "Thanks for the vote of confidence."

"You've got Krampus blood flowing through your veins, Gina. We still don't know if that will have a negative effect inside Flitterndorf."

"Chill, Dad. I have a plan." I place a new log on his chopping block. "And blood doesn't determine our course in life, as Papa Campi would attest to."

Dad drives the ax through the wood fibers. "It has the power to separate families—and friends."

"Or bring them together."

His lips compress. "What did your mother say?"

"She has her reservations." I pile the kindling scattered around the snow-encrusted ground in the crook of my elbow. "Listen, as much as I love you guys and want to please you, I'm twenty-one. I make my own decisions."

"And your aunt?" He sets another log in place and raises the ax. "What did you tell her?"

"That I'm dog-sitting for a friend of mine."

Quirking an eyebrow, Dad blasts the log apart. "I'll try to remember that so I don't slip up on your lie."

I dump the kindling into the metal wheelbarrow nearby. Dad needn't worry. Aunt Cat won't ask about me, because I told her the truth.

She already knows about Santa. Why not explain how Kristof's related, that my BFF is a Christmas elf, and I visited Santa's village just the other day? When I then suggested I could act as Ina's new liaison, Aunt Cat's face brightened, and she gave me extra bottles of mistlefeude.

I didn't mention Krampus, however, since my one inquiry about him had produced a blank expression. Best not to complicate things. "Before you ask"—I bend to gather more kindling—"I've already talked to Mikal and Titus, and they're cool with taking on the extra workload at the café this week. And that was before I promised them each a bonus for their help."

"What of Kristof? Can I talk candidly about Krampus when he comes to pick you up in an hour?"

I clutch my armful of kindling. "Absolutely not."

"Gina—"

"Dad, no. He can't know about this skeleton in our closet."

Dad plunks the ax head on the chopping block and stacks his gloved hands atop its handle. "When it comes to ordinary folk, I'm all for keeping quiet. But Kristof knows Krampus exists, so—"

"Which is why I can't—won't—say anything. Krampus is, like, his

195

enemy. If Kristof discovers I'm part of that family, he'll never look at me the same way again." While I'm not seeking romance in the arms of a Kringle, no matter how delicious his hugs, I refuse to forfeit a friendship that has been a staple for almost half my life.

Dad sighs. "I hope you're not making a huge mistake."

I toss the kindling into the wheelbarrow. A niggling of doubt invades my confidence, but I brush it away as easily as I brush the wood fibers from my coat. Dad doesn't know I pack a secret weapon to dispel the elves' troubles.

"Actually, Dad, I'm making one of the best decisions of my life."

Thirty-Two

Tinsel—Nov 30 Hidden Tunnels

Weihnachts Manor

"Ready for some snooping?" Niklas whispers when I meet him in the stairwell at one-thirty in the morning. His eyes twinkle in the lamplight as he presses an extra flashlight into my hand.

I grin, and together we slink our way to Herr Stoffel's office. Ever since I recognized Dieter Bote, my mind has been whirring. I'm sure I glimpsed him mucking stalls in the Prep Stables last month when I met with Herr Verwalter about feed supplies, so when did he begin working here at the manor? How did he get here? Where'd he get a key to the closet? He exited Herr Stoffel's office with a set of keys. Did he steal them? Borrow them? Door Number Five is locked again, so did he replace the keys once he completed his work, or did someone lock it behind him?

What kind of work does Herr Bote do here, anyway? And whom does he serve—Herr Stoffel or Meister K?

Or, given his sour disposition, perhaps he serves Krampus.

Such an idea seems preposterous, but with no other lead, it's as

197

good a place as any to start.

Concerned we might find Herr Stoffel's office door locked, too, I give a silent clap when Niklas turns the knob effortlessly. He ushers me inside and closes the door before flicking on his flashlight. The beam passes over two chairs facing an imposing desk centered in the room, behind which stand a coat rack and file cabinets. Framed pictures hang on the walls, and a narrow door is partway open in one corner. A closet? Something glints inside, and Niklas moves to open it further—

He jumps as a snarling, devilish creature springs at him. A scream jets into my throat, and I clap a hand over my mouth, meeting Niklas's wide-eyed gaze. We can't get caught in here.

Niklas lets out a quiet, pent-up laugh. "That shocked five years off my life."

I glare at the Krampus costume hanging from the closet door. The wooden mask exudes malice with its vacant, slitted eyes and yawning, fanged mouth. "What is your great-uncle doing with a symbol of our enemy in his office?"

Niklas shuts the door with a shudder. "Probably for the Krampus Run in a few days. It's tradition in this area to dress up as Krampus, remember?"

"Or maybe *he's* Krampus." Yet he doesn't have the right bloodline. I rub my arms and put the desk between me and the closet. "Let's find the keys and get out of here."

With another chuckle, Niklas crosses the room. "Why don't you concentrate on the desk, and I'll start with the shelves and file cabinet?"

"Fine." Keeping a wary eye on the closet, I slide the drawers open and closed, rifling through papers, clattering through miscellaneous office supplies, thumbing through file folders. After several minutes, I've found journals, cubbies, a lollipop stash, and a shoebox, but no keys.

"What are these?" Niklas says, his words strangled.

I abandon the bottom desk drawer and join him at the cabinet. A folder lies open atop the other files in the cabinet drawer, several papers fanned out. Muscles tense and breathing stalled, Niklas holds one aloft, shining his flashlight on long German words in official script.

"Some kind of application form?" I tap a finger on *N. Kringle* scrawled at the bottom. "That isn't your signature, is it?"

"It's Pa's. This is a *Ledigkeitsbescheinigung.*"

"*Gesundheit.*"

"It's not funny, Tinsel. It's a form used in the marriage application process to show that one is single, and this"—Niklas moves the flashlight beam to the top sheet on the file folder, highlighting a line where his name is printed—"is an *Ehefähigkeitszeugnis*, which says I'm legally free to marry."

"Okaaay ...?"

He highlights another line, another name. "Free to marry Gretel."

My stomach drops, and I scan the paper. "Is there a date? It could be several years old. You know, before you made it officially clear you weren't going to marry her."

"I keep telling you, it was never official."

I wave the paper in his face. "This looks official to me."

Scowling, he snatches it back and studies the page. "Here. It's dated in August." He gulps. "Of this year. Why would Pa sign this?"

We stare at each other, Niklas's eyebrows jammed together, my heart constricting. I give myself a shake and take the paper from Niklas. "What we have is a couple of forms, that's all. It's not like anyone can force you to marry Gretel, right?"

"Right. Right?" Niklas tugs at his shirt collar, backing away. "I don't like this." He bumps into the coat rack and barely catches it before it falls over. Something jingles to the floor.

"Candy crumbs, I hope no one heard that." I stuff the paperwork into the file drawer and crouch for whatever fell. "Look." I hold up a loaded key chain. "Do you think—" His squeamish expression quells my words, and I lower my hand. "Maybe I should continue this alone."

"No." Niklas helps me to my feet, folding his fingers around mine, which fold around the keys. The muscles bunch in his jaw. "I have more reasons now to unravel what's going on and how it's all linked. We're trying every single one of these keys in that closet door."

* * *

We sneak back to Door Number Five. Niklas must sense my skepticism, for he mutters, "I'm fine," while glaring at the door.

I pass the flashlight beam over his stern features. "'FINE,' as in Fed up, Insecure, Neurotic, and Emotional?"

He awards me with a wry purse of his lips. "Open the door, Kuchler." The lock clicks on the fourth key. "Got it."

Everything looks the same as last time, though the vintage coat is missing, leaving behind an empty hanger. While Niklas crouches to give the wooden boxes a thorough inspection, I step over them to the back wall, determined to unmask its secret.

"I don't get it," Niklas says. "They don't budge. They don't open. There aren't any knobs or switches or doohickeys that would activate something. So why are they here?"

Assessing where the draft comes from, I glance behind me at the boxes. "They look like stairs."

"Going where?"

I shrug. A crack runs down the back corners of the closet, and I push against the wall. It holds firm. I spin about to Niklas. "You should try—oof!" Stumbling into the boxes, I lose my balance, flail, and catch the hanger as my knee hits the top box. I grimace and rub my knee. "You'd think I'd have learned my lesson the first time."

Niklas stands with mouth agape, his gaze fixed on something behind me. Cold air brushes the flyaways at my temple. I turn. A dark recess yawns where the back wall had been. Niklas shines his flashlight into a long, chilly corridor leading into blackness, and I exhale. "We found it."

He directs the beam above my head. "The wooden boxes must be steps that allow the elves to work the rod and access the passageway. You had the right door, after all." Skirting the boxes, he kisses my cheek. "I love your clumsy nature." He moves the beam over the stones and holds out his hand. "Shall we?"

I close the closet door behind me. "You lead. I'll follow."

"Scared?"

"There's a reason I don't watch horror movies with Gina."

The passageway slopes down for several meters before it makes a ninety-degree angle and becomes a flight of stairs. Going down. Down. Down. It drops us into another tunnel, which turns, and we pull up short at a fiberglass door with a lever handle. I meet Niklas's eyes. "What if it's locked?"

"What if it isn't? Do we have a plan for whatever we find on the other side?"

"Run if necessary?"

One dimple appears. "Here goes nothing." Niklas grasps the lever, and my pulse accelerates when the door clicks open. A bluish glow fills in the widening crack. He peeks his head around the doorjamb, then beckons me with the flashlight. "All clear."

I step into a large, square, tiled room, the blue glow bathing the walls and glinting off glass objects set atop long tables. Flasks, condensers, a convoluted maze of rubber tubing, and a Bunsen burner dominate the nearest tabletop. "It's like we're back in Herr Chemie's classroom,"

I whisper, "complete with lab benches and glass beakers."

"Except his experiments weren't so complicated." Shutting off his flashlight, Niklas wags his eyebrows. "Best not to touch any of it. You remember what happened last time."

I stick out my tongue, easily recalling the smoke plumes from the explosion that charred an entire wing at Flitterndorf School of Talents. "I was set up. Don't forget that part."

Niklas winks, moving to a thick shelf burdened with equally thick books. More books fan across a narrow table at waist height.

I sniff and glance around. "Do you smell that?"

"Hmm?"

"It's jasmine. And some other scent I keep smelling but can't name."

In the far corner, several human and elf-sized white lab coats hang from wooden pegs. I shine my flashlight at the poster pinned above them. Santa's rosy-cheeked, vintage face smiles back—with added devil horns, fangs for teeth, and a dripping, dark line slashing his neck. I quiver. "I'm guessing whoever runs this lab loathes Santa."

Niklas glances at me, and I point to the poster. His jaw hardens. Turning away, he examines an open book propped on a mini pedestal.

"Why do you suppose this science lab is linked via underground tunnels to Weihnachts Manor?" I finger my choker. "Does Herr Stoffel know about it? The elves obviously do. So, is it his lab? With that kind of poster on the wall?"

Niklas shakes his head, frowning at the page. "Good questions, Tins. Wish I had the ans— Mistlefoil?"

"Miss-what?"

His lips move in silence as he scans the page. His eyes flare. "Of all the holly, jolly, merry Christmases …."

"What is it?" Coming alongside him, I glimpse a picture of an animal before he snaps the book closed. "Hey!"

"We should get out of here." He spins away. "Where's the door?"

I flip open the cover and thumb through several pages of chemistry experiments. "What just put the fear of the Christmas spirit in you?" "Seriously, Tinsel." Niklas's voice sounds tight, urgent. "Where's the frostbitten door?"

I look up. Niklas paces along the wall we came through, yet there's no door. Just a stone wall with a few floating shelves and a console table pushed against it. Atop the shelves stand several reindeer figurines, like the ones I've seen Ina Donath carry. Each one is unique—different color, body position, set of antlers—and each looks eerily realistic.

The area brightens behind me. Light fills the crack below a door on the opposite wall, and my heartbeat falters at a moving shadow. "Someone's coming." I yank Niklas toward the last door in the room, a broad, steel one, and my hip knocks against a lab bench. The precarious tubular structure wobbles. Glass clinks as I turn the doorknob, and something crashes to the floor. *POP!* White light flashes behind us, illuminating an emblem recessed in the tile above the door. An emblem with intertwining leaves and berries. I hesitate, despite the shouts outside the room.

"Tinsel, what's with you?" Niklas shoves open the door, pushes me into a dim cavern, and scurries after me. The door shuts, plunging us into blackness.

* * *

Cold, dank air seeps through my sweater. I feel for where I last glimpsed Niklas, and my fingers close around his sleeve. With a bit of fumbling, he takes my hand and gives it a squeeze. After a few seconds, there's scuffing on the floor, his body heat evaporates, and a tug on my arm forces me to blindly step forward. A faint *slap* sounds ahead, then Niklas's lips brush my earlobe. "I wanted to get out of

203

immediate view, in case someone opens that door," he breathes, "but there's a stone wall right here. We can't go any farther."

I nod against his cheek as exclamations rise in the science lab. A barked command. Hurried footsteps. My pulse races. "I'm so sorry. Thanks to me, they know someone's been in that lab."

"You do have impeccable timing." He wraps his arms about my waist. "But I shut the book, Tinsel. That would've eventually tipped them off."

Clatters and other muffled noises continue. Voices wax and wane in volume. At any moment, the door could open. A tremor courses through Niklas's body, as though his thoughts track with mine. I wriggle from his hold and switch on my flashlight, muting the beam with my palm.

"What are you doing?" he whispers.

"I'm not waiting like some trussed-up Christmas goose for them to catch." I move the light around our immediate area. "I want to know where we are and if we have any options."

"They could be friendlies."

"Then why'd you run?" I shake my head. "We both know it won't end well if we're discovered."

The dimmed light reflects off high stone walls at my back and to my left, and a shorter, interior wall to my right. Massive crossbeams overhead support a lofty ceiling. "This place is immense," I murmur, moving forward. And somehow familiar. The interior wall stops at a six-foot gap before continuing again on the other side. At the gap, I peer around the corner.

More short walls break up the cavernous room in equal intervals on either side of a center aisle. Recognition ignites. "Niklas, these are the stables from my dream." Tiptoeing along the aisle, I aim the flashlight into the areas between the shorter walls. Hay covers the ground in these spaces; clean hay in some, soiled in others. I wet my lips. "What if my nightmare is a type of premonition? What if these are Krampus's stables? Could he be after the Third String?"

"Look at these stalls," Niklas says, his voice strained. "They're huge. Nearly twice the size used for the Big Eight."

"Yeah." The beam accentuates deep gouges in the wood. "Yeah, too big for the Third String. They're safe in Flitterndorf, anyway, right? Recuperating from whatever ailed them last week?" Niklas doesn't answer. My light slides along several lengths of burly chain anchored to the stall's rear wall. Unease slithers down my back. "What kind of animal does that hold?"

"The kind I don't want to meet in person. C'mon, we've got to find another exit." He hurries down the aisle, anxiety rolling off his body like waves of heat. "Ah, sweet gingerbread"—his pace increases—"there's one up ahead." His flashlight unveils a pair of humongous doors, black as pitch with iron rings for handles. A solid wooden beam lies across them like an amped-up version of what we saw in the Hohensalzburg Fortress.

"That thing must weigh a ton," I say. "How will we—"

"Here." Niklas hands me the flashlight. Readying his arms under the beam, he hoists it and, with grunts and his neck muscles straining, arcs it upward. I stare.

Kristof might have ended up with the broader build, but my man has got himself some brawn.

The beam settles upright into place beside the door. Niklas shoulders the doors open, and they swing outward on well-oiled hinges. We escape into a small clearing under the concealment of night. Fresh air kisses my face, and we break into a run toward the tree line ahead of us. The ground slopes downward. As we race under the branches, I pant, "Where are we?"

Niklas tosses a glance over his shoulder and stumbles to a halt, steadying himself against a nearby tree trunk. "Snowflakes and blizzards."

I look back and stumble, as well. Rising pale in the moonlight is the abandoned castle we hiked to a few days ago—and that door I couldn't open before stands wide open now. "How did we end up here?" Where are the stables?

A slim figure appears in the doorway, moonlight splashing across grave features as she scans the area. Niklas and I duck behind the tree—but not before I recognize the woman.

Ina Donath.

Thirty-Three

Gina—Nov 30 Workshop Jitters

Flitterndorf

Perched on the miniature couch in Tinsel's living room, knees level with my chest, I wait for Kristof to take me to the Workshop, much like I waited last night for him to bring me to Flitterndorf. My parents' pained looks had dogged me around the house as I pulled together a week's worth of belongings into one of Logan's old duffle bags. I would have crumpled beneath their concern had Aunt Cat's covert smiles not lent me strength.

Chimes on the Kuchler's cuckoo clock announce the half hour. My knee bounces, and I pinch the wristlet holding my phone and a bottle of mistlefeude. I told myself to wait until I'm situated among the Doll Makers before applying the elixir, but my nerves could do with a spritz right now.

Tinsel's mom, Kandi, emerges from the kitchenette, a human-sized mug dwarfing her petite hands. "Here, *Liebchen*. Some drinking chocolate to encourage you on your first day of work."

First day of work. My insides flop about like a hooked fish. You'd think I was some young teenager embarking on her first job. To be fair, we are talking about Santa's Workshop.

I force my knee to still and take the steaming mug with a breathy, "Thank you." The combo of salted caramel and chocolate hits my tongue, and my eyes widen. Then they close, and I melt into the tiny couch cushions. My first Kandi Cup. "This is heaven in a mug."

Kandi chuckles. "I thought you might be a salted-caramel kind of girl. Niklas is a steadfast peppermint guy, whereas Tinsel tries each new flavor I create."

My mouth lifts as I recall their orders at the Huggamugg Café over the years. "Kristof's dark chocolate all the way, isn't he?"

She nods, squints at me, and smiles broadly. "Like the color of your eyes."

The possible connection shouldn't bring me pleasure, and I hide behind another swallow, another moment of bliss. "How does Tinsel endure my paltry attempt at drinking chocolate when she has *this* at home?"

Kandi pats my hand. "I could share a secret or two with you while you're here."

"Would you?" I get giddy all over again. "That would be amazing."

In the background, the clock ticks away the seconds. With an occasional *pop*, flames dance in a fireplace outlined by tiles painted in Christmas-themed rosemaling. Blue Willow china plates dress the windows overlooking the Town Square, while vintage cooking utensils and worn heirlooms decorate the walls and occupy floor space. Two inset shelves display a collection of medals and trophies.

Old-world charm melds seamlessly with the present, much like what I found in the Kringles' apartment. Something deep within me hungers in response.

"This is surreal." My grip tightens around the mug. "When I was a child, I dreamed of living in Santa's village. Most kids probably do, but how many of them realize one day that their hometown practically borders Santa's village?" I grin. "Or that they've befriended a Christmas elf?"

Kandi chuckles again, then her lips drift downward. "Have you heard from Tinsel much since she arrived in Germany?"

Her wistful tone keeps me from mentioning the book-length texts I have yet to read. "Occasionally. You must be thrilled for her. Going abroad. Meeting new people. Gaining new experiences."

"Yes. Provided she doesn't expose her ears, I suspect she's in a better place at the moment."

"Oh?"

"It's no secret something strange is going on with us elves lately." Kandi gestures at me. "You wouldn't be here, otherwise. Everyone complaining. Questioning. Discontent. Wishing for—" She clears her throat and smooths the long skirts of her dirndl. "I'm not innocent of these things, mind you. Just aware." Her voice drops. "And concerned."

Does she suspect the dark shadow Aunt Cat mentioned?

"Never mind the prattling of a middle-aged elf." Kandi waves aside her words and stands. "Enjoy your day, Gina. I must join my boys downstairs. Chocolates don't make themselves." She winks and leaves by way of the apartment's back staircase.

Once her footsteps fade, I withdraw the mistlefeude from my wristlet and hurry to her bedroom. A few spritzes on her comforter should clear away the disquiet in her eyes.

* * *

Kristof arrives minutes later, a dark gray fisherman's sweater hugging his torso, his legs clad in green lederhosen. My stomach swirls at another visual of old-world charm. He smiles, and my mouth goes dry.

Settling behind him on the snowmobile, I tamp down this developing chemistry. It serves no purpose and promises heartbreak. No, thank you.

We pull away from The Flaky Crust and wend around the Town Square with its gigantic snow globe. A pungent odor momentarily eclipses Kristof's sandalwood scent, jarring a memory, but the village's miniature scale distracts me as we ride through the narrow streets. I savor the sights like I savored Kandi's cocoa.

Soon, the houses give way to an open area that stretches to meet the pine-and-snow-covered hill I first ascended, bound and gagged. (Current position much preferred.) Kristof points to our left, calling above the engine, "Over there's the hockey rink. Herr Trainer coached the Tiny Tykes while I was overseas, and the plan was for me to resume my duties once I came back."

"'Was'? That's not the plan anymore?"

"Not now, anyway. I won't have time while filling in for Grandpop at the Workshop."

"You love coaching hockey."

"The Workshop is more important, especially with Christmas on the line. Besides"—Kristof shrugs—"this isn't the first time I've had to ignore what I want."

I mull over his words as we ascend Huff 'n Puff Hill's switchbacks. In the distance, the mountains rim the horizon like a wall, hemming us in. Hemming in Kristof? How often has he put off what he wants for the sake of family duty? I would have thought that, as second-born, he'd have more freedom in his life's choices than Niklas.

When he parks outside the Workshop and kills the engine, I hitch my chin at the craggy view. "Do the mountains ever make you feel claustrophobic? Do the elves ever begrudge their confines?"

"Some do. Tinsel's great-grandmother did, likening the Clandy-Stein Mountains to prison walls. She left, then returned when she realized they were walls of protection." Kristof leans close, extending a hand toward the mountain peaks. "To the southwest, you have Mount Gnade and Mount Frieden. To the east, you have Mount Trost. Then there're Mounts Freude, Hoffnung and Liebe." He catches my eye, his own shining. "In English, Gina, we're surrounded by mercy, peace, comfort, joy, hope, and love."

We dismount the SnoMo and head for the Workshop entrance. "So, you don't feel confined?"

"No. There's freedom in boundaries." He opens one of the grand doors, motioning for me to precede him. "Freedom, though not necessarily my future."

Another comment I want to unpack, but as we step into the warm interior, Meister K puffs down the stairs to our right.

"Good, you're here," he calls to us. "Kristof, I need you in my office immediately."

"Yes, sir. As soon as I get Gina set up at her new job."

"I'm afraid we don't have time for that. I must get to the Prep Stables and"—Meister K adjusts his spectacles, his eyebrows pulling together—"Frau Bereits has quit. You'll have to pull double-duty between my job and hers until I can find a replacement."

"Uh, come again?"

Meister K runs his thumbs up and down his suspenders. "She said something about always wanting to work in textiles, and that the way we allocate jobs for the elves is unfair." His blue eyes glisten behind his lenses. "How is it unfair to give elves an education that helps them discover their talents, and afterward, give them jobs in those respective fields?" He shakes his head. "Why would Frau Bereits work for me for ten years without breathing a word of discontent? Did you know she was unhappy?"

"Grandpop, I've been gone for eleven months."

"Is this why more elves quit each day? Because they're unhappy?"

Meister K pulls at his beard. "They should come talk to me about it first."

I bump Kristof's shoulder with mine. "Go help your grandfather. I can find my way to the Production Wing." I hope. "I was there, like, five days ago."

His eyes crinkle. "You couldn't find your way out of a Christmas stocking, let alone back to a place you visited in a semi-state of shock." His attention flits past me, and he lifts a hand. "Herr Bücher!" A green-clad elf hurries up to us. "Herr Bücher, this is Gina Donati. She'll be working with the Doll Makers for the week. Would you please show her to the PD Wing?"

The elf gives a slight bow and too-bright smile. "Yes, sir. I'd be happy to."

As soon as we move out of earshot of the Kringles, however, Herr Bücher begins to grumble. "Happy to? Happy to? Of course I'm not happy. What do they take me for, a tour guide? That because I'm away from my desk I have nothing to do? Well, I have news for them. Thanks to the walk-out the other day, I'm swamped with work. I'd leave myself if I … if I …" He stops in the middle of a nondescript hallway, fists on his hips. "Why don't I leave?"

"Because you love what you do?" I suggest, forcing my own too-bright smile. "Because you're an elf who helps make Christmas morning magical for children worldwide?"

The elf blinks. He relaxes and his eyes soften. "The children. Of course. Wonderful squirts." He scratches his head. "Funny. I forgot about them for a minute. Well"—he waves me along—"*los gehts.* Let's go. The PD Wing is out of my way, but I'm happy to do anything for Santa."

This time Herr Bücher sounds like he means it. I cast him a wary glance, fingering my wristlet and following him along corridors and through doorways. Earlier, I'd decided to first take stock of where mistlefeude would be best utilized before liberally spreading my cache of liquid treasure, yet one extra spritz while I fortify myself won't do any harm.

As we travel down the hallway that houses the lone Production door on the right, I withdraw the bottle and spray my neck. A hint of jasmine billows into the air. Discretely, I spray in Herr Bücher's direction when he reaches for the door. He sneezes. Blinks. Huffs with a frown. "We're here. My task is done." He marches back the way we came, grumbling about Santa and his job duties again.

Wow. I hope Ina has several liaisons working for her here. Infusing joy into these elves will require far more mixture than I have with me.

Thirty-Four

Gina—Nov 30 Doll Makers

The first hour working with the Doll Makers goes as well as one can expect when one is an outsider joining a party to which she kinda invited herself. I have an ally in Bellamy, however. She seats me at the wig-making table and goes over their routine and procedures, shows me where they stock supplies, and how they check their list of children's doll requests against Santa's official list. Twice.

Armed with mistlefeude's confidence and skill, I catch on quickly and settle into a groove, knotting lengths of yarn around thin wooden dowels and combing out their fibers. I amass a decent pile in my work area before picking up the straight iron—the elf-sized straight iron, which my palm swallows. Drat. Why didn't I think to bring my own doll-making gadgetry? If I don't burn myself at least once before lunch, I'll consider myself blessed.

I operate the iron in a careful hold, and a snicker issues across the table from the one elf who hasn't introduced himself. "Hope you're not as clumsy as your friend."

"My friend?"

"He means Tinsel," Jipper says beside him. They have the same face, except Jipper has kinder eyes.

The other elf glowers, scoops up his dowels and wefts, and moves to another table. Jipper loads his dowel with more yarn. "Don't mind Jopper. He's in a snit because Leela broke up with him last night."

"Leela from the ski shop?" Bellamy lines up inch-wide sections of ironed, multi-colored yarn on a plastic surface.

Jipper nods. "She thinks jobs in the Workshop are more important than those in Flitterndorf-proper. Said she'd hinder Jopper from future prospects or promotions if they continued their relationship."

I pull the straight iron along my brushed yarn to make it smooth and shiny. "She broke up with him because of some hypothetical future job?"

"It wouldn't have worked out, anyway." Bellamy applies glue along the top edge of her sections. "She's Green, he's Red."

"Oh?" I iron the yarn a third time. "Is that a problem?"

"It never was before."

"Then why is it a problem now?"

Bellamy opens her mouth and shuts it again with a puzzled brow. "I don't know."

I hide my confusion, and an awkward silence cloaks the table. Shifting in the child-sized chair, I nod to Bellamy's wefts drying on the plastic sheet. "Did you decide on a wig for the goth doll you were making last week?"

Her little nose screws up. "No, I'm still stymied, so I switched to a different project for the moment." Capping the glue, she slumps. "This has never happened before. Why am I stuck?"

"You're making too much out of a wig," Jipper says, working his yarn through his straight iron.

I shake my head. "I don't think so." They raise their brows. "I used to be a hairstylist, and if there's one thing I learned, it's to never underestimate the effects of a cut, style, or color. A good style can enliven a soul as easily as a bad style can douse it, whether we're talking about a person or a doll."

"Then you must help." From a zippered bag beside her chair, Bellamy pulls out the goth head. "I was going to make a black wig, but that's boring. Expected. This warrants something different."

I cradle the head, assessing painted lashes around empty eye sockets, faint rosy cheeks, lips cocked in a mischievous expression. "You haven't baked it."

"I don't dare. Not before I can mentally picture his wig."

"Color of his eyes?"

"Purple."

Closing my own eyes, I envision the possibilities. "What about pale mint green hair with an exaggerated spiky cut?" I straighten and smile. "Since you haven't sent him to the kilns yet, you could add a facial element. You know, like a tattoo on his cheek. Nothing too edgy. Maybe a soft scroll design. It would totally give him character and—" I cover my mouth, my gaze jumping between Bellamy's and Jipper's wide eyes. "I'm sorry. I got carried away."

"Why apologize? It's nice to see someone passionate around here again." Bellamy takes the doll head and places it back in her bag. "If you ask me, we've become a morose group."

Jipper nods, and we return to our individual tasks. A number of chairs remain vacant in the loft, even though it's now mid-morning. Empty chairs represent work not getting done, dolls not being made. Dolls that children specifically asked for.

It'll be okay, I reassure myself. Once the mistlefeude takes effect, the elves will come back in time to make quota.

Noon arrives and slowly the area empties as workers leave for lunch. I remain hunched over a doll's head, pressing a weft of hair into place with a minuscule wooden tool. New wig ideas fill my brain faster than I can implement them.

"Tell me—"

I jump at the deep voice near my ear as Kristof crouches beside me. He chuckles.

"Is the reason you're not answering my texts," he continues, an impish grin tugging at his mouth, "because you're absorbed in your work, or are you blowing me off?"

His presence brightens the loft's atmosphere. "What texts?" I ask. "My phone's been quiet all morning."

"I wanted to know if you'd join me for lunch. When you never responded, I decided to ask you the old-fashioned way. Face-to-face."

Wincing, I dive into my wristlet for my phone. "I put it on airplane mode so I wouldn't get distracted on my first day. Sorry."

Kristof's grin widens. "No rejection?"

"No rejection."

"Then you'll have lunch with me?"

Bellamy stiffens beside me, her mouth tight as she continues to work. I glance at my doll's head, analyzing where to glue the next weft. "I shouldn't leave right now. A Frau Spielen came by earlier. She says we're falling behind and must work faster."

"Gina." Kristof lays a hand on mine, stilling my movements. His eyes are a captivating mix of green and gold bands. "Making toys requires creativity, but creativity is fickle. It will flee if you don't take a breather once in a while. As your quasi-boss, I insist you both"—he glances at Bellamy—"enjoy a lunch break or you will be useless to me this afternoon."

Considering his electric touch has shorted out my brain, I'm already useless. "So, concern for my productivity is what prompted your invite to lunch?"

"No, G." He draws a lazy circle on the back of my hand, sending shivers up my arm. "I just want your company."

* * *

Kristof brings me to the Workshop cafeteria, where I attempt to load an elf-sized tray with a Greek salad, a baguette, and a bowl of homemade lobster bisque—times two since the portions are small. Smiling, Kristof produces a human-sized tray, and I gratefully transfer my dishes. I'm about to fill a to-go cup with coffee from a machine when he stops me again and leads me back to the coffee kiosk in the Production Wing.

"They serve better hot drinks here," he says as we approach the thigh-high counter.

I quirk my eyebrow. "As long as my food's still warm by the time we sit down to eat."

He brandishes an arm toward the nearest wall. "There's a microwave, Your Highness, if the temperature doesn't meet your expectations."

"Thank you, kind sir. Such information is extremely valuable."

"To think I gave it away for free." We share a playful grin before he turns to the barista and orders a mocha. To me, he asks, "Is a caramel latte still your favorite?"

"Yes. How'd you know?" He wasn't the one working at the Huggamugg Café, learning customers' preferences.

"I observe." Kristof nods to the barista, and she moves away to prepare our drinks.

"I observe things, too. Why didn't you order your usual drinking chocolate?"

A half-laugh escapes him, and he gives a sheepish shrug, toying with a straw wrapper on the countertop. "You and Kandi are the only two who get it the way I like."

Warm fuzzies burst like fireworks inside me. "Europe didn't convert you into a tea or coffee addict?"

He wads the wrapper between his fingers, his gaze catching mine. "I will forever be in love with dark hot chocolate."

Kandi's earlier words about my eyes spring to mind, and my cheeks grow warm. Must deflect. "So, your grandmother's adage holds true."

His brow furrows as he accepts our drinks from the barista and sets them on his tray.

"When she said once you fall for something, it's unlikely something else will tempt you away." We choose a secluded table in the corner, and I sink into a chair with a tufted red gingham cushion.

Kristof's lips part in a smile. Definitely nice lips. "She was referring to people, not hot drinks."

I pluck my latte from his tray. "Specifically, she was referring to your crush."

"We're not going there, G." Kristof takes a bite of his sandwich.

I stare at him while uncapping my soup and stirring it with my spoon. Waiting.

He rolls his eyes. "I'm surrounded by three-foot females, Gina. Who would I crush on?"

"You're a warm-blooded, eighteen-year-old guy." I knock his leg with mine under the table. "You've crushed on a girl at least once."

His leg knocks back, but he doesn't deny it.

"So?" I take a sip of bisque.

"So what?"

"Does she still have your heart?"

Kristof hesitates. I hold my breath. Why does his answer matter to me? He smiles over the sandwich, his lone dimple materializing. It doesn't come around as often as Niklas's, which is a relief since my stomach trips every time. "Yes. She does."

My spine straightens at a new thought. "She's more than a crush. You have a girlfriend."

Kristof freezes, like a reindeer in headlights. Caught. Exposed.

A foreign, sickly substance coats my insides. I squirm. "Kristof Kringle, you never told me you were dating anyone. Is she from Russia? Germany? It's Germany, isn't it? That's why your texts became random once you transferred there."

Confusion joins the shock in his expression. "Random?"

I swirl the bisque with my spoon. "You texted nonstop from Russia—about your internship, how welcoming your distant relatives were, the crazy stories your cousin-thrice-removed told at dinner. You even sent pics of your meals. Then you went to visit the Kringles in Germany, and your texts, like, dried up." Kristof scoffs and takes another bite. I lean forward, the soup's steam warming my face. "What happened in Germany? Your great-uncle's grandkids live with him. Did you fall for the girl?"

He wrinkles his nose. "Elke's my second cousin."

"You fell for her best friend."

"She's also fourteen."

"Love can wait."

His gaze finds mine. "Can it?"

"Why not?"

"Because we live in a day when people want what they want when they want it."

"True." I scoop a wedge of potato. "But then, that's not love."

"Hmm." Kristof contemplates me as he chews. "Well, my silence had nothing to do with a girl. I came across a ... complication ... that required most of my attention. Unfortunately, I think parts of it followed me back to Flitterndorf."

"You mean the stuff happening with the reindeer and elves." Brought on, most likely, by Krampus. To whom I'm related. The reminder lands like claws upon my shoulders. "I did notice a number of empty chairs in here before lunch."

Kristof looks from station to station around the vast room. "More elves walked out an hour ago from both Assembly and Carpentry."

"What?" I set down my spoon. "Why are you wasting your time with me? You should—"

"I need the distraction." A shadow skims across his features. "Whatever's going on, I hate that it's affecting the elves and stealing their joy. Take Bellamy, for instance. She grows more serious every day."

"I'm sorry." I want to reach for him. Instead, I poke at a bread crumb on the tabletop. "You'll figure this out. I know you will."

"Glad one of us has confidence in me." Kristof sits back and kneads his neck. "As it is, I don't know what to do about Grandpop. He woke up this morning, ranting about taking an immediate vacation—with Christmas less than four weeks away. What will he do when he finds out this latest group of elves quit? Start packing?"

I flick the crumb, and it shoots onto the floor. "I won't tell if you won't."

An ironic smile tugs his lips. "With anyone else, that might work. Santa, on the other hand, has an irritating knack for figuring out who's been naughty or nice."

Thirty-Five

Gina—Nov 30 Broken Vessel

Laying aside the straight iron, I flex my fingers and eye the basket I'm using to corral my growing pile of yarn wefts. I've set myself up to cruise through several wigs tomorrow, and I still have fifteen minutes before five o'clock, when my first day comes to an official end. Who knew I could see such productivity in one sitting!

I take my phone off airplane mode and wait as several texts chime in. One's from Mum, two from Aunt Cat, and a recent one from Tinsel.

I read hers first to make up for the fact I still haven't read her earlier texts.

There are days I wish I had a desk job like yours. You claim it's boring, but boring is underrated sometimes. ;)

My heart plummets. Niklas hasn't told her I'm in Flitterndorf? Does that mean she still doesn't know about the reindeer? **It's almost one in the morning over there,** I reply. **You're still awake?**

Three dots undulate, then: **I'm meeting Niklas in a few min for another night of snooping (found a creepy science lab last night).**

Wanted to catch up w/ you first. What's new on your side of the globe?

Um, everything. And I can't breathe a word of it—not even (especially even!) about Krampus. But another message comes in, saving me from having to answer.

Hey, you never showed me that doll you were working on. How'd it come out?

I didn't? Hold on a sec. I scroll through my photo app and send her the video I'd sent Kristof yesterday. Gracious, a lot has happened in twenty-four hours.

After a moment, my phone buzzes again. **Gina, they're stunning!! Santa needs you on his team. :D**

Funny she should mention that.

Beside me, Bellamy stands with a stretch and pushes in her chair. "Time to call it a day." She studies my wefts and the few wigs I've partially completed. "Nice work. Santa will be impressed." She smiles. "You know your way out?"

Not exactly. "I'm hoping to catch Kristof before I leave. He's working in Meister K's office. Do you know how I can get there from here?"

Once Bellamy gives me detailed instructions that I type into my phone, I finish ironing my last few dowels, straighten my workspace, and head down the stairs per her instructions. Though I recognize where I am through the first few directives, I soon enter unfamiliar territory. And when I should be staring at a door with "an oversized metal candy cane hanging in the center," I stare at a dead end, instead. The hallway I've traveled down stops at a window with a view of hills, trees, and snow.

I study the many doors lining the hall. Fine. I'll check every one.

Three conference rooms, a broom closet, and one stairwell later, I open the next door to find wood pieces scattered at my feet. The hallway light reflects off a lone bulb in the ceiling, and I pull the cord dangling beside it.

The room is little more than a glorified closet. In the middle stands a jagged, wooden structure in the process of being built—or rather, reconstructed. Broken lengths of wood litter the floor, their ends splintered and cracked. Some have been joined together like puzzle pieces, and they lean against the base of the busted ... what even *is* this structure? A dresser? Cabinet?

A wardrobe.

Tinsel was temporarily banished for destroying a wardrobe a couple of years ago. Is this the same one? I pull out my phone and snap a pic. Once Nik tells Tinsel everything that's going on, I'll send this and ask.

But why would someone bother rebuilding something so fractured and unsalvageable? Even if the person succeeds in connecting every piece, it won't be structurally sound to function properly.

More pieces cover a narrow table to my right, above which hangs a calendar tacked to the wall. I venture closer. Red "X's" cross out each previous day in November, marking the month almost complete. A pale green post-it note with handwritten words clings to the calendar at the bottom. **Must be ready by Krampuslauf.**

Krampuslauf. Is that related to the Krampusnacht Kristof had mentioned?

I flip the calendar to December. Red marker encircles the first Saturday. Obscured by the circle's bottom arc is the printed word *Krampusnacht*. An arrow points to the previous Thursday, and in the same script as the post-it note, someone has written: **Krampuslauf in Brückenstadt**. That's three days from now.

I chew the inside of my cheek. Why is it so important this wardrobe gets ready by then? What is meant by "ready"? And what does Brückenstadt have to do with it?

On the table beneath the calendar, a wooden emblem sits among the pieces. Broken in two, its familiar branches crisscross, blending into rounded leaves and berry clusters. My heart pounds. The last time I saw this emblem, it brought me to an office in Brückenstadt. I glance at the busted wardrobe, its incomplete doorway gaping at me. Once repaired, will it bring a traveler to Brückenstadt, too?

A door closes in the distance, and I jump. In case this room is off-limits, I pull the cord to extinguish the light and leave the room to resume my search for Meister K's office.

I haven't gone five steps when Meister K himself turns down the hallway, tugging at his beard. "Spoiled ... that's what ... become," he mumbles. "Take me for granted ... Ungrateful, like the elves—Oh." Seeing me, he lifts his eyebrows. "Gina. H-how was your first day on the job? I trust everyone treated you well."

"Yes, sir. I had fun."

"*Ausgezeichnet.*" He glances around, then frowns. "Are you looking for something or someone in particular?"

"Kristof, actually. I think he's in your office. Bellamy gave me directions, but I managed to get mixed up, anyway."

Meister K gives a strained smile. "I believe there's a new app for that." He asks for my phone, downloads a Santa's Workshop Map, and locates where we're standing among the Workshop's many floors. After tapping the screen a few more times, he hands it back. "The red dot is you. The green line will bring you to Kristof."

"Thank you, sir."

He waves and shuffles along the hallway. As I head in the opposite direction, tracking the green line, he slips into the same room I left moments ago.

He's rebuilding the wardrobe? Why?

* * *

Five minutes later, I approach the large oak door Bellamy told me about, the oversized candy cane decoration listing to the left. I straighten it, and the door opens a few inches. Kristof's voice carries through the gap. Another voice follows, sounding tinny. Speakerphone?

"You know what their continued rebellion means." The voice belongs to a female. "We got lazy. The good times and prosperity we've enjoyed these last few decades have lulled us into complacency, and we allowed Krampus to flourish in his hidey-hole."

"We'll make it right, Gram. It's not too late."

"No. No. Never too late. Sometimes, our bleakest moments usher in the greatest miracles."

Kristof grunts. "I'll be sure to pass that along to Nik."

"Oh?"

A chair creaks, followed by a tap-tap-tapping. "He claims the Silver Reindeer attacked Tinsel yesterday when they were in Salzburg."

"But the legend says the SR is on our side."

"Apparently, the live version doesn't hold to legend, Gram. Besides which, Tinsel's lost her ability to communicate with reindeer."

Madam Anne sighs. "That complicates matters."

"Nik also mentioned something called mistlefoil. You ever heard of that?"

"No. Frau Chemiker might have."

Do they mean mistle*feude*?

"He was going to do more research and get back to me and Grandpop," Kristof says. *Tap tap.* "By the way, where *is* Grandpop? I haven't seen him all day."

"He's working on a project. Told me not to expect him for dinner. What about you?" Madam Anne asks. "Will you be home for dinner or have you become a workaholic in so short a time?"

Kristof chuckles. "Yes, I'll be there. Give me ten minutes."

They sign off, and I press my lips together. Does it count as eavesdropping when the door's ajar and one party is on speakerphone? I smooth out my tunic dress and knock.

"Come in."

Pushing the door wide, I give a tentative smile. Kristof sits at a large table strewn with gizmos and gadgets, his phone propped on the surface beside him as he taps the toe of his hockey stick against a table leg.

His face brightens. "This is a nice surprise. What's the occasion?"

Feeling superficial in the wake of his somber phone call, I shrug. "Came to say goodnight." I pick up a metal toy axle from the table, useless with one wheel. "Wanted to see a friendly face before I left."

"You didn't get lost on your way?" Kristof's smile widens. "I'm impressed."

Should I tell him *I* know where his grandfather is? "It seems someone at the Workshop devised a map app while you were away." I fit a spring over the one-wheeled axle. "What're you working on?"

"Supposed to be making toys."

"I thought the elves made the toys."

Kristof leans his forehead against the shaft of the hockey stick. "They make most of them. But Santa does his part. Usually. With Grandpop focused on his ailing reindeer, however"—(or tinkering in small rooms with broken furniture)—"he hasn't the time to make toys. So, it falls to his grandson to do the job for him." Kristof's gaze narrows at the table's surface. Many parts. No assembled toys. "How hard can it be, right? Niklas could do it with a stocking pulled over his head."

"And yet?"

He flicks a random bolt with his finger. "Turns out making toys is harder than it looks. And for many toys, if one part is out of whack, the whole thing can't operate."

"Like the Workshop," I murmur, rolling the one-wheeled axle in a circle atop the table. "Talk to Nik. Does he have to attend this Initiation Ceremony? What if you two switched places?"

His mouth quirks. "Eager to get rid of me, huh?" He rises from the chair, giving the hockey stick an absentminded twirl, and moves to the windows behind Meister K's desk. To the left, a picture has been flipped to hang backward on the wall. Weird.

"Couldn't you have done something to help while you were in Germany before?"

"I'm not the future Santa. Plus, with Nik already scheduled to fly out, my family needed me here."

I pinch the tiny spring. "So that's why you came home early."

He nods. "Leaving a piece of my heart behind."

His heart? Oh, he means his mystery girlfriend.

An image flashes in my mind of some nameless, flirty, blonde chick with "dark chocolate eyes," perfect skin, and a flouncy dress. Cute-as-a-button, like a doll I'd seen waiting on the shelf labeled *Fertig*, German for "finished" (yes, I had to ask).

I drop the spring and axle on the table. Kristof's love life doesn't concern me. "Well, with everything going on, your grandparents must be grateful to have you around." When he responds with another distracted nod, I take that as my cue to leave. "See you tomorrow, yeah? Let me know if I can help in any way before then."

"You spent the last seven hours helping me."

With a soft laugh, I reach for the doorknob. "You know what I mean."

Movement sounds behind me, and the toe of Kristof's hockey stick hooks around my waist. "G, wait. You got dinner plans?"

I face him, crossing my arms. "Tinsel's family might be expecting me, and your grandmother's expecting you."

"If I cleared our schedules, will you have dinner with me?"

The hockey stick presses into my back, forcing me to step forward. "I'd suspect you of trying to finagle a date out of me, except I now know you've got a girlfriend."

Kristof snorts. "If believing that is what gets you to hang out tonight …" He tugs the toe toward him, hand over hand on the shaft, and I stumble along with it. "How is it you can be brilliant and completely dense at the same time?"

"*I'm* dense? I figured out you have a girlfriend—something your grandmother doesn't even know."

He draws me ever closer, a lop-sided grin playing about his mouth. Fireworks shoot off inside me, and I try to corral them.

"Dinner, G. Yes or no?"

"What will the elves think?"

"Do I care what the elves think?"

"We don't want them getting the wrong idea."

Kristof pulls until I'm so close, he fills my entire view with his Christmas-candy scrumptiousness. An unspoken current pulses between us. "Guaranteed they'll jump to all sorts of wrong conclusions, Donati," he murmurs. His eyes dance, more brown than green in this light. "So whaddaya say? Want to help contribute to the rumor mill?"

Would he flirt like this if he had a girlfriend?

But I can't entertain the possibility that Kristof's single. Some nameless girlfriend of his is just what I need to force my interest elsewhere and prevent a romance destined to fail. Because I will fail, and our friendship will be ruined. I can't have that on my conscience.

So, someone please explain why I respond to his banter with a smile?

Thirty-Six

Gina—Dec 1 More Than Coffee Brewing

Flitterndorf

My smile temporarily falters the next morning as I glare at my dead phone and shimmy into a pair of leggings. After spending hours with Kristof last night—dining at his favorite restaurant, The Pleasing Palate, then meandering the streets bundled in our coats, yakking until we yawned ourselves into incoherency—I forgot to charge my phone. When it died overnight, it took the alarm feature with it.

Now I have ten minutes to ready myself before Kristof arrives.

I accomplish it in seven despite reliving last night's most memorable moments. Like when I said something witty enough that Kristof's dimple made another appearance. Or when he slid a finger along my wrist to get my attention. Or when he gave me another delicious hug goodnight.

Dreamy sigh.

The one downer to the evening was another unspoken reminder that Kristof wishes to return to Germany. Dare I hope his parents won't allow him that satisfaction for at least another year or two ...

or five or more?

Petulant sigh. My lagging spirits could use a Kandi Cup right now. Convenient that I don't have to travel far to find one.

I take the stairs two at a time, exit through the back door, and walk around to the shop's entrance. A line of elves snakes to the counter, behind which stands Tinsel's mother, eyebrows raised at the female customer opposite her.

"… remark on my dirndl?" says the customer in a shrill voice. "Why not simply say, 'It's lovely to see you today, Lulu'?"

"It's lovely to see you today, Lulu," Kandi responds. "I merely commented on your skirt's unique embroidery. The Green Clan can't boast such exquisite stitches."

Lulu raises her chin. "That's because you're inferior."

Kandi's posture stiffens. The other customers shift mutely, attuned to the face-off at the register. Even Tinsel's father, Pan, hovers at the kitchen door, flour dusting his forearms and apron.

"In the art of embroidery, perhaps," Kandi says. "But not in everything. Herr Schoko doesn't come close to replicating the succulent notes of my ganache."

Several elves elbow past me in their haste to leave, the bell jangling every time the door opens and shuts.

"He makes fabulous delicacies," Lulu hisses.

"Yet the Workshop has showcased *my* creations for the last five years in their cafeteria."

"Kandi." Pan pats her shoulder. "Let it go, *meine Liebe*."

"What are you saying?" Lulu flails her arms. "That the Green Clan is better than the Red?"

"If the stocking fits …."

Lulu scoffs. "You are nothing without the Red Clan."

"Prove it."

"I will, starting with my exit. And if you doubt my sway in the community, think again. This is the last time a member of the Red Clan sets foot in your shop."

Kandi crosses her arms. "Then I have no further reason to do business with *your* shop. Consider our order for the Sunrise Festival flyers canceled."

"Done." Whipping about on her heel, Lulu marches through the shop, nose in the air, cheeks red. Her eyes glisten with moisture.

As she sails out the doorway, I startle at Kristof's presence behind me, his gaze on Tinsel's mum. "I've never known Kandi to be baited into a quarrel," he murmurs, Red Clan members jostling against our hips as they exit in Lulu's wake.

I tug on a lock of my hair. After returning to the apartment last night and finding everyone asleep, I'd spritzed the air with mistlefeude. I even put a drop in the coffeemaker already set up for the morning brew. What went wrong?

Kristof sighs and motions us toward the door. "Let's go. My SnoMo's around the corner."

Outside, elves gather on the sidewalk, grumbling, complaining. Some whisper behind mittens, others argue outright, little fingers jabbing at little chests. I thought Aunt Cat said Ina has others working for her in Flitterndorf. How come things are getting worse?

I follow Kristof to his snowmobile. "I suppose it's too much to hope Meister K won't hear about this?"

"He won't." Kristof straddles the seat, his expression grave as he offers me a helmet. "Grandpop's gone."

Thirty-Seven

Tinsel—Dec 1 Just a Game

Weihnachts Manor

Snowflakes dance in the air and catch in my eyelashes. I blink them away. Pursing my lips around the cold metal whistle, I issue a series of blasts, and the reindeer trot in a line before me. I give another few tweets and they about-face, take two steps, and stop as commanded.

My gaze drifts toward the stables and its empty doorways. Where's Niklas? I check my phone messages again. He texted this morning before I'd even come down for breakfast, saying he had an errand to run with Meister Nico, and we could catch up after lunch. I told him he'd find me with the reindeer.

Lunch was a few hours ago. Thanks to yesterday's busy schedule filled with a lengthy dance practice, preparations for the Initiation Ceremony on Saturday, and private meetings involving Niklas but excluding me, we haven't had a chance to discuss the stables and science lab. I thought we'd chat last night when we were to meet up for more sleuthing, except he never showed.

And I have so many questions beyond the Santa-hating lab owner's identity.

Like, why does the lab connect to Weihnachts Manor? What's with those reindeer figurines? What unnerved Niklas in that book? What type of animal gets chained within the stables' humongous stalls? How did we end up escaping through an abandoned castle so far from the manor?

I can speculate all day with little to go on, yet I can't ignore the apprehension that shrouded me in that lab. Whoever heads up the experiments conducted there, they're not "friendlies," as Niklas suggested.

"Focus, Tinsel."

The whistle tumbles from my fingers. I shoot Fritz a tight smile and pluck the whistle from the ground. "Sorry." Blowing off flecks of snow and dead grass, I glance at the expectant reindeer. "Is it me, or are there even fewer reindeer than yesterday?" Bonbon is still missing, and now Muskat has gone MIA.

Fritz shrugs though worry lines crease his brow. "Come. Practice."

I bring the whistle to my lips. "I don't suppose you know where Niklas is?"

"You have a phone." He gives an impatient flick of his hand. "Do you not text?"

"He hasn't answered."

"Maybe he does not want to be found." Fritz gives three long blasts with his whistle, and the reindeer prance in a circle. "Gretel was going to stop by before lunch. Perhaps they are somewhere together."

I know he says it to get a reaction from me, so I refrain from making a face. *Relax. She taught you how to tie a hemp bracelet yesterday and reapplied essential oil to your choker. She's not after your fiancé.* "Do you like her?" I blurt out.

Fritz looks away. "Gretel is off-limits to me."

"So that's a *yes*."

His expression darkens. "I am not the best choice for her."

"Says who?"

"Does not matter. I want what is her best."

"And that is ...?"

Fritz points his whistle at my engagement ring. "Niklas proposed to you, yet he will not marry you. We are pawns in this game. Accept it, before you get hurt worse."

I gape at him. "I'm not playing any ga—"

An elf bursts from the stables and looks wildly about the area. Spotting Fritz, he fires off a rapid slew of German. Fritz scowls, whistles a command at the reindeer, and as they break formation to graze, he follows the elf from the field. No backward glance, no promise to explain himself later.

* * *

I return to the manor, where elves continue to prepare the first-floor rooms and ballroom for the surge of exclusive guests arriving on Saturday. My dress hangs in the wardrobe upstairs, a symbol of hope, commitment, excitement. I'm supposed to be introduced as Niklas's fiancée that evening, but Fritz's comment sours my anticipation.

Pausing by the Norway spruce, I remove from my wrist the hemp bracelet I attempted to make yesterday and place it on a lower branch. This poor tree needs a pick-me-up as much as I do. My gaze falls to the dingy packages underneath. And the elves need a review on how to properly wrap a Christmas present.

Sharp heels click across the entrance hall floor. "No, no, no," a woman says, approaching the spruce from the other side. Its thick branches obscure her face. "She agreed to this. There's no backing out," the woman continues in perfect English. "We do not give up that easily."

235

Ina Donath. Is she talking on the phone? I shift to keep the tree between us as she walks past, my heartbeat rushing in my ears.

"Niklas is not your average guy," she says. "The girl he marries will be the future Mrs. Claus. A woman with position. Influence. Power. We need that power on our side." She pauses, then laughter bursts from her as her heels march toward the morning room. "When was the last time an elf became Mrs. Claus? We need the right lineage, and Tinsel is not worthy. Niklas must be convinced he made the wrong choice." Another pause. "So increase the mistlefoil."

Mistlefoil. Niklas mentioned that word last night, his tone implying he knows what it is.

A shout issues from far off, and the woman sighs. "What is the fool mismanaging now?" Her steps click in a new direction.

I remain frozen until her footsteps have completely faded and the elves working in the entrance hall send me odd looks. Why would Ina want to sabotage my engagement? Is *she* Krampus? Whatever the answer, mistlefoil seems to be involved, and might even be part of the game Fritz mentioned.

My fingernails dig into my palms. I refuse to be anyone's pawn or play according to their rules.

Thirty-Eight

Tinsel—Dec 1 Missing Santa

Weihnachts Manor

More galvanized than ever to find Niklas, I begin my search with the common rooms on the ground floor. After peeking into an empty breakfast room and equally empty morning room, I open the door to the music room. Meister Nico lifts his head where he's hunched over the grand piano, and Madam Marie turns from the window in the alcove.

I smile. "Sorry to interrupt. Do you know where Niklas is?"

Meister Nico depresses a key with his forefinger. "I think he and Gretel are in the ballroom, practicing for the ceremony."

My fingers tighten around the doorknob. "Just the two of them? But…" I trail off at the Kringles' serious expressions. "Is everything all right?" My thoughts jump from Niklas to Flitterndorf, to my family and worst-case scenarios.

Meister Nico waves me into the room, and I cross the floor to the piano. Madam Marie meets my gaze across its polished surface, her eyes red-rimmed. "Meister K is missing."

237

My mouth parts, and I lean into the piano for support. "Missing?"

"Kristof called a little bit ago," Meister Nico says, his voice rough and monotone, "to inform us my father left sometime during the night. It's unknown where he went or how he traveled, however, since the Big Eight and all SnoMos are accounted for. Mother and Kristof found a note from him on the kitchen counter that read more like a rant. He's tired of playing Santa and feels under-appreciated since the children only see him as a genie. He complains about the unmerited elf strikes—"

"Elf strikes?"

"—and claims we shouldn't give gifts to children who aren't *always* good." Meister Nico stands and paces the room. "He finished by saying he's taking a vacation, effective immediately."

"He'd never leave Flitterndorf this close to Christmas," Madam Marie says in a tone that implies they've already had this discussion.

"Yes, well, Mother admitted he hasn't been himself lately," Meister Nico snaps. I compress my lips at the uncharacteristic display.

"He didn't leave willingly," his wife maintains.

"Then, what?" Meister Nico grips his suspenders. "He was Santa-napped? Forced to leave? Rubbish. No one overpowers my father, let alone forces him to do anything, no matter his state of mind."

The lines about Madam Marie's mouth tighten, and she stares out the window again.

I hug my stomach. "What did the Clans say when they heard the news? Out of twenty-five hundred elves, someone's got to know something."

Madam Marie stiffens. Meister Nico clears his throat. "You're the only elf who knows."

"What?" On wobbly legs, I move to the piano bench and collapse onto its tufted cushion. A flowery scent hits my nose. "Why?"

Silence hangs in the air until Madam Marie says softly, "What do you think the elves will do, Tinsel, when they learn their boss—the linchpin of Christmas—has gone AWOL?"

My shoulders slump. "They'll freak out." I want to freak out.

"Exactly. Things are shaky enough there as it is."

I frown. "What's going on? You mentioned elf strikes?"

They exchange looks, and Meister Nico turns ashen. "Nicky didn't tell you?"

"Tell me what?"

Madam Marie sinks beside me and takes my hand. Uh-oh. "You know that something's been festering among the elves these past few months, yes?"

I nod.

"It's gotten worse since we left last week. Kristof has texted us daily about businesses warring along clan lines, walkouts at the Workshop, discontentment and jealousies rising. The elves aren't the only ones affected, however. The reindeer are also getting sick."

Her words sink in, the breath stalling in my lungs. "Which reindeer? How sick? Is it because of this mistlefoil?"

Madam Marie tilts her head. "I don't know anything about that. The sickness began among the herd near the Prep Stables." She places her other hand atop mine. "Some of them have died."

"A-and the Third String? They weren't feeling well when we left. Are they … did one of them …?" My throat closes over the question.

Meister Nico glares. "I'll have you know half my Second String is sick. Two of the Big Eight are ill. As for the Third String, has Nicky told you nothing? They went missing. Last week!"

A desolate chill sweeps over my heart like hoarfrost. "He didn't tell me." I swallow. "Why didn't he tell me?"

"That's what I'd like to know." Meister Nico harrumphs, his demeanor hardening. "What kind of engagement are you two playing at, that you don't communicate?"

"One that seems doomed to fail." I tug from Madam Marie's hold and rush from the room.

* * *

My legs tremble as I ascend the grand staircase. My eyes grow hot. I tug at my choker and suck in a breath. Why didn't Niklas tell me about the reindeer? *Why?* I rack my jumbled brain for a reason. Because he didn't want me to worry? Didn't want me to stress over something I couldn't change, being on the other side of the world?

Sprightly music drifts from the ballroom, grating against my internal conflict. Is it true that we could do nothing? I pinch the reindeer pendant between my fingers. Or did Niklas keep the truth hidden because he thought I'd bungle things in trying to help? Or maaaybe, he wanted me to look a fool in front of his parents. Give them more reason to question our engagement.

I choke on the bitter realization as I pause in the doorway to the ballroom. Niklas and Gretel whirl across the elegant floor, laughing into each other's eyes, their steps precise, smooth, coordinated. Two people moving as one.

That's it, isn't it? Our relationship was a setup for my epic failure. Niklas spent two years playing me. Perfect humiliation for a human-sized elf that has no business aspiring for more than mucking stalls.

Set him free. He belongs with Gretel.

Like it's done before, the notion flits through my mind, but this time it anchors itself. Talons hooking into their prey.

Or a lifeline keeping me from making a huge mistake?

I fidget with my engagement ring, suddenly too tight on my finger. *Gretel was meant for him,* soothes the notion. *If you love Niklas, you'll let him go. What can a talent-less elf offer the future Santa Claus? He needs a strong, competent woman by his side.*

The couple dances past, their outlines softening, and the atmosphere around them quivers. I rub my eyes. When I look again, they've paused in their dance, and a blurred Niklas cups Gretel's cheek, their heads angled close together.

Air whooshes from me like a reindeer kicked me in the stomach. I clutch the doorframe. Anger, betrayal, hurt, and sadness churn in my gut, warring for dominance. They coalesce into one bleak conclusion: if Niklas's heart belongs to another girl, why bother fighting the inevitable?

I push away from the doorframe, my shoes squeaking on the hardwood floor as I approach the couple. Niklas's gaze wobbles to mine, eyes flat. I twist off the engagement ring. "Here." The ring drops into his palm, and I close his fingers over it. "I can't do this anymore."

Niklas takes a ragged breath. "Tinsel." My name comes out strangled, and he looks wildly between me and Gretel. A flame rekindles in his eyes, and he backs away from her, a flush racing up his neck and into his cheeks. "Roasted chestnuts, I don't know what you saw—"

"Doesn't matter." I clench my teeth against the clog of tears. I. Will. Not. Cry. "I'm freeing you, Niklas."

"What?" Niklas opens his hand, and his face blanches at the ring. "No. Tins—"

"That's what you want, isn't it? You set up stumbling blocks for me along the way so that I'd look foolish. Unfit. Unworthy. But since you lied in order to accomplish it, how worthy does that make you?" Turning on my heel, I stride from the room.

"Tinsel, wait." Niklas hurries after me and plows between me and the top of the stairs. He lowers his voice. "Whatever you think you saw, I was helping Gretel get something out of her eye. That's all."

"Whoever believes that is an idiot."

He grips my upper arms. "You saw what Krampus wanted you to see. He's trying to split us apart by using mistlefoil."

"What even is mistlefoil?"

"I don't know."

"Then how do you know he's using it?"

"I saw it referenced in that lab book. How else can we explain these mind games?"

I scoff and break from his hold. "That's quite a jump, to go from a chemistry experiment to mind games. Yet it makes for a convenient excuse, blaming your antics on something abstract." Edging past him, I jog down the stairs.

Niklas jogs after me. "Tins, you gotta trust me."

"How many times will I hear that, before you own up to everything that's going on?" I spin about at the terrace doors. "When, exactly, were you planning to tell me about the Third String? Before or after I got home and faced a set of empty stalls?"

He winces, his gaze falling away. "I'm sorry. I didn't know how to tell you. You love those reindeer more than any of us—"

"That much is clear." I flail an arm toward the ballroom. "I can't believe you were up there, dancing like you haven't a care in the world, when your team disappeared a week ago."

Niklas pulls himself taut. "You think I don't worry about them?"

In the background, Gretel stands at the gallery railing, watching us. My eyes narrow. "Let's just say, you've spent less time searching for your furry, four-legged reindeer and more time attending to a curvy, two-legged brunette."

The muscles pulse in his jaw. "Kinda hard to track animals that can fly."

"An entire team of reindeer doesn't vanish without explanation."

"This team did. No rhyme or reason, no clues left behind. Just damage to the FTA's rear entrance to signal their escape. That's all

242

we've had to go on, Tinsel." Niklas jams a hand into his hair and whispers, "What if they left willingly? What if they don't want to serve a flight-averse Santa?"

"You mean a flight-averse, secretive Santa with a wandering eye? Maybe they're onto something, and the rest of us should follow their example."

The words shoot from my lips like barbed needles, impaling Niklas with stinging accuracy. Shock swirls across his features. I flee the manor before I can name the other emotions taking root.

Fresh sleet pelts the ground, and I slip and skid across the terrace, acid burning in my throat. Niklas once said I could empower or cripple him with my words. Shamefully, I've accomplished the latter. Doesn't he deserve it, though? Why should I feel guilty when *he* was the one making goo-goo eyes at another woman?

Dashing at my tears, I race past the elf village and into the woods beyond. My boots kick up slush against my shins. Cold seeps into my shirt sleeves, for I didn't stop to grab winter accessories, but anger heats my core. My lungs burn. The choker chafes my skin. I trip over a root hidden by debris and catch myself before I fall. Up and up the slope I run, no destination in mind, propelled by a need to escape, to breathe clean air—

The Silver Reindeer stands in the path ahead. I windmill to a stop, skidding in the slush. She raises her head, regal despite her small stature, her coat sparkling like sun-kissed diamonds despite the cloud bank and sleet. She steps forward.

I throw out my arms to ward her away, recalling her fond hello in Salzburg. "Listen, I've already lost my talent and just lost my guy. I'm in no mood to deal with you right now."

The SR sniffs the air, still approaching me.

"I'm serious. Stay back."

A branch snaps behind me. I glance over my shoulder, my romantic side hoping Niklas pursued me. Will I always be a sucker for his Kringle charm?

Antler tines thrust into my vision as heat flares along my neck. I cry out, stumble backward, and land on my rear. The SR shakes her antlers, a stringy object flying into the brush, and brays at me. Bobbing her head once more, she bounds away into the woods.

I stare after her and touch my throbbing neck. Sugarplums and figgy pudding, what was that about? If she wants to harm me, why not finish the job before racing off again? I pull my hand away and gulp at my blood-stained fingertips. Maybe she means for me to bleed out, alone in the woods.

The idea of returning to Weihnachts Manor tangles my insides, but I won't give the Silver Reindeer the satisfaction of killing me. I struggle to my feet. By the time I reach the side doors in an unfurnished part of the manor, the bleeding has stopped.

It's not until Poppy helps me disinfect and bandage the wound that I discover I no longer wear my choker.

Thirty-Nine

Gina—Dec 1 Got Questions?

Flitterndorf

I pace in front of the Workshop as the sun sets behind Mount Frieden. Swirling snowflakes create a snow globe effect on my hilltop view of Flitterndorf. Lights twinkle from windows, woodsmoke drifts above chimneys, fresh snow coats everything in soft white. From way up here, the scene looks like a classic Christmas movie, complete with sentimental mush. The close-up view reveals a disturbing reality.

Meister K is gone, the Clans are feuding, and the mistlefeude isn't working as intended. Aunt Cat says I'm expecting too much, too soon, since I've been here less than forty-eight hours, yet shouldn't it work as fast for the elves as it does for me?

The hum of a snowmobile carries on the breeze, and I peer along the visible section of switchbacks. Kristof? I pull my coat tighter. He's been searching for his grandfather all day, off the grid. I offered to help, but since he and Madam Anne are trying to keep a semblance of normalcy—as if Meister K simply fritters away in another section of the 'Shop—Kristof asked that I report to the loft for work instead.

Like that helped. Before I even had time to reapply the elixir on my wrists, Jipper greeted me with a scowl instead of a smile, looking frighteningly like his twin. After lunch (during which I ate alone), Bellamy's smile had cooled off, as well, and by one-thirty, a third of the chairs in the PD Wing sat vacant. It doesn't take a genius to know that the low volume on the Doll Makers' *Fertig* shelf is mirrored across all departments in the Workshop.

Kristof crests Huff 'n Pull Hill and pulls to a stop when he comes alongside me, letting the engine idle. A smile pushes at his lips, though it doesn't reach his eyes. "Waiting for me, or feeling hemmed in again?"

I cross my arms on a shiver. "I take it you didn't find him."

He blows out a breath, his shoulders falling. "No. I even checked his office at the Prep Stables, hoping something there would give me a hint as to what might've happened to him."

"You're sure he didn't take a vacation, like his note said." It's a question disguised as a statement. What if Santa got burnt out?

"Kringles don't vacation this time of year, Gina. And certainly not when it appears that Krampus is up to no good." He hitches his chin at the Workshop. "How'd it go in there today?"

I squeeze the tasseled ends of my scarf. "Considering some of the elves questioned what took both you and your grandfather away from the Workshop all day, it's a miracle we didn't have more than one walkout."

Kristof groans and tugs the brim of his beanie over his eyes.

"They also don't like that you're replacing the elves with strangers from outside." I tie two tassels together, pull them apart again. "Strangers who don't meet Workshop standards."

He tugs the brim farther. "One stranger," he says, voice muffled. "Desperate times and all that."

"Yeah, I tried that angle." I yank off his beanie and clap it to his chest, leaning close, holding his gaze. "It didn't work. They decided they were done giving you Kringles their loyalty, time, and energy."

The Workshop doors bang open. Two female elves hurry out, one of them crying, the other consoling. I straighten away from Kristof, but the damage is done, and they glare as they pass. Kristof's brows rise. "What else did I miss?"

"Nothing. Unless you count the elves who voiced a less-than-favorable opinion about us having dinner together last night. If I had a weft for every comment about your preferential treatment of me, I could make, like, two dozen wigs."

Kristof rubs a gloved hand along his scruff. "I'm no good at this. Niklas would know how to handle these situations better than I do. He has a way with the elves and the family business that I'll never have." He stares at the entrance, above which the numbered sign reads 0-2-3. Twenty-three days 'til Christmas Eve. Enough time for the Kringles to get things functioning again.

And plenty of time for more things to go wrong.

"It's right that Nik's in line to be Santa, not me," Kristof murmurs.

I frown. "Did someone say otherwise?"

"Implied it." His jaw muscles bunch, the chiseled lines blurring beneath his scruff.

"I kinda think the hockey player might be what we need now, like your grandmother said."

"Don't see why."

"You process things differently. You come at problems from a unique angle. And since this whole Silver Reindeer-Krampus issue is different, perhaps you're what we need."

"Hasn't helped me figure out how the Workshop and reindeer shenanigans are connected to Krampus. It's almost like he infiltrated our borders, except he can't make it past the barrier, so—"

"You know that for sure?"

"Elves have been patrolling the border ever since you made it through. No other humans have shown any questionable actions when it comes to the barrier's stability."

The breeze trails wisps of hair across my face, and I push them away. What if I got through because of my bloodline? "When was the last time you met a Krampus in the flesh? If the family is known for their mischief, their interference, could it be possible they found a way in?"

"I told you—no one has passed through the barrier."

I huff and loosen the scarf from around my neck. "Fine, then how about another way? One that bypasses the border?"

"What are you talking about?"

"Hopefully nothing. Come with me." Tapping into the Workshop App, which saves the user's past history, I retrace my way to the small room with that semi-rebuilt wardrobe. Worrying my lip, wondering how many questions I'll have to field, I open the door and snap on the light.

Other than a few missing pieces here and there, the wardrobe stands almost fully restored. Even the mirrored door hangs on its hinges.

Behind me, Kristof sucks in a breath. "What is that?"

"I was hoping you'd tell me. I think it's the wardrobe Tinsel busted a couple of years ago. Why would someone repair it?"

He smooths a hand over its surface. Centered above the mirror rests the oval emblem. "This is the wardrobe, all right."

"Forget Niklas and his perfect timing. Tinsel needs to know I'm here, and I want to ask if she knows anything about this wardrobe." I unzip my wristlet, but it's empty, save for the mistlefeude. "Drat, my phone's charging in Tinsel's bedroom."

"Use mine. I agree she needs to know." Kristof passes it to me, and I've barely pulled up his text thread with Tinsel when he asks, "How did you find out about this?"

I snap a new pic of the wardrobe and include it in a message to Tinsel, my thumbs dancing across the keypad. To Kristof, I say, "I stumbled upon it by accident yesterday afternoon." Just yesterday? Someone's been busy. "And I saw your grandfather working on it." Technically, I only saw Meister K enter the room, but what else would he be doing in here?

"You saw Grandpop …?" His question fades in puzzlement. "Why would you think this has anything to do with Krampus?"

My thumbs hesitate for a nanosecond before I send the text and raise my head. He poses a good question. Now, how to answer it? "I've, um, seen that emblem before. In a, uh, book. And …" I pick at the edges of his phone case. *And I've seen it above a hidden door in my house, which transported me to Brückenstadt, and so maybe this wardrobe is some kind of portal, too.*

Kristof angles his head toward me. "Yes? And?"

"What are you doing in here?"

I vault into the air with a yelp and face the growled question. An elf stands in the doorway and hikes a thumb over his shoulder. "Out. Out. You shouldn't be snooping—Meister Kristof!" His face blanches.

"Herr Bote?" Kristof urges me into the hallway, his hand at my back. "What are you doing in the Workshop? Shouldn't you be at the Prep Stables?"

The elf clears his throat. "Yes, well, Meister K asked me to complete a project for him."

"A project."

"Yes. This here wardrobe."

Kristof's eyebrows rise. "You know about the wardrobe?"

"O-of course. It's a surprise. For Meister Niklas's ceremony."

"That's only a few days away."

Herr Bote gives a bright smile. "Exactly, so if you'll excuse me, I best get to work." As he closes the door, it bumps a drawstring pouch at his waist, which *clinks*. My eyes narrow at its red color and gold filigree pattern. Does he work for Ina Donath?

"You don't believe him."

I blink up at Kristof, who studies me. "Who? What? Believe Herr Bote? Uh …" Confusion trips over my tongue. The post-it note said the wardrobe should be completed by the Krampus Run, not Nik's ceremony. I move down the hall, away from the room. "What does the wardrobe have to do with the Initiation Ceremony? It's not like anyone can transport it overseas." But could someone transport *through* it?

"We'll have to wait for Tinsel to text back. See if her response matches Herr Bote's."

"Mmm." I tap the phone against my lips. How much should I disclose to Kristof? How much *can* I disclose without him finding out about my Krampus lineage?

"You know what this means, don't you?" Kristof says.

My heart races. Does he already suspect something? "What?"

He grins, dimple and all. "You'll have to hang out with me until she answers. That might take a while. I haven't heard from either her or Nik since yesterday."

So he doesn't suspect. A relieved laugh bursts from me, and I wiggle the phone. "I could always call her." I pretend to swipe its screen, but he makes a grab for it. With another laugh, I angle away, and he seizes me from behind in a backward hug, capturing my hand at my breastbone. I still, his sandalwood scent teasing my nose.

"Have dinner with me," he murmurs, his breath tickling the hair by my ear.

"Again?"

"I owe you a rain check. Plus"—he spins me out of his arms, at once freeing his phone and keeping hold of my hand—"I haven't talked to

Gram all day, and she's not going to like what I have to say. I could use some emotional support."

The corner of my mouth lifts. "Is this your way of roping me into another non-date?"

"Well, it's not romantic enough to be a real date."

"You have a girlfriend. I can't real-date you."

Kristof's gaze drops to my lips, and my tummy scrambles. "You'd consider a real date if I were single?"

Wait, what? How'd I walk into this one? I try to wrench my hand free. "Th-that's not what I meant."

He grins. "What did you mean?"

"I ... you ... we ..."

"So there is a 'we.'"

"No!"

Chuckling, Kristof releases my hand to drape an arm across my shoulders and guide me to the stairwell. "Has anyone ever told you, you're cute when flustered?"

"Has anyone ever told you, you're annoying?"

"Only the girl I'm crushing on."

"Hmph." I duck out from beneath his arm. He laughs again, and I playfully elbow him in the ribs.

Forty

Tinsel—Dec 2 Connections

Weihnachts Manor

"You do know what time it is, right?" Gina asks, her voice hushed.

Back on the terrace, I yawn behind my mitten. "Roughly nine o'clock your time, and well before your bedtime, so why are you whispering?"

"What I mean is, why are you up so early?"

"It's more like I've barely slept." When I still couldn't relax after Poppy came to rekindle the fire a half hour ago, I used it as an excuse to call Gina.

"I'm sorry. Did I worry you with the text I sent?"

"What text?"

"From Kristof's phone."

"I haven't received anything from Kristof all day."

"Oh. Wait, really?" Gina says. "That's weird. He said the same thing about you and Nik. Here, I'll resend the original pic I took."

I wait a moment for it to pop up. "Is that a wardrobe?" I zoom in on its façade.

"Kristof thinks it's the one you busted."

"He may be ri—hold the mistletoe." I adjust my newsboy cap. "You said you took the picture. How? The wardrobe's in Flitterndorf."

"Right, you didn't get the text," Gina mumbles. "Um, are you sitting down? You may want to sit down."

"Omigoodgarland, you're in Flitterndorf." I thump against the manor wall. "How did that happen? Have you been there long? Why are you …? I don't understand."

"I've been here a couple of days. We're trying it out for a week or two. To help the Doll Makers, though I don't know that I'm making much of a dent. Too many elves have walked out. You do know about the walkouts, right?"

"Found out today. But, Gina, you're a human. Other than the Kringles, no human has ever worked in the 'Shop. How did you pull it off?"

"Remember last weekend when I did those doll repaints? I showed them to Kristof, one thing led to another, and here I am, staying with your family, sleeping in your bed. Oh." She pauses. "I hope that's okay."

I frown at a second-story window, imagining Niklas's room on the other side. "Does Niklas know you're in Flitterndorf?"

"I don't know. As I said, I arrived the other day."

"He must've known about the walkouts, however, and he didn't tell me. And he knew about the Third String but didn't tell me—"

"You had enough on your mind with the Silver Reindeer."

"That's the least of my problems." I reach beneath my scarf for my parents' choker and find Poppy's bandage instead. "In the last week, I've lost my talent, learned my reindeer are missing, Santa's AWOL, the elves have turned mutinous, Herr Stoffel doesn't respect me, Ina Donath seeks to sabotage my engagement—"

"Ina Donath?"

"—though she needn't have troubled herself, because I took care of that yesterday afternoon." Wait. Did I play right into her hands? "Holy frankincense and myrrh, I may have made the biggest mistake of my life."

"If you just admitted in a roundabout way that you broke off your engagement with Niklas, then yeah, I'd say you made a mistake."

I groan. "G, it's complicated. I don't know how to tell truth from lies over here. One minute, Niklas warns me about Krampus and something called mistlefoil. In the next minute, he acts like he likes Gretel. You know how it feels to find your guy mooning over another girl."

"Isaak wasn't just thinking about another girl, he was *kissing* another girl. Was Nik kissing Gretel?"

"He might have, had I not interrupted them." Or was it the mistlefoil *foil*ing my vision? Did this have less to do with body chemistry and more to do with a chemistry experiment? My jaw clenches. I don't like being manipulated. Neither does Niklas.

"Tins, you need to patch things up with him. I promise he's not attracted to Gretel. He loves you. Good gravy, he defied his family, community, and an ancient edict for you. You can't give up on him."

Promise you won't abandon him, Meister Nico said.

I rub the ache in my chest. My heart might be wrecked, but Gina's right—I can't sever ties with Niklas. Not yet, anyway. I owe it to Christmas to keep digging until I unearth what's going on before Niklas fully succumbs to some toxin.

"Gina, I've got to go." Pushing away from the wall, I stride across the terrace. "I have a science lab to raid."

But my impetuous hopes don't last long, and twenty minutes later, I stumble back to bed, emotionally drained. Door Number Five is locked again. And this time, so is Herr Stoffel's office.

Forty-One

Tinsel—Dec 2 Mistle-foiled

❧

By mid-morning, an empty stomach compels me out of bed and downstairs for breakfast. I'm halfway across the entrance hall in a sleepy stupor when I stop and turn on my heel, jaw dropping. The Norway spruce is gone, along with the presents. A few elves sweep and vacuum the floor tiles, stray pine needles the lone evidence that something grand once stood there.

"What happened to the Christmas tree?" I ask.

A female elf looks at me with vacant eyes. "We're ushering in a new era."

"A new era? Where did the presents go?"

She lifts a tiny shoulder and resumes sweeping. I hasten to the breakfast room, hoping to find someone with an explanation. It's empty. Not even dirty breakfast dishes remain to indicate a recent occupant.

Light, tinkling laughter dances from the morning room, and my head snaps around. Gina? Can't be. I cross the entrance hall to the morning room and push its door wider. A heavy layer of jasmine and that unnamed scent assaults my nose. I falter in the doorway, my mood darkening as though encased in smoke. Around the room, Herr Stoffel, Gretel, Niklas, Madam Marie, and Ina converse, the sunlit windows and cheerful fireplace a cozy backdrop to the surreal scene I've interrupted: Gretel snuggling against Niklas's side.

Such a perfect couple, comes that soothing voice.

I blink against the image. "What's going on?"

Niklas stiffens. Gretel whispers in his ear and snakes a hand through his arm, angling him away. Something flashes on her ring finger.

Herr Stoffel marches forward to stand like a guard between me and the others. "Congratulations are in order." His stern gaze pushes me into the floor. "Niklas and Gretel are getting married."

A reindeer couldn't deliver a sharper kick than those words. "Excuse me?" I gape at Niklas's back, then turn to Madam Marie. Her expression is blank. *Don't fight the inevitable,* says the voice, soft and compelling.

"Niklas proposed an hour ago." Ina gives a brittle smile. "Gretel accepted."

"That's impossible. He and I were engaged only yesterday."

Gretel avoids my accusing stare as Herr Stoffel says, "And you broke it off." *You were right to do so,* adds the voice. "Once freed, Niklas came to his senses and went back to where he belongs."

I press a hand to my temple. More like his senses fled ... or were suppressed.

"Niklas must be convinced he made the wrong choice," Ina said on the phone yesterday. *"Increase the mistlefoil."*

Is mistlefoil the smell I can't identify? My eyes narrow at Ina and Herr Stoffel. "Whatever you're giving the Kringles, you better hope you have enough to keep them brainwashed, because given time—"

"Your time has run out." Herr Stoffel lowers his stern chin. "By

Saturday, they'll be married."

An invisible noose cinches around my neck, and I struggle to breathe. Niklas stands like a wooden nutcracker, his back to me. "But the Initiation Ceremony—"

"Rest assured Niklas will go through the formality of vowing to uphold, honor, and protect Christmas as the future Santa," Herr Stoffel says. "We must observe tradition, after all. Yet this ceremony will end as a marriage celebration, with Gretel featured as Niklas's wife, not an elf as his fiancée."

Don't fight. Accept.

I hug my arms, the future I envisioned with Niklas disintegrating into a yawning black hole. "This isn't Las Vegas, where people get married on the fly. It must happen at the registry office, and the formalities surrounding a civil ceremony require several months' worth of planning."

"Brava." Herr Stoffel mocks me with a slow clap. "Someone's done their homework. But, so have we. Why do you think we acquired Niklas's necessary paperwork back in the summer? He and Gretel have a ten o'clock appointment at the registry Friday morning."

The noose tightens. "You're lying."

Stepping around a side table, Herr Stoffel retrieves a manila folder from the couch. Atop the side table stands a reindeer figurine, perfectly balanced on its hind legs—and missing a brow tine. Like Muskat. A telltale white patch surrounds his left eye. I reach for the 'deer—

Herr Stoffel flourishes two sheets of paper before my gaze. The forms from his file cabinet.

I point to one. "That's not Niklas's signature."

"Mmm, yes, we had to improvise. Funny you should instantly recognize these, though." He pins me with a knowing glare. "You didn't, perchance, invade my private office and go digging where you aren't allowed?"

I lift my chin. "I'd like to speak with Niklas alone, please."

Herr Stoffel snorts. "Absolutely not."

"He owes me an explanation." *Whenever circumstances look questionable, feel free to plant one on me.* I move toward Niklas.

Herr Stoffel blocks me. "He owes you nothing, and your time here is done." He grips my arm and wrenches me backward to the door. "Go home."

Yeees, home, the voice chimes.

Shut up! I project my thought at the voice, and it shatters. Fighting against Herr Stoffel, I catch Madam Marie's eye. "Where's Meister Nico?" She flinches. "Please, will you do nothing to help?" Yet, why should she? Gretel was the Kringles' initial choice for a bride.

Managing to rip away from Herr Stoffel, I race for Niklas. "I'm sorry. I'm sorry for doubting you. All I want is one minute." One kiss. Grasping his arm, I spin him around and press my lips to his.

Gretel lets out a cry. Niklas convulses, smelling of ylang ylang and cedarwood rather than cloves. His lips begin to soften, then he jerks back. "Go ho—away, Tinsel," he says through clenched teeth, his usual twinkling eyes lifeless and dull. "I don't wa—" Wincing, he squeezes my hand in a painful grip. "You're not wanted here."

The kiss didn't work? I swallow the tears clogging my throat. "You don't mean that."

Something pricks my palm. "Get ... out."

A sob escapes me, but I obey, fleeing the room and slamming the door on Herr Stoffel's triumphant grin.

* * *

Breakfast forgotten, I race across the entrance hall, inhaling gulps of air, nausea roiling in my gut. Niklas has succumbed to the mistlefoil.

This is worse than a Christmas Eve blizzard without Rudolph. Is there an antidote? Can I find an antidote when I don't understand mistlefoil's properties in the first place?

My palm stings. Still. With watery eyes, I open my fist. A key's jagged edges press into the meaty base of my thumb. The key to the hallway closet. Who gave me this?

Something pricked me when Niklas squeezed my hand. *Go away, Tinsel*, he said. *You're not wanted here. Get out.*

Harsh words that came out in fits and starts. A warning rather than a rejection? Maybe he *hasn't* fully succumbed. If he slipped me the key, he expects me to return to the science lab. Perhaps I'll find an antidote in that experiment book. Ascending the main staircase, I slip the key into my dirndl pocket and swipe at wayward tears. I can't afford to entertain hope right now, yet its embers glow a little brighter.

As I near the top of the stairs, Fritz strides along the gallery. I force a wan smile. "Grüß Gott."

"Grüß—" He slides in front of me, analyzing my face. "So, you have heard the news. I warned you, nicht wahr?" With a smirk, he brushes past me down the stairs.

I whirl about and scowl at the top of his head. "Why don't you do something to stop this? You know it's not right."

Fritz hesitates, then turns. "I want Gretel to be happy. If she thinks Niklas will make her happy—"

"He won't. He doesn't love her."

"He will come to love her. She's sweet. Kind-hearted. Selfless—"

"Not from where I stand."

Fritz inclines his head. "You cannot fault a person—or a family—for having goals."

"Is that what this is? An attempt to impose your family's will upon the rest of us?" I descend a few steps, closing the distance between us.

259

"Ever wonder if they're poisoning Gretel, too?"

Fritz stiffens, his nostrils flaring. "They wouldn't dare."

A flame jumps among my embers of hope. "So they are poisoning Niklas."

"I never said—"

I hold up a finger. "You contradicted my use of 'too,' not 'poisoned.'" His eyes twitch, his gaze flicking to my neck. I rub the bandage there. "Why do you want Christmas destroyed?"

"Not destroyed. We must purify it. It has become corrupted."

"The Christmas message remains as pure as that night in Bethlehem, spreading Hope, Light, Peace—"

"Santa spreads greed."

"Man spreads greed. Santa encourages generosity."

Fritz's lip curls in a sneer. "Kids get rewarded for bad behavior."

"Kids get rewarded despite bad behavior."

"Why be good if there's no punishment for being bad?"

"Because it's not about performance, it's about the heart. One's belief. Where faith is sown, there's opportunity for growth. When there's growth, then love, joy, kindness, self-control, obedience—all that and more have a chance to blossom."

Conflict wavers in his eyes. "That is not what I was taught."

"You've been lied to. Manipulated. I hear Krampus is a master at deception." I poke his shoulder. "But I'm going to expose him, before Niklas is forced into a marriage neither he nor Gretel—were she in her right mind—wants."

Fritz seizes my wrist. "Remember what I told you. We're pawns. You cannot defy Krampus and win. If you force the issue, you won't like the results."

Forty-Two

Tinsel—Dec 2 Strung Out Third String

After checking that I stand alone in the hallway, I use Niklas's key to unlock the closet door. Stepping into its shallow confines, I close the door behind me, activate my phone's flashlight, and pull the overhead rod. Displaced air brushes my face as the back wall moves aside.

I shiver. At the end of this corridor lies a science lab, and beyond that, monstrous stables. Darkness, gouged wood, and heavy chains pop into my mind. Those stalls were made to constrain power, and I'm a meager elf.

But Christmas is on the line, with Niklas in mental bondage. Someone once said the only thing necessary for evil to triumph is for good men to do nothing. In this case, Krampus wins if I do nothing.

With a fortifying breath, I throw back my shoulders and march down the corridor.

Bright fluorescent light hits my eyes as I inch open the fiberglass door to the lab. Squinting, I cautiously peer into the room. A soft sigh escapes me. Empty.

I let the door close and memorize where its outline fades among

261

the shelves of reindeer figurines. Then I scan the room. The tables have been pushed against the walls, their surfaces wiped clean. Bits of hay and mud trail between the stable door and the one I assume leads to a hallway. I gulp. Are the stalls occupied today?

Suppressing my unease, I move toward the narrow table where Niklas found the experiment book. The pedestal sits vacant. Where's the book? I open and shut drawers and cupboard doors, rifle through papers, metal instruments, glassware, peek behind the lab coats in the corner. Gingerbread man, where did it go?

A muffled grunt and a *thwack* come from behind the stable door. My fingers freeze between a pair of beakers. Other sounds prick my ears from beyond the third door: clicking heels, clip-clopping hooves, a mix of male and female voices. I race to the wall through which I'd entered and explore its surface for the exit.

No seam. No way out.

The sounds grow louder. A bead of ice shimmies down my spine. I spin in a circle and dash behind a human lab coat, praying my feet and lower legs go unnoticed.

As the coat settles around me, my nose wrinkles at the strong stench of … what I smelled in the morning room earlier. What I've smelled underlying the essential oils rubbed into my choker. The fragrance in my bedsheets. The powder Poppy tosses into the fire. Mistlefoil?

You should have never come here, says the derisive voice inside my head. My chin lowers. *You're no hero. You don't even have a talent—*

"Three reindeer down, five to go," says a female voice, nasally and high-pitched. "Who would you like next?"

"Chip," a man says.

My breath jams in my lungs. They better not mean *my* Chip.

"It's time we dealt with the troublemaker," he adds in a thick accent.

Okay, that sounds like my Chip. Tangled lights—do they have the Third String?

A door opens, and the hooves and footsteps retreat. Shuffling, heavy jangling, and growls ensue. "Stop resisting," chirps the high-pitched female, her voice growing faint. "You'll be magnificent when …"

A shadow passes over my lab coat. "After your clumsy behavior the other day," the man jeers, "did you think you could come through again, undetected?" The fabric scrunches by my face and the lab coat is wrenched away.

The mustached man—Gretel's dad—stands there, his countenance spiteful as he gives me a once-over. "*Blöde Elfe.* Neither you nor your ex-fiancé can thwart plans set in motion long ago. Come, see my creations." Clenching my upper arm, Herr Brunner yanks me toward the stable door. "I think you will agree my upgrade suits them."

He pushes me across the threshold and along the aisle between the two rows of stalls. Ina Donath stands before a middle stall, arms crossed, frowning. How does she get around so fast?

She looks over as we approach, yet her glare is aimed at Herr Brunner. "You said enhanced powers. You didn't say anything about turning them into monstrosities. What did you do to my elixir?"

"I *enhanced* it." Herr Brunner chuckles. "Why should you care? You get your own lab after this."

Ina's gaze falls to me. "What is she doing here?"

"Causing trouble, like her animal friends. Tinsel"—his beefy fingers dig into my shoulders, rotating me to the stall's opening—"meet my first patient."

My throat closes at the gargantuan mutation struggling against its chains anchored to the back wall. It stands twice the size of Santa's Big Eight, muscles rippling beneath its patchy fur coat. Dagger-like antlers slice the air. Contorted claws rake the ground. Eyeballs bulge from a disfigured skeletal face with angry slits for nostrils and fangs as long as my hand, wrist to fingertip. It lunges, its maw snapping inches from my face.

I scream and jump back into Herr Brunner, but the shackles restrain the creature. For now. "What is that?" I ask in a strangled voice, wiping spittle from my cheek.

"Surely you recognize the leader of the Third String," Herr Brunner mocks.

"Leader of—" My brain screams in disbelief. "Butterscotch?" Nothing about the fiendish, oversized body resembles my friend. "What have you done to him?"

"You don't like my upgrade?"

"Upgrades are for machines. This is an animal."

"These are a means to an end," Herr Brunner counters.

I glance around. Eight reindeer fill eight stalls—three of them monsters, five of them normal. "Peppermint!" I wrench from Herr Brunner's grasp and fling an arm about Peppermint's neck in the stall beside Butterscotch. She doesn't react. I frame her head. "Peppermint, it's me. Tinsel." Her expression remains empty, and a tear slips down my cheek. Across the aisle— Aw, gingersnap. "Bonbon? You're here?" Like Peppermint, she stands unresponsive.

"I wouldn't linger near that one," Ina warns, nodding to Peppermint. "We recently administered the transformative elixir."

"You mean poison."

Herr Brunner shrugs. "A poinsettia by any other name …."

"He's ready, Frau Donath," says the high-pitched voice. A female elf backs out of the stall beside Bonbon's, leading a droopy-headed reindeer into the aisle via a rope.

"Chip!" I grab the rope. "Chip, it's me. Please, you gotta fight this. We can't let them win—"

"Oh, what melodrama." Herr Brunner yanks the rope from me. "You do not know who is even your enemy. What chance you have in winning a war, let alone a battle?"

Suddenly, Chip bucks and rears in the aisle. Ina cries out. Herr

Brunner drops the rope to shield his face, and Chip's hooves clip his forearms. He exclaims in pain, stumbles back, and hollers something in German. The elf scurries away.

Chip tosses his head. "Run!"

I can hear him! "I'm not leaving you."

An alarm blares overhead. Chip pushes at me with an antler. "Out … silver … save—" His eyes roll back into his head, and he collapses on the ground at my feet.

"Chip, no!" My gaze snaps to Ina, who brandishes a thick needle. "What did you do?"

"Nothing we won't enjoy doing to you next," Herr Brunner answers, cradling his forearm.

Thudding feet sound in the lab. As blue- and white-clad elves spill into the stables, I race for the humongous, barred doors. Herr Brunner shouts again in German.

Fueled by desperation, I grapple with the beam, hoisting it a few inches before an elf leaps to hang from my arm. Another snatches my dirndl from behind, and I stumble, dropping the beam. With rallying cries, several more bodies attach to my back. My knees buckle. Despite my thrashing, my blind kicks and strikes, the bodies keep pouncing, overpowering in number. Someone claps a cloth over my nose and mouth. I gag, but the raunchy stench fills my lungs. A prick flares in my neck, and a black cloud balloons across my vision. My body goes limp.

The elves cheer. Unnatural sorrow radiates from the center of my chest out along my limbs, dragging me down faster than the elves did. As I succumb to the sweeping blackness, one word echoes in my head.

Failure.

Forty-Three

Gina—Dec 2 Illogical Logic

Flitterndorf

Tinsel knows Ina Donath.

The words float to me as my phone alarm jingles and I fumble to shut it off. Grabbing clothes and shampoo, I plod into the tiny bathroom ahead of Tinsel's family.

Tinsel knows Ina.

All night, this newfound knowledge ricocheted in my dreams after our phone call. It makes sense. Ina's in Brückenstadt. So is Tinsel. Tinsel's a Christmas elf, and Ina's trying to help Santa and his elves. Why wouldn't there be a connection?

My elbow smacks a shower wall.

Yet, Tinsel said Ina wants to ... how did she put it? *Sabotage my engagement.* In that, Tinsel must be mistaken.

Like she's mistaken about mistlefeude, when she used the word, mistle*foil*, instead. Or are we talking about two different substances?

My knee tips a bottle of body wash from a low, tiled shelf, and I roll my eyes. How does Tinsel shower in these tight dimensions? As I dry off and get dressed, I topple lotion bottles from the vanity, bang my shin against the toilet, and bump into the free-standing towel rack.

"She's worse than Tinsel," her brother, Mash, hollers from another room.

Red-faced from more than getting dressed in cramped quarters, I hover at the kitchenette doorway as Mash and Kandi bustle around within. They pull dishes from cupboards, jam from the fridge, butter from the counter, and lay everything out on their corner table. The one time I tried sitting there, I ended up on the floor.

"We're almost ready for Frühstück." Kandi gives a weak smile, her eyes red. "Waiting for Tinder to return with some *Brötchen*, croissants, and bear claws." She offers me a mug filled with drinking chocolate, the liquid rippling inside.

"Does your shop open later on Wednesdays?" I ask. "I didn't think you took leisurely breakfasts."

Her throat convulses. "I'm not working today. I ruined the batch of chocolates yesterday, my measurements are fluky, and this"—she holds out her childlike hands, which tremble spasmodically—"won't stop." She gestures to my mug. "Try it. You'll see."

"Hmm?" Tilting the mug, the dark liquid steaming into my face, I take a sip. Bitterness bites my tongue. And salt! Too much salt! I grimace, and Kandi sinks into a chair at the table. Mash gives her shoulder an awkward pat.

"We're ruined," she whispers.

The front door slams. "Vati burned the bread!" Tinder pounds into the kitchen and edges past me to brace his arms on the table. "Mutti, it's a catastrophe. Vati burned three batches of bread, he's mixed up the sugar and salt, and now the dough won't rise."

Kandi's head lowers.

"Plus, I overheard customers say that Meister Kristof likes the Red Clan more than the Green Clan."

"Meister Kristof has no favorites."

"Herr Wurzeln heard Meister Kristof himself. The other night when he ate at The Pleasing Palate. She was there." Tinder motions toward me. "You heard him, didn't you?"

"This has always been my favorite place to eat," Kristof said as I preceded him into the restaurant. *"But now I can better appreciate the dishes, having been overseas myself."*

I clench the mug. "Having a favorite restaurant doesn't stop Kristof from enjoying the others. Nor does it mean he favors one Clan over the other. To draw that conclusion is asking for trouble."

"Oh, yeah?" Tinder crosses his arms. "Well, I think *he's* asking for trouble."

"Tinder, hold your tongue. Gina, I'm sorry we don't have pastries for you this morning." Kandi indicates the kitchenette with quaking hands, which she then hides in her lap. "But our cupboards aren't bare. Please, help yourself—"

"That's okay." I wave aside her invitation. "I'll grab something at the Workshop. I should head there now, anyway. Kristof can't pick me up today, so I need extra time to trek the hill." I slide the mug onto the table and ease out of the room. "May I borrow Tinsel's snowshoes?"

Mash grunts as he pours drinking chocolate down the sink drain. "It's not like we can use them."

Back in Tinsel's bedroom, I pluck my phone and wristlet off the nightstand, and Papa Campi's journal tumbles to the floor. I flipped through his entries last night, hunting for any clue that would suggest he knew about mistlefeude, or give more info about the emblem. My search proved fruitless. Brushing off its cover, I set the journal back on the nightstand, then corral my winter accessories and escape the apartment's bleak atmosphere.

The Workshop's atmosphere isn't any improvement. Of the few elves who show up for work, most of them spend more time grumbling over Kristof's Clan-comment, which becomes embellished in the retelling. I keep my head down, fortify myself with mistlefeude, and concentrate on making wig wefts.

Aunt Cat assured me the best way to help Ina—help Santa—was to continue applying mistlefeude where and when I had the opportunity. Except, Kandi fares worse today, and as I made my way through town earlier, the same elves who smiled two days ago glared at me instead. Either the stuff works differently on me than on the elves, or it takes twice as long to work on them because they're half my size.

A notion so illogical it kinda makes sense.

From a few tables away, a female elf in a forest green dirndl hops up, flailing her arms. "How dare he say we're expendable! It was the Green Clan that first stood with the Kringles during the Christmas of '44."

"What if he's convinced Meister K that we're expendable?" whines the elf beside her, also wearing green.

The first elf tugs on her coworker's arm. "We'll just go see about that."

"Good luck getting an audience with him," shouts another elf as they head for the stairs. "Meister K hasn't shown his face in days."

Angling away from Bellamy, I pull out my phone and tap into my text thread with Kristof. **Head's up**, I tell Kristof. **Two elves are on the warpath, seeking Santa. You might want to hide.**

A moment later, he texts back. **I've been hiding all morning.**

Then you've heard?

About how they misconstrued my comment at the restaurant? Oh yeah. And they keep asking me and Gram about Grandpop. We've exhausted all excuses.

Still no lead?

Kinda. No. Maybe.

I hesitate, then type: **Want to talk about it over lunch?**

Do we have another non-date I'm not aware of? I can't break away.

So, lunch is a no-go. Sigh. Who knew I'd miss seeing his cute mug. **Break away from what?**

Scrounging through a storage room under the Lower Stables. I remembered last night that Nik found old documents and logbooks down here when serving a Penalty a couple of years ago. Thought I'd try looking for anything about the SR or Krampus or this "mistlefoil" Nik mentioned the other day.

Documents and logbooks? Krampus? What if he finds something that reveals my Dad's Krampus lineage? *My* Krampus lineage? My stomach twinges. I should be with him to explain, to soften the blow. Or even better, to intercept the discovery.

With the help of more mistlefeude, I make it to mid-afternoon before giving in and asking Kristof the question gnawing at me: **You want company in your hideout?**

After an agonizing ten minutes, he responds. **Admit it. You miss me.**

I squirm in my chair and straighten a pile of wefts. In situations like these, I'm grateful for texting—he can't see my face to realize how close his words hit home. But I have no business missing someone who has a girlfriend. **You were gone eleven months. What's a few hours? ;)**

Meet me outside the Lower Stables in thirty min. Out of curiosity, how many non-dates does it take to count as one real date? I think we're up to four.

How can he pretend away his girlfriend so casually? And why do I find a two-timer appealing when I, myself, have been two-timed?

Huffing out a breath, I shove my phone into my wristlet and straighten my work area under Bellamy's disapproving eye. I'm an idiot. Maybe Kristof should know about my lineage. If a girlfriend can't create a wedge between us, Krampus sure will.

Cranky and conflicted, I head across Huff 'n Puff Hill to the stables. The grand building with its three distinct rooftops houses the Upper Stables, the FTA (Flight Training Arena), and Lower Stables. I sit on the bench outside the Lower Stables' entrance and extract a bottle of mistlefeude from my wristlet. Spritzing it in front of me, I take a deep breath. Confidence powers along my veins, and I welcome it.

Something that feels so good couldn't possibly harm the elves.

I slip the bottle back into the wristlet as the door to the Lower Stables opens. Kristof aims a smile my way despite the haggard lines around his eyes and mouth. "Afternoon."

My eyebrows rise. "Was the omission of 'good' deliberate?"

With a half-laugh, he sinks beside me and leans against the wall. He sighs. Then he frowns and straightens again. "Do you smell that?"

I fiddle with the wristlet's zipper. "Smell what?"

"I don't know. I never know. I smelled it occasionally in Germany, and now it's cropping up here. Sometimes I think I'm going crazy." Collapsing once more against the wall, Kristof mumbles, "I almost did go crazy once. Not one of my better moments."

"No?" I knock his knee with mine. "Sounds like a juicy story."

Kristof crosses his arms, tilts his head back. "I got jealous of Nik while visiting my kin in Germany."

I exaggerate my shock. "A definite mark of insanity. No wonder you're chagrined."

His mouth lifts. "Shut up. I'd never been jealous of Nik before. Until several weeks ago." He shakes his head along the wall. "I became jealous of his extra abilities as future Santa, his easy-going manner with people, the way everyone fawns over him. Jealous he was the firstborn. Why should my birth order automatically make me unfit to be Santa Claus? What role exists for Santa's second son? Does my life have purpose? What if I wasn't wanted?"

271

His words twist my heart, and I grasp his hand. "Of course you were."

Kristof chuckles. "I told you I almost went crazy."

"What stopped you?"

He glances at our hands, and I withdraw mine before he misconstrues my intent. "I wrestled through my feelings. Zeroed in on the kernel of truth to help me recognize and dispel the lies. Once I did that, it was like deception's power over me snapped. Not until I was freed, however, did I realize I'd been enslaved."

"But your circumstances haven't changed."

"My perception has." He stretches out his legs and crosses his ankles. "A head is useless without a spine to support it, right? Likewise, Santa is only as good as his support system—his family and the elves. When Nik becomes Santa, I'll be part of his support system, and when he succeeds, I succeed."

"Isn't that settling?"

"Not when I'm doing what I'm called to do. Accepting my role rather than fighting it brings peace and satisfaction. I can focus on being the best Kristof Kringle, not the best Kristof-trying-to-be-Niklas Kringle."

I study his face, identifying the assuredness that has radiated in his eyes and influenced his bold manner since returning from Germany. Why must I find his confidence so darn attractive? I shift away, crushing my wristlet in my lap. "What if someone doesn't know what their best version looks like?"

"You mean, you?" Kristof motions across the hill. "I swung by the PW loft early this morning and saw the dolls you've completed. They're extraordinary, G. Both in quality and quantity. *You're* extraordinary. I had no idea how skilled you'd become so quickly. My opinion? Your best version includes doll-making in some form."

A grin breaks free, then something slimy writhes within me. If my skills exist because of the mistlefeude, I shouldn't take credit for the work. If, however, the mistlefeude enhances what I already possess, I should take credit. So, which is it? Why this grimy feeling?

"Hey." Kristof cocks his head, trying to catch my eye. My knee bounces. "You looked pleased as rumberry punch one second and sadder than a coal-filled stocking the next. What gives?"

"It's insensitive."

His mouth quirks. "Now you've piqued my curiosity."

My knee bounces faster. "Other than this past weekend, I never devoted so much time to making dolls. Never let myself daydream about that possibility." I duck my head. A curtain of hair shields my face from Kristof. "Yet, since I've been here, it's like a piece of my soul's come alive. A piece I didn't even know was missing. Working with the Doll Makers has given me an unexpected level of joy and satisfaction."

"That's wonderful."

"It's terrible."

Kristof brushes my hair over my shoulder. "Why?" His hand trails down my back, and though I wear a jacket, his touch penetrates to the marrow of my bones.

"Because I wouldn't be here if Flitterndorf wasn't having problems. I wouldn't be having fun if the elves weren't suffering. I'm benefiting from your pain. From their pain."

"The elves used to derive the same pleasure in their work as you do now. I believe they will again, once we get to the root issue." His steady gaze compels me to look at him, and my heart trips at our proximity. The green flecks in his eyes gleam. "Right now, you're stepping in at my family's greatest hour of need, and frankly, I'm glad someone's having a good time around here."

"Yeah, but you didn't see the Workshop today. It's like church on Monday morning. Empty."

"Then let's discover what secrets hide among the forgotten documents downstairs"—Kristof stands, pulling me with him—"before our enemy wins by default."

Forty-Four

Gina—Dec 2 Hockey Player

Too many hours and who-knows-how-many-boxes later, our futile searching results in hangry frustration. Kristof doesn't need to ask twice before I agree to another non-date dinner. We end up eating at The Pleasing Palate again since the Green Clan restaurants refuse to serve us. Their rejection sobers Kristof. By eight o'clock, he drops me off at The Flaky Crust and leaves with a distracted wave, the giant snow globe puffing out snowflakes in the Town Square beyond him.

Huggamugg Café spreadsheets await my perusal, but rather than head to the Kuchlers' apartment, I cross the street to the snow globe. It towers over me, fat flakes eddying around a replica of Weihnachts Manor inside. Like a big dollhouse. I flatten my gloved hand against the curved glass dome, and my mood lifts despite Flitterndorf's troubles. How will I return to my normal life after helping at the Workshop, when I prefer dolls and wigs over numbers and coffee?

Hooking my thumbs in my coat pockets, I stroll through the streets. Notes of mistlefeude twirl in the air. I grin. As I pass the windows of one quaint home after another, however, my smile fades. Inside, elves

275

wear somber faces and move as though burdened by a heavy load. The food in my stomach curdles. What if the mistlefeude never—

No. Averting my eyes, I hurry on.

Houses give way to the open field, and the path I follow cuts across to the switchbacks on Huff 'n Puff Hill. A gust of wind wriggles down my neck, bringing with it the scrape of blades on ice. Spotlights illuminate the outdoor rink, and a human-sized figure races back and forth within the guardrails. Kristof. My feet redirect me to the rink.

Another gust has me tugging my hat lower and hunching into my coat collar. In contrast, Kristof shucked his outer layer and zooms across the ice in his heather gray sweater and forest green lederhosen. Lowering his hockey stick, he nears a black puck, strikes, and the puck sails across the rink. Goal!

I sink onto a bleacher made for a community of elves, knees at my chest. I've tried skating. No matter how polished the ice, its little bumps and nicks inevitably trip me up, and I'm on my butt more than my feet.

Not Kristof. He glides across the glass surface, pivoting with ease on those thin blades. Forward. Backward. Forward again. Goading a puck with his stick, he nears the net at one end and takes a shot. The netting jerks from the puck's punch, and Kristof circles away, slapping the ice with his stick. Gone are the tight lines that rimmed his eyes during dinner. Gone are the hardened features. A grin curls his mouth as he speeds across the ice with a grace born from years of experience.

Who knew a guy could make the sport so appealing?

Or is it the sport that makes the guy more appealing?

Something tells me I'm not holding out for Legolas anymore.

If Kristof were single and could get over his first crush; and if he planned to stay in Flitterndorf, and I threw out my three-date policy; and if I didn't have Krampus blood running through me, and he ignored the Kringles' dating restrictions; could there, as he once joked, ever be a "we" out of he and I?

Those are a lot of "if's."

Kristof skates past again, toying with another puck, and my heart clenches. When Niklas defied his family's ancient edicts, at least he chose someone within the Christmas community. I'm an outsider and their enemy's relative. Kristof and I don't stand a chance.

This is why I keep my heart reined in. Reality hurts too much. Sighing, I rise to slip out the way I slipped in: unnoticed.

"Where're you going?"

Or not.

On the other side of the guardrail, Kristof cuts to a stop, ice crystals spraying in an arc beyond the rink. I pull my gloved hands into my coat sleeves. "I didn't mean to intrude."

"You're not intruding." His skates weave atop the ice, backing away and sliding forward again in a seamless motion. "How long have you been here?"

"Not long. I chose a walk over work, and this is where it brought me." I descend the elf-sized stair treads three at a time and join him at the thigh-high guardrail. "Sorry if I pulled you out of your zone."

"It's just as well I stop." He glides in a circle. "I think better while skating, but skating doesn't get the job done."

I toe the guardrail post with my boot. "If you dream up better ideas and concoct better plans on the ice than when surrounded by office walls, skating is where you need to be sometimes."

"Perhaps." Kristof moves in perpetual zigzags and semi-circles before me. "Did you know the elves in both Russia and Germany could use a hockey team?"

I shake my head.

"After I dealt with my big-brother jealousies, I considered staying abroad. Supporting Nik from one of the outposts. Coaching hockey."

"And then you discovered the Silver Reindeer, which forced you to come back."

"I wouldn't say forced, but yes, that influenced my return." His gaze rests on me, then veers away again. "Not that it's done any good. Things are fast spiraling out of control, and now I can't even reach Nik—" Kristof smacks the ice with his hockey stick. "Somehow Krampus has infiltrated Flitterndorf and probably Weihnachts Manor, too, and I'm helpless to stop him. I hate that his family might have what it takes to undo everything my family stands for."

Will he eventually come to hate *me*?

He strikes a lone puck. It hits the goal post and ricochets off. "And I hate that, despite my determination to step in wherever needed, I'm not much good to anyone outside my skill set." He takes another shot and the puck goes wide. "Or inside, apparently." Skidding to a stop, Kristof yanks off his hockey gloves. "Now more than ever, Flitterndorf needs a leader"—he tosses the gloves at my feet—"and they're stuck with the likes of me."

I lean toward him, pressing my legs against the guardrail. "Sometimes the best leaders aren't those groomed from birth. They're the ones pushed into positions they never wanted, thinking on their feet, making decisions based on their unique life experiences and wisdom rather than on a book of tactics. Sometimes the best leaders"—I tug him forward on his skates—"arise from the team players."

Kristof studies my face in silence, his hazel eyes steady and intense. With a crooked smile, he tucks a lock of hair under my hat brim. "Wise and captivating. Now there's an irresistible mix."

"Careful." I fight the heat building inside. "Somewhere there's a girl holding your heart who wouldn't appreciate you talking like that."

"So you keep reminding me." His fingers trail down my cheek and along my chin, burning a path where they graze my skin. I command my body to move away. It doesn't comply.

"Why date someone so forgettable?" I whisper. Dark blond stubble blurs his jawline, and the straight slope of his nose draws my focus to the indent above his top lip. A perfect pair of lips ... to go with his perfect girlfriend. "Does she know you're flirting with me?"

Kristof's gaze drops to my mouth. "You think I'm two-timing," he says, his voice husky, "but I'm not."

"What do you call this?"

"I admit to having a little fun at your expense, but come on, Gina"—he cradles my neck—"when will you realize you and the girl I'm crushing on are one and the same?" And he dips his head to claim my speechless mouth.

Sparks shoot off behind my eyelids. He tastes like Christmas morning—full of promise, expectation, joy, giddiness, adventure. Without breaking the connection, Kristof backs along the ice, pulling me with him over the railing. I loop my arms around his neck and stand on tiptoes atop his skates as he hauls me against him, deepening the kiss. Melting the barricades around my heart. Hugs and kisses. Delicious in different ways, complete without the other, yet what a formidable combination.

"So, you don't have a girlfriend?" I ask between kisses.

"No." He nips my lower lip. "You jumped to that conclusion all by yourself."

"You helped." More kisses. "You admitted to having a crush."

"Not the same thing."

"You didn't correct my error."

After an exceptionally dizzying kiss, Kristof lifts his head. "You could've figured it out, had you been ready to consider a relationship with me." His stare sears me. "You may still not be ready, but I'm tired of dancing around the subject."

I press my lips together and step off his hockey skates. "Your friendship's more important to me than a tourist's."

"What does that have to do with giving us a chance?" He scowls. "Are we back to your silly three-date policy? Be honest, G—I've trounced that multiple times, and if that kiss was any indication, you're not sick of me, nor are you losing interest."

"I could screw things up, though." My heart pounds. "If I risk going after what I want, be it relationships, jobs, careers, I'll fail, proving I shouldn't have tried in the first place. It happened with Isaak—"

"His cheating wasn't your fault."

"—and it's why I didn't take the job in Alberta." I cross my arms to warm my body. "When it comes to you and me, you're a Kringle and I'm a—I'm not. Someday, you'll leave for Germany, and I'll stay behind. I don't want to be responsible for our friendship's demise or for breaking your heart."

"You let me worry about my heart." His forehead wrinkles. "Who said you weren't good enough, G?"

"What?"

"Someone once told you, you weren't good enough, and you believed him. Or her."

"You no have talent." Nonna rips up my colored picture all over again in my head.

"That person was lying, Gina. Everything you need to be amazing is already inside you. You just have to water the seeds with a little faith." Kristof jabs the air with a finger. "You want to create dolls? Go for it. You want to run a coffee shop? Do it. You want to travel the world? Don't let anyone stop you. You want to stay close to home? Don't let anyone make you leave." His eyes blaze with fervency. "Like the elves, you were created with unique talents. Don't be a paler version of your potential because someone once pushed you down in order to prop themselves up."

My throat convulses. "Thanks," I whisper. Grabbing the front of his shirt, I yank him in for another kiss.

Kristof stumbles forward on his skates, catches me around the waist, and we topple to the ice in an awkward heap. "Ow," he says on a laugh, then meets my lips to kiss away our pain.

Forty-Five

Tinsel—Dec 3 Krampuslauf

Brückenstadt

The cage in which I'm imprisoned jostles and rattles atop the flatbed wagon pulled by two draft horses. Haunting music and wisps of artificial smoke curl through the bars. My heart pounds in time to the drums beating nearby. Ever since the elves overtook me, I've drifted in and out of a reality akin to a horror movie—and something tells me I'm an expendable extra on set.

I lean against the bars, heavy chains shackling my wrists and ankles. Hopelessness has drained my energy, my impetus to escape. Nevertheless, I attempt a feeble kick at the opposite bars, the chain clinking against the cage floor. Spectators line the sidewalk in the darkness of evening, laughing, pointing.

"If you try to make a scene, the crowd will simply think it's part of the Krampuslauf festivities," Ina had warned after Herr Brunner tossed me into the cage. "Even if you did manage to attract attention, you're a foreigner in this country and an elf. What do you think the authorities will do with a foreign freak like you?"

Herr Brunner slammed the barred door in my face. "After watching you parade about with Niklas for two years, I will enjoy witnessing your humiliation behind bars during the show."

Surrounding me now, ghastly horned creatures affect limping gaits in the cobblestone street, creeping and lunging at the crowd. Guttural sounds issue from their throats like the Uruk-hai in Gina's Lord of the Rings movies. They lash out with their birch whips, striking unsuspecting children and adults on their legs or arms. Their victims shriek in good-natured fun.

At times, a Krampus will look my way and rush at me, fangs glinting, serpentine tongue lolling. Some poke their bundle of birch twigs between my bars. Laughs ripple through the bystanders at their antics while panic congeals along my veins. The masks look so lifelike, one forgets humans inhabit these costumes.

As we turn a corner, I glimpse a pale blond head in the crowd. Niklas! Light flickers within me, nudging aside the dark. He stands between Gretel and Fritz, observing the Krampuslauf with an impassioned gaze, Gretel latched onto his arm possessively. Inspired by the glimmer of light, I push to my knees and shake the bars, my chains rattling. "Niklas! Niklas, it's me. Help!"

A birch whip strikes my exposed knuckles, and a distorted face presses against the bars, snarling at me to shut up. But fresh defiance courses through me, and I rock the cage. "Niklas, over here. Please, help!"

His body jolts, and he blinks, turns his head. Our gazes catch—

Three Krampuses converge on him as a fourth leaps in front of me, blocking my view. He crams his whip through the bars and jabs my shoulder, pushing me back. "You've lost, elf." The mask muffles his words, yet I'd recognize that contempt anywhere. Herr Stoffel. "There is no knight-in-shining-armor to rescue you."

Glaring, I lurch to the other side. "Niklas!" He's no longer in sight.

No. I rattle the bars again, beseeching the crowd. "Help! Help me, please!" They laugh, wave, and shift their focus to the creatures parading behind me. The wagon moves on. I slump and squeeze my eyes shut as my inner fickle light dies.

No hope.

No talent, no reindeer, no promotion, no fiancée, no Santa Claus.

What's to become of me?

What's to become of Christmas?

Forty-Six

Gina—Dec 3 The Two Are One

Flitterndorf

I stare at my wristlet on the tabletop, willing it to vibrate with a text from Tinsel. She's been silent ever since our phone call. Did she ever patch things up with Niklas? I want to dish to her about my kiss-a-licious evening with Kristof, but not until I know where her own love life stands. Hello, I'm not that insensitive … although I do have my faults.

Like not telling Tinsel about jumping time zones and thousands of miles through a secret passageway in my parents' house because I don't want her to know about my heritage.

Like taking advantage of Kristof's warm gazes and sweet kisses without first confessing to *him* about my heritage. Our time together already has a limit, thanks to the many obstacles between us. Why shouldn't I postpone the day his admiration crumbles into repulsion?

A knot lodges behind my diaphragm, and I wriggle in my chair at the Workshop. Time for more mistlefeude. Contrary to what Aunt Cat said, mistlefeude's effects don't last longer with each application.

(If she's mistaken about that, what else did she get wrong?)

After three spritzes, I slip the bottle into my wristlet and withdraw my phone. One peek can't hurt. Little chance I'll get caught slacking off, as most elves didn't show up for work, including Bellamy. Their absence results in an unhealthy silence throughout the Production Wing. No hum of distant machinery. No piped-in Christmas music. No happy chatter.

Even if the few of us remaining cranked out toys as fast as we could, we wouldn't make up for the lack of productivity. And the longer it takes to determine how Krampus has affected Flitterndorf's citizens, undo the damage, and reassemble the elves in the Workshop, the less hope we have of making quota by Christmas. Umpteen times worse than two years ago when Tinsel unintentionally destroyed a portion of Christmas presents.

Heaving a sigh, I tap into Tinsel's text thread. Where is she? Have I missed something from previous texts that would explain why she's MIA? I scroll back through our conversations and her myriad pictures. Back. Back. Back. Oh. Here are some pictures and texts I never saw. Christmas kiosks strung with lights. A pretzel twice the size of Tinsel's hand. Funny nutcracker dolls—

Whoa whoa whoa. Aunt Cat?

I stop scrolling and frown at the corresponding text: **Personality-wise, you outshine this woman in every way. Visually, Ina Donath reminds me of you. Miss you!**

Tinsel thinks my aunt is Ina Donath?

I zoom in on the details. Yes, there's Aunt Cat's small mole on her left cheek. And she wears her favorite chic leather pea coat. And I suppose even though I saw Aunt Cat in Waldheim Saturday morning, she could have used my parents' hidden passageway to arrive in Brückenstadt for the Weihnachtsmarkt Saturday night.

But why would Tinsel think she goes by another name? Unless …

My fingers tremble. Images of the connecting office flit through my mind. The chemistry accessories. The reindeer figurines like the one Aunt Cat carried when I caught her in the hallway. The letters addressed to Ina Donath.

Aunt Cat's full name is Caterina.

Cate*rina* Donati.

Ina Donath.

The room swims, and I hunch forward, dropping my head in my hands. Aunt Cat said she worked with Ina Donath—not that she *was* Ina.

Ina Donath seeks to sabotage my engagement.

"No." I knead my forehead. "No, she's supposed to be on the Kringles' side. On the side of Christmas." But if Aunt Cat lied to me about Ina's identity, what else is she lying about?

The mistlefeude bottle peeks out from my wristlet.

Oh, crud.

"Frau Donati?"

I jump, "nah-tee" echoing throughout the loft where four elves work in silence. Frau Chemiker stands at the top of the spiral staircase. "Meister Kristof would like to see you." Her countenance reveals nothing. Is this a good summons, or a not-so-good summons?

Closing my eyes, I gulp. Kristof had thought Aunt Cat looked familiar when they met last week. What if he met Ina while over in Germany? And what if he just now remembered where he saw my aunt's face?

I think I can kiss Kristof's admiration goodbye.

Forty-Seven

Gina—Dec 3 Busted

The door to Meister K's office stands ajar. Kristof sits at the worktable surrounded by half-finished toys, looking like I must have in the loft: elbows propped on the tabletop, head in hands. Feeling as defeated as I do?

Frau Chemiker knocks on the door and pushes it wider. "Meister Kristof?"

He lifts his head, dark shadows beneath his eyes. When he sees me, his mouth tightens. Not good. "Vielen dank, Frau Chemiker." At his nod, she enters the room behind me and closes the door. As she hoists herself onto a high stool opposite Kristof, he waves me to an armchair beside the door. "Have a seat."

I perch on the edge of the cushion. "What's going on?"

Though he smiles, his expression lacks its usual warmth. "We had a major breakthrough with the mistlefoil."

"That's great. So, why do you seem upset?"

Kristof rubs a hand over his face. "Tired, I guess. We were up all night."

Frau Chemiker adjusts her glasses. "It was actually quite thrilling. You've heard of mistle*toe*, yes?"

"Of course. We hang it over doorposts at Christmastime, hoping to, uh"—I avoid looking at Kristof—"give or receive a kiss."

"That's the holiday version. Did you know mistletoe does not grow on its own?" I shake my head, and Frau Chemiker continues, her voice oozing enthusiasm. "Mistletoe requires a host in order to thrive. Throughout its life, it taps into that host's supply of water and nutrients, which weakens the host and sometimes results in death. Its berries provide nourishment to birds and other small woodland creatures, but they're harmful to humans and elves." She clasps her hands in her lap. "As for mistle*foil*, we came across it rather fortuitously and conducted a sleighful of experiments. We now believe mistlefoil behaves in similar ways to mistletoe by tapping into a host's reserves, although instead of doing so to flourish, it does so to corrupt."

"Corrupt what?"

"The host," Kristof says.

I bite my lip. "And mistlefoil's host?"

"Flitterndorf," Frau Chemiker answers. "Or, rather, her inhabitants. The reindeer become sick physically, while the elves become sick both emotionally and in character."

That would explain their increasing hostility, except ... "*You're* not sick."

She spreads her hands. "A few of us remain healthy, but we haven't figured out why."

I grip my wristlet. "Is there an antidote?" Perhaps I carry it on my person.

Or was I tricked into carrying the poison?

Would Aunt Cat betray me like that?

It's Frau Chemiker's turn to shake her head. "There's still a lot we don't know about mistlefoil's properties. We intercepted it as a liquid, but it may also come in a powder form. Essential oils like jasmine or ylang ylang mask its telltale, rancid odor, yet how it's being administered, the amount in each dose, if a cure exists—those questions remain unanswered."

My scalp prickles at her description of the smell.

"My assistants continue to run experiments," Frau Chemiker adds. "I'm confident we'll have more information before the end of the day."

Kristof gives her a smile, this one genuine. "Thank you, Frau Chemiker. Now, I'd like to speak with Gina alone, please."

"Certainly, sir." She hops from the stool and leaves the office, the door closing with an ominous *click*.

Kristof leans his elbows on his knees, steepling his hands at his mouth, and holds my gaze. Something tells me he didn't ask for time alone to steal a kiss or two. "Mind enlightening me on what, precisely, we're up against here?"

My knee bounces, and I quell it with a hand. "Why would you think I know anything?"

He gestures to my wristlet. "May I have a look?"

I wince, my insides sinking. "This isn't what you think—"

"The elves have seen you spritz the air at times." He extends his hand. "I'd like to know what that is."

I slap the wristlet into his palm. "It's mistle*feude*. Not the other stuff." Because Aunt Cat wouldn't betray me.

Kristof unzips the wristlet and removes two glass vials. Uncapping a bottle, he sniffs. His features harden. "Why are you lying, Gina? This is mistlefoil."

"No." I jump up and hug my arms. "She told me, herself—feude means joy, and we must circulate it among the elves to ward off the dark shadow threatening Christmas. That's what the elves saw me doing."

"Yeah? Well, it's not working."

"It works on me." I can't have been doling out poison these last few days! "When I use it, I feel fabulous. Like I can access portions of my brain previously closed to me. My creativity is off the charts." I point at him. "You've seen the results—the dolls I made this week. You know I speak the truth."

Kristof stands and walks to Meister K's desk, where he reaches toward a stack of papers. "I think I can guess why the mistlefoil affects you differently. Can you?"

"Oh, please, do tell."

"Because you're a Krampus." He holds up two objects, one in each hand. A red pouch with gold filigree … and a leather book. Papa Campi's journal.

The room spins, and I drop back onto the armchair. "Where'd you get those?"

"Tinsel's father gave them to me when I brought you back to The Flaky Crust for the second time last night." His gaze skitters away. "Mash found them in Tinsel's room."

"What is he, a kleptomaniac?" My fingers squeeze the seat cushion. "No one had a right to go through my things."

"You had no right to keep this information from me. Did you think I wouldn't figure it out? You made it through the barrier, you wigged out over a Krampus portrait, you know something about that wardrobe you haven't told me." He reclaims his chair, shaking the pouch. "Gina, this is what I've been searching for—the key to the sickness plaguing both the reindeer and elves. You had it the whole time."

"I didn't know that."

"And this?" He fans through the journal's pages. "Google Translate wasn't perfect, but I was able to connect enough dots. To think that in allowing you access to the Workshop, I was welcoming an enemy into my camp."

I jerk, his words a physical strike. "You don't believe that."

"You're a Krampus."

"Descendant. I'm a Krampus descendant."

"What's the difference?"

I scowl. "I don't know, diluted bloodline?"

"This isn't a joke!" Kristof slaps the journal onto the table. "Christmas is at stake here. The reindeer are dying, the elves hover one step shy of mutiny, my grandfather and Third String are missing, we haven't dialed in on the SR—am I forgetting anything?"

"Nik and Tins broke up."

His eyebrows spike. His mouth opens, closes, opens again. "How? Why?"

"Who knows? I haven't heard from Tinsel since she told me. With everything else going wrong, consider it the straw that broke—no, no, it's the 'ornament that toppled the Christmas tree.'"

Kristof pulls himself taut. "Putting it into terms I can understand? Or does being a Krampus descendant give you license to use Christmas jargon?"

"That's not fair."

"When did you learn about your pedigree? Years ago?"

"Days ago!"

"And you had the guts to kiss me, knowing how I feel about the Krampus family?"

"You enjoyed it."

His eyes narrow. "It happened under false pretenses."

My insides shrivel at his rejection. I predicted it, but not how much it would hurt.

"What triggered your newfound knowledge?"

"The Krampus portrait in your apartment," I mumble. "He looks like my grandmother. When I confronted my parents, they told me the truth, gave me that journal, and then …" I chew on the inside of my cheek.

"What? Don't stop now."

I let out a huff. "Then I went to Germany through a magic portal in my hallway, ended up in Ina Donath's office, found the leather pouches, and couldn't resist taking one—"

"Magic portal?"

"Yes. I think the wardrobe might be another portal, and one in the Prep Stables's supply closet, too, since they all have the same emblem."

"Portals? Emblems? Germany? You're talking nonsense."

"This, coming from a guy who lives in a town hidden by invisible borders, whose grandfather slides down chimneys, drives a sleigh pulled by flying reindeer—"

Kristof raises his hand. "Hold the mistletoe. You said Ina Donath a moment ago."

"I did?" Drat.

He curses and jumps to his feet. "I met her while visiting Weihnachts Manor. I didn't trust her then, and if she's involved with what's going on in Flitterndorf, I was right not to like her."

I stiffen. "She's not all bad."

His gaze swivels to mine, and I press my lips together. *Gina, you're an idiot.*

He fists his hair. "Sweet little drummer boy, why didn't it click into place last week? Ina Donath is your aunt, and she's working for Krampus. She could *be* Krampus."

"Before you fly off with these crazy conclusions, let me talk to her—"

The office door bangs open, and a disheveled elf hops up and down. "Meister Kristof, come quick. Someone's sabotaged the torches down in Welding. We need you immediately."

"Now?" He pinches the bridge of his nose, then looks at me. "Stay here until I get back. We're not done talking."

I bat my eyes. "Can't wait for another round of verbal ammo."

His jaw muscles bunch. Bracing himself on the arms of my chair, his handsome face inches from mine, Kristof whispers, "This would've been a lot easier had you kept your lips to yourself."

I inhale to memorize his scent, doubtful I'll get this close to him again. "You kissed me first."

"A move I'm beginning to regret."

I flinch.

Straightening, Kristof motions toward the door, and three elves enter the office. The ones who had chased me with water guns. "Guard her until I return," Kristof says, and without another glance, he exits behind the original elf.

Benny smirks and pats his water gun.

I sit in the resulting silence, staring at my mistlefeude bottles lying on the worktable. Would these half-pints drench me if I reclaimed the bottles? Kristof can have Papa Campi's journal. He seems determined to translate the whole thing, and my secrets have already been laid bare.

We're not done talking. Pff. What more could he have to say? "You repulse me"? "I never want to see your face in Flitterndorf again"?

"I could never love a Krampus"?

Whoa, whoa. Nobody said anything about love. Several non-dates do not equal love.

Yet, I've known Kristof for over a decade. How many unofficial non-dates have we had in that time? And how many does it take for feelings of friendship to morph into something more when no one's paying attention?

Something moves in my peripheral vision, and Benny slumps to the floor.

I recoil. "What the—?"

Tibbs drops next, and I glance over as Herb wrestles with … Herr Bote! Herb's face slackens, and he, too, drops to the floor.

"I'm told you work for Frau Donath," Herr Bote rasps, pocketing a syringe. "You want to see her or not?"

"W-what? But—" I kneel beside Benny and feel for his pulse.

"They're not dead." Herr Bote curls his lip. "Just unconscious." He checks the hallway. "You coming? This is your chance. No telling what Meister Kristof will do once he gets to her."

I press a hand to my chest. I love Aunt Cat. Even if she and Ina are one and the same, I owe it to the family—the Donati family—to learn the truth and let her explain. Surely this is a massive mistake.

Standing, I tuck my phone into the wristlet, snatch the mistle-what-ever-it-is from the table, and follow Herr Bote from the room.

Forty-Eight

Gina—Dec 3 Through the Cabinet

Once outside the Workshop, Herr Bote points to a human-sized SnoMo. "Take that to the Prep Stables. Inside the supply closet is a cabinet with berry-and-vine emblems on its doorplates. That will bring you to Weihnachts Manor—and Frau Donath."

A direct link to the manor itself. I straddle the SnoMo and glance back at Herr Bote. "Why are you aiding the enemy?"

Herr Bote lifts his chin. "Krampus values my skills, which is more than I can say for Santa." He shoos me away. "Go. She'll be waiting for you."

Does Krampus value the elf's skills, or simply manipulate them to the fiend's advantage?

Twenty minutes later, I enter the Prep Stables. At this time of day, elves bustle about, intent on their individual duties, and expressionless reindeer either stand or lie in stalls. I loop a blue lock of hair around a finger. Which way to that supply closet?

"Have you come to help again this afternoon?"

I turn at the hopeful request and straighten before the elderly stable manager, ragged and worn around the edges. "Herr Verwalter. Yes, sir, here to help. In a way. Except, I can't remember where the supply closet is."

Chuckling, he nods down the wide, central hallway and gives me directions like one might for a child. While I don't have time for the slow pace, neither do I have time to get lost, so I listen with forced patience and take off at a jog when he finishes.

After an unintended detour through the community kitchen (seriously?), I stand before the cabinet door. On the other side, I'll find Weihnachts Manor. Ina Donath. My aunt. If I call Aunt Cat right now, would she answer in German or English? I didn't even know she spoke a second language.

Emotions roil within me. Anger, confusion, disillusionment, guilt. What should I believe anymore? What's right? What's wrong? Who's right? Am I wrong?

Seizing the door pull, I give it a yank. A dark, empty interior and solid back wall greet me. I lean in as jasmine-tinged air wafts my face. Where's that coming from? I step back and study the outside cabinet depth. The rear wall inside extends farther, like the hall passageway went beyond the boundaries of my parents' house.

Heart fluttering, I slip into the cabinet and close the door behind me. A faint outline appears on the back wall in the measurements of a narrow door. I give it the merest nudge, and the new door inches open.

Yellow lamplight brightens the room in which I find myself, the dark windows a good indication I'm no longer in Flitterndorf. But did I make it to Weihnachts Manor?

A grand piano takes up prime real estate in an alcove across the room, and a cello and guitar rest in their stands nearby. On the wall hang more instruments. An Oriental rug adorns the floor. A posh enough place to be the manor. So what now? Do I roam the halls until I find Ina Donath? What if someone spots me?

Footsteps sound to my right. I duck back into the cabinet (on this side, it's an intricately carved armoire), and leave the door open a crack. Pale blond hair and a familiar profile speed past. I tumble out again. "Niklas."

Nik rotates, though it takes an extra second for him to focus. His eyebrows rise. "May I help you?"

He doesn't recognize me? "It's me, Nik. Gina."

"Gina. Gina." He tilts his head. "Where have I heard that name? No matter." A vacant smile replaces his confusion. "Did you know I'm getting married tomorrow?"

"Tomorrow!" I grip his arms. "Then you and Tinsel patched things up?"

Nik sneers. "Why would I marry Tinsel?"

"Um, because you love her." Whom else would he marry?

"Tinsel rejected me. She thinks I'm a failure and is ashamed I can't fly."

"Never. Not Tinsel."

"They told me she said so."

"Who told you?" I snap.

An elf passes outside the doorway and glances into the room at my outburst. I give him a tight smile. He glowers before moving on. As friendly as the elves in Flitterndorf, I see. Who, according to Kristof, are under the influence of mistlefoil.

A.k.a, mistlefeude, which enriches me even as it destroys my friends.

"That's it! Nik, you're being poisoned. It's affecting your mind, your thoughts. You would never consider marrying someone other than Tinsel." I shake him. "You gotta fight this."

His face contorts. "I ... know ... that," he struggles to say, teeth gnashed. "I've been ... trying to fight it ... ever since"—doubling over, he takes a deep breath—"we got here." He grasps my arm, his expression anguished. "Gina, she … took Pa."

"She, who?"

"And they've … got Tinsel. I … saw her. At the Krampuslauf—"

"Niklas?" A female voice drifts from outside the room, and I retreat toward the armoire.

Niklas clutches his head. "Mistlefoil too strong. Too much. Can't fight—" He winces, emitting a shuddering breath. "Get out, G. Tell Kris … Ina Donath is—"

"Nicky, where are you?" the voice calls again.

He stiffens and the fire fades from his eyes, like a flame being snuffed out. I hop into the armoire and peer through the crack as the voice purrs from the room's doorway, "There you are."

A curvy brunette slides a hand up Nik's shoulder and around his neck. I grind my teeth. She leans in to kiss him, but he jerks his head at the last second, and her kiss lands on his chin.

Atta boy, Nik. Keep fighting it.

He murmurs something incoherent, and they move out of sight. I worry my bottom lip. Maybe I don't want to meet Ina. I can't deny anymore that the woman is, in fact, harming my friends, so she couldn't possibly be my aunt—

The armoire door swings open. An elegantly dressed woman stands before me, cradling a reindeer figurine. "Hello, Gina."

Or maybe she can. I manage a smile. "Hey, Aunt Cat. Or should I call you Ina? Or do you have a third personality I know nothing about?"

Forty-Nine

Tinsel—Dec 4 Jailed

❦

Weihnachts Manor

Despair has eclipsed everything, eroding my ambitions and plans, dismantling my future. It infects my surroundings, coating every crude stone wall in this dungeon cell. And Herr Brunner called the switch from my cage an "upgrade." Ha.

An unseen source of light casts a feeble, gray glow against the iron door I tried kicking down before Ina stuck me with mistlefoil again. Now, I sit amongst the dirt and straw littering the floor. A tin plate lies upside down partway into the cell, where it came to rest after a delivery elf shoved it across the ground. Moldy cheese and stale crackers flew in every direction.

It didn't take long for a pair of mice to spot the food. They scurry between the cheese crumbs and a two-inch hole in the far corner. If my talent included shape-shifting, I could escape and help save Christmas. But no. I merely talk to reindeer.

Even that ability deserted you. The one thing that made you special. Now, you're nothing. You're useless. So useless, the word should display your face beside its entry in the online dictionary.

The truth is, you never had what it takes to save Christmas or help the reindeer. You never were suited for life as Mrs. Kringle. Never special.

Ugh, someone make the voices stop.

But mistlefoil slinks along my veins, staining as it goes, toying with my mind, and I can't shake free. Tighter and tighter it coils. Deeper and deeper I sink.

What's the use in fighting anymore? Niklas gets married tomorrow. Or is that today in a few hours? Or has it already happened?

Pressure and heat build behind my eyes like water straining against a dam. I drag my knees to my chin, the stone wall digging into my spine, and stare at my naked ring finger. Have I truly relegated myself to fading into the background, mucking stalls again now that my talent's gone, while Niklas goes about his married life with someone else? If, after all this, we still have reindeer to make messes and Christmas to celebrate … and I don't start mutating like the Third String.

You weren't good enough for him, anyway. You abandoned him.

Heels clip across the floor. "Aw, Tinsel."

I shiver at the cold voice. Please, no more mistlefoil.

Peep-toed shoes come into view as scuffles sound in the distance. "Having a rough night, are we? Here I thought the Krampuslauf would've cheered you up." Ina crouches into my line of sight. "I never wanted to see you like this, you know. Not after I learned you were Gina's best friend."

"How do you know Gina?" I struggle to sit up straighter. "You leave her alone."

"Oh, I couldn't ignore her meddling ways. A pity—she had promise." Ina's gaze flits to the opposite wall as a shout rises from the corridor.

"If you hurt her—"

"Relax. It's temporary. As are your surroundings, provided you behave when this is over." She grasps me by the chin, scrutinizing my face. "The buildup of mistlefoil has done a marvelous job on you. I'm impressed." She pinches my chin before releasing me. "We should have injected you a while ago."

I raise a limp hand to scratch my neck, the skin inflamed at the injection site. "You planning to mutate me, too?"

"Nothing so drastic, sweetie. We just need you sidelined until Niklas gets married, Gretel settles into her new life as Mrs. Claus, and we dismantle Christmas from the inside-out."

So Niklas isn't married yet!

"The elves have already indulged in the bickering and jealousies, the doubts and abdications," Ina continues. "It's delicious. They're destroying themselves without realizing it."

"You won't succeed. Meister K—"

"Santa is two dungeon cells away. And his son is a blubbering jellyfish by this point."

The pressure wells in my eyes, seeking a weak spot in the dam.

Ina's cherry lips lift. "Did you know Nico's claustrophobic? He's ruined from ever cramming down chimneys. It's no wonder Santa caved to mistlefoil so quickly, what with a son who's afraid of tight spaces and a grandson afraid to fly. Who wouldn't be ashamed? Even if Krampus wasn't slated to destroy Christmas, Santa's offspring would complete the job eventually."

Anger tunnels into my arm, and I swing at her. She catches my wrist in a vise-like grip, chuckling. "Now, now. That's no way for a Christmas elf to act." Her eyes narrow. "You're proving as difficult as your reindeer friend. What was his name? Ah, yes. Chip. Had to get him out of the way, in the end."

I let out a cry. "What'd you do to him?"

One hand still wrapped around my wrist, she crooks a finger at the doorway, and an object soars through the air to land with a soft clatter on the floor beside me. A reindeer figurine.

My jaw drops. "How many 'deer are you planning to destroy?"

"As many as it takes."

I jerk to pull from her hold, but Ina gives a painful squeeze, and I suck in air with a hiss.

"You can't win, Tinsel. Failure runs through your veins. Remember that, because if you cause trouble, I'll try my hand at doll-making—with you as my lab rat. Got it?"

I assess her words tossed among the shadows … and the ones she holds behind her back. "You're afraid I'll figure out how to escape." That means a way exists. Her mouth purses, and she withdraws a pen-like object from her pocket. I shrink back. "No."

"I can't trust you to play nice." Quick and precise, Ina pricks my neck and shoves me against the wall. I slump as she rises to her feet, her outlines fuzzy. "If you'll excuse me, I must get some beauty sleep before the marriage ceremony. We'll send you a slice of wedding cake after Saturday's celebratory ball." She laughs and leaves the cell, the door closing on silent hinges.

A coldness drifts around me as the fresh mistlefoil takes effect. In a few hours, Niklas will be married. To Gretel. It's for the best I'm not the bride. Clumsy elves have nothing worthwhile to offer Santa.

I roll my head and dip my chin, my brain taking an extra second to catch up with the movement. My gaze bounces about the familiar set of antlers attached to a familiar tawny coat by my leg. I reach for Chip, but my body won't respond. I try again. And again. My arm flops out, landing on his torso.

I slide down the wall to lie beside him on the floor and whisper, "I'm so sorry."

At last, the dam breaks behind my eyes.

Fifty

Gina—Dec 4 Don't Hate Me

***

Weihnachts Manor

I sit curled on the wooden pallet against one wall. In the dungeon cell next door, Tinsel has been talking to herself for forever, her words carrying through the mouse hole in the corner near my head. Despite the fact she's having a full-blown pity party, her familiar voice comforts me in my dreary surroundings.

"Languish," she says now. "Great word. Sounds as pathetic as I feel."

My mouth quirks. She tried lifting her spirits with Christmas carols earlier, but I could've told her "Blue Christmas," "Where are you, Christmas?" and "I'll Be Home for Christmas" don't conjure up the warm fuzzies.

Time has escaped me, yet it must be a couple of hours since Aunt Cat's minions tossed me in here while she spoke with Tinsel. I haven't made my presence known, though. How do I tell my best friend I messed up and brought disaster upon her peers, family, and hometown? That I may have ruined Christmas for everyone, for all time?

"Who am I kidding?" Tinsel grumbles. "Gretel is a way better match for Niklas. Even if her dad does want to destroy Christmas."

"Totally makes sense," she adds in a higher voice.

"Nothing makes sense," she says in her normal voice.

"And I don't care," she says in that higher voice.

Omigoodness, Tinsel's lost it. Has the mistlefoil seared her brain?

"Perhaps Christmas *should* be destroyed," Tinsel continues. "If Meister Nico can't handle chimneys, Niklas can't fly a sleigh, and Meister K chose a vacation over children's happiness, why bother forcing Christmas along on limping limbs?"

"Meister K didn't choose a vacation," I holler at last. Someone needs to stop this train wreck. "Ina told you—he's down here with us."

Silence meets my words and then a stage-whispered, "Gina?"

"Present."

"Whoa. Since when do you turn invisible and walk through walls?"

I laugh. "You really are addled. I'm in the next cell over, dummy."

"Huh?"

I shift on the pallet and look at our shared wall. "See that hole in the back corner? I'm on the other side."

Scuffs and slaps and an "oof" emit through the little opening. "G?" Tinsel sounds like she's right beside the hole.

"Hi."

"Hiiii! I'm so glad you're here." Her voice wavers. "I mean, I hate that you're locked up, but if ever I needed a friend …. Is this how Ina's taking care of your meddling? What'd you do to her, anyway? How do you know each other?"

An ache begins in my throat. During my last conversation with Aunt Cat, she tried to convince me to help her and Krampus take over Christmas.

"I thought you didn't know about Krampus," I accused.

"I lied. I found out about our ancestry on a trip six years ago. Yes, I

struggled with the knowledge at first. *Who wants that kind of pedigree? In time, however, I came to appreciate the work our relatives—distant and close—were doing."*

"The work? You mean their attempt to destroy Christmas and the Kringles?"

Aunt Cat let out a heavy sigh. *"It's a matter of perspective. Krampus has promised me my own lab and endless funding. He'll bring us freedom—"*

"At the expense of my friends? I can't let you do that."

Her countenance froze over. *"I'm sorry to hear that, because I can't let you stop me."*

"Gina?"

I blink, clenching a bottle of mistlefoil. Aunt Cat left me my stash, expecting me to surrender and use it. I could do with the confidence boost. And anyway, there's no harm in using it on myself. Such intoxicating delight that comes with those enhanced abilities.

Fake abilities.

"G? You there?"

My forefinger trembles atop the fine mist spray nozzle. Intoxicating. "It's a long story, Tins."

A spurt of laughter breaks from her. "I've got time."

"You'll hate me."

"I could never hate you."

"You say that now, but you haven't heard my story." One spritz. One more can't hurt.

Tinsel remains silent for several seconds. Then she takes a loud, shuddering breath. "Gina, despite a promise I made, I abandoned the guy I love in his most vulnerable hour, with disastrous results. I'll regret it forever." Another pause. "I'm not about to do that to our friendship. Whatever you tell me, I might get mad, but I won't stay mad. And I won't hate you."

Tears tinge her voice. Mistlefoil did that to her. Mistlefoil upended her world. My finger slips from the spray nozzle, and I return the bottle to my wristlet. I roll off the pallet and crawl over to the hole.

"Ina Donath ... is my Aunt Cat."

Fifty-One

Tinsel—Dec 4 Simple, Not Easy

Weihnachts Manor

On the dungeon floor, I pad my head with one arm and stroke figurine-Chip's fur as Gina tells her surreal story. Space travel. Mislabeled elixir. Heightened abilities. An aunt's lies and trickery that brought Gina—and more poison—into Flitterndorf. And the zinger: Gina's a Krampus descendant.

My enemy.

With numb detachment that is likely (thankfully?) caused by the mistlefoil in my system, I accept her story, her confession, while Chip's glassy eyes stare at me. Had Gina been open from the start, could we have pieced together this mistlefoil mystery before my reindeer got altered?

"Tinsel, I'm sorry," she pleads now from the other side of the mouse hole. "I'm sorry I didn't tell you earlier, and I'm sorry about the danger I've put everyone in. You know I didn't mean it, right?"

"Yes." She loves me, loves Christmas. The fact she's in a dungeon cell proves she chose me over her aunt; the Kringle family over her bloodline. Forgiveness coaxes my comatose heart.

"I thought I was helping," Gina continues, "and I couldn't understand why things weren't getting better. Frustrating, and yet—oh, Tins, I made the most incredible dolls. Nonna said I'd never be able to do it. That I wasn't creative enough. Thanks to the mistlefoil, I proved her wrong."

"She was never right to begin with. You've always been creative, G. Think of the customers you made happy with your creative cuts as a stylist. Look at the imaginative ways you revived the Huggamugg Café. And when it comes to dolls, your ideas didn't originate with mistlefoil. I bet that along with heightening your natural abilities, mistlefoil also suppressed your grandmother's cynical voice, which freed you to try new things and take some risks." The opposite effect it has on us elves.

Quiet follows. Then a slap as she strikes the wall or floor. "How could I be so stupid?"

"You're not stupid, G," a deep voice says from the corridor. "You have a wonderful mind, capable of remarkable things."

Rolling onto my back, I gape at the cell door. "Kristof?" I will my body to stand, but it remains limp like a rag doll. "Snowballs and icicles, you're here, too?"

"He must've used the portal in the Prep Stables." Gina sounds fainter, as if she's moved away from the hole. "What time is it? How'd you sneak past everyone in the manor?"

"I didn't," Kristof says. "Thankfully, Tinsel's elf-friend bailed me out of a predicament involving three other elves. A Pansy? Or Peony?"

Poppy!

"But how'd you know we were in the dungeons?" Gina asks.

"Herr Bote and his gang ambushed me, and he talks too much when he thinks he's got the advantage."

"Ambush?"

Kristof grunts, and something hard strikes my door. "We've no time to chat, ladies. By now they might have realized I escaped and sent someone to investigate. So, Tinsel, you need to fight the mistlefoil and free yourself fast."

I snort. "I'm trapped in a dungeon cell behind a solid iron door. Hello."

"To which you have the key. Or rather, the antidote."

I struggle to rise on my elbow. "Did Herr Bote force-feed you tainted fruitcake when he ambushed you? Because you're talking nonsense."

Kristof grunts again. "I discovered the antidote when translating the last few entries of Gina's great-grandfather's journal. Right before the ambush. Apparently, the Krampus family has been manipulating and perfecting mistlefoil for centuries, playing up its positive attributes for the Krampus bloodline, and exaggerating the negatives for Christmas beings like Kringles, elves, and reindeer. In us, mistlefoil deposits seeds of doubt and fear. Those grow into lies, which deposit more seeds of doubt and fear, which grow into more lies—"

"And the vicious cycle keeps going," Gina says, once more near the mouse hole.

"And deteriorating. Plus, I think someone must've recently modified it to where mistlefoil attacks and disables the body's unique strengths and talents."

I hug Chip to my chest. "And mutilates the reindeer."

Gina sighs. "That would be my aunt."

Another tap echoes in the hallway. "Thanks to Herr Bote and several other traitors—"

"Meaning me," Gina interrupts.

"—the parasite has been permeating Flitterndorf and its citizens for months now, undetected and unrestrained. Instead of fighting the Kringles and elves on a tangible level, Krampus has been fighting on an abstract one, nullifying my family's powers, dousing the elves' talents, messing with our heads." Kristof punctuates his words with more taps.

"Did you bring your hockey stick?" Gina asks, amusement lacing her voice.

A pinprick of truth pierces my darkness, and I straighten. "Doubting our abilities and talents paralyzes us from honing our skills. When we fear the 'what ifs,' we avoid taking risks. Without risks, we don't grow."

"And a town comprised of insecure, skeptical, inward-focused citizens," Kristof says, "is vulnerable to an outward attack."

My mouth falls open. "Krampus would immobilize and divide our community without ever lifting a finger."

"But Kristof hasn't been affected," Gina points out.

"Because I'd already unwittingly discovered the antidote."

Gina gasps. "When you overcame your jealousies of Nik."

I push to a full sitting position. "Kristof, jealous? Since when?"

"It began after I arrived here in October." He briefly explains his inner conflict under mistlefoil's influence, adding, "Who wouldn't question his worth as a second son? Grandpop never bothered to have more children, and he sent his own brother—a second son—halfway across the world, out of sight, out of mind. Unwanted, perhaps?"

My lips purse. "How'd you fight the mistlefoil?"

"I realized Onkel Stoffel, strangely enough, envied Grandpop in the same ways I envied Nik, and that suspicion pricked a hole in my mistlefoil bubble. Truth had the chance to shine through, expose the lies, and eventually shatter the bubble. So I'm not the firstborn. I was still created with purpose, for purpose. A different purpose than Nik, and that's okay."

I rub my eyes and drag my hand through my short, frazzled hair. "So, while mistlefoil's been saturating Flitterndorf, you haven't succumbed to it because…"

"It whispered the same lies I'd already exposed and defeated with the spirit of truth. Cycle of fear and doubt broken."

"Sounds too simple."

"It is simple. Just not easy. That's why most have fallen for the lies, both in Flitterndorf and here at the manor."

Except for Kristof. And Poppy, because she embraced the truth of her talent and position and lives in contentment. Didn't I embrace my position with the Minor Flight Team, and in being Niklas's fiancée?

… No. Even Niklas called me out on pushing myself with the reindeer so I can prove something to the other elves and outrun my bungling. Always proving, always striving. And when it comes to being Niklas's significant other, there's no question I dance around that issue.

Because you know you don't have what it takes.

Seeds of doubt and fear, Kristof said. Growing into lies. A vicious cycle on repeat. "Break the cycle," I mumble. "Combat the lies with the truth."

You're too clumsy.

I wince. Where's the lie in that?

Except, doesn't my fumbling sometimes leads to fortuitous happenings? Like when I tripped in the closet and revealed the hidden passageway.

You're not smart or talented enough.

"I am when working with the Third String." And they need my help right now.

Energy flows into my body and thrums along my limbs.

"Tinsel?" Kristof asks.

Niklas needs a strong woman, like Gretel, if he's to achieve his highest potential. He can't afford to settle for a lesser partner.

A memory surfaces of a Penalty I'd served in Flitterndorf's library.

Followed by another memory of a Penalty in the Vittles Mart. And another in the boutique. Many Penalties over the years for my gaffes—Penalties that required both physical and mental strength.

"So, I am strong." I use the wall to push myself to a standing position. "And I can take my unique experiences working with those businesses to help improve relations between the elves and Kringles."

Beams of light fracture the darkness in my mind, like sunlight dispersing a fog.

Failure runs through your veins. Ina said so.

I glare at the dungeon door. "Failure happens when I choose to give up. I'm not giving up." Cradling Chip against my torso, I approach the door, strength returning with each step. "It's time I viewed my qualities and quirks as tools to aid me along my path. I may be short on poise and abounding in height, but I'm still a Christmas elf, born to partake in the Kringles' mission to ignite hearts with the Hope of Christmas. Something I can't do from inside a dungeon cell."

Ignite? Please. You'll never shine as Mrs. Kringle.

Gritting my teeth, I target the lie embedded in that mistlefoil-laced tentacle. "You don't get to trap me any longer, Krampus. According to Niklas, shine is what I do best." Dropping a shoulder, I slam against the iron door—

—and careen, unhindered, into the dimly lit corridor.

Fifty-Two

Tinsel—Dec 4 Too Late

Kristof catches me by the shoulders, the end of his hockey stick bobbing near my eye. He pulls me in for a quick hug. "You did it."

"I don't understand." The door remains closed, and I stretch toward it. My fingertips pass through the metal surface like they sweep through air. "It's an illusion? Why didn't you say that?"

"It's real to me." Kristof raps the door with his knuckles. "But this wasn't my prison. And it only had power while you gave it power—believing the lies spoken over you instead of testing them against the spirit of truth."

"Lies that keep us imprisoned." My hand fades in and out of the door. "An illusion. Gina!" I pound on her door. "G, it's your turn."

"It won't work on her," Kristof says.

"Why not?"

"Because I'm a Krampus descendent," Gina chimes in from the other side. "Right?"

My gaze jumps to Kristof. "We can't leave her in there."

Something shifts down the hall, and my blood chills. Have we been found out already? The figure pauses, bracing himself on the wall, and I squint at the dirty white shirt, the lederhosen, the pale hair and beard. "Meister K?"

Nodding, he shuffles forward a step. Kristof drops the hockey stick and rushes to wrap him in a hug. "Grandpop, you're here. I knew you didn't abandon Christmas."

"No." Meister K pats Kristof's back. "Although I'm ashamed to admit I succumbed to the mistlefoil for a time."

His waistband sags, his suspenders more a requirement than tradition now, and my eyebrows hike. "Have you been down here since you disappeared?"

"Yes, and I'd still be in my cell if I hadn't heard your conversation." Meister K grips Kristof's shoulder. "I'd like to set the record straight on some of that, if I may."

Kristof lowers his gaze. "It's okay, Grandpop. I know I'm loved."

Meister K continues nonetheless. "Nico is an only child not because your grandmother and I didn't want more children, but because complications with your dad's birth made it impossible. We never spoke at length about it, since we didn't want Nico burdened with misplaced guilt. In hindsight, however, we should have been candid about the past, especially once you were born." He gives Kristof's shoulder a squeeze. "My boy, we were overjoyed when you entered the world—your father most of all."

Kristof's eyes glisten. "Thank you." He clears his throat. "I, uh, haven't heard anything from Pa in a couple of days. Is he ...?"

"Ina Donath has him squirreled away somewhere. With help from my brother." Meister K grimaces. "Stoffel acts under the influence of mistlefoil, of course, yet I suspect the poison found an easy purchase. Once Stoffel graduated from school, our father sent him here to stabilize the European outpost. I thought Stoffel enjoyed preserving our traditions in the place of our roots. Now I realize he may have felt we were kicking him out of his home. No wonder he's jealous." He tugs at his suspenders. "When this is over, I must remind him how much I depend on his accounting skills each month."

His words rekindle my sense of urgency, and I readjust figurine-Chip so his antlers quit poking me. "If we're hoping for a happy ending when this is over, we need a plan. Meister Nico—"

"You leave Nico up to me." Meister K lets out a weak chuckle. "Since I was able to escape my prison, I suspect my powers have returned. In which case, I can locate Nico on my own."

"What about Gina?"

"I've got an idea to get her out." Kristof withdraws a hockey puck from his coat pocket and winks.

Meister K dips his chin. "Tinsel, your task is to locate the Silver Reindeer."

I suck in a breath. At my neck, the bandage tingles. "She's not on our side. And I can't communicate anymore—oh. The mistlefoil masked my talent, didn't it?" Maybe I can talk her out of attacking me again. "But Niklas is about to get married. Shouldn't I—"

"Locate the Silver Reindeer?" Do Meister K's eyes twinkle? "Yes, you should."

"No, I mean—"

Kristof points me down the corridor. "Take two rights, then a left, then a right, then a left. That'll bring you out behind the manor's east wing."

I rub my thumb along my bare ring finger. "Are you sure about this?"

Meister K cocks an eyebrow. "Are you questioning Santa?"

"No, sir." With a tremulous smile and a goodbye to Gina, I hasten down the corridor. It ends in a "T," and I turn right, following Kristof's directions. Too many dungeon cells and several minutes later, I burst into early morning light. I inhale the fresh air—and freeze.

What have I agreed to? How can I possibly waste time searching for the Silver Reindeer? She could be anywhere, and in looking for her, I'd lose my opportunity to rescue Niklas. I abandoned him once. I won't do it again. And at least I know where to find him.

But will I make it to the Standesamt in time? Breaking into a jog, I run parallel to the manor and skirt around an oak tree—

"Now!" someone shouts.

Several elfin bodies drop onto me from the overhead branches. I crash to the ground, Chip tumbling free, and the elves pin me down. One hand presses my head into the hardened snow as more hands wrench my arms behind me and lash my ankles together. Bound again!

Dark blue elfin booties come into my line of vision. Their owner leans down, tilting his head to look me in the eye. "You shouldn't be out of your cell, *Fräulein*." He makes a tsk-ing sound. "Frau Donath warned what would happen if you caused trouble."

"My niece will love a new doll," says the elf on my back, still pressing against my head. A shudder wracks my body.

"Was ist hier passiert?" someone hollers from a distance. Fritz.

No! I wrestle with my binds. He'll throw me back into the dungeons—in a real cell this time.

Herr Blue-Boots straightens, responding in German. Something about Herr Bote and Kristof. Fritz replies in kind, then addresses all the elves present, after which they scatter toward their village, the elf sitting atop me shoving my head into the snow for good measure.

Frostbitten mistlefoil.

Fritz hauls me to my feet by an arm. I yank free and hop about on bound ankles. "Don't even think about sticking me with more poison." Losing my balance, I land on my rear, almost crushing Chip in the process. "It won't work anymore." I hope.

Fritz's attention snags on Chip, and he crouches to pick him up.

"Careful. That's one of Niklas's reindeer."

He flicks Chip's antler with a finger. "This is a toy."

"*Now* he is. Thanks to Ina and Herr Brunner. They're the reason your reindeer keep disappearing." I shake the snow from my frazzled hair and nod at Chip. "In an attempt to perfect a poison to mutate the Third String, they've been snatching your 'deer and changing them into home decor."

Fritz's mouth mashes, a vein popping in his temple. Rattling off a stream of German words, he puts Chip in the crook of his elbow, tugs something out of his back pocket, and snaps his wrist. Metal glints in the morning light. His arm arcs down—

"No!"

—and he slashes my ankle ties. "You think I would kill you?" He pulls me to my feet again.

I glare at him. "Who knows what you're capable of anymore? To stand mute while the guy I love is forced to marry the girl you care about requires a particularly cold heart." I stomp a foot. "How is this ceremony even taking place? Niklas would've had to present himself—in person—alongside Gretel at the Standesamt in order to apply for marriage, except that never happened, so—"

"I did it." Fritz inspects Chip. "I dyed my hair this summer, pretended to be Niklas, and faked his signature on the documents."

"That wasn't his signature."

"*Stimmt.* I studied Meister Nico's when he signed the original marriage agreement with the Brunners years ago. It was close enough."

Frosted windowpanes, that thing needs to be burned. "You did this to please Gretel?"

"She says she wants Niklas, so I go along, and we both want Christmas pure ... eh, purified. But I think about what you said

Wednesday morning. Two hours ago, I learn Gretel is being poisoned, though it affects her differently than you. Now you tell me her father abuses my animals." He shakes his head, turns me around, and the ties binding my wrists jerk, then fall away. "Pieces fit into place like a … puzzle. I see it now, yet we are too late."

My heart trips. "Why? What time is it?"

He checks his phone. "Ten minutes to ten."

"Then we're not late." I rub my wrists, relief swirling through me. "The ceremony's at ten. They won't sign papers right away, so you can drive me to the Standesamt and—"

"Tinsel." Fritz grips my upper arms. "My grandfather lied to you. The civil ceremony was at nine-twenty. Niklas is already married."

Fifty-Three

Gina—Dec 4 Dangerous in the Wrong Hands

Weihnachts Manor

Fidgeting with my wristlet's zipper, I pace the craggy floor of my cell as Kristof and his grandfather converse in the corridor. They speak softer now that Tinsel has left. I can't make out their words, and my imagination runs wild with what they could be discussing.

Did Kristof know I was here when he used the portal? Will he still try to free me? Does he hate me for lying? For being a Krampus? After spending years worrying about another guy hurting me, I end up doing the hurting.

I stop pacing and cock my head. Silence greets my ears. They can't have gone! I rush to the door. "Hello?" No one answers, and I pound on the iron surface. "Kristof, you there?"

"Which side are you on?" he asks.

Oh, whew. Still here. "What do you mean?"

"You told Tinsel you didn't know you were poisoning the elves. Are you lying?"

320

"Would my aunt have locked me up if I were?"

"It could be a trap."

I flatten a palm against the door. "I never meant to harm anyone."

"Then why'd you knock out my elves?"

"What?"

"In Grandpop's office. I told you to wait for me, yet when I returned, my elves were unconscious and you had run."

My eyes narrow. "Who told you I ran?"

"Herr Bote."

"You're trusting the words of an elf who later coordinated your ambush?"

A series of taps on the door fill the quiet. "What's *your* story?"

"Herr Bote knocked out your elves." I recall the syringe he tucked in his pocket. "He probably used a hefty dose of mistlefoil to do it. They went down immediately." My wristlet grows heavier. It carries potent stuff. "He said to follow him if I wanted to see Ina. I'd recently learned she was Aunt Cat, so of course, I jumped at the chance to talk to her. Better than waiting for you to return and ream me out for being a Krampus descendant."

"C'mon, Gina, you lied to me."

"You never asked."

Kristof scoffs. "You lied by omission."

I rap the door with my wedge-heeled shoe. "It's not the type of news one shares, spur of the moment. Or during a non-date. And definitely not during a date-date—"

"I let you into Christmas headquarters."

"Okaaay. I'm sorry." I sag against the door. "It wasn't easy to hear that I'm, like, related to someone you hate, and I didn't know how to tell you. I thought I could show you I was on your side, but it got complicated, and ... well, I botched things, haven't I?"

Silence.

"Kristof?"

Thwack—CRACK!

The door vibrates, and I leap back. What the—?

A rattling ensues, and the door swings inward, weak light from the hallway pooling around Kristof's silhouette. A busted padlock dangles from his hand. "C'mon. We don't have long before someone comes to investigate that noise."

"Thank you!" I throw my arms about his neck, relishing the sandalwood scent embedded in his ribbed sweater. He stiffens, and I withdraw. "Sorry. Sorry. You must hate me." I clench my wristlet and lower my eyes. "I promise not to do that again."

Sighing, Kristof ushers me into the hallway. "I don't hate you, Gina." He grabs his hockey stick, scans the corridor, and crouches to snatch a black object from the ground.

I choke on a laugh. "You used a hockey puck to smash the lock?"

"I had no idea what I'd be up against here, and hockey is one thing I do well." Kristof closes the cell door behind me and works the broken padlock into place. "At a glance, this'll look like you're still inside and buy us some time." He heads along the corridor toward a dead end.

"Where are we going? Where's Meister K?"

"He went to find Pa, and I'm returning to Flitterndorf. You can go wherever."

"Then I'm coming with you. If we can make it to that armoire—" Kristof whirls about, and I collide into him, bracing my hands against his chest. I whip them back to my sides.

He leans close, and my heart pitter-patters like a schoolgirl (most inconvenient timing). "I left Flitterndorf in turmoil, Gina. I wasn't kidding about the ambush. Gram and I spent the last few hours under house arrest. Thank Christmas for the conference balcony one story below the living room window, or I couldn't have escaped—"

"You jumped?"

"Yes, and there's no telling how I'll make it back without being found out. You helped put me in this predicament—"

"So let me help you out of it. Tell me what to do, and I'll do it."

"Convince me I can trust you."

"How?"

"I'll know it when I see it. In the meantime, you're not going anywhere near Flitterndorf."

"If you go back and I stay here, how can I prove anything?"

"That's for you to work out." His gaze flits past me and widens. I turn. At the end of the corridor, bobbing light glows around the corner. Kristof spins in the opposite direction. "We've lingered too long."

"You're heading toward a dead end—"

He yanks me into a run. After the last cell, at the corridor's apparent end, Kristof ducks into a slim opening not visible until one reaches the back wall and looks to the right. I slip through the narrow gap as elves round the far corner.

Blackness shrouds me, the smell of dank stone assaulting my nose. My breath falters, and I hold fast to Kristof. "Please don't let go."

The air shifts. "Watch your step," he murmurs, his lips moving against my ear. My breath falters for new reasons. "Spiral staircase ahead."

His presence fades, and he pulls me after him, my steps hesitant until I get the feel for the treads' depth and height. "How did you know about this passage?"

"Lukas. The dungeons are his favorite place, and he showed me all the hidey-holes he's explored over the years. This will bring us to the kitchen."

Shouts sail up to us from the dungeons. They must have discovered their prisoners escaped. Kristof and I quicken our pace as best we can in the dark. We travel one, maybe two, rotations, and gray light trickles to us from unseen windows above. Kristof pauses beside a door on the next landing, faint clangs and voices coming from the other side.

"I may have figured something out," he says, hand poised on the doorknob. "When talking to Grandpop downstairs, I asked about the busted wardrobe, and he confirmed it has space-traveling abilities. That's why he was repairing it. Once fixed, the wardrobe will connect the Workshop directly to the Manor. He wanted it finished in time for the Initiation Ceremony so he could surprise Nik, and Nik could use it to walk—not fly—home. But Grandpop didn't know about a portal in the Prep Stables or the one at your house. Herr Bote knew, though. Niklas mentioned in a text that he'd seen Herr Bote here."

"Which means Krampus probably knew."

"And could've used it to his advantage in spreading the mistlefoil." Kristof kneads his neck. "At some point, Herr Bote must've learned about the wardrobe repairs and reported his findings back to Krampus, because thanks to the traitorous blabbermouth, I now know that Krampus plans to use the wardrobe—and soon."

I grip Kristof's arm. "You need to get to Flitterndorf and destroy both portals."

"Destroy?" He winces. "Yeah, you're probably right."

"So why have we stopped?"

He hitches a thumb at the door. "We need to get past the kitchen elves on our way to the music room."

Elves. I tap my wristlet against my thigh. An idea sparks. "Play it casual, like we're supposed to be here," I say. Kristof rubs his scruff, frowning. "It works in the movies. Sometimes." His frown deepens, and I cock my hip. "Do you have a better idea? Once we're past the kitchen, we race to the music room, into the armoire, and destroy the portal from Flitterndorf's side before they can follow us through. Er, follow you." *Please, us?*

324

Footsteps patter on the stairs below, and Kristof nods. "Okay, let's go." Opening the door, he saunters into the kitchen, me dogging his steps. Work comes to a halt among the elves. Kristof waves. "Grüß Gott," he says. "Don't mind us. Just passing through. Food smells great."

I poke him in the back. "Quit drawing attention."

Voices shout in German from the stairwell behind us. Not good.

Kristof and I break into a run. Elves swarm around, hopping onto Kristof, clinging to my legs, and as Kristof shouts at them, I fumble with my wristlet. Grabbing the first vial I touch, I spritz mistlefoil in random directions, random faces. Elves blink, cough, sneeze ... and desist. I continue spritzing, inhaling the fumes myself, euphoria overtaking me, unblocking brainwaves, allowing me a glimpse into unchartered creativity. Ah-MAZE-ing!

A moment later, Kristof and I are surrounded by elves that either squabble, stand in a depressed stupor, or have fainted altogether. I swallow. Once again, our escape lies unhampered, but at what cost?

Kristof stares at the vial I hold. His solemn gaze lifts to mine. "That's dangerous in the wrong hands."

I clasp it close. "And miraculous in mine. It enhances my abilities—"

"Enhances, maybe, but that stuff doesn't create something you don't already possess. You have the skills, G. You'll just need to work harder without the mistlefoil to access them."

My breathing escalates, and I shake my head. "Without this, I revert to boring, normal Gina Donati."

"You mean the beguiling, fun-loving Gina Donati I fell in love with, prior to all this happening?" His jaw muscles pulse. "C'mon, let's go before the elves revive themselves."

I hurry behind him in my own kind of stupor, fixated on his confession. Love? I knew he had a crush, but *that* word? We speed walk through an area three stories high, and although elves rush to and fro, no one confronts us. I stare at Kristof's back. He used the past tense. Could my Krampus genealogy have put the kibosh on his feelings?

Not that my actions in the kitchen did me any favors.

We enter the music room on our left. Soft morning sunlight stretches across the grand piano in the alcove. Kristof wrenches open the armoire door and hesitates, internal conflict visible in his bunched eyebrows. "Gina, I can't—"

"Here." My throat burns as I stretch out my hand, the vials of mistlefoil in my palm. "Dispose of them when you get to Flitterndorf."

He studies my face. "You're willingly giving them up?"

"Just take them." If I think too much, I'll lose my nerve. "I'd rather struggle through creative blocks than lose the last of your respect."

Kristof accepts the bottles, slipping them into a pocket. The resulting emptiness hits me like a void in my soul—and then Kristof's warm fingers thread through mine, filling that void. I meet his gaze in surprise.

He grins and tugs me to the armoire. "You wanted to come, right?"

Fifty-Four

Tinsel—Dec 4 The Silver Reindeer

Weihnachts Manor

Niklas is already married!

My mind revolts, and I wrench from Fritz. "That's impossible. You're the one who's lying. I can't be too late."

His gaze turns pitying, and pain scalds my heart, swelling and straining against my rib cage. Unshed tears blind me. Knees buckling, I crumple to the ground. Niklas is married? The snow seeps into my leggings. He belongs to another woman.

Only over the last two years did I begin to entertain dreams about us, but gingerbread man, how deep and fast they grew. Dreams that feature me working beside the man I love, the teammate I respect. Dreams of raising a new generation of Kringles; influencing a new generation of believers. Dreams that eclipse my former ambitions to become Chief Operations Elf and my present goal to lead the Minor Flight Team.

An invisible door now slams on them.

Tears slip from my nose and chin, melting away a patch of snow one dot at a time as my hopes melt away. How could I let my doubts about becoming Mrs. Santa Claus beat me? How could I choose fear over love?

Mistlefoil, that's how.

My hands fist in the snow.

The surrounding area brightens, and Fritz makes a strangled noise. I lift my head.

His eyes are as round as a slice of yule log cake, staring above and beyond me. I follow his gaze—and spring to my feet. The Silver Reindeer stands before us, her majestic silvery coat exuding a light that doesn't stem from the morning sun.

My limbs shake, yet newfound anger surpasses the fear her presence evokes. "You were supposed to help us! Instead, you threatened me and Niklas, and now the mistlefoil's out of control and Krampus has practically won."

She bobs her head, her thick, overloaded antlers sweeping the air. "I regret how my actions must have looked," she says, her voice calm and even. "But I did help. Your necklace was corrupted with mistlefoil, after all."

"Corrupted?" I touch my neck where the choker used to lie until my last run-in with the SR. Had Gretel offered to rub essential oils into it as another way to expose me to mistlefoil and stifle my talent? I clear my throat. "That doesn't explain why you took off with Niklas in Salzburg."

"I wanted to show him he needn't fear flying."

"Well, you failed."

Fritz points between us, his jaw hanging open. "Are you speaking to the reindeer?"

The Silver Reindeer curls a leg beneath her in a type of bow. "My name is Bliss."

"Fritz, meet Bliss." I take Chip from Fritz and bob a curtsy. "I'm

Tinsel."

Bliss narrows her eyes at Chip. "Why does your toy reek of mistlefoil?"

"Because he's not a toy." I give a quick explanation of the reindeer-turned-figurines, ending with, "If you don't know about this, how much help can you give?"

"It wasn't until the young Kringle came into my stall several weeks ago that I became aware of matters related to Krampus. That initial contact activated partial knowledge within me, and I've been seeking answers ever since. Once I learned about mistlefoil, I sensed it everywhere. In the air. The food. Your clothes. In that toy reindeer." Bliss contemplates Chip and flicks her ears. "I've seen a reflection of my magnificent rack a time or two. I wonder ..." She shifts on her front legs, takes a breath, and lets it out again, murmuring, "This is no time for vanity." Jerking her head, she punctures Chip's torso with an antler tine.

"Hey!" I yank Chip away. "This is also no time for violence. Are you on our side or not?" Scowling, I assess the damage, but Chip's torso remains intact. No wound. No insides spilling out. Nothing. Except, a tine on Bliss's antler is now missing. "What's going on?"

Bliss cocks her head at Chip. "I thought—"

Bells jangle in the distance, rapidly growing louder and more obnoxious, like clanging. It comes from the sky, and I shield my eyes from the sunlight to search. Seven deformed monstrosities swoop into view from the direction of town, chained to a gigantic black sleigh. Their skeletal maws strain at their bits, their claws thrashing the air as they circle above the manor.

I grip Fritz's arm. "That's what they did to the Third String."

"Ho, ho, hahaha!" the driver calls, his face hidden from view.

"And that sounds like Opa Stoffel." Fritz pulls out his phone, lips tightening. "It should be Herr Brunner, yet he is not to leave until

329

tomorrow." Fritz's thumbs fly over the screen.

"Leave for where?"

His gaze connects with mine. "Flitterndorf."

My lungs constrict. "Omigoodgarland, Herr Brunner—Gretel's *father*—is Krampus?" Of all the times the Kringles have been exposed to him, the visit he paid to Flitterndorf, we did nothing—because we knew nothing. All the while, he took advantage of our ignorance and plotted our demise. I glare at Fritz absorbed with his phone. "How long have you known? No, never mind that. Why is Herr Stoffel taking the sleigh?"

A sleigh that finishes a second loop above the manor and jets off to the west.

"Wait, where are they going?" In seconds, sleigh and beasts are specks in the sky, and I smack my forehead. "It's not even Christmas Eve. They're flying in broad daylight with no magic to shield them. Any watchful government eye wouldn't hesitate to blast them out of the sky."

Bliss grunts. "Did you see those beasts? They possess heightened abilities. No doubt protection from detection is one of them. Now, are you ready?"

"For what?"

"To go after them."

"There's no catching up with them now."

"You doubt me?"

My gaze flicks over her small form. "Um ..."

Bliss arches her head back and inhales, her torso expanding. "I am sustained by the spirit of Christmas. Do you doubt that power?"

Not when it helped get me out of the dungeons and fuels my talent. My waning hope rekindles. Krampus might have succeeded in marrying off Niklas, but in whatever nefarious plan he's concocted that involves my Third String, I won't let him succeed without an additional fight.

I gesture to Bliss's back. "May I?" She kneels on her forelegs, and I settle behind her slim shoulders. "What happens if we—"

"When we."

"—overtake them?"

"I don't know." She rises from the ground. "I'm figuring this out as I go."

"Tinsel, wait." Fritz waves his phone, but his next words are lost to my outcry as Bliss vaults into the sky and chases after the Third String.

Fifty-Five

Gina—Dec 4 Chaos

⟡

Flitterndorf

Kristof and I emerge not from the cabinet into the supply closet, but rather from a now fully restored wardrobe into a darkened, empty hallway. I run a hand over the wardrobe's surface, unmarred save for a few faint cracks. Like it was never broken in the first place. Magic?

I glance around. Light angles in from an archway at one end of the hallway—along with shouts, scuffling, and general mayhem. "Where are we?"

Kristof's face turns stony. "The portal brought us inside Santa's Workshop. Exactly as Grandpop planned, and as Krampus counted on."

We approach the sounds of combat. "What's with the noise? It's the middle of the nigh—" I step onto the third-floor balcony, and my mouth drops. A battle rages on all three levels of the Workshop foyer.

Elves flail at each other with foam swords, batting heads, whacking arms. One level below them, a pair face off with wooden spears, their shafts colliding with dull *thwacks*. Cornered in front of the nativity scene on the first floor, the hockey team uses their sticks to shoot a battery of toys through the air. Some toys hit their targets, others bounce to the floor and roll away—to be picked up by other elves and hurled in random directions. Along the two flights of stairs, elves have set up toy canons and aim them around the room, firing off plastic balls and candy bombs. And in a shocking twist, the fighting doesn't just happen along Clan lines.

Next to me, Kristof grips the rail. "Look at us. We're not prepared to fight Krampus when he walks through that wardrobe." His knuckles whiten. "How am I to speak order and reason into this chaos?"

I tug at his elbow. "First, let's destroy the wardrobe before Krampus or any other enemy barges through it."

With a grimace, he accompanies me down the hallway. "I hate to do this." He jockeys into position beside the wardrobe. "Not only would Nik have benefited, but easy access to Europe could have improved relations with our German kin."

I mirror Kristof's stance on the other side. "I'm sorry."

"Me, too." With a tremendous heave, we rock the wardrobe onto its face. Whatever magic held it together severs on impact, and it shatters like glass with an echoing racket. Kristof rubs his chest. "That was painful." He stares at the wreckage, then gives himself a shake and points down the hall. "Now for the second one. Take the stairs to the bottom level, turn left, and keep going until you see the green striped door. That will bring you to the rear of the Workshop. Use my SnoMo and get to the Prep Stables."

"You're not coming?"

Kristof motions toward the balcony and the in-fighting. "I need to deal with that."

"What if I lose my way?" I pull my hands into my sleeves. "Bad sense of direction, remember?"

He gives a teasing rap on my forehead with his knuckle. "A

wonderful mind, remember? What did you tell me about your attention to detail?"

I bite my lip to hide a grin. "Okay. I'll go. Promise me, though, that at the end of all this craziness, if I haven't shown up again, you'll come search for me."

"Promise."

I move toward the stairs.

"G, wait." Kristof grabs my arm. "For what it's worth, knowing your bloodline doesn't change my feelings for you." Angling close, he captures my lips with his. I gasp, and he deepens the kiss. Heat curls in my belly, and I slide my arms about his neck as the kiss turns deliciously thorough. Assailed by his encouragement, forgiveness, and love, my heart can't help but take the plunge.

Too soon, he withdraws, a boyish grin lifting his lips. "I couldn't let you go without telling you—" His eyes flare. "You're crying."

"Am I?" I swipe at my damp cheeks. "Sorry."

"*I'm* sorry. I shouldn't have assumed—"

"Yes, you should have." I emit a half-laugh, half-sob. "You make me feel what no liquid in a vial ever could, and I'm grateful for it." I kiss him again, then make for the stairs.

Time to take out the second portal.

Fifty-Six

Tinsel—Dec 4 Ready or Not

Somewhere Between Brückenstadt and Flitterndorf

Astride the Silver Reindeer, I grip one of her main antler beams and hug Chip with my other arm. Freezing air numbs my skin as we race several thousand feet above the ground. I've never flown so high with any reindeer. No seat belt. No helmet. Were I to fall—

Bile rises in my throat. Is this how Niklas felt as a little boy when flying with Meister K? Vulnerable. Helpless. At the mercy of someone else and the unfamiliar.

No wonder he has a phobia.

As we travel from daylight back to the wee hours of the morning, we gain on Herr Stoffel's sleigh wavering in the sky, roughly a mile away. "What's the plan for when we overtake him?" I holler, the wind whipping at my voice.

"I shall focus on the reindeer." Bliss stretches her neck forward, upping her pace. "You focus on the man."

"You're going to leave me to wrangle Herr Stoffel by myself? You're going to tackle eight monsters by yourself? This has failure written all over it."

"We each have a part to play in this fight." The sleigh zooms ahead of us, now a half mile away. "Stopping Herr Stoffel is yours. Let me do mine."

"What if I—"

"Get ready," Bliss calls. The sleigh looms ever larger.

I clench my teeth. *You can do this, Tinsel. You* must *do this. For Christmas. For the Third String.*

Bliss closes in on the sleigh. Something slumps on the seat beside Herr Stoffel, who glances over his shoulder. Exclaiming, he slaps the reins.

I clutch Chip tighter. "I'm ready." With a burst of speed, Bliss leaps above the sleigh, and my heart clambers over itself when I recognize the slumped form. "Niklas."

Then Bliss tips.

I yelp, slipping from her back, and land in a tangle of elbows and reins.

"Get off me." Herr Stoffel thrusts me aside as he juggles the reins. I tumble to the floor, and he kicks me in the shoulder.

Son of an abominable snowman! I kick back, catching his shin. He strikes again as I shift out from under his feet. Pain flares in my hip. When he kicks a third time, I catch his boot, wrench it off, and throw it at him. It hits his shoulder, then bounces over the side and disappears.

"You'll pay for your meddling," he shouts, striking with his stockinged foot, his attention split between me and the mutant reindeer.

"Niklas." Fending off Herr Stoffel's blows with Chip in one hand (so sorry, buddy!), I jostle Niklas's inert form on the bench seat before me. What's he doing here? Where's Gretel? "Niklas, wake up." His eyelids flutter. "What have you done to him?" I yell at Herr Stoffel.

"He did it to himself, foolish boy. No matter. I still say Christmas should have new ownership."

"Nobody owns Christmas." I shake Niklas again. "But you're on your way to destroying it."

Niklas's eyes crack open. "Tinsel?" he croaks.

"I want *you* destroyed!" Herr Stoffel snatches Chip from me.

"Give him back."

"Go get him," he snarls and tosses Chip from the sleigh.

"Chip!" White-hot anger drills through me, and I launch myself at Herr Stoffel. The sleigh tips. He shoves. Momentum smashes me against the top edge of the sleigh, and I spin out into thin air, shrieking, grasping.

I catch the lip of the sleigh with one hand and bang into the hull. Herr Stoffel pounds on my fingers. Stars prick my vision, and I grapple for purchase with my other hand. Just as he pries my fingers from the sleigh, I snag a length of rein. And plummet.

My stomach lurches. "*Heeelp!*" I kick the air and squeeze the rein connecting me to the frenzied beasts above. Jerked off-balance from my weight, they bump into each other, snapping and snarling and trying to stay on course. A petite Bliss fights antler-to-antler with a lead beast, while the second, smaller leader nips at his slackened harness.

Smaller? Crumbling candy canes! It's Butterscotch, reverted to normal. Did Bliss do that?

My numb hands slip, the rein chafing my skin. "No. No, help!" I slip again—and the sleigh shrinks as air rushes through my clothes and across my face.

I'm falling. Tumbling. Thousands of feet above the earth. Sky and ground flip over and over. Tears freeze in the corners of my eyes. I'm not ready to—

Oomph.

A solid object knocks the breath from me. My arms dangle over one side, my legs over the other. Hooves pump across the sky. A reindeer.

Bracing against the warm hide, I turn my head. I know the coloring in that neck. "Chip!"

He arcs his head in acknowledgment. "Is it too much ta ask that ye let a reindeer fully transform afore needin' a rescue?"

His endearing brogue resettles a piece of my capsized world, and I give him an awkward hug in my sack-like position. "Bliss fixed you, after all."

"Goin' ta need therapy after this shindig is over, but I'd rather be turned into a toy than a devil-monster." He nods ahead where the sleigh zigzags in the sky. "D'ye have a plan fer savin' our friends?"

Moving carefully, I rotate to straddle his back and hitch forward behind his shoulders. "Bliss is working on part of it, although—" A faint glow materializes on the horizon, and my insides congeal. "Snowflakes and frostbite, that's Flitterndorf. Chip, we can't let Herr Stoffel make it there." The town's glow expands as an idea sprouts in my mind. "Can you bring us closer to the sleigh?"

"With pleasure."

"Stay out of Herr Stoffel's sight until I say."

Chip gains on the sleigh until he trails directly behind and to the right of it. Two reindeer have transformed back to their old selves, and Bliss struggles with a third. Evading a desperate kick from the monster, she does a funny drop-and-swerve to jab an antler tine into its side. It squeals and convulses, tethers jerking like Christmas lights in a windstorm. As I gape, the claws retract into hooves, the head morphs from some grotesque Halloween creature into that of a reindeer, and within seconds, Licorice pummels the air in the monster's place.

Three down, four to go. Flitterndorf looms closer, and I pat Chip's side. "Okay, get me up there."

Lengthening his stride, Chip pulls ahead of the sleigh, and as we parallel the tethered reindeer, I cup my mouth. "Peppermint Twist!" The restored members of the Third String glance my way. "Peppermint Twist. In honor of Cocoa—ow!" Pain stings my back, and Chip bucks and veers away.

"That bloke whipped us." Chip growls at Herr Stoffel. "I oughtta—"

A hand stretches up to wrest the whip from Herr Stoffel, a blond head appearing over the rim. Niklas.

Then the sleigh tilts.

Down the row of animals and monsters, the three restored reindeer have tangled the traces à la Cocoa, and now rotate in sync ... again ... and again ... and again, forcing the others and the sleigh to rotate with them. They gain speed as they go, making a dizzying, bumpy trajectory toward Flitterndorf.

Chip races after them, and I hang onto his main beams. My heartbeat rushes louder in my ears the closer the whole contraption gets to the ground. I did not think this all the way through.

Fifty-Seven

Gina—Dec 4 Invasion

Flitterndorf

I zoom down Huff 'n Puff Hill on Kristof's SnoMo. Early December air nips my exposed face and hands, but the heat from his sultry kiss keeps me warm.

Not that any number of kisses lessens the hurdles we must jump to make a complicated relationship work. Kristof might return to Germany, yet I'm on my way to destroy the second of three portals linking our worlds together. What could have been easy visits between us will now be time-consuming. And expensive.

Though it appears my Krampus lineage isn't a deal-breaker. As to the three-date policy ... yeah, that went the way of snow in July. So maybe there aren't many hurdles aside from the pesky long-distance issue. What would Claire think of opening a Huggamugg Café in Brückenstadt?

But I don't want to manage a café. I want what I've had this week with the Doll Makers.

A stab of regret burrows between my ribs. I relinquished that dream when I relinquished the mistlefoil.

As I drive through town, elves mill about the sidewalks, and I frown. It's past two in the morning. Why is everyone awake? And not just awake. They're squabbling with each other—even as whispered encouragement blooms within me, lifting my spirits, expanding my mind.

Mistlefoil.

The fighting escalates the closer I get to the Town Square. Some elves shout insults, some resort to fisticuffs, others have taken up random items to wield as weapons. A broom jabs like a sword, a side table defends like a shield, and a candlestick whacks like a club.

Glass shatters behind me. I stop the SnoMo, swiveling on the seat. The Skate 'n Ski Shoppe's front window lies smashed on the sidewalk, and elves scuttle through the opening to … loot? Plundering in Flitterndorf.

Okay, where's that mistlefoil coming from?

A slow clap sounds from the far corner of the Square. "Ausgezeichnet." A mustached man smiles, though his black eyes remain cold. Beside him stands Aunt Cat.

I'm too late in destroying the second portal.

"Our work here is almost finished, and I barely got my hands dirty," the man says in a thick German accent. Elves clad in blue and white, their mouths covered by cylindrical masks, fall into formation behind him. They carry blasters similar to Benny's, yet sleeker. "I feel my powers growing exponentially."

"Stop!" I shout above the chaos, speeding around the square. Shock blooms on Aunt Cat's face as I swerve the SnoMo in the street to block them. "Whatever you're planning, you must end it. This isn't right."

"I do not take orders from little girls," the man sneers.

I purse my lips. "I wasn't talking to you."

His nostrils flare. "See here, child. I'm Krampus."

"You?" My gaze travels over his plain features and average, middle-aged form. "I was expecting someone scarier."

Glaring, he yanks a whip from his side and strikes a random red-clad elf, who drops to the ground. "Step aside and join me or reap the consequences."

My fingers tighten on the SnoMo's handlebars. Has Flitterndorf lost before it even knew to fight? I eye the blue- and white-clad elves as they fan around the Town Square and trickle down side streets. The squabbling red- and green-clad elves don't notice. Unease creeps into my muscles.

"You won't win." Thankfully, I sound more convincing than I feel.

Krampus laughs. "I already did, several months ago"—he indicates the oversized snow globe behind me—"when Stoffel sent that as a present." My mouth parts as comprehension takes hold.

Aunt Cat raises a familiar vial. "You've tasted mistlefoil's power, Gina. You've experienced the enlightenment it gives. All Krampus descendants do. Who could fault us for utilizing the benefits? Think of the good we'll bring about, empowered alongside Krampus."

"You call this good?" I gesture to the mayhem. "It's destroying the elves, destroying my friends. And you knew it would. You lied when you said mistle*feude* would benefit them and convinced me to spread it."

"But it is beneficial. In the end. You'll see. Krampus will make things right when this is over."

"A world without Christmas? Without a message of hope? Of love? The most sensational Gift mankind has ever known? How is that good?"

"Enough!" Krampus slashes his whip through the air. *"Meine Elfen! Bereit!"*

The foreign elves aim their guns upward at an angle.

Good gravy. I leap off the SnoMo and run to the nearest bickering elves. "Elves of Flitterndorf"—I shake them—"you're being invaded. Stop fighting each other." I turn to the next group. "Fight for Christmas!"

"*Feuer!*"

Shots sound off like firecrackers from the blasters, ricocheting among the buildings. Multi-colored dust particles shoot into the sky and scatter among the Flitterndorf elves.

"*Feuer!*" Krampus shouts again.

A second round issues into the air, and as a layer of dust builds, the Flitterndorf elves either faint or lapse into slack-jawed stupors. The foreign elves, protected from the mistlefoil by their masks, holster the blasters and pull lengths of rope from their pockets. Meeting no resistance from those unconscious or dazed, they begin tying up their Flitterndorf kin.

"No!" I shove a blue-clad elf away from Tinsel's mum.

Arms grab me from behind and wrestle me backward. "The Kringles and this antiquated holiday have oppressed me for too long," Krampus snarls in my ear. "It needs to be routed."

"Don't give in to the mistlefoil," I holler to the elves. "Don't listen to its lies." Straining against Krampus, I glare at Aunt Cat, her own eyes wide. "Can't you see he's deceiving you? He's using the poison for selfish gain—not to repair a holiday, or improve your personal life, but to put himself in a place of power. If he can get the elves to question the truth, if he can get them to fear, he can control them. Bondage. That's what he wants—"

"No more from you." He flings me aside with extra-human strength, and the world blurs as I fly through the air.

I crash into a parked SnoMo, pain splitting in my head and my shoulder as I land. Dots of light flare and spin. I blink to clear them.

"I was thwarted two years ago when Niklas chose a measly elf over my daughter," Krampus declares, straddling Kristof's SnoMo. "I will not be thwarted now by a measly girl." He zooms inches from me and cuts down the street that leads to Huff 'n Puff Hill.

Feeling the back of my head, I struggle to sit up. "Gotta stop him."

Aunt Cat rushes over and drops to my side, her hands skimming my arms. "He promised not to harm you."

"Like you care. You locked me in a dungeon cell."

"I didn't physically hurt you."

I push her away, wincing at the twinge in my shoulder. "Hurt comes in many forms, Aunt Cat. Look around." I blink against a fresh wave of stars and cradle my head. "These clans are fighting over nonsense and destroying each other in the process."

"Because Christmas is destructive. It's a faux holy day meant to part one from one's money. A beacon pointing people to restrictive rules and narrow-minded thinking. When we rid this world of the Kringles and Christmas, we'll be free from its constraints."

Kristof's explanation of the Clandy-Stein Mountains pounds alongside my growing headache. "The constraints aren't the enemy, and doing away with them won't bring freedom, because the real entrapment waits on the other side. The boundaries are the last defensive line protecting us from the bondage."

Aunt Cat's eyebrows pull together. "But the mistlefeude feels so good. And my lab …"

"It has to start out feeling good. That's how we're enticed to cross over. Yet look where it's brought you. You're willing to hamstring four elf clans and aid someone bent on destroying a message of love for a cold, steely science lab." I glare through the bickering elves at the snow globe spewing filthy air. Gritting my teeth, I push past the pain to stand. "We've got to disable that thing—"

"Paß auf!" shouts an elf, pointing at the sky. Others scream and run, tugging their hampered Flitterndorf counterparts away as massive, demon-like creatures descend from the sky. They crash onto the Town Square, sliding along the ground in a web of straps, while an inky black sleigh smashes into the slow globe.

The globe explodes in a shower of glass and rancid air.

Fifty-Eight

Tinsel—Dec 4 Rally the Elves

Flitterndorf

Chip and I hover above the destruction as glass, dirt, and snow balloon around the scattering elves. Pitching to one side, the sleigh plows across the street and into the Vittles Mart, brick and mortar walls crumbling on impact.

Niklas.

Ribbons and bows, what have I done?

We land several yards from where Bliss shakes off the fall and confronts a monster reindeer. Two other beasts use their razor-edged antlers to slice themselves free from the traces. The fourth mutation lies tangled, sides heaving, breath fogging.

I slip from Chip's back and race to the sleigh half-buried in rubble, one runner missing. Herr Stoffel is hunched over on the bench seat. Where's Niklas?

The monsters shake free and rampage through the street, tossing their skeletal heads, attacking elves. Shouts, roars, fights, and screams coalesce into pandemonium, all blanketed by a fetid smell. How can we withstand such calculated hatred?

We've lost. There's no hope. We're worthless. I'm worthless.

No. Not again.

"Tinsel, look." Chip jumps up and down on his hooves. "'Tis Bonbon! We need ta free her." I hesitate. What about Niklas? What if he fell from the sleigh while still in the air? My pulse pounds in my temples.

Chip approaches the monster trapped in strappings. It growls, its claws ripping through the cobblestones as though pawing through mere sand.

"Chip, wait." I start after him. "She doesn't recognize—" High-pitched screeching rents the air, and I turn. A skeletal monster stares me down. Tremors wrack my body. The monster launches, jaw opening.

"Tinsel!"

Someone knocks me aside, covering me with his body. I cringe, expecting the gouge of an antler tine, a bodily toss. Nothing comes. I chance a peek.

Bliss tussles with the monster, their antlers locked in battle. Dwarfed by the creature, she nonetheless drives it back, empowered by the Christmas spirit. She yanks free, contorts her body, and sinks a tine deep into the monster's flesh. The monster howls.

"One of these days, you'll learn to move out of the way."

My rescuer's voice pulls my gaze, and I squeak. "Niklas!"

He gives me a dimpled smile. "Hi."

"You're alive."

"And trying to keep it that way." He hauls me to my feet. "I'd appreciate it if you did the same. No more jumping out of sleighs in mid-flight, okay?" He wraps me in a hug, pressing his face into my hair, and my body ignites. "I thought I'd lost you up there, Tins. I blacked out at the Standesamt and awoke in the sleigh, only to see you go overboard—" Niklas's voice cracks, and he shudders. "I kinda went all Yeti on Onkel Stoffel after that."

I ache to stay snuggled against him, but technically he belongs to someone else (can Kringle marriages get annulled?), and I withdraw from his arms. Behind him, Cocoa stands where the monster once did, giving himself an overall shake.

"You blacked out?" I ask. "What happened? Where's Gretel?"

Gretel won. You lost. You'll always be a loser.

"Long story. First"—Niklas scans the Town Square, brows drawn together—"let's figure out what in the winter wonderland is going on."

Of course! How could I forget we stand in the middle of a mini-war zone? *See? You're not good enough for Flitterndorf.*

The immediate chaos died away with Cocoa's recovery, but some Flitterndorf elves continue to fight, while others stand with their wrists bound, lost expressions on their faces. "It's the mistlefoil." The source of my angst. "Question is, where's it coming from?"

"Bonbon!" Chip's cry rises amid the group of recovered reindeer.

Frosted holly berries, what's happened now? I hurry to join their circle, but anxious questions die on my tongue when I see the Silver Reindeer at the center, stabbing the remaining beast. As Bliss loses another tine, the disfigured monstrosity melts away into Bonbon's slender form. She struggles to breathe, however, her eyes pinched shut.

"Bonbon," Chip whispers, nosing the traces from her body. He folds himself on the ground by her head and extends his muzzle toward her. "Will she be okay?"

Bliss's no-nonsense expression softens. "She will be." Bliss touches the tip of her main beam to Bonbon's side. The tip dissolves, and Bonbon's breathing relaxes. Her eyes flutter open. Seeing Chip, she brightens and touches her nose to his.

I exchange a smiling glance with Peppermint and Licorice. Chip has a girlfriend. Then I frown. "How do you know Bonbon?"

Licorice tosses her head. "After Herr Bote drugged us an' forced us ta fly ta Weihnachts Manor, we stayed with their herd fer a few days."

"Afore that evil lady whisked us away," Peppermint adds. "'Twas love at first sight fer Chip an' Bonbon."

While you remain unloved. Unlovable.

Rubbing my head, I push away the soiled words. Bliss extracts herself from among the other reindeer and meets my gaze. "I must leave."

I rub harder. "Why? How? You solved the reindeer's problem, but the elves still suffer."

"There's nothing more I can do. As long as the Clans quarrel with each other, as long as the Kringles wallow in doubt, Krampus maintains the advantage."

"But you're the key to defeating him."

"A key to unlocking *how*." Bliss noses my breastbone. "Which you and your friends already figured out. Now I'm needed elsewhere. More toys await to be changed back into reindeer." She glances at Chip. "And it seems they require extra time to transform."

My gaze flits to Bliss's antlers, her once-resplendent rack broken and irregular after her skirmishes and willing sacrifices. Less magnificent, yet far more beautiful. "Vielen dank for all you've done. Will we see you again?"

"Perhaps." She limps to the sleigh and presses a tine to Herr Stoffel's head. "He will sleep until his return to Weihnachts Manor. Would you help secure him to my back?"

"What's going on?" Niklas strides forward, and I explain the situation. He shakes his head. "We can't let Onkel Stoffel go free without answering for his behavior. He wanted to destroy my family."

"He was deceived," Bliss says as I translate. "Once the mistlefoil clears his system, you'll find him a different person. There might even be an opportunity for healing between the brothers."

"Besides, the real enemy is headed to the Workshop."

My heart jumps at Gina's voice, and I race to hug her as she emerges from between groups of tussling elves.

She sucks in a pained breath. "Careful. I got banged up." I spring back, apologizing, but she grins. "A hug is worth the discomfort." Then she addresses Niklas. "We need to rally your elves and go after Krampus. Last I knew, Kristof was facing a mutiny of Toy Makers by himself. We can't leave him to face Krampus alone, too."

You can't stop him. You're pathetic. Deficient.

I grimace. "How do we rally the elves when the mistlefoil is so strong here? Even I want to give into its whispers."

"It's coming from the snow globe." Gina glances around and beseeches someone in the crowd. "Please. Help us."

Ina Donath steps forward in dusty high heels. I clutch my throat, checking her hands for hidden syringes, and move in front of the Third String. "What are you doing here? Gina, we can't trust her."

Ina narrows her eyes. "Stoffel wasn't the only one deceived." She pivots on her heel and marches to the shattered globe's base, picking up a broken sleigh runner in the process. Wedging the blade behind the electric panel, she pries it off. Screws pop and bounce to the ground, and some elves clamor in confusion.

"You were led to believe Herr Stoffel gifted you the snow globe," Gina explains to the elves as her aunt kneels and reaches inside. "When, in fact, it came from Krampus."

"And this"—Ina withdraws a palm-sized disc—"is how Krampus infiltrated Flitterndorf." Brushing snow and dirt from her pants, she brings the disc to Niklas with a skittish glance at Gina. "Herr Bote applied concentrated mistlefoil on this device each night, which was then diffused through the snow globe's filtration system into

Flitterndorf."

Niklas rotates the disc in his fingers, his jaw muscles jumping. He pockets it and nods. "Danke."

"Forgive me," Ina whispers. "I let resentment and greed blind me to the truth." She turns to Bliss. "If you take me back to Brückenstadt, I can show you where to find the reindeer figurines."

Bliss bobs her head, and Butterscotch and I help Niklas transfer Herr Stoffel from the sleigh to her back. Giving her niece a sad smile, Ina situates herself behind Herr Stoffel's prone body, and the Silver Reindeer takes a running leap into the sky.

As they fade from view, I slip my arm through Gina's. "You okay?"

"I will be. One day. You?"

Watching Niklas greet his reindeer, I struggle beneath the weight of a thousand felled Christmas trees. "Herr Stoffel lied about when the marriage ceremony took place. I was too late."

"Oh, Tins." Gina puts her arms around me. "I'm so sorry."

It's your own fault. You abandoned Niklas. He's moved on.

He doesn't need you. No one needs you.

You're useless. Lacking—

"No!"

Gina starts. "Tinsel?"

"I'm not defined by my past mistakes," I say through clenched teeth. "Nor is my worth tied to a singular person or job."

"I never said you were ... or it was," Gina responds warily.

Climbing onto the back end of the busted sleigh, I cup my mouth. "Elves of all Clans! Red, Green, Blue, White—listen up." A few elves nearby pause their bickering and squint at me. "I know the kind of poison that clouds your minds. For months, mistlefoil has polluted our air and tainted our food. Even now, we breathe it in. It suggests we're not good enough. That our lives are meaningless, purposeless. Fearing it speaks the truth, we doubt our value, question our abilities, and distrust others' motives."

More elves fall silent, lowering their fists and makeshift weapons.

"Krampus planted the mistlefoil with the intent to enslave us in this mental bondage." I spread my arms. "For how could a community threaten his plans when paralyzed by fear and doubt?"

"We're a threat to Krampus?" someone shouts.

Niklas hops up beside me. "As long as we can reach one more person with our message of hope and love," he calls out, "that's one more light in the darkness. A light that exposes, and therefore threatens, Krampus's greater deception on an unsuspecting world. To stop the light from spreading, Krampus must snuff out its source—but he didn't count on us having a secret weapon."

"What secret weapon? We have no real weapons."

I spot the elf who spoke. My older brother, Chorley. He sports a black eye and shakes a pool noodle for emphasis.

"Who are you?" Niklas asks.

My brother scoffs. "You know me. I'm Chorley Kuchler."

"No. You're not just Chorley Kuchler. You're a Christmas elf. I'm a future Santa Claus." Niklas sweeps his arms to include the rest of the crowd. "We are, all of us, Christmas beings, and as such, we have the Christmas spirit, the spirit of truth"—he taps his chest—"right here. To aid us. Unite us. To dispel the lies."

"How do we recognize the lies?" Exasperation lines Chorley's words.

"Condemnation is a lie," I say, drawing from my own experience. "Self-doubt is a lie. Negative thoughts are lies."

Niklas finds my gaze. "It helps to remember—as someone once had to remind me—that we're equipped with the tools needed to complete the tasks we're purposed to do. Whether that's making toys at the Workshop, or teaching the next generation of elves, or mopping floors at the Vittles Mart." Niklas slips an arm about my waist. "Or becoming the next Mrs. Kringle."

I long to melt against him but push instead. "You're already married."

He chokes. "Who told you that?"

"I didn't make it to the ceremony. Fritz said I was too late."

"Well, yeah, the ceremony almost happened. But"—Niklas frames my face, his green eyes twinkling—"you know I won't marry anyone other than you."

He's not married?

Gina stands before the sleigh and speaks to the crowd. "So, what will it be, elves of Flitterndorf? Will you remain bound by lies, or break those chains with the truth? Even now, Krampus is bent on defeating Meister Kristof and the rest of your kin, the few standing between him and a Christmas takeover. They need your help. Will you unite and march against Krampus? Will you fight for Christmas?"

Murmurs travel among the elves, and someone shouts, "Fight for Christmas!" Suddenly, the crowd erupts with rallying cries, and elves from the different Clans drop their weapons to hug each other or shake hands. Niklas kisses my cheek, but Gina drags me off the sleigh before I can claim another, saying, "We don't want to be late to our own battle."

Niklas winks and energy zings along my limbs. He's not married. Grinning, I join the ruckus with shouts of my own, hope restored as we race for Huff 'n Puff Hill in one colorful wave.

* * *

We crest the hilltop to find Herr Brunner lashing out blindly with his whip. Volleys of toys, hard and soft, big and small, arc toward him from a circle of elves brandishing new hockey sticks. Kristof leads the crossfire, his expression set in determination.

353

Herr Brunner may be armed with mistlefoil and some special "Krampus" powers, but he's no match for us now that we won the greater battle below. He snarls as the four elf Clans close in on him, his contorted face resembling a Krampus mask. Using the new distraction to his advantage, Kristof charges in to seize Krampus's whip and yank it free. We pounce. In seconds, we have our adversary trussed tighter than a Douglas fir in a Christmas tree lot.

A cheer rises from the crowd, and elves break into spontaneous jigs. Kristof enfolds Gina in a bear hug, and Mutti tugs me low for a tearful kiss.

"We won, *meine Liebling*," she says as Vati hobbles over to embrace us. "We won."

"Genau, Mutti." Despite the elves' minor injuries, the maligned toys strewn across the ground, the broken windows in the Workshop that mirror the store windows in town, we saved Christmas for another generation.

And as my gaze collides with Niklas's across the way, victory tastes very sweet indeed.

Fifty-Nine

Tinsel—Dec 4 Second Chances

I shake the last load of straw into the Lower Stables' ninth stall, then bring the pitchfork and wheelbarrow back outside. "It's all set," I call to Bonbon, where she and the other reindeer munch lichen in the corral. "You can sleep the rest of the day away if you like."

That's what I'd do, if I could, after having been awake through the night and morning hours, European time.

"An' Tinsel'll petrify yer own chew toy today." Chip bounces from hoof to hoof and looks at me. "Won'cha?"

I droop my arms over the top rail of the corral fence. "Today?"

"Nay, she's givin' me a bath afore makin' any toys." Licorice stomps her hoof. "I was never so dirty as when I was a mutant and want all remnants off me as soon as possible."

"Sounds like some things are back to normal." The familiar timbre laced with humor shimmies down my spine, and I spin about as Niklas steps from the stable's back entrance.

I haven't seen him since his parents and Meister K returned through the Workshop portal and the whole family retreated into their apartment. He looks dapper in his gray Trachten jacket and deep red lederhosen. As he nears, his gaze flits over me and he chuckles. "You're a mess."

"Thanks a lot." I cross my arms. "I was in a dungeon not too long ago."

"Let me rephrase that. You're a beautiful mess, and I could stare at you all day." Eyes twinkling (I'll never take that for granted again), Niklas pulls straw from my coat collar. "I noticed the stall inside. Is that for Bonbon?"

I nod. "I hope that's okay. Ever since Eggnog quit, we've—I mean, you've been down a member, and because Bonbon and Chip …" I pinch my biceps. "But I shouldn't have assumed—"

"It's fine, Tins." Niklas dips his head close. "Adding Bonbon to the Third String is a great idea."

"Oh." I sway toward his oh-so-missed clove scent. "Good." He smiles, dimples showing, and my stomach flips. "So, um, how'd family time go?"

"It went. We're all in one piece, for which I'm grateful." Niklas tiptoes his fingers along my waist, inching me closer. "The Initiation Ceremony has been canceled, though. Or at least postponed."

"I'm sorry."

"I'm only sorry I won't see you in your Initiation dress." He kisses my nose. "We need to come up with a reason for you to wear it."

My eyes prick with unbidden moisture. There's a lot we haven't talked about yet. "I still can't believe you're not married. When Fritz told me the ceremony had already happened, I thought …" A lone tear escapes my eyelashes.

Niklas thumbs it away. "I'd like to say I didn't come close, but Ina and Herr Brunner had to pump me with so much poison just to get me to the Standesamt that I stood there unrestrained, pen in hand, about to sign the marriage document."

"What stopped you?"

He links his hands behind my waist. "I caught sight of a silver ribbon from Gretel's bodice. It reminded me of tinsel, which reminded me of you, and I remembered your words in Salzburg."

I play with the top button on his coat. "Which words?"

"You said if I saw myself through your eyes, I'd never doubt my worth or potential. When I recalled that truth, it was as if light pierced the darkness holding me hostage and renewed my resolve, my defiance. I snapped the pen, and something like shackles snapped inside *me*. For a moment, I felt fully free and awake." Niklas frowns. "Then I blacked out."

"So, you don't know how you got in the sleigh?"

A shudder visibly rips through him, and he withdraws to lean back against the corral fence. "Pa said Herr Brunner's been nursing a grudge ever since I officially rejected his daughter and, as it happens, foiled his original plans to usurp Flitterndorf." Niklas stuffs his hands into his lederhosen pockets. "Once his second attempt—this marriage ceremony—flopped, Herr Brunner got desperate and decided to charge Flitterndorf a day earlier than planned. Onkel Stoffel took me along as leverage."

"What will happen to Herr Brunner—to Krampus—now? We have no dungeons in Flitterndorf, and it's not like we can throw him in a Canadian prison."

"When Grandpop's strength has returned, he and Kristof will transport Herr Brunner to our outpost in Russia. They're equipped with special chambers for entities like Krampus, the Abominable Snowman, mutant reindeer." Niklas winks at the nearest members of the Third String. "The Silver Reindeer will head over to patrol the area once she completes her principal mission in Brückenstadt."

"Okaaay." I lean against the rail beside him. "What's to keep us from being deceived again, though? We have a powerful message, and there will always be people—Krampus or otherwise—who want to silence us."

"We learn from our past mistakes and move into our future with a little more humility and a lot more wisdom. And we cling to truth, Tins. Truth will always vanquish the lies in the end."

"Promise?"

"It's been promised *to* us."

I smile. "You're gonna make a great Santa."

"Only with you by my side." Niklas trails a fingertip along my cheek, his green eyes sparking with intensity. "Your love is what helped me quell the mistlefoil's effects for so long, after all."

A rush of gratitude steals my breath. "Then you forgive me for abandoning you? For cutting you down when I should have spoken life?"

"You didn't abandon me for long." Niklas takes my hands. "Tinsel, we're going to do and say things that hurt one another. I don't expect you to be perfect, but you're perfect for me—"

Chip's head appears beside mine, his brow tine pushing aside my newsboy cap.

"Ach, ye flake." Butterscotch pokes Chip's rump with his own antlers. "Yer ruinin' the moment. Git out o' the way."

Licorice snorts as I readjust my cap. "Can't blame him fer wantin' ta make sure the eejit gets it right this time."

Chip nods. "We didna witness the first one, an' look what happened."

"Yer sayin' we're good luck?" asks Butterscotch.

"*I'm* good luck," Chip counters. "Dinna ken 'bout you, Butterball."

"Thanks, Fuzzbucket." Niklas nudges aside Chip's snout. "But I think I can manage." With a lop-sided grin, he reaches into his pocket and pulls out a ring. My engagement ring.

My heart soars—then dives as Gretel's ring from that coal-corrupted morning flashes in my mind. "Did Gretel ...?"

"She came nowhere near this ring. She wore her grandmother's, and I didn't even put it on her."

Relief manifests itself in a fresh prickle of tears.

Niklas knuckles my chin. "This ring was made special, for the brightest, prettiest, most courageous elf in the entire world." His throat bobs. "And when I'm nothing but a few lines in a history book, future generations will remember that any success I enjoy as Santa is thanks to her."

Licorice sniffs. "No' such an eejit after all."

Dimples winking, Niklas drops to one knee for the second time in a month. "Tinsel Kuchler, will you do me the honor—"

"Yes." Laughing through my tears, I pull him up by his coat lapels and press my lips to his. "Yes, you charming eejit, of course, I'll marry you."

Sixty

Gina—Dec 24 Christmas Surprises

Waldheim

Curled on the couch, I doodle a new idea for a doll wig in my sketchbook as I wait for Kristof to arrive. Nat King Cole plays on the vintage phonograph, its veneer surface reflecting the colored lights from the nearby Christmas tree. On the coffee table sits my laptop displaying Huggamugg Café's budget spreadsheets.

I tap my chin with the pencil. Mikal managed the café beautifully while I worked in Flitterndorf …. Perhaps she'd like a promotion and go halfsies with me while I develop my doll-making skills and explore a career change.

A knock sounds on the front door, and my tummy scrambles. Kristof.

I toss the sketchpad beside the laptop. "I'll get it," I holler to my folks in the kitchen. Smoothing my figure-hugging Icelandic tunic dress, I take a deep breath and open the door.

Kristof stands beneath the porch lamplight, drool-worthy in dark brown lederhosen and a thick moss sweater that brings out the green in his eyes. His hair is gelled into soft curls, and a grin lifts the corner of his mouth, his appreciative gaze sweeping over me. A trill skitters along my limbs.

I've seen Kristof a total of three times since the Krampus debacle. Meister K required all present and former Toy Makers to finish as many Christmas presents as possible, while the Kringles and the rest of the elves repaired the buildings around the Town Square. Every inch of my heart has noted his absence.

Wordlessly, I step into his embrace, looping my arms about his neck as our lips meet. The frozen winter air doesn't stand a chance against the heat our kisses create.

"Hi," he whispers against my lips.

"Hi."

He pulls back, assessing me. "I wasn't sure what kind of reaction to expect today."

I lift on my toes for another kiss. "Why's that?"

"Because I'm here for date-number-four." His hands slide up my back, his eyes crinkling. "Rumor has it you have a three-date policy."

"Policies like that are made to be broken." Grinning, arms still linked behind his neck, I back into the foyer and pull him with me. Kristof kicks the door closed, his mouth seeking mine again.

A few minutes—and several heady kisses—later, we sit on the couch, my legs draped over his as he draws lazy circles on my legging-clad calves. He casts wary glances at the kitchen door. "I've never been this nervous when visiting you."

"A dinner date with my parents will do that." I kiss his freshly shaven cheek. "How did the Santa Claus sendoff go earlier?"

"As well as can be expected."

"Did the elves make quota?"

"Almost. Grandpop didn't stress, though. Any presents we didn't finish, we're giving gift cards in their place."

"Gift cards?"

"Yep. To whatever local shops the kids enjoy in their respective hometowns. Supporting the little guy and all that."

"How do you know which shop each child prefers?"

Kristof wags his eyebrows. "Letters to Santa. Well, more like, emails if the child is older."

"The whole idea is genius."

"Pa gets the credit."

My smile falters. "Any improvement on your dad?" Aunt Cat had put Meister Nico in solitary confinement in a room no bigger than a broom closet. She and I have had limited contact since she left Flitterndorf.

Kristof scratches his chin. "Physically, yes. His phobia has returned, however, so he won't go near a chimney."

I grimace. "I'm sorry."

"No one blames you."

"But Tinsel said Meister K was hoping to retire after next Christmas."

"He may yet, still. There's plenty of time for Pa to recuperate." Kristof looks back toward the stairs. "Is your aunt …?"

"She's not here." I slip my legs from his. "She betrayed us simply because she'd grown tired of being passed over for grants and promotions. Mum and Dad took it hard, so she's keeping her distance."

Kristof winds a blue lock of my hair around his finger. "How're you taking it?"

My lips press together, my emotions running just below the surface these days. "I'm working through it."

He hitches his chin at my drawing. "Is that part of the process?"

"Maybe. Tinsel's wedding invitation inspired that wig."

"I heard she invited your parents."

"Is that okay?"

His eyebrows rise. "Of course."

"Oh, whew." I sink against the couch. "They're stoked to see Flitterndorf. And during the Sunrise Festival, no less." Only a twosome who has dated and waited for two years would be crazy enough to plan a wedding in a month. But the festival makes sense. The entire community will be gathered in the same area with plenty of food and games to entertain, and Tinsel claims she already owns the perfect dress.

Kristof transfers my sketchpad onto his lap, and a piece of paper slips to the floor. Picking it up, he squints at the writing, then gives me a knowing grin. "Another doll contest?"

"The deadline isn't until March, so I have time to brush up on my skills. Not that I'll be as good as when I had the—" I clear my throat, clamping my wrists between my knees. "Anyway, four lucky winners get an all-expense-paid trip to a week-long summer workshop in the States with three prominent doll artists. I figured my recent bout with rejections has toughened me up, so what have I got to lose?"

Kristof contemplates my drawing. "In the meantime, how would you like to apprentice with Frau Spielen?"

My mouth opens several times before words come out. "I didn't think the elves wanted me taking one of their jobs."

"Bellamy visited with me a few days ago. She and the other Doll Makers would love to have you back."

I shake my head. "I don't possess the skills anymore."

"You possess the aptitude, and you're teachable." He returns the sketchbook to the coffee table. "Frau Spielen confirmed Bellamy's claim and is offering you the apprenticeship. If you're interested."

"Heck, yeah." I bounce my knee. "Except, I can't abandon the café like that."

Kristof puts a hand on my knee. "I'm sure we could come up with a plan that would allow you to do both for a time."

"Really?" A hesitant smile works across my mouth.

"Really."

I lean into his shoulder. "Think we could throw in some lunch dates when I'm at the Workshop?"

His gaze fixes on my lips as he bends close. "What's there to think about?"

"Ahem," comes a voice from the kitchen doorway.

We spring apart as Dad walks over, and Kristof stands to shake his hand. "Merry Christmas, sir."

"Merry Christmas," Dad says. "I trust your grandfather got off all right."

"Yes, sir."

"What will you do, now that the holiday rush is over?"

"I'll stick around until after Nik's wedding, then head to Weihnachts Manor in mid-January when my great uncle comes here for an extended visit."

My jaw drops like the nutcracker Tinsel gave me. So soon?

Kristof tosses me a confused look but addresses Dad. "While helping run the Workshop, I developed some ideas for improving the toy and goods production at the Manor. I'd like a chance to test those ideas. I also have marching orders from my soon-to-be sister-in-law to address the rundown state of the elf village." His lips quirk in a boyish grin. "And the elves need a hockey team."

Dad chuckles. "Well, good. Good to hear you have a vision."

A vision that leaves me behind. Mum and Dad bricked up the portal upstairs, and last I heard, Meister K shut the one in the Prep Stables.

"Marco!" Mum hollers from the kitchen.

"Speaking of marching orders, I better get back to the drill sergeant." Dad winks and points at us. "I just came out to say dinner's in five minutes."

As the kitchen door closes behind Dad, Kristof turns to me. "Why so sad?"

"Because you're taking off for who-knows-how-long this time." I push against the ache in my sternum. "All the portals are gone, so I can't walk to Germany anymore—"

"Gina—"

"—yet neither can I afford to buy a plane ticket whenever I want to see you." The ache intensifies. "I don't like this."

Kristof sinks beside me. "G—"

"No, it hurts too much. I never should've let you in—"

He shuts me up with a kiss, hot and unrelenting. My body responds immediately, and though I whimper, I fail to push him away. Our breaths mingle when he withdraws a fraction. "You'd rather go through life not knowing love," he whispers, "than taking a chance with me?"

His words evoke an empty future, one shackled by the fear of a broken heart. I shiver.

"Remember that once this Kringle falls for someone, he's a goner for life." Kristof caresses my cheek with a thumb. "I'm the one taking a risk, G. And I'm happy to do it. Besides"—his mouth quirks at one end—"Grandpop decided to keep the portal open in the Prep Stables."

I gasp. "And you didn't tell me?"

"Sometimes it's hard to get a word in edgewise with you."

I give him a playful shove. "He's truly keeping it open? That means easy connection to the Manor, right?"

Kristof pulls me onto his lap. "I think what you mean to say is, easy connection to me."

Nuzzling his neck, I inhale his signature notes of sandalwood and vanilla. It's become my favorite combo. "Guess I better locate my passport. I have lots of international trips to plan."

Sixty-One

Tinsel—Jan 6 Sleigh Ride

~⁕~

Flitterndorf

"Seriously, hold still, or you'll end up looking like Rudolph." Fingers on my chin, Gina angles me into position under her portable cosmetic lamp and sweeps blush along my cheeks.

"Sorry." I fist a tissue in my lap and straighten on the vanity stool. Voices drift under my bedroom door from the living room as my parents converse with Madams Anne and Marie, who came to help with wedding day preparations.

Gina moves to her cosmetic case by my bed, and a floorboard creaks. Our apartment has never entertained so many humans at once.

She flourishes a liquid eyeliner pen. "Close your eyes."

The pen skims along my lash lines one at a time. A tendril of hair tickles my forehead, but I refrain from touching it. Gina already worked her magic on my curly bob and wouldn't want me "smudging" her masterpiece.

"What's the deal with you, anyway?" she asks. "What's with the anxious vibes?"

"I'm getting married in an hour. I'm allowed to be nervous."

"Look up." When I comply, she works on my lower lash line, shaking her head. "This isn't nerves. It's worry. Why? Meister K revoked your suspension, so that's irrelevant." Stepping back, she studies my eyes, then steps close again. "Would it help to know the entire Flitterndorf community is clambering to make sure your wedding ceremony goes without a hitch?"

My fingers shred the tissue. "I didn't ask them to, G. Niklas insisted on having the wedding the same day as the festival." Niklas, who remained distracted throughout the festivities and disappeared after the fireworks display.

Gina cups my face. "The elves are clambering because they want to, not because someone issued a command. You've won them over."

A knot eases in my shoulder. Madam Marie laughs in the other room.

"Have you seen the Production Wing yet?" Gina exchanges the eyeliner for mascara. "Kristof gave me a sneak-peek earlier."

For the rare Kringle weddings, elves temporarily empty the Production Wing floor of workstations, as it's the one area large enough to accommodate the entire Flitterndorf community gathered to witness the exchange of vows. "I've heard it's gorgeous. Chorley's wife took charge of decorating, and she's a master at her craft."

"I'll say. Picture garland swags with white lights and holly berries swooped over loft railings and ceiling beams. Chandeliers embellished with pine cone clusters, greenery, and red and white roses. White linen draped along the archway next to the double-sided fireplace." Gina touches my shoulder. "That's where you and Niklas stand, right?"

"Mmm-hmm. Along with Meister K." The first Kringle wedding to take place in my generation. Provided Niklas still wants to get married and his disappearance means nothing.

I blow out a tiny breath. For the love of reindeer, what's my deal? My gaze narrows at Gina brushing something along my cheekbones and forehead. "You're not wearing mistlefoil, are you?"

She huffs and plants a hand on her hip. "I gave my stash to Kristof, thankyouverymuch."

I tear the tissue into teenier bits. "Sorry."

"Is this about the Third String? Are they still sluggish?"

"No. I mean, yes, they're sluggish, even though the vet assures me the mistlefoil is out of their system, so I haven't worked them hard. But even if they're not ready to perform the Peppermint Twist in the Mastery Tournament, I'm okay with that now." I know my career doesn't hinge on that one event.

She rifles through her bag. "And you told me Jangles and the Minor Flight Team love your idea about the whistles."

A grin flits across my lips. "We'll start implementing them into our lessons after the tournament."

"Then I don't get it. What's the matter?" Gina raises the slim bottle of setting spray. "Hold your breath."

"Again?"

"I don't want your makeup budging one millimeter all night."

As she mists my face, a gentle knock sounds on the door, followed by a soft sigh. "Oh, Tinsel, you are a vision," Mutti says.

"Isn't she? And she's not even fully dressed." Gina lobs her mascara into her cosmetic bag. "My work here is finished." She grips my shoulders as I rotate toward the mirror. "No peeking until the final product! Madam Marie has your circlet in the living room when you're done getting dressed. Then you can look." She flicks a hand at her paraphernalia. "I'll come back for this later."

Mutti watches her slip out and close the door. "Gina seems happy, nicht wahr? I saw her meandering through the crowds before the fireworks, arm-in-arm with Meister Kristof, beaming like a kid on

Christmas morning." She plucks at her dirndl apron. "She's good to have forgiven us so quickly for our poor behavior when she stayed here."

"You're good to forgive her for the part she played, as well."

Mutti smiles and draws a step stool to the end of my bed. "Shall we?"

My Initiation Ceremony gown with its matching apron lies atop my comforter, the green velvet skirts flared to keep from wrinkling. I pull in my bottom lip. Niklas suggested we use the ceremony outfits for our wedding since we can't use them for their original purpose, and while I love the unique spin on an old tradition—

Mutti pats my knee. "Liebling, was ist los?"

My eyes grow hot, and I blink rapidly. "It's Niklas," I whisper, squeezing the tissue remnants in my lap. "He's been acting secretive lately. He's tired a lot. And today at the festival, he was über distracted." Sighing, I toss the tissue wad into the trashcan. "It sounds foolish, but what if he's having second thoughts? What if the reality of married life has freaked him out and—"

Mutti chuckles. "Ah, sweet thing. I've never seen a boy more eager to make a girl his wife than Niklas. Now come." She hops onto my bed and lifts the dress by its shoulders, winking. "You'll know soon enough what drives his behavior."

* * *

A few minutes later, sheathed in the exquisite dirndl and long sleeve blouse, I join the others gathered in the living room. They exclaim with gasps, claps, and squeals (this last from Gina). Glimpsing my reflection in the mirror, I gape, myself. Gina subdued my unruly curls into springy copper coils, and gave my skin a dewy sheen and my hazel eyes a smoky look for the evening ceremony.

369

Madam Marie steps forward and presents a grapevine circlet bedecked with red holly berries and baby pine cones. "May I?"

I lower my head, and she nestles the circlet in my curls. After Gina makes adjustments, Madam Marie takes my hands. "My dear, we haven't spoken of our time at the manor, and I want to apologize for not taking a stronger stance against Stoffel that day he announced Niklas's engagement to Gretel."

I shake my head. "You were poisoned—"

"I know my son's heart, and I should have fought for him. Though you wavered, you never fully stopped fighting, and for that I'm grateful." She squeezes my fingers. "Do you know why Niklas will make a great Santa someday?"

"He's a Kringle?"

"Because you will be at his side to encourage him, support him"—she gives an impish grin—"keep him humble." She kisses my cheek. "We couldn't have asked for a better elf or human to become our son's wife."

"Danke," I whisper, moisture collecting in my eyes.

"Don't you dare cry!" Gina warns, and laughter dances around the room.

The door to the back stairs slams open. My brother, Mash, stumbles in, scanning the room until he spots me. "Tinsel—whoa, you clean up nice. Come quick."

"What's wrong?"

"Just come." He waves an impatient hand. I glance at the others, and they shrug or turn away with suppressed grins.

Hmm. Draping my wool capelet over my shoulders, I follow him down the stairs, navigating the treads carefully in my full skirts. Outside, elves gather on the sidewalk around the Town Square, barren without the gaudy snow globe. They lift their gazes toward the sky. Vati and my other brothers wait in their formal lederhosen and coats, their faces also raised. A faint jingle meets my ears.

"Who is it?" one elf says to another.

"Dunno. It's not the Big Eight."

Vati elbows Tinder. Gripping my capelet lapels, I look up.

High above, against the twilight backdrop, a reindeer team makes a slow arc over Flitterndorf from the direction of Cookie Meadow. The new practice sleigh, outlined in colored lights, trails behind the 'deer, and a trim figure stands at the dash. Who …?

The team and sleigh complete a wide circle before descending toward the Square. "That's Bonbon!" I cry. "And Chip. That's the Third String." The person standing at the helm, however, is too tall to be Jangles.

I cover my mouth. It can't be.

The matching smiles on my family's and Gina's faces say it is.

Alighting across the Square, the sleigh fills up the street. Showered by claps and excited shouts, the two rows of reindeer prance their way around to The Flaky Crust, where they stop in front of me. I stare at Niklas, resplendent in his Initiation Ceremony coat and corresponding lederhosen, his blond hair tousled from the wind.

His gaze rakes me from head to toe and back again. "I was going to say, 'Surprise!' But, 'You're stunning,' is more appropriate."

"You flew," I breathe as he steps from the sleigh.

"Still a little shaky." Niklas splays his quaking fingers, yet his green eyes twinkle brighter than I've ever seen.

Behind him, the reindeer wear collars adorned with holly berries and pine cones that match my circlet. Licorice prances in place. A dazed smile pulls at my lips. "I don't … How did …? Niklas, you *flew*."

He draws me close and nods at the reindeer. "We've been secretly practicing at night. These 'deer are troopers. Patient. Attentive. Obedient."

I chuckle. "You sure you're talking about the Third String?"

"They've gone easy on me."

Now I raise my eyebrows. "You're *sure* you're talking about the Third String."

"Give us some credit, gel," Chip says halfway down a row of reindeer. "We can behave when we want ta."

"I don't understand. This helps explain your exhaustion as of late, but"—I study Niklas's face—"how did you overcome your fear?"

"Once again, I have you to thank for that." He runs his palms down my arms. "You know how we possessed mistlefoil's antidote all along? That drawing strength from the truth helped nullify its effects?"

"Mmm-hmm."

"It's the same for flying." Lifting our hands, he weaves his fingers between mine. "It goes back to what you said in Salzburg—I'm purposed to become the future Santa Claus, so I already possess the courage and confidence to fly a sleigh. I had to exercise faith in that truth, however, and view myself through the lens of my potential rather than my inadequacies, before I was set free to experience it."

"I take it you've been 'exercising' these last two weeks."

A wry smile tugs at his lips. "Which is why you've barely seen me."

Beaming, I tuck our hands under my chin. "I knew you'd fly."

"It'll be even better with you by my side."

"Then let's fly on up to the Workshop," Gina says, reminding me we stand in the figurative spotlight of many bystanders, "and get you two hitched, shall we?"

I settle beside Niklas on the sleigh's padded bench seat and accept my bouquet from Madam Anne. Behind her, our families linger on the sidewalk. "How are the rest of you getting there?"

"SnoMos. Reindeer." Gina motions across the Square, where Kristof waits astride Blaze, surrounded by other members of the Big Eight. "Don't worry about us. But don't start without us, either."

As she and Madam Anne back away, Niklas blows out a breath. I touch his arm, and a smile wobbles on his lips. "I'm fine. Steeling myself for what's ahead." White-knuckling the reins, he gives them a slap. "To the skies, team!"

The Third String takes off amid the cheering crowd, but Niklas's profile tightens as we ascend into the air. I tuck my hand under his arm. "You're amazing, you know that?"

His gaze fastens on mine, and the fog clears from his eyes. "Together. You and me."

"Unstoppable."

He gives me a sound kiss, tightening his arm to anchor my hand at his side. When he pulls away again, his face has a determined look despite its ashen pallor. "Get ready, Tins. This is for you."

Niklas tweaks the reins, and I let out a whoop as the reindeer rotate into their most coordinated Peppermint Twist yet.

* * *

Glossary

German words/phrases:

Alles in Ordnung?—Everything all right?

Auf Englisch—In English

Ausgezeichnet—excellent

Bitte—please

Blöde Elfe—stupid elf

Brötchen—bread rolls

Dirndl—traditional German dress

Es tut mir leid—I'm sorry (informal)

Es war fett—It was awesome.

Feuer!—Fire!

Frau—Mrs.

Frühstuck—breakfast

Guten Morgen—Good morning.

Guten Tag—hello

Grüß Gott—hello in southern Germany

Herr—Mr.

Ist das richtig oder?—Is that right?

Ja—yes

Kann ich Sie helfen?—Can I help you?

Kein Problem—no problem

Kinder—children

Komm schon—come on

Konditorei—bakery

Lederhosen—traditional German leather pants

Liebchen/Liebling—an endearment, like sweetheart or darling

Materialismus—materialism

Mein Auto—my car

Meine Elfen! Bereit!—My elves! Ready!

Meine Familie—my family

Meine Freunde—my friends

Mischling—half-breed

Nein—no

Nicht wahr—isn't that right, isn't that so

Oder—Coming at the end of a sentence, it's similar to how we say "right?"

Paß auf!—Watch out!

Schnell—fast/quickly

Sie sollten nicht hier sein—You shouldn't be here.

Sind Sie eine echte Elfe—Are you a real elf?

Sprechen Sie Englisch?—Do you speak English?

Stimmt—agreed

Und—and

Verlassen Sie sofort!—Leave immediately!

Vielen dank or **Danke**—thank you.

Vorsicht—careful

Wann können wir die Dungeons sehen?—When can we see the dungeons?

Was ist hier passiert?—What is going on here?

Was machen Sie hier?—What are you doing here?

Weihnachtsmann—Santa Claus or Father Christmas

Weihnachtsmarkt—Christmas market

Wieviel kostet es—How much does it cost?
Wunderbar—wonderful
Wunderschön—beautiful

Scottish words:
  Eejit—idiot
  Gel—girl
  Ken—to know

Acknowledgement

I can't begin to express how hard it was to write this sequel! It was a monster at 156K words by the time I'd fleshed out the second draft, and from there, it took me way too long to chop, cut, snip, and basically overhaul it into a manageable novel. A huge THANK YOU goes out to Leah Schwabauer and Robyn Hook for reading that monster, and for all the phone calls, texts, emails, critiques, and encouragement thereafter. :)

Thank you, Lea Freitas and Rebecca Mildren, for tackling a later draft, and for your input along the way. Thank you, Storyteller Squad, for your crits, encouragement, and prayers, especially Candice Yamnitz, Michelle Welsh, Michelle McCorkle, Gretchen Carlson, Tracy Popolizio, and Kristen Johnson. I appreciate each of you taking the time to read my work in one big chunk. <3 And thank you, Kelsey Gillespy, for your fresh eyes on my last draft and for checking in with prayers and encouragement.

As always, no written work would exist without the support of my family: my girls, who knew when to leave their mother alone, and my hubby, who listened to my rants and frustrations, whether or not he could understand and relate to them. ;)

Lastly and most importantly, God gets the ultimate glory for this book's existence. So many times when I was about to call it quits,

He would give me a little breakthrough—an idea, an *ah ha!* moment, a new way of coming at a scene to improve it—and that would be enough to nudge me a little farther along my writing journey. Like Tinsel, I have to remind myself God has equipped me with whatever tools needed to accomplish what He's purposed me to do. I won't always have the same calling throughout the different phases of my life, but I will always have His Spirit to aid me in fulfilling the task at hand.

About the Author

Laurie Germaine is the author of the clean Christmas fantasy romance, *Tinsel in a Tangle*, the forerunner to *Tinsel in a Twist*. As a New England native, she once dreamed of raising a family in Europe, but thankfully God knew what her heart truly desired. She now lives quite happily in Montana with her husband of twenty-one years, two teenage daughters, two horses, an Alaskan Malamute, and an ever-changing number of chickens. When not immersed in writing or honing skills as a mom and homemaker, you can find her knitting anything from clothes to toys to phone cozies, or working on random crafts around the home.

You can connect with me on:

🌐 https://scatteredwhimsy.com

f https://www.facebook.com/lauriegermaineauthor

✎ https://mewe.com/i/lauriegermaine1

Subscribe to my newsletter:

✉ https://www.lauriegermaine.com/contact

Also by Laurie Germaine

Tinsel in a Tangle

In the arctic town of Flitterndorf, generations of elves have worked alongside generations of Kringles to make gifts for believing children worldwide. But never have they endured a tall, blundering elf like Tinsel. Despite her setbacks, Tinsel is determined to prove her worth by nabbing an internship at the Workshop. When her chemistry lab explodes, however, destroying gift reserves and putting Christmas in jeopardy, she lands a punishment mucking reindeer stalls for Santa's hotshot grandson, Niklas.

Now if she wants a second chance at that position, she must collaborate with the twinkle-eyed flirt to redeem herself in everyone's eyes without messing up. For one more mishap will not only bring about the holiday's demise, she'll be immortalized as the elf who shattered children's faith in Santa Claus.

So not the way she wants to go down in history.

CPSIA information can be obtained
at www.ICGtesting.com
Printed in the USA
BVHW082056240921
617501BV00003B/369